ROMAN'S HAVING
SEX AGAIN

NIKKI ASHT♡N

Cover design – ebook-designs.co.uk

Edited by—Bernadette Kearns of Book Nanny Writing & Editing Services
Formatting by—JC Clarke from The Graphics Shed

1

This book is dedicated to all those women who struggle to conceive, or never conceive at all. I can't give you hope, but I may make you smile.

Nikki x

PROLOGUE

♥

'Oh God, please kill me now,' I muttered to myself as Mr. Barlow, my boss, continued to drone on about terms and conditions of sale. He was selling his building and structural engineering business to a guy who had recently returned to the area, and had been banging on to the new owner's accountant for the last hour. As his PA, he wanted me there to take notes. To be honest, all I had written on my pad was: *'blah, blah, blah'*. I just hoped he didn't ask me any questions later.

'Are you okay, Sarah?' he asked, as I squirmed in my chair.

I nodded and smiled, not really meaning it. I felt uncomfortable having had to sit for over an hour already. I was also feeling a little sad, because although Mr. Barlow was a bit dippy at times and wasn't the best businessman, he was always jolly and treated us all fairly, and I was going to miss having him as a boss. So, no, I wasn't okay. Life was changing and I wasn't sure I liked it.

'Sarah's recently had an operation,' Mr. Barlow told the stiff-backed accountant. 'She's only been back a week.'

Yep, definitely kill me now. Not only did I not want everyone knowing that I'd recently had an ovary removed, but my bloody name was Summer, not Sarah. At seventy-five, Mr. Barlow was a little doddery and always called me by his granddaughter's name.

1

It was easier to answer to it than explain otherwise.

As my boss continued to chatter on, the accountant's mobile phone buzzed with an incoming text.

'Oh,' he said, looking down at it. 'Mr. Hepburn has arrived.'

Yipee, I thought, another boring old fart to add to the mix. A little over two minutes later, the door was flung open and the most beautiful man I had ever seen walked in. He was tall, broad and confident, and if someone had asked me to describe my ideal man, well, he would most definitely be it. With chestnut-coloured hair, perfect stubble and dark-brown eyes that I would happily lose myself in, he was simply knicker-wettingly handsome.

'Sorry I'm late,' he said breathlessly. 'Had a few issues that needed sorting on a job.'

'No problem, Mr. Hepburn,' his accountant smarmed, with a thin-lipped smile. 'We were just discussing the finer points of the sale.'

Mr. Beautiful held his hand out to Mr. Barlow. 'Nice to see you again, Richard.'

'You too, Roman, you too.'

Oh my God, he even had a sexy name!

'I'm sorry,' he said, looking at me with twinkling eyes. 'We've never met before.'

'I do apologise, Roman,' Mr. Barlow said, with a shake of his head. 'This is Sarah, my PA.'

Mr. Beautiful took my hand in his and shook it, and I couldn't ignore the zing of electricity that shot from his palm right down to the pit of my stomach—and lower, if I was being honest. He gave me a soft smile and then turned back to Mr. Barlow and the accountant.

'Okay, Nigel, fill me in on what you and Richard have come up with.'

As I shifted in my seat, he gave me a quick glance and I saw him take a deep breath, before blowing it out slowly.

He was so damn sexy that the only thought in my head at that point was: *'Oh shit, there goes my remaining ovary.*

CHAPTER 1

♥

It was the first working day of the week, and, with a slight feeling of dread, I turned on my PC. Today was the day that Mr. Hepburn started as my new boss, and I was as nervous as hell. He'd seemed a perfectly nice guy at the meeting a couple of weeks ago, so it wasn't that I was worried he'd be an awful boss: it was because I already had an almighty crush on him. Throughout the meeting with the accountant, we kept snatching glances at each other, and, each time I did, I found myself getting turned on just a little bit more. So by the end of the almost two-hour meeting, I couldn't have felt more horny if Jamie Dornan himself had been giving me a lap dance.

As I worked through the day's worksheets, I heard voices in the corridor outside my office. My stomach gave a flip, nervously anticipating meeting the man who would now be paying my wages. Trying to look industrious, I put my head down and carried on typing.

'Ah, and here she is,' Mr. Barlow said gaily. 'My marvellous PA, Sarah. Sarah, your new boss, Mr. Hepburn.'

I looked up with a ready smile and almost peed my pants. Standing in front of me was Mr. Beautiful—Roman—looking just as handsome as that day at his accountant's office. As he approached my desk a small, knowing grin appeared on his

3

gorgeous face, and he flicked out his tongue to wet his lips. My heart rate quickened, and I could feel the heat creeping up my neck as he held his hand out to me.

'Sarah, nice to see you again, and call me Roman.' He took my hand and gently rubbed his thumb across the back of it as he shook it. 'I look forward to working with you.'

Swallowing back the sigh I sooo wanted to let out, I smiled. 'Thanks, Mr. Hepburn, but my name's actually Summer.'

'Oh of course it is,' Mr. Barlow said, wafting his hand at me. 'I always get it wrong. I have a granddaughter called Sarah, you see, Roman.'

I looked up at Roman, expecting to see a sexy smile. Instead, his face was thunderous, and I had no clue why.

CHAPTER 2

'Summer!' Roman bellowed from his office so loudly that it rattled the pictures on the walls. 'Get in here now!'

Rolling my eyes, I scraped my chair back from my desk and walked to the doorway. 'Yes?'

'I didn't say, 'Summer stand in the doorway'; I said, 'Summer get in here now!''

Resisting the urge to stick my tongue out at him like a toddler, I plastered on a smile and took one step forward so that *technically* I was standing in the office. Roman looked at me, shook his head and huffed loudly.

'Where the hell is the report for The Palisade's development? I asked you to put it in the folder on the shared drive, and it isn't there.'

'It is,' I stressed, moving towards his desk. I leaned forward and brushed his hand away from his computer mouse, making a couple of clicks. 'There.'

'That's not where I asked you to put it.' Roman snatched the mouse back and clicked on the file. 'That folder is called "Shopping Centre". I asked you to call it "The Palisades".'

I looked down at him, my eyes wide with frustration. 'Seriously, how many shopping centres are we actually working on?'

'Just do as I ask in future, and don't backchat me.'

I shook my head and returned to my desk leaving a grumpy boss muttering away behind me. I had no idea why I stayed working for him as we seemed to wind each other up without even trying. Mr. Barlow had been lovely and never raised his voice. We had mutual respect for each other.

I'd thought that Roman was grumpy on that first day—once Mr. Barlow had left—but he was a pussycat then compared to how his mood had declined over the last month or so. He'd gradually been getting more impatient and testy. Finally, yesterday, when I came in late after a visit to the dentist, he hit the roof: bawling and shouting that he had needed me to help with the details of a new contract—information that I had already added to the shared drive and also emailed to him earlier. Me being me, and unable to hold my tongue, I gave it back to him with both barrels. And so, a shouting match ensued. It lasted for a good ten minutes before he told me to get back to my desk and do some work. I had waited with bated breath all day for him to tell me I was fired, but he didn't: he simply carried on all day ordering me around and being a miserable sod. The memory of those furtive glances and how nice he'd seemed at his accountant's office all those weeks ago was getting hazier, with every mean comment he made.

As I continued typing up the Statement of Works Roman had given to me for another of our contracts, I tried to get my head around why he was so angry with me all the time. Fifty people worked for Roman—if you didn't count the contractors he used—made up of forty tradesmen and ten office staff, including me. Out of all those people, I was generally the only one he didn't get along with. When clients or other members of staff came to see him, he was Mr. Charm himself. I knew that we were under pressure with The Palisades project, and, as I worked the closest with him, I put our somewhat fraught relationship down to that. Yet it had all started off so well, until his mood had flipped like a wet fish on a river bank when Mr. Barlow had introduced us that first day. Well, I was getting to a point, where I just wanted to tell him to stick his job up that tight little ass of his.

The Palisades project was a small, thirty-unit shopping centre which our company was building. We had been experiencing some problems with it, the latest being the discovery of a Marsh Harrier's nest in the reed beds that skirted the edges of the shopping centre on one side. Not only were Marsh Harriers a protected species of bird, they were rare in the North-West of England, and so the building work on that side of the site had been halted for almost three weeks, despite the fact that no Marsh Harriers had actually been spotted near the nest. This meant that we were unlikely to reach the deadline and would therefore incur huge financial penalties. Losses that could potentially ruin the company.

As I read back over what I had just distractedly typed, the office door pushed open and a gorgeous, long-legged, brunette sauntered in: Tiffany, Roman's younger sister. She had visited her cantankerous brother at least once a week over the last month.

'Hi Summer,' she greeted me brightly. 'Is he in?'

'Hi Tiffany,' I replied with a genuine smile. 'I think he's on the phone.' I looked down at my telephone and did indeed see the light for Roman's extension glowing red.

'Okay if I sit and wait then?'

I nodded and got up to make her usual green tea that she liked. While I waited for the kettle to boil, I had to wonder how Tiffany and Roman could possibly be related. Like Tiffany, Roman was gorgeous, and even covered by his designer suits, you could tell that his body was ripped: the glimpse you got of his corded forearms when he rolled up his shirt sleeves was a tempting sight. Despite the fancy packaging though, they were extremely different in temperament. Tiffany was not only beautiful, but also a decent person: always happy, polite, and interested in how I was. She was the complete antithesis of Roman, and she seemed perfectly lovely to me.

'So how are things going with The Palisades?' Tiffany asked. 'I know Ro is stressed about it, but he won't share anything about what's going on.'

I sighed and passed Tiffany her cup of tea. 'Nothing has changed really; we're still waiting to hear when we can continue building.'

'There must be something you can do?' She smiled at me as she took a sip of her drink.

'Roman is looking into flipping the plan, building on the other side instead.' I wondered why he hadn't shared any of this with her, because Tiffany obviously cared.

'And is that feasible?' she asked softly.

'We don't know yet,' I shrugged. 'He was working with the architect yesterday and is meeting with the planning committee tomorrow.'

At that moment Roman's office door burst open.

'Summer, where the hell ... oh hey, Tiff, I didn't realise you were here.'

Tiffany's face lit up as Roman took a step towards her: it was so bright she could have short-circuited the national grid, even more so when he bent to kiss her cheek. Blimey, she really did love her big brother.

'I wondered whether you fancied lunch,' Tiffany said.

Roman rubbed a hand over his face and then let out a strangled grunt. 'I can't, Tiff. I'm really sorry, but I need to get this plan finalised before my meeting tomorrow.'

Her face fell briefly before she plastered on another sparkling smile. 'Okay, no problem, it was a last-minute idea anyway.'

Roman's face softened. 'Sorry.'

'I'll go and get something instead, and bring it back here,' Tiffany said, as she put her cup on the edge of my desk.

Roman hesitated momentarily, before shaking his head. 'Tiff, seriously, I'm fine.'

'No, Ro, I'm getting you something. You never eat properly.'

'Tiffany,' Roman warned.

'Roman?' Tiffany beamed at him and I had to wonder how someone could be so smiley when she was dealing with someone so argumentative.

'But I don't want anything,' Roman groaned, raking a hand

through his hair.

'Well, I'm getting you something. Summer?' she said, turning to me.

'I'm fine thanks, Tiffany,' I replied with a smile nowhere near as glowing as hers. 'I've got some sandwiches.'

'Okay. Well, I'll pop back later then.'

'Whatever, Tiff, do what you like as usual, and leave whatever you get with Summer,' Roman said waving a hand in my general direction. 'I'm going to be really busy.'

'Alright, will do,' Tiffany replied brightly, winking at me. 'See you later then, Summer.'

Tiffany left and, Roman, like the miserable troll he was, retreated back under his bridge. I couldn't understand why he just couldn't give her a little bit of his time. It was his loss, though, as she evidently cared about him a great deal. He was her big brother and she idolised him. I know I did mine, even though I didn't wholeheartedly like how Dylan treated his 'girlfriends'. I sighed. Who was I to criticise how my brother conducted his love life? I might not agree with his conveyor belt of women, and his one-night stands, but women were attracted to him like teenagers around a *Primark* sale, and were always desperate for more, so he must be doing something right. The most action I'd had in the last few months was ... none. Not since finishing with my boyfriend of three years. When I was diagnosed with Polycystic Ovary Syndrome and told I'd have to lose an ovary, Alex had dumped me, two days before my operation, because, according to his text—I kid you not—'*he couldn't cope with the thought of not being able to have kids*'. That was a joke. And an excuse: he hated kids, and avoided his sister's two boys at all costs.

As I pondered this, Roman's office door burst open.

'Summer, where the hell is the latest blueprint that the architect sent over yesterday!'

From where I was sitting I could see the cardboard tube propped up against Roman's filing cabinet. Biting my tongue on the sarcastic comment I was *dying* to make about him having painted-on eyes, I heaved myself up from my chair with a sigh and considered how much money I would need to just take off backpacking around the world.

Yep, my life was shite, and more boring than an iced finger. It's basically bread, for goodness sake, where's the cream? To top it all off, my boss, Roman 'The Ego' Hepburn, hated me.

CHAPTER 3

♥

It had been over two months since my operation, and tonight was my first big night out. Me and my best friend, Emma, were at the recently refurbished and re-opened local nightclub, Ziggy's. I was finally off my medication and I was going to have a good time.

I had to say, the club was looking good, and whoever had done the work had done a fantastic job. It was over two floors, the top floor being a mezzanine overlooking the lower level, in the middle of which was a large, round dance floor with a circular bar at one end

'So, Alex still hasn't been in touch?' Emma asked as we stood people-watching.

'Nope,' I replied, staring out over the masses of dancers. We had positioned ourselves on a small landing halfway down the stairs overlooking the dance floor, and we had a great view of everyone.

'And you're okay with that?'

I heaved a sigh, and contemplated that question for a few seconds.

'Yeah, I think I am. I never really expected it to be a *Hallmark Romance* love story, Em. So no biggie.'

'It would have been nice if he'd shown you a little support, though,' Emma grumbled.

'I certainly didn't expect that from him,' I laughed.

'But why not? You'd been going out for three years. Surely that meant something?'

Her little chin was determinedly set, and I knew she was wishing all sorts of hate upon Alex. We'd been friends for almost fifteen years, and from the day we'd met at school, we'd always had each other's backs.

When her last boyfriend, Tyler, disappeared with her credit card and a thousand pounds of her cash, Emma was going to put it down to experience, but I couldn't let it go. I stormed around to his dad's tyre-fitting business and refused to leave until I had a cheque for a thousand pounds for her. Thankfully, it only took two hours before Tyler's dad caved, and it only took that long because he didn't have his cheque book on him.

'I may have to hurt him,' Emma said. 'Not sure how, but I'll think of something.'

I started to laugh at the thought of my tiny little friend bringing hurt upon Alex, who, at six feet, towered over her.

'Seriously, Em, I really don't care. I have no illusions that life is full of hearts, flowers and unicorns, and that all women fart fairy-dust. I'm a realist and I always knew Alex wasn't to be counted on. I shouldn't have let it go on as long as I did.'

'Maybe, but he'll get his one way or the other,' she said, pulling me into a hug.

God, I loved her; she might look like Barbie and be totally spoiled by her parents, but she had the biggest heart of anyone I had ever known. Almost half of what she earned working in her dad's car showroom, she gave to charity, and she was forever rescuing animals and taking them to my elder brother, Dylan, who was a vet, so that he could give them the once-over before she found them a new home. As well that, Emma had the innate ability to make me smile when no one else could: not even my brother, and he made me smile a lot.

'How are you really feeling, though?' she asked. 'And none of your usual bravado bullshit.'

I couldn't help but smile: she had me. 'About Alex, I'm not

lying, I'm fine. About losing one of my ovaries and my inability to have children ... well, no, that's not so good.'

'Oh Summer,' Emma cried, 'don't think like that. They've not said it's impossible, just that it'll be more difficult.'

'It was going to be difficult with two,' I said with a huff. 'Now I've only got one of the damn buggers, and that one almost exploded of its own free will when I first saw Roman.'

I giggled at my little joke, because that was the only way I could cope at the moment: make light of it. I hadn't told Emma, or anyone—other than Mum and Dad—that my consultant had said my remaining ovary was covered in cysts: so it definitely was *Mission Impossible* as far as babies were concerned.

'Just wait and see what happens. As for Alex,' Emma grumbled, 'I'm glad you're fine about that specimen. Let's face it, you're not going to be missing much are you?'

She was totally right about that. He'd never been the most attentive of boyfriends: dumping me at the first hurdle had proved that. To be honest, I wasn't missing him at all, and the sex had been mediocre at best. Alex's style of foreplay often had me wanting to shout: 'They're not radio knobs, you know.' He just had no idea how sensitive a woman's nipples could be. I'd even asked him to rip my knickers off once, but he'd had to go and get a pair of kitchen scissors to do the job.

'Come on then, let's dance,' Emma cried.

We placed our empty glasses on a nearby table, pushed our way onto the dance floor, and both got lost in the beat of some old-school Ibiza club music: swaying our hips and waving our arms in the air; all we were missing were the glow sticks and fluffy boots. I had my eyes closed, feeling the music, when I felt a pair of hands on my hips and I was suddenly jerked back against a hard, broad chest. My eyes snapped open as I fought to pull myself away from whoever was holding me against them.

'Oi,' I said over my shoulder. 'Do you mind?'

'I don't mind, no.'

Hot breath that smelled of sour alcohol, whispered against my neck and made me shudder. As I pulled away again, his grip tightened.

'Hey, come on,' he murmured, 'I only want a dance.'

I turned the top half of my body around and pushed my palms against the guy's chest. He was built like an Eastern European weightlifter: squat, wide and with a short neck.

'Get off me!' I pushed again, but he barely moved. He just laughed and carried on gyrating, not particularly rhythmically or to the beat.

'Leave her alone,' Emma cried, appearing at my side.

'It's just a dance, sweetheart.'

The man's fingers loosened. He didn't let go of me totally, but it was enough for me to get free of him.

'Prat,' I snapped, as I slapped a hand against his chest. 'If I'd wanted to dance with you, I'd have asked.'

'Who the fuck do you think you're hitting?' he growled, his eyes darkening.

'You. Now, if you don't mind, I'd like to dance with my friend.' I turned to walk away, but he grabbed hold of my arm. 'I said, no!'

'Yeah, well, I don't like being slapped.'

I was about to raise my knee when a large hand landed on my shoulder. If the enticing smell of lemon and musk hadn't invaded my senses, I might have been scared. I turned my head around.

'Roman,' I gasped.

'You heard her,' Roman spat at the squat guy. 'She said she didn't want to dance; now get your fucking hands off her.'

Squat Guy dropped his hand from my arm, but he took a step towards Roman. 'You got a problem mate?'

The guy was a little shorter than me, but I was wearing four-and-a-half-inch heels. That being said, it still made him a good couple of inches shorter than Roman. Squat Guy was, however, extremely muscle-bound, so I was a little worried about how this might end up.

'Leave it, Roman,' I said, pushing him away with the palm of my hand.

'No, he doesn't get to manhandle you like that and get away

with it.'

'Emma!' I pleaded. 'Do something.'

Emma shrugged and looked wildly around. 'Where are the damn bouncers when you need them?' she cried.

'You don't need them.' Roman's jaw tightened as he looked at Emma.

'Roman, stop it now!' I demanded. 'I don't need you beating up the little guy just because he doesn't understand when he's not wanted.'

'Hey, who you calling "little", bitch?'

It all happened in one quick movement. Roman hauled me behind him with one hand, while the other shot out, the heel of his hand smacking hard against the man's nose, sending him reeling backwards and landing him on his arse.

'Nice one,' Emma whooped and did a little jig.

'You idiot. Do you want to get us thrown out?' I pulled at Roman's shirt as he shook his hand, still looking down at his victim.

At that moment the bouncers kindly made an appearance, shuffling through the crowd that had now congregated around us.

'What the fuck, Ro?' a huge ginger-haired man dressed all in black asked. 'You've fucking broken his nose.'

Roman nodded towards the man on the floor. 'See he gets sorted, Jimbo.'

'Will do. What's the damage, Dec?' Jimbo asked the other bouncer who was kneeling down next to Squat Guy.

'Yep, pretty sure you've broken his nose.' Dec, a bald-headed guy with pock-marked skin, grinned up at Roman. 'You've still got it, boss.'

Roman quickly turned to face me. 'Are you okay?'

'I'm fine, thank you, Mr. Bloody Terminator. What the hell did you do that for?'

'He was all over you,' Emma said sticking her hand out to Roman. 'Emma White, the best friend.'

'Hi, Roman Hepburn, the boss.'

Emma nudged me as she smiled up at Roman. I turned to her

15

and tutted.

'Like Emma said, he was all over you.'

'Yes, well, I had it covered, thank you very much.'

Roman let out a huff. 'I don't think so, do you?'

'Ooh no,' Emma grimaced. 'You don't want to call her out on being able to deal with Mr. Handsy.'

'Sorry?'

'You heard her,' I snapped. 'How dare you question whether I can look after myself?'

'Because you evidently can't,' he replied crossing his arms over his chest.

'As entertaining as this is, I think you two should move this somewhere quieter,' Jimbo said, leaning towards us both. 'You've got a bit of an audience.'

I spun around on my heels to see we did indeed have half a dozen or so people circled around us and watching everything that was going on. I grabbed hold of Emma's hand and stormed away towards the bar.

'Summer!' Roman growled in that warning tone that he liked to use on me—a lot.

'Wow,' Emma gasped as we reached the queue for the bar. 'He's freaking sexy. Why have you never introduced us before?'

'Because he's a miserable twat who gets on my tits on a regular basis. Is that a good enough reason for you?'

Emma bit on her bottom lip and nodded. 'Yes, but you might want to consider updating your CV.'

'Why?'

I turned to where she was pointing. Roman was striding towards me with a face as dark as a November morning.

'I think you might be about to get fired.'

'Hah, let him try,' I snapped, trying to sound more confident than I actually felt. 'I'll take him to a tribunal.'

As Roman reached us, I opened my mouth to speak, but he grabbed my hand and pulled me behind him. He moved forward a few paces, then turned back, still dragging me with him, and reached into his pocket. He pulled a note out of his wallet and shoved it at Emma.

'Get whatever you two are drinking and two bottles of beer and a shot of whisky.'

'O-okay,' Emma stammered.

'My friend will be here in a few minutes. You can't miss him, tall blonde guy with tattoos and a beard. Looks like a model. Probably got his hair in one of those twatty man buns.'

Emma nodded as Roman pulled me away from her, past the bar, and towards a door marked *'Private'*. He pressed a few numbers on a keypad and pushed the door open, before dragging me inside.

'What the hell are you doing?' I asked as he flicked on the light. 'We *can't* go in here.'

'Yes, we can; I'm co-owner of the place. As for what am *I* doing? What the hell were you doing dancing near a sleazebag like that? Couldn't you see that all the wanker wanted to do was to get into your damn knickers?'

'For your information, I was dancing there first.' The air rushed from my lungs. 'And don't speak to me like that.'

'I've just saved you from getting felt up,' Roman cursed. 'So I think I'll speak to you how I like. And did I get any thanks for it? No, I didn't.'

I gasped and glared up at him.

'I did say thank you,' I exclaimed. 'You ask Emma.'

'I think your words were "I'm fine, thank you." I don't recall the words, "Oh thanks for saving me, Roman" coming from your mouth.' Roman turned towards the door, his breaths deep and heavy.

'Can I just ask, what your damn problem is?' I asked. 'Was it totally necessary to drag me in here and tell me off like a child? We're not actually at work now, or hadn't you realised?'

He turned again and looked at me.

'It was necessary because you're rude, and I hate rudeness. Christ, you're just like Tiffany—got an answer for bloody everything and no manners to go with it.'

'Tiffany is perfectly lovely,' I snapped. 'And if I must, I apologise for my lack of manners, and please let me thank you for saving me from a dance worse than death.'

I gave him a sarcastic grin, and made to walk past him.

'Oh and next time ...'

I didn't finish whatever snarky comment I was about to make, because Roman was pulling me towards him, his jaw tight and his eyes dark. His gaze never left mine as he grabbed me, cupped my chin, tilted my head upwards and kissed me. His kiss was deep and strong, taking the breath from my lungs. The hand under my chin moved to thread through my hair, while his other hand pushed into the small of my back. My arms flailed at my side for a few seconds, but then as Roman's kiss became more insistent and I opened up my mouth to him, I snaked them up his back and gripped his broad shoulders. His muscles tightened beneath my fingertips, and he pulled me closer to him so that I could feel his growing erection through his trousers. I moaned gently as my whole body lit up, sagging against him, wanting him to hold me tighter.

'Shit.' Roman gently pulled away from me. 'I shouldn't have done that.'

I stepped back and felt my legs hit a desk. I reached behind me to grab hold of it for support. My chest heaved with the exertion and exhilaration of the kiss, my body buzzing with need.

'Seriously, it's not a problem,' I gasped. 'None whatsoever.'

'I just had to, and at least it shut you up,' he said. 'You've always got something to say.'

'I'd better go then,' I bitched, pushing off the desk onto shaky legs. 'Let you have some peace and quiet.'

'Summer.' Roman reached out his hand to me, but then pulled it back.

'Forget about it, Roman,' I said breathlessly. 'I need to find Emma.'

'She'll be fine,' he said, his eyes burning into mine, 'if she's with Henry. He's a good guy. But if you have to go, you have to go.'

I nodded and moved past him, the electric charge that zapped me when I brushed his arm not escaping my notice.

When I got back to the bar, Emma was leaning against the wall laughing at something the blonde man with her was saying. I guessed it was Henry. He was exactly as Roman had described him: tall, blonde, bearded, tattooed, with a *sexy* man bun, and he was very beautiful. He and Emma looked like they'd been handmade for each other. She certainly seemed to like him because I hadn't seen her smile at a guy like that in a long time. He'd obviously made an impression as I'd only been gone for ten minutes. But, shit, what a ten minutes they were! Not wanting to spoil her fun, I walked over to Jimbo, the bouncer, who was standing near the entrance door.

'Hey Jimbo,' I said shyly, 'I just wanted to say thanks for earlier.'

'I didn't do anything, love,' he replied with a grin. 'It was all down to the boss.'

'Was the other guy okay?'

'Yeah, nothing a free drink and a month's free entry wouldn't sort out. I don't think his nose was actually broken.'

'Oh, that's good. I'd hate for there to be any trouble. Anyway, I was wondering could you do me another favour, please.'

'It depends. If you want me to punch someone else, then the answer is no.'

'No, it's not that,' I giggled. 'My friend, Emma, she's over there with your other boss and, well, I don't feel too good, but if I go over and tell her, she'll want to come home with me and I don't want to spoil her night. So would you mind doing it for me, once I've gone?'

Jimbo looked over at Emma and Henry, who were now laughing hysterically together and standing distinctly closer to each other.

'Yeah, no probs.'

'Thanks.' I started to walk away and then a thought struck me. 'He is a good guy, isn't he? She will be safe with him?'

Jimbo threw his head back and started to laugh. 'Yes, love, she'll be perfectly fine with Henry. He might look a bit rough with all those tattoos, but he's one of the nicest blokes you'll meet. Him and Roman are two of the best. Both really top blokes.'

I looked over at Henry again. Despite the tats, he didn't actually look rough to me. He looked quite distinguished and as though he had impeccable manners. Unlike his business partner, who just took kisses from girls without asking. But—oh my God— Roman might not have manners, but he definitely had sexiness. In abundance! *And* he was my boss —deep joy!

'Cheers, Jimbo, tell her to call me when she gets home. No matter what time.'

Jimbo saluted me and then held the door open, letting me slip out into the cool night air towards the taxi rank.

As I climbed into the back seat of a cab, I looked back towards the club and saw Roman standing in the doorway watching me.

***

I barely slept that night thinking about Roman and waiting for Emma to call. I eventually got a text at four o'clock in the morning to say she was home. At just gone nine, Mum called us down for breakfast and, while I wasn't feeling my best, there was no way I was passing up one of her fry-ups.

'Morning.' Pippa, my younger sister yawned, scratching at her hair which resembled a bird's nest. 'You have a good night last night?'

'Yeah, great thanks.'

I'd had a couple of minutes: the rest of the night had been— *meh.*

'What about you, Pip?' my dad, Ray, asked as he folded up his paper.

'Not bad, Pater, not bad at all.' She grinned widely and gave Dad a peck on the cheek.

Dad gazed at her with pride, as he did with all three of us.

With two years between each of us, my brother, Dylan, the vet, was the eldest at twenty-seven. He was Ma's pride and joy, not only because he saved animals for a living, but he was her only boy and her eldest. Even though he lived in a flash apartment in town, Mum still liked to cook and wash for him. He was extremely handsome, and looked just like my Dad: tall and slim with a shock of honey-coloured hair and dark green eyes. With a cheeky grin, perfectly straight white teeth and the obligatory man-V, Dylan was every girl's wet dream. He had even done some modelling to help him through university.

Pippa, the youngest of us at twenty-three, and I looked a lot alike. We were both pale-skinned with black hair and blue eyes, but Pippa's hair was waist-length, whereas mine was cropped short and cut a little longer on top. It was usually styled according to whatever I was doing: straightened and tidy for work and quiffed and punky for pleasure.

Slim and long-limbed, we both appeared to be delicate, but as the saying goes: 'Never judge a book by its cover.' The James girls might look fragile and ladylike, but you wouldn't want to cross us, my mother included. Although Pippa's battles tended to be fought by the rest of us: she was the baby. She still had one hell of a temper, though.

'Didn't see you in Ziggy's,' I said to her as I sat down at the table.

'Nope, people to do, places to see.'

We both started to giggle just as my phone rang. It was Emma.

'Leave that,' Mum said, placing a large cooked breakfast in front of me. 'Whoever it is will have to wait.'

'Yes, Mum,' I sighed.

'This looks good, Sue,' Dad announced to Mum as he cut into his sausage.

'I know how you like your sausage,' Mum said, triggering another stupid giggle from me and my sister.

While Mum was distracted, dishing up Pippa's breakfast, I took a quick look at my phone:

Emma: Ring me when you can – got so much to tell you xxx

After breakfast, I sprinted back up to my room to call Emma

back. I felt bad for leaving her alone the night before, but Jimbo had promised me that Henry was a good guy.

As soon as she answered, Emma gave a little squeal down the line.

'Oh my God,' I cried, 'I take it that you had a good night.'

'Summer, he is so lovely. He's really respectful and, God, he's gorgeous.'

Her enthusiasm made me smile. She'd been steering clear of men since Tyler, so I was really happy that she seemed to like Henry.

'You're seeing him again?'

'Yes, but he's off to Barbados tomorrow for a week to see a friend, so he's going to take me out a couple of days after he gets back.'

'Did you sleep with him?' I asked. I was pretty sure I knew the answer, but I wanted to be certain that Henry hadn't slept with Emma and was then giving her the brush-off.

'No!' she snapped. 'I didn't! I told you he was very respectful. We sat in the office at Ziggy's until almost three. Then he said he'd better take me home, and when we got there we sat in his car for another forty minutes.'

'Just talking?' I giggled.

Emma paused and I heard her clear her throat. 'There may have been a lot of kissing involved.'

'Underclothes groping?'

I knew this answer too: Emma was a little more reserved than I was.

'Certainly not. But he did hold my hand.'

I burst out laughing at her sweetness. She was so adorable.

'Just because you probably let Roman feel your breasts! Because I'm assuming something did happen when he dragged you into his office like a frustrated caveman.'

Despite wanting to vehemently deny the accuracy of that deduction, I couldn't help but laugh again. Emma liked to use different words than I did to describe body parts. What were 'knockers' or 'boobs' to me, were 'breasts' to her, and what was a 'cock' or 'dick' to me was—believe it or not—a 'disco stick' to her.

'For your information, no, I did not let him feel my knockers.'

I heard Emma groan at my use of the word and couldn't help but smile.

'No wonder he looked so miserable when he was cashing up. Henry asked him to have a drink with us, but he just mumbled something about needing his sleep.'

'He didn't say anything else?' I asked, trying not to sound too desperate for information.

'No,' Emma sighed. 'Although, to be honest, I was more interested in Henry. Roman is very good-looking though, Summer. So, did something happen?'

I blew out a breath, and braced myself to explain about one of the hottest kisses that I'd ever had.

CHAPTER 4

♥

I was in the pub, groaning into my glass of wine, while my sister and my brother grinned inanely at my predicament.

I know it's unbelievable that I told Dylan that I'd kissed my new boss—most women wouldn't divulge such things to their brother —but that's how it's always been with the three of us. We told each other everything. Which is how I knew how many women he gets through in a month, and that Vicky Steadman was the best lay he's ever had. 'Hands down, Sum' and swear on the magnificent arse of Nicki Minaj,' he'd informed me.

'Just think of all the quick gropes you can get working in the same office,' Dylan said as he nudged me with his elbow.

'That is not going to happen!' I snapped, half-hoping it would.

'Wouldn't be so bad?' Pippa said with a shrug as she took a swig of her pint of cider.

'Seriously, what am I going to do?' I asked, pinching a crisp from the packet in Dylan's hand. 'I can't work with him. I'm going to have to find a new job.'

'Why do you?' Dylan asked, moving his crisps away from me. 'Didn't you say he was the one that snogged your face off?'

'To-may-to, to-mah-to, Dylan,' I cried. 'He hates me at work, and then kisses me last night. I just don't get it.'

Every day was the same with Roman. Him complaining that

files were missing, or they were incomplete; he'd even told me that my coffee was crap earlier in the week. Who does that and then sticks their tongue down your throat?

'He'll probably forget about it, especially if you were a shit snog,' Dylan said, not being at all helpful.

'He won't forget, stupid,' I hissed. 'Anyway, if I remember correctly, he seemed to enjoy it.'

'Did Biggus Dickus feel your boobies when you kissed him?' my sister asked.

'No,' I sighed. 'And stop calling him Biggus Dickus. For one, that's not even a proper Roman name; two, it's the most tenuous nickname I've ever heard; and three, you have no idea whatsoever whether he has a large appendage or not!'

'Sorry, sis,' Dylan sighed. 'I really have no idea what your problem is. You kissed him, he's your boss, get over it.'

'Well, if I fancied my boss, I think I'd find it awkward too,' Pippa said, rather sensibly for her. 'I mean, Mr. Devine is pretty hot for an older guy, but I can't imagine lusting after him all day. He's too particular on how he likes his cup of tea. Plus, he's too damn soppy about his wife.'

'Exactly,' I cried dismissively, 'I keep looking at him and thinking how sexy he is, while all the time wanting to strangle him. It's confusing and takes up too much energy trying not to drool while he's acting like a dick.' I swallowed hard and tried not to think of Roman's pert backside in his perfectly fitted trousers. It was so hard being faced with it in the office: him pacing up and down all day, that rock hard bum always in my view.

'Maybe he'd be up for a bit of sadomasochism,' my stupid brother added. 'You strangling him while he has a quick grope.'

'Is that the sum total of your advice?' I asked, with more than a hint of disgust.

Dylan nodded. 'Yep. Now, if you don't mind, I've just seen a girl at the bar whose cat I castrated last week. She kept flirting with me the whole time I was telling her all about Sid's undescended bollock, so I may be some time, girls.'

My brother winked at us, picked up his jacket and sauntered over to the bar to greet a tiny brunette who giggled and flicked her hair furiously as she gazed up at him.

'Want another?' Pippa asked, 'or shall we go home and get Ma to make us some hot chocolate?'

I looked across at Dylan, who already had his hand on the girl's backside. 'Hot chocolate.'

'Excellent choice,' Pippa said and drained her glass. 'And we'll also ask her what she thinks you should do about your sexy-as-hell grumpy boss.'

I groaned inwardly because I had no doubt that my mother would indeed have some thoughts on the subject.

CHAPTER 5

♥

Thankfully, I didn't see Roman for the week after our kiss, which was an even bigger relief than that wee you have after holding it in for two hours. Yes, I was nervous about what he'd say, but I was also tired of the constant sniping from him. He'd been in contact by email from the site he was on, but no phone calls or visits to the office. I had to wonder if he was avoiding me, but he *was* busy and didn't seem the sort of person to shy away from his mistakes.

When Friday rolled around again, I was thankful for my two days off, but also a little less stressed after four Roman-free days. When I saw his parking space was empty, I breathed a little sigh of thankfulness as he obviously wasn't coming in again. Roman was nothing if hard-working and usually was in the office long before and long after anyone else, so evidently I was to have another day of peace.

With a lovely strong cup of coffee in my hand, I started to look through my emails, contented at the peace and tranquillity of having the office to myself. However, that contentment didn't last long, when just after lunch Roman called me.

'Summer!' he barked down the line. 'Clear your diary and mine for next week, we're going to France.'

'W-what?' I stuttered. 'What do you mean, *we're* going to

France?'

'Exactly that. We. Are. Going. To. France,' he repeated slowly and deliberately. 'I take it that you've got a passport?'

'Yes, but—'

'Good. Get us a couple of flights to Nice, leaving on Monday and returning on Thursday.'

I scribbled the details down on a pad. 'What about a hotel?'

'Erm, well, book one,' he said as though I was stupid.

'I know that, but do you have a preference? A spa hotel, one with a gym, one without a gym, one with—'

'One with less narky women would be preferable,' he griped. 'May I suggest you check the Internet. It's that thing that's on your PC where you can search for anything.'

I huffed quietly. Who was being narky now?

'I'll call my friend Holly; her husband Liam used to run hotels all over the world. I'm sure he can recommend somewhere.'

'Whatever, Summer. Just make sure there's Internet, oh, and a gym.'

Now I had just about reached the end of my very thin tether with him. Why didn't he say that in the first place!

'Oh and our prospective client will be flying over too,' he said. 'So make sure you pack a couple of decent outfits as we'll be going to some top restaurants. We're going to have to do some serious wining and dining, and we need to impress him. You do have something suitable, I take it?'

'Yes,' I snapped, disgruntled that he was questioning my sartorial elegance. 'Do you?'

The short, sharp burst of laughter shocked me. Okay, it was very short and sharp, but it was definitely laughter. Roman rarely cracked a smile, never mind chortled.

'Let me know flight times,' he snapped, back to his usual self, laughter forgotten. 'And don't book anything too late going out so that we end up wasting a day travelling.'

'What is it we're going to be doing there, anyway?'

He sighed. 'Not that you need to know, but we've been approached by a guy called Alan Cromwell. He's from Rickeby, but wants us to refurb a farm and outbuildings that he's bought in France. He's turning it into an exclusive villa with adjoining apartments. It's going to be a top-end holiday let for people who have so much bloody money that they have no idea what to spend it on, apparently.'

'So not the sort of place I'll be going to on a girlie holiday, then?' I joked.

'No.' Was Roman's short reply. 'Now get those flights booked. We'll talk more on the flight over.'

'Can I just ask, why do I need to go?' I said.

Roman sighed. Because, Steve, the structural engineer can't go, and I'll need you to take notes and synchronise calendars. Believe it or not, you're pretty good at organising me.'

Then, before I even had chance to register the compliment, I heard the dial tone as he abruptly ended the call.

Rocking in my seat, and chewing on my lip, I stared down at the phone, desperately wanting to call him back and tell him that I couldn't go. I could hear my blood pumping in my ears as it had a drum battle with my thudding heart. How the hell was I supposed to spend time with him away from the office? We would be with each other all day, and all evening, and the thought petrified me.

By the end of the afternoon my nerves were in shreds, and I decided that I needed to talk to Emma about it. We agreed to meet at the pub just across the road from the office, but as I locked up the building, my phone beeped with a text from her:

Emma: Sorry, going to be 20 mins late. I'll have a white wine — large. Dad has got on my nerves today. x

I smiled as I put my phone back into my bag. Emma's dad, Ronnie, was a nightmare to work for. According to Emma, he never kept to time, always double-booked meetings and appointments without either consulting with his diary or Amy, his PA. His business lunches lasted all afternoon and often resulted in Amy having to make her way to wherever he was so that she could drive him home because he'd had too much to drink. No, Roman was an irritable cuss at times, but at least I knew where he was when I needed him.

Pushing through the double doors of the pub, the smell of stale beer was strangely comforting and I felt myself relax. I was being stupid: going to France with Roman wouldn't be so bad—would it?

Getting two glasses of wine, I made my way towards a table that I'd spotted over by the window. I was just a couple of feet away from the table, when a tall good-looking guy, with raven-black hair, plonked himself down at it.

'Shit,' I muttered, loud enough to get his attention.

He looked up at me and grinned. 'Sorry, did I just beat you to it?'

I gave him a weary smile. 'It's fine, I'm sure I'll find another one.'

I looked around the pub, but it was six-thirty on a Friday night: the place was packed.

'Hey,' he called, 'I'm not staying long. I only popped in because I'm early for meeting. Take a seat.' He pushed a chair out with his foot and nodded towards it.

'Are you sure? My friend will be here soon and if I know her, she'll have ridiculously high shoes on that are crippling her.'

'I'm sure,' he said, laughing.

'Thank you.' I plonked onto the chair next to him, placed Emma's glass of wine on the table, and took a huge gulp of mine.

'Bad day?' he asked.

'Bad week to be honest.'

'Well, glad I could help improve it then.' He put his own glass down and held his hand out to me. 'You don't remember me, do you?'

I looked closely. 'Oh my God, Jack Abbott,' I cried. 'It's got to be, what, nine years?'

'It has indeed, Summer James. How are you doing?'

'I'm great. Well, as great as you can be after a long week of work.'

'You work around here?' Jack asked.

'Yeah, just across the road at Barlow's.' I pointed through the window to our office and yard.

'So you're working for the infamous Roman Hepburn, then?' Jack's eyes widened as he watched me over the top of his glass. 'I heard he'd taken over the place.'

I almost spat my wine over the table. 'You know him?'

'Oh yeah,' Jack said nodding vehemently. 'Our paths have crossed, let's say.'

'Why, are you in the building trade too?' As I drank I watched him carefully.

He was very handsome, in a smooth, debonair way, with his neatly styled hair and pristine white dress-shirt tucked into dark blue jeans. His problem was, and had always been, that he knew he was good looking. He'd been fully aware that at least three women had given him a second glance in the last couple of minutes.

'Yes,' he replied. 'Not on Roman's scale, though. I'm more in the conservatory-attic-bedroom sector of the trade.'

I nodded and looked outside to check for Emma. I'd only grabbed a sandwich at lunch, and the wine was already making me feel a little tipsy. I was desperate for her to get here, so if we weren't eating, at least I wouldn't get plastered alone.

'You busy over there, then?' Jack asked.

'Fairly busy, yes. We have a shopping centre on the go, although that's on hold because of some stupid birds, and Roman and I are flying out to France next week to meet a possible client, a local guy who wants some holiday accommodation built.'

'Really, nice work if you can get it,' Jack laughed. 'My work takes me as far as exotic Manchester, if I'm lucky. There's not much call for small-time builders like me in France.'

'I'm sure you do okay. So you still see anyone from school?'

Jack shook his head. 'Nope. You?'

'I'm meeting Emma White actually, that's who the wine is for.' I pointed at the other large glass of wine on the table.

'Bet you'll be drinking the expensive stuff next week, if Roman is paying.'

'Oh I'm not sure about that.' I shook my head. 'He's not exactly your friendly type of boss who'd share a bottle with you.'

Jack nodded and played with a beer mat. 'I heard that about him. Heard a few things about him, actually.'

My interest was definitely piqued, but wasn't sure that I should ask. The less you know, the less you can get into trouble for. It seemed Jack, though, was a gossip, because I didn't need to ask.

'Listen, Summer,' he said. 'I know that he's your boss, but be careful out there in France.'

I tilted my head to look at him. 'Sorry?'

'Just be careful in France. It's probably not my place to say anything, but one of the things I've heard is that Roman likes to use his female employees to entice his clients.'

My heart dropped to the bottom of my empty, growling stomach, and I could feel the colour drain from my face.

'W-what? I'm sorry, what do you mean?'

Jack stood up and gulped back the last of his drink. 'I shouldn't have said anything. It's probably a load of old bollocks; just a girl I know, who knows another girl. You know how it is?'

'No, I don't,' I said, my shaking hand gripping my glass tightly. 'Tell me, Jack.'

'She just said that if Roman's having a struggle getting the client on board, he'll offer a little incentive in the form of some alone-time with his female employees.'

I shook my head. No way, Roman may well be a miserable bastard, but he was no pimp. Christ, was that what he was planning on doing to me?

'Hey, nothing major,' Jack insisted, leaning down to look me in the eye, and putting a reassuring hand on my shoulder. 'He just leaves them alone so the girl can flirt with the client a little bit, then he'll come back when he thinks the deal might be done.'

I swallowed the huge lump in my throat, as Jack took a step away. Was that why Roman had asked me about my clothes, to ensure that I had something that I could entice Mr. Cromwell with?

'Honestly, Summer, You'll be fine. Like I said, it's probably just a rumour, but just be aware. Okay?'

'Okay?' I whispered.

He pulled his wallet out of his back pocket, and flipping it open, drew out a black-and-silver business card and passed it to me.

'If you find it all gets a bit much working for him, then give me a call. And, I'm sure France will be fine. Who is it you're going to see out there, anyway? You said it was a local guy?'

Dazed, I stared down at the card, before snapping my gaze back up to Jack.

'Erm, yeah, a man called Alan Cromwell.'

'Al Cromwell, oh okay. Yeah, he's a nice enough bloke. You should be fine with Al.'

'Okay, well, thanks and good to see you.'

'Yeah, you too. Take care.'

As I watched Jack leave, I knocked back the rest of my wine and wondered how on earth I could get out of going to France. Just at that moment, my phone beeped again. Looking at it, I saw that it was a text from Roman, and my stomach lurched.

Grumpy: Thanks for sorting flights and hotel. See you at airport at 6. DON'T BE LATE.

Without hesitation, I picked up Emma's wine and knocked it back in one go. I may as well get pissed now, because there was no way I'd be getting drunk in France, not if I was to be on my guard at all times.

CHAPTER 6

Monday morning had dawned and my stomach was in series of Girl-Guide knots. Not only was I worried that Roman was going to expect me to charm Mr. Cromwell, but also because I would be spending a lot of time with him. For starters, in close proximity on the flight to France. He had never mentioned the kiss in Ziggy's, but then I'd hardly seen him since then, so maybe he'd want to talk about it while we were away. Suddenly my palms were sweaty and my heart was beating faster because, despite the fact that he could be the most grumpy man on the planet, I couldn't ignore that he sent my libido into warp factor.

As Roman and I were finally ensconced in our seats, the sun was slowly rising and I couldn't help that think that most people, i.e. those with a reasonable boss, were still sleeping and not getting on a plane.

'Couldn't you get anything a little later?' Roman grumbled as he shifted in his seat. 'We're not due to meet Mr. Cromwell until four this afternoon, I don't want to be fannying about all day.'

'*You* said to get an early flight,' I hissed as a stewardess stopped to check our seatbelts. 'So that's what I did.'

'You are aware of our relationship, aren't you?' he said, pointing a swirling finger between the two of us. 'That I'm actually your boss.'

'Yes. Why?' I said, unable to take my eyes off his lips.

'Oh no reason. I thought maybe you'd forgotten seeing as you talk to me like shit.'

And I was back in the room.

'Oh I'm sorry Mr. Hepburn.' I replied, with attitude. 'Please excuse my rudeness.'

I knew that I pushed the boundaries with Roman on a daily basis, but I couldn't help it. He knew how to wind me up and, to be honest, he didn't seem too perturbed by my backchat. To my way of thinking, he'd have fired me by now if he didn't.

Proving my point, Roman ignored my comment and continued to grumble on about the lack of leg room and general state of the plane that we were flying in. The flight was only a little over two hours long, but Roman complained the whole time. And, while it was annoying, it distracted me from thinking about *that* kiss in his office at the club, the kiss that thankfully he never mentioned. It didn't, however, distract me from his gorgeous smell. Because, to be honest, it was taking all my effort not to run my nose up the length of his body, it was so damn sexy.

It also hadn't helped that when he'd ambled into Departures earlier, a little drool had formed at the corner of my mouth. He was dressed casually in loose-fitting jeans and a worn grey T-shirt that stretched nicely across his broad chest. It wasn't the first time that I'd seen him out of a suit—he often came in wearing work clothes if he was going on-site—but it was still a lovely surprise so early in the morning. It was, however, the first time I had ever seen his arms bare of shirt sleeves, whether it be a flannel work shirt or a cotton dress shirt, and, God, they were ripped. His biceps, while not huge, were impressively big and a vision of me gripping them while looking up at him did flicker through my mind. Then Roman made some dismissive comment about my bed hair and I started to envision me gripping his throat instead. Thus, by the time we were in the taxi to go to the hotel, any good thoughts I had about Roman were almost gone. Only *almost*, because I couldn't *not* admire his hair. Its style wasn't unlike mine, shorter at the sides and longer on top, and today it wasn't combed straight and gelled into submission: it was all messy and sexy—so, yes, if I had a crush on anything, it was his hair; but I could live with that. There was the usual stubble on his jaw too, but I tried to ignore that as it drew my gaze to his lips again, which were full and kissable ... okay, this was getting ridiculous.

'Right,' Roman said as we exited the lift on our floor of the hotel. 'I've got some work to do, so I'll meet you downstairs in three hours. I've hired a car to drive us to the site where we'll meet Mr. Cromwell. It takes about an hour to get there, and I'd like to have a quick look around before the meeting.'

I glanced down at my watch, it was almost eleven-thirty. 'What about lunch, do you want to grab something to eat before we go over there?'

'No. If you want something get it and keep your receipt or charge it to my room.'

With that he picked up the handle of his case and strode away leaving me gawping after his gorgeous bum.

***

'You can see it's a big job,' Mr. Cromwell said to Roman as we wandered around the grounds of the villa. 'But I want the best of everything, and by that I mean the best materials and the best workmen and craftsmen that you can find.'

'That's a given,' Roman replied, running his hand down the stonework of the main house. 'There doesn't appear to be anything too wrong with the basic structure of this. Obviously, the barns are a different matter, but I'm confident that we can retain the rustic look and feel, even if we have to rebuild them from scratch.'

'You think you'll need to?' Mr. Cromwell rubbed a hand across his chin, seemingly contemplating the costs.

'On first inspection, the larger one is in better condition than the other two, but I don't want to commit until my structural engineer has looked at them. Once he has, I can work out the exact costs.'

'When will that be? Getting the structural guy here, I mean.'

Roman looked at me. I tapped at my iPad to find the calendars and timetables that I had stored on there.

'Steve can be out here next week.'

'Okay,' Roman replied. 'Get him a flight booked.'

'Already done.' I smiled at Mr. Cromwell.

'Well, that's what you call efficient,' he said, returning my smile.

'Summer is extremely organised, Mr. Cromwell. She'll be my contact for the project if you can't get hold of me. She will be able to provide you with any information that you need. And if she doesn't,' Roman said looking directly at me, 'then I'll want to know why.'

'Can't say fairer than that.' Mr. Cromwell paused and looked from Roman to me, and then back to Roman. 'Okay, Mr. Hepburn, as long as the numbers stack up, then I think we have a deal.'

He held his hand out to Roman, who took it and shook it firmly.

'Oh and call me Alan.'

'Roman.' Roman dropped his hand and then turned to me. 'Summer can you organise a table in the hotel restaurant for this evening. I take it that you're free, Alan?'

'Yes, I am. That would be great. But may I suggest somewhere other than your hotel?' he asked, turning to me.

I looked at Roman, who gave me a quick nod.

'Please do,' I replied.

Mr. Cromwell gave me the name of a restaurant and the telephone number. ,Seemingly, he and his family had holidayed in the area for many years, so he was very familiar with good places to eat.

I moved away from Roman and Mr. Cromwell to call the restaurant, pleased that the girl on the phone spoke good English, and I didn't have to use my schoolgirl French. After a few more minutes looking at the barns, Mr. Cromwell left with a wave and a promise of seeing us later.

'That went well,' I said, thankful that I hadn't been required to flirt.

'Hmm, too well,' Roman grumbled. 'He's not spoken to anyone else, and that worries me.'

'Why, surely that's a good thing?'

Roman shrugged and started to walk towards the car that he'd hired.

'I don't know, Summer, something about it all seemed a bit too easy, which usually means it won't be. But I guess we'll see.'

'Can we manage this and The Palisades?' I asked getting into the car.

'Because of the problems with The Palisades we *have* to do both. The other smaller projects that we've got going on aren't enough to sustain the workforce. The warehouse conversion is fairly substantial, but we need this. So, yes, we can manage. I'll use some of our own guys, but also local workmen as well.' Roman buckled up, turned the ignition, and we sped out of the farmyard.

'Do we need to be here until Thursday?' I glanced at Roman, trying not to stare too much at his profile as he concentrated on the road.

'I guess not. I was expecting to have to work harder to get the job.' He turned to me and gave me the briefest of smiles. 'When we get back to the hotel see what you can do with the flights.'

I nodded and then sat back, enjoying the view of the sea as we followed the coast road back to the hotel in silence.

***

I studied my reflection in the mirror and the butterflies in my stomach started to flap manically. Ever since I'd started to get ready for dinner with Roman and Mr. Cromwell, I'd felt sick. My main worry was what Roman expected of me. Would he really do what Jack had suggested, or was it simply a rumour? I hoped so, because there was no way I'd be doing any flirting with some man, just to get Roman a contract. If he expected me to, I didn't care whether he sacked me on the spot, I wasn't doing it. Something about what Jack had said was bugging me, though. Roman had saved me from Squat Guy in the club, so why would he then expect me to flirt with a potential customer? It just didn't make sense. I would still be on my guard, though.

Bizarrely, I did want to impress him, and prove that I could wear a nice dress and behave impeccably. I stupidly cared what the miserable goat thought about me, and I had to question my own sanity.

Despite my chagrin when Roman had asked me if I had an appropriate outfit, I hadn't. Oh I had the shoes and bag, but not the dress. Shoes were my particular drug of choice, and I thought nothing of spending hundreds of pounds on a pair that I would be happy to team with a pair of jeans. That was why I'd not only had to raid Pippa's vast and expensive wardrobe, but also rush into town on Saturday and buy something suitable. Hence, here I was studying the short, pewter-and-black striped dress that I was wearing. It was a skater style with a faux crop top and full skirt. I had loved it on the hanger in the designer boutique: it was fun and flirty, while still being sophisticated. Now I had it on, I wasn't sure it was appropriate. As I was quite tall—five feet seven—the skirt seemed even shorter, and I was sure if I bent over you could see my black, lacey boy shorts. Would Alan Cromwell see that as a green light to feel me up? While I contemplated changing into the cobalt-blue body-con dress that Pippa had loaned me, my mobile shrilled on the dresser next to the bed. It was a text message from Roman:

Grumpy: Hurry up, I feel like a prat standing in reception waiting for you.

I sighed and picked up my clutch bag. It was too late to change now; I hadn't even had chance to tone down my hair that I had styled it into a quiff. I wondered if I should have gone for my more conservative workplace style? Oh well, it would have to do. So with a quick touch-up of bright red lipstick, I left my room to meet Roman.

***

As I made my way across the reception towards Roman, my black-studded *Louboutin* shoes clipped on the marble, alerting

Grumpy's attention. He turned towards me, still looking down at his mobile phone in his hand. I took a few seconds to take him in and drew in a sharp breath. He was wearing a charcoal-grey suit, with a white open-necked shirt. He'd tidied up his stubble, but it was still there. He looked handsome—swoon-worthy handsome. As I got closer, he raised his head and stared wide-eyed at me.

'Summer.' His voice was so quiet I could barely hear him. It was almost reverent.

'Hey,' I said holding my hand up in greeting. 'Sorry you've had to wait.'

'Yeah, well,' he said with a cough, 'it gave me time to answer a couple of emails. You're here now, so let's get going.'

Roman strode ahead of me and pushed through the door to the hotel vestibule. He did at least hold the door open for me while nodding to the doorman to call us a taxi. The man stepped forward and clicked his fingers, indicating for the car at the head of the line to move forward. As the sleek, silver Mercedes pulled up at the pavement, the doorman bent to open the door. I stood back expecting Roman to get in before me, but he placed a hand in the small of my back.

'After you,' he said softly.

My breath hitched slightly as I felt a small shock throughout my body. Unnerved by Roman's touch, I clutched my bag to my chest and lowered myself into the back seat of the car, in as ladylike fashion as possible. I thought that Roman was going to sit in the front, so was surprised when I felt his knee pressed against mine.

'Oh sorry.' I shuffled further along the seat, not missing how hot my leg felt where Roman's had touched it.

'L'Aromate, s'il vous plait,' Roman said leaning between the seats to the driver.

'Oui, Monsieur.'

'Ah, so you speak French,' I said lightly, grinning at Roman.

'Only the basics,' he replied. 'But if this deal goes ahead, I think maybe we both need to get a better grasp of the language.'

'What, me too?'

Roman didn't look at me, but messed with the cuffs of his shirt that were peeking out from his jacket sleeve. 'Yep, you too. They may speak good English, but we'll gain more respect if we learn their language. It will also mean that we will know exactly what is being said about us.' He turned to me and gave me an absolutely glowing smile. It caused my heart to flip.

'Oh shit,' I muttered, shocked at how hard his smile had made my heart beat.

My head felt as though it was in a blender, he had me so confused.

'What's wrong?' Roman frowned.

'N-nothing,' I stammered like an idiot. 'I just … I just realised I didn't water my plant before we left.'

I groaned inwardly and lowered my head to stare at my clutch bag on my lap. *Hadn't watered my plant*—was that the best excuse I could come up with?

'Don't you live with your parents?' Roman asked quizzically. 'Just ring them and ask them to water it.'

'Yeah, I'll text my mum,' I mumbled as I fiddled with my mobile.

'Sometimes you're a bit weird, you know.'

I looked up at Roman and frowned. 'Well, thanks for that.'

He grinned and laughed—two smiles in a matter of minutes. 'You're welcome.'

My heart sank. Not only was his smile beautiful, but his laughter was rich and deep, and I actually felt a little excited down below. What the hell was he doing tonight? Where was the rude, abrupt dick that I usually worked for: the one that I wanted to strangle on a daily basis? This was all too confusing and making my head hurt.

CHAPTER 7

Dinner was going well: the food was excellent, the wine extremely fine, and the conversation was pleasant. The only problem was that Roman was being charm personified, not only to Alan Cromwell, but to me too. As the night had worn on, his bitching and sniping started to fade from my memory, and I found myself desiring him more each minute. Gone was my irritation with everything he said; now all I could think of was how I'd like that slight stubble of his to irritate me between my legs.

'Would you excuse me, please,' Roman said throwing down his napkin. 'I just need to visit the bathroom.'

My stomach lurched as he got up from his seat. He hadn't said anything, but was this when he expected me to turn Alan Cromwell's head? He'd be sorely disappointed if it was.

As the waiter came over to pour us some more coffee, I glanced at Mr. Cromwell, who had shifted his chair a little closer to mine.

'So, Summer,' he said as the waiter moved away, 'I have to say you look beautiful tonight.'

He reached across the table and ran a finger down my cheek. 'So very beautiful.'

I dragged in a sharp breath and inclined my head away from his touch. As my heart thudded, it felt as though my dinner was about to make a reappearance.

'Well, that's a lovely thing to say,' I replied, shifting my chair back a little. 'But I think maybe you're being too generous.'

'I certainly am not.' Mr. Cromwell moved his chair forward and leaned closer to me. 'You're just my type.'

My stomach roiled at the thought of being his type. I was probably young enough to be his daughter. He certainly looked older than my dad.

'Why don't you and I go on somewhere?' he asked.

I glanced over my shoulder wondering how to make an escape. I had to get out of here, and once I was back at the hotel, I'd be packing my things and getting the first flight out in the morning. Roman Hepburn could stick his job if this was what he expected me to do to get a client.

'I'm sorry,' I said through a clenched jaw. 'But I don't think so. I'm really tired.'

As I reached for my bag, Mr. Cromwell grabbed my arm and rubbed his thumb along my wrist. 'Oh come on, Summer, you know it's part of your job to keep the client happy.'

My heart sank. Damn it, his words just proved that Jack had been right! My palms started to sweat as I wondered what Roman would expect. The fear of being here with the two men was palpable. As I opened my mouth to tell Alan Cromwell to get his hand off me, the words wouldn't come. My tongue was sticking to the roof of my mouth, and I was trying desperately not to cry. I couldn't show any weakness.

Trying to make ready my escape, I dragged my chair further away from the table and took hold of my bag. Mr. Cromwell's hand tightened on my arm. I snatched it roughly away and grabbed my bag. Then out of nowhere, Roman appeared at my side.

I looked up at him with trepidation, tears brimming at my lashes, scared that he was going to insist that I let Mr. Cromwell letch over me. I should have just run when I had the chance.

'I'm sorry, Alan,' Roman said in a tight voice, 'I've had an urgent call about a problem with a job we're doing. We need to get back to the hotel. Summer?'

The relief was immense as he held a hand out for me. I just wanted to sag into his arms, but the uneasiness was still pulling at my stomach. He didn't look happy, and I guessed it might be because I hadn't played nice with Alan Cromwell. Well, I didn't care whether he was pissed off, because as soon as we were away from Alan the Creep, I'd be telling Roman Hepburn exactly what I thought of him.

'Goodnight Alan,' Roman said holding out a hand. 'I'll be in touch soon with the quotation.'

Alan shook Roman's hand and shifted in his seat. 'Pity we have to cut the night short,' he said looking straight at me. 'But work calls, I suppose.'

Roman gave him a short nod. 'Yes, sorry, Alan, but we really need to go. I'll settle the bill on the way out.'

I suppose he thought it was the least he could do, seeing as I had to go back to the hotel with him.

'Goodnight Roman,' Alan Cromwell called. 'Goodnight Summer, and hopefully I'll see you soon.'

***

As we got into the taxi, I glanced at Roman who still hadn't said a word. He was definitely angry because his jaw was tight and was pulsing rapidly.

'How could you?' I said my voice breaking. 'I'm not something that your clients can use as a plaything just to seal the deal.'

Roman breathed in heavily and turned to face me.

'I know and I'm sorry,' he replied.

I felt the nausea rising at the realisation that he was acknowledging it. Yes, he was sorry, but sorry for what? That I hadn't sealed the deal?

'He had no right touching you like that,' he snarled. 'I was on my way back when I saw him creeping you out. I know that you like to look after yourself, Summer, but he blatantly took advantage of you being alone, and his position as the client. It's damn not acceptable.'

'W-what?' I didn't understand. I thought he was mad because I'd brushed Cromwell off. I wasn't expecting him to be mad at

Cromwell.

'Did he hurt you?' Roman asked, looking down at my arm. 'When I got back to the table and saw that he had hold of you, I felt like punching him. If I'd known that's what he was like, I'd have never left you with him.'

'Oh,' I whispered, relief that Jack Abott was totally wrong about him sweeping over me like a comfort blanket. 'Thank you.'

'Wow, a thank you,' Roman said with a hint of grin. 'We are making progress.'

***

As we pulled up outside our hotel, Roman got out first and held out his hand for me. When I stepped out onto the pavement, he leaned into the taxi and asked him wait. Gripping my hand tightly, he then led me inside and stopped us in front of the highly polished lift doors.

With a sigh, he stabbed at the button with his finger.

'Why did you ask the taxi to wait?' I asked.

'Because I'm meeting a friend.'

My heart lurched as I wondered what gender that friend might be.

'He lives out here.'

I shouldn't have, but I grinned widely and did a little dance of joy—in my head, obviously.

When the lift arrived, Roman waited as I walked inside. He then held the door and I thought maybe he was coming up with me.

'I'll work on Cromwell's figures in the morning, so you can have some free time. But get to my room by one o'clock.

'Wow, a whole morning off, thank you Mr. Hepburn,' I said with a grin.

'I can always find you something to do in the morning if you'd prefer,' he sniped back, with a shake of his head.

'Nope, that's fine, thank you.'

'Fuck,' he muttered, 'another thank you.'

I should have been annoyed at his little dig, but I was far too distracted about him saving me, and the fact that he'd seen me safely into the hotel.

'Thanks again for tonight,' I said, giving him a small smile.

'Don't forget, one o'clock,' he said without acknowledging my thanks. 'We've got plenty of work to be getting on with.'

He then turned on his heels and walked back towards the hotel doors.

'Grumpy idiot,' I moaned while still taking time to appreciate the damn splendid bum that was disappearing through the doors.

CHAPTER 8

♥

Ugh, my mouth felt like the bottom of a budgie's cage and my head felt as though someone had cut the top off it and shoved a woolly hat inside. Champagne was a killer, and I had drunk far too much of it the night before.

My head spinning about the enigma that was Roman, I had run myself a bubble bath to try and relax. I also decided that one of the half bottles of champagne from the minibar, would be a great accompaniment while I soaked. That would have been fine, except, once I was in my pyjamas, I felt bad for the other half bottle left all on its own in the cold, dark fridge, so I drank that one too.

With a groan I checked the time and rolled out of bed— literally. I landed on the floor and contemplated staying there. After a couple of minutes of being nose to carpet, I heaved myself up and into the shower. The early May weather was gorgeous outside, and I decided that my free morning would be spent lazing by the hotel pool. While Roman worked on his figures for Mr. Sleazy I wasn't going to waste my time lying on my bedroom floor and lamenting the invention of champagne.

Almost an hour after shifting my body into the shower, I made it down to the hotel pool. The sun was high in the sky, and I was

47

glad for my huge sunglasses, and the two painkillers that I'd had for breakfast. There weren't many people around: a couple with their two young boys, an elderly couple sunbathing fully clothed and a middle-aged woman with a smooth, line-free face, pert boobs, but a wrinkled neck and arms—she was evidently working her way down her body with the plastic surgery.

I found myself a spot in the corner away from everyone else and close to a little cobbled path that led into the gardens of the hotel. Having stripped off my white, crochet cover-up, I slapped on some sun cream and made myself comfortable, surreptitiously pulling my red bikini bottoms out of my bum cheeks. With a contented sigh, I lay back on the sunbed, closed my eyes and let the warmth of the sun lull me to sleep.

'Where the hell have you been?' The loud growl dragged me from my blissful dozing.

'Roman? What the …'

'Where have you been?' Roman demanded as he towered above me, hands on hips. 'I've been looking everywhere for you.'

I shaded my eyes with my hand and pushed up onto my elbow. What the hell was his problem?

'You said you didn't need me until one.'

'Well, I do now. I've been trying your mobile for the last hour; I even got housekeeping to open up your room for me.'

'Did you not think that I might be by the pool, perhaps?' I hissed, looking around at the other guests, who were casting worried glances in our direction. 'And stop shouting, people think that you're going to hit me or something.'

Roman turned around and glared at everyone. They all went back to their own business, except the wrinkly woman: she was still prone on her sunbed and hadn't moved a muscle—but that could have been because she couldn't move due to vast amounts of Botox.

'I wouldn't have had to come looking for you, if you'd just answered your damn phone,' he said, his voice now a little quieter. 'That's if it's actually on, of course.'

I reached down into my bag and pulled out my mobile. There

were twenty missed calls from Grumpy, one from an unknown number, and a text from Pippa that simply said: *'Have borrowed your new push-up bra!'* Hah! Typical of Pippa, I hadn't even worn it yet.

'I didn't hear it. I must have been in a deeper sleep than I thought,' I explained.

'Yeah, well,' he huffed, 'maybe you should turn the volume up in future.'

'So what did you want me for?' I asked, choosing to ignore the last comment.

Roman scrubbed a hand over his face, but didn't speak.

'God, you infuriate me,' he sighed, flopping down onto the sunbed next to me. 'I need you to help me with the quotation.'

My breath caught in my throat as I stared at Roman. His jaw was set hard, but his eyes looked tired as he returned my gaze, yet he looked spectacularly handsome.

'Okay,' I replied, 'I'll come up with you now.'

'As long as you don't mind dragging your backside off that sunbed,' he snapped, standing up. 'After all this isn't a damn jolly, Summer.'

'Okay,' I huffed, 'I've said I'm coming.'

Roman shook his head and picked up my cover-up. 'I'll see you in my room, but get some damn clothes on first.' He threw the white top at me and strode away. I think he even growled in the direction of the two small boys splashing about in the pool.

'What the hell is his problem?' I muttered to myself, dragging my cover-up over my head.

'Lover's tiff, honey?' the elderly lady with the husband asked in a Southern-American drawl.

'Sorry?'

'That man of yours, he sure is feisty,' she laughed.

'Oh he's not my man,' I replied as I pushed my feet into my flip-flops, 'he's my boss.'

'Jeez,' she whistled. 'They didn't make bosses like that in my day. He's one damn fine man. Although, don't tell Harold I said that.' The woman burst into laughter as she looked at her husband, who was snoring loudly next to her.

'Well, nice to meet you,' I said, as I passed the end of her sunbed.

'You too, honey, and take my advice, make that man your boss in the bedroom too. He looks as though he'd be *darn* good.'

As I walked away, she was still chortling to herself, whereas I was feeling all hot and bothered at the thought of Roman ordering me around in the bedroom.

***

A little over three hours later, and we had finally finished the first draft of the quote for Mr. Cromwell's villa and luxury apartments. It would need adjusting once Roman had received the report from Steve, our structural engineer, but the bulk of it had been written. While it was a lot of money Roman was quoting, I also knew that the margins were tight to ensure we got the contract.

Since I'd been working for him, I seen how hard he worked, and that he was a much better businessman than Mr. Barlow. He took ownership of far more than his predecessor ever had: *he'd* been more than happy to delegate every little task to me and other members of staff. Roman took responsibility for finding the work, quoting the right amount for it and then ensuring that we always came in within budget. However, it had only really hit home today, helping him with the Cromwell deal, *how* much stress he was under. Normally he locked himself away in his office taking direct calls and dealing with clients; today I'd been there when he'd taken call after call about not only The Palisades and the warehouse project, but all the other smaller projects that we were involved in. I had also heard him on the phone to Gareth, the company accountant, who was stressing about unpaid invoices, penalty clauses, and wage bills. I knew that the company had been in trouble when Roman took over, and I also knew that in a short time he'd started to turn things around, bringing with him not only his expertise, but a good reputation in the building industry. I now understood totally why he was so grumpy most of the time. Who wouldn't be with that amount of stress?

'Do you want a drink of anything?' I asked Roman as he stretched his arms above his head.

'No thanks, a hot shower and I'll be fine.'

I looked away quickly as his T-shirt rode up and gave me a glimpse of flat stomach and a happy trail disappearing into the waistband of his undies. I really ought to get back to my room and maybe call Emma, or Pippa, anything to distract me from that stomach! Oh and his smell *again*, it was so sexy and was addling my brain.

'Okay, well, if we're finished, I'll go.'

Roman gave me a hint of a smile. 'Thanks for today. You know how shit I am at typing up proposals. I'd have still been doing it on the flight home tomorrow.'

'Hmm, it does take a while when you insist on using one finger to type.' I picked up my bag and walked towards the door. 'What time shall we meet for dinner?'

'I don't have time for dinner,' Roman muttered as he started to tap away on his mobile. 'I've got other stuff I need to do. You go for it, though; same as yesterday, either keep the receipts or charge it to my room.'

My shoulders dropped as my whole body seemed to deflate with disappointment.

'Oh okay, I'll see you in the morning then.'

'Yeah, and make sure you're in reception on time,' he grumbled. 'The taxi is picking us up at seven-thirty.'

'I know, I booked the damn thing.'

'I'm simply reminding you, that's all. I know what you women are like, fannying around getting ready.'

'Well, I'm not like other women,' I snapped flinging the door open. 'And if I'm late, then have a go at me, otherwise keep your thoughts to yourself.'

'Hey, remember who's the boss,' Roman snarled with his back to me.

'As if I could ever forget.'

I slammed his door behind me and stomped back to my room. Working with him recently had become a pain in the backside, even more so than ever before. One minute he was being nice, the next a total tool. Well, when I got home, I was definitely going to look for another job. Somewhere that the boss was old, grey, un-fanciable and gentlemanly.

Still grumbling to myself, I let myself into my room and walked over to the bed, throwing my bag on top of it. I turned to my dresser and stopped. My heart thudded. On top of the dresser was a *Chanel* gift bag. I peeped inside the bag to see a bottle of *Coco Mademoiselle*, my favourite perfume. Propped up against the gift bag was a note:

Summer
Just a thank you for all your hard work recently, especially as I'm not the easiest boss in the world.
Grumpy

I gasped at the signature. How the hell did he know I had him in my phone as Grumpy? And—more to the point—what my favourite perfume was? Then the thoughtfulness behind the gift brought a lump to my throat, and I decided to have a rethink about my job search.

CHAPTER 9

♥

Once we got back to the office, Roman was his usual self: irritable and cranky. If anything, he was getting worse, even complaining about the style of my internal emails—who the hell cared whether I started them with '*Hey Guys*'.

Roman had almost brought me to the end of my very short rope when he decided that the Cromwell quote needed some amendments. I was just trying to decipher his scrawled changes, when Alfie Chambers, one of our carpenters, swaggered into the office with a huge grin on his face.

'Hey, Summer, how you doing?' he asked, perching on the edge of my desk.

I tutted at the sawdust that settled on some paperwork and gently nudged at his bum with a ruler.

'Get off, you're messing up my desk,' I moaned good-naturedly.

'Sorry.' He stood up and pulled over a chair. 'Where were you earlier this week? I missed you.'

'France, with Roman.' I opened my drawer and picked up a packet of biscuits, handing them to Alfie. 'Here, I know that's all you've come in for.'

Alfie grinned and took a couple of biscuits from the packet. 'No, your beautiful face drew me here as well.'

'Whatever. Now, what can I help you with?' I asked, putting the biscuits back in the drawer.

'Is the boss man in?' Alfie said around a mouthful of biscuit.

'He's just popped out,' I sighed, thinking of the icy atmosphere there had been over the last two days. 'He shouldn't be much longer, if you want to wait.'

'Any chance you can check whether he's left me a worksheet for the Hutchinson extension?' Alfie asked with a cheeky grin. 'He said he'd leave it on his desk.'

'He'd have left it with me,' I sighed, 'but I'll check.'

I got up and went into Roman's office, finding the worksheet that Alfie wanted. Needless to say, it was under a load of other papers, but it I found it after a little bit of tidying.

'Here you go.' I handed it to Alfie and returned to my desk.

'Cheers, although I still need to speak to him. Okay if I wait?'

I'd rather he didn't, I'd got work to do, but Roman was due back any time.

'Yeah, if you like.'

'Okay, good. So is this a good time to ask you out for a drink … again?' he asked, winking at me.

'Alfie,' I groaned. 'How many times do I have to tell you, I'm not interested? Besides which, you remind me too much of my brother.'

'I look like him?'

'No. The masses of women that you have in and out of your bed.'

'I do not!' he protested with a smirk.

'Oh you so do, and, even if I was single, you would be the last man I'd go out with. Some of us want to be a bit more to a man than a one-night stand.'

Alfie started to laugh. 'Yeah, but what a night it would be. I'd make you feel amazing, I can promise you that.'

My heart did a little pitter-patter because I was in no doubt that he would, but Alfie was someone women should avoid if they had any self-respect. Unlike Dylan, Alfie wasn't charming when he got rid of the women he slept with. An old school friend of mine had been on the receiving end of Alfie's brush-off, and it hadn't been pleasant.

'Go on,' Alfie said interrupting my thoughts. 'What about it? Just once.'

He leaned across the desk and pushed a lock of hair behind my ear. Just as I lifted my hand to push his hand away, Roman decided to return.

'What the hell is going on?' he demanded standing in the doorway, hands on hips.

'N-nothing,' I stammered.

Alfie pulled his hand back from my face slowly and grinned at Roman. 'I was waiting for you, and Summer and I thought we'd use the time to arrange a date.'

I waited in trepidation for Roman to blow a gasket. He hated people shirking at work, and was well known for being a hard taskmaster. When he turned up on site, it wasn't unusual for him to get stuck in laying bricks or sanding floors, and if anyone wasn't working as hard as him, they soon knew about it. So for Alfie to admit that he'd been messing around meant he had some balls.

'Well, I don't pay either of you to arse about fixing up dates.'

Yep, he was mad.

'I wasn't,' I said, trying to protest my own innocence at least. 'Alfie's only got here, and he's messing with you, aren't you, Alfie?'

I looked at Alfie pleadingly. I know I didn't normally care what Roman said to me—I could hold my own with him—but for some reason I didn't want him to think I'd been arranging to go out with Alfie.

'Yeah, unfortunately she won't take the bait. I keep trying, but she ain't interested.'

Roman stared at me, his eyes blank and his face unreadable.

'Have you sent the final quotation to Alan Cromwell?' he barked.

'No, not yet. I'm trying to decipher your handwriting.' I gave him a smile that barely touched my lips.

'Right, well, I suggest you get on with it then, and, Alfie, I suppose you'd better come into my office,' he said as he turned and stalked away.

'Oh dear,' Alfie whispered leaning closer to me. 'Sounds like someone is in a bad mood.'

'Nothing new there,' I muttered turning back to my PC and halting any further conversation.

***

For the rest of the day Roman barely spoke, unless he was barking orders at me. It was all very stressful. I'd be working away quietly, then all of a sudden Roman's office door would be flung open and he'd bellow something, scaring me half to death. I almost jumped off my chair the first time he did it. I shouldn't have been surprised because it wasn't as though that sort of behaviour from him was unusual.

Finally it was time for home and I had never been so glad. I was just packing up my things when, in my peripheral vision, I saw Roman standing at my desk.

'I need you to work late,' he said without any preamble.

I looked up at him and smiled. Not a nice happy smile, but a 'I-hate-your-guts-and-I'm-pretending-not-to-so-that-I-can-kill-you-when-you're-least-expecting-it' sort of smile.

'No, I don't think so,' I replied, heaving my workbag onto my shoulder. 'I have plans and you can't just spring something like that onto me. Plus, it's Friday, I am not working late on a Friday.'

'I need you to work and, as your boss, I can request you do that.' He folded his arms across his chest causing the cotton of his shirt to stretch against his biceps.

'Yes, Roman, you can request it, but I can also say no. And that is what I'm doing.'

'What plans have you got? Can't you cancel them?'

I looked at him wide-eyed and gave an empty laugh.

'Hah. No, I can't and you have no right to ask me to.'

Roman ran a hand over his face and turned, taking a step away from my desk.

'Can I go then?'

'I suppose so,' he grunted turning back to face me. 'Where are you going to anyway?'

'Ziggy's,' I said with a shrug. 'Why?'

'Just wondered what was so damn important that's all. With your boyfriend, or your friend, Emma?'

'No, my sister. I don't have a boyfriend. Anything else?'

What the hell was with all the damn questions? He could barely say hello most days.

Roman shook his head and stormed back into his office.

'Christ,' I muttered under my breath. 'If I didn't know better, I'd be sure he was on his period.'

'I fucking heard that,' Roman shouted. 'If you're going, go now before I make you damn well stay.'

Resisting the temptation to shout a response, I left the office wondering what the hell had twisted his undies more than usual.

CHAPTER 10

♥

Pippa and I sat in silence people-watching at a tall table in Ziggy's, and I was not feeling the joy like everyone else in there appeared to be.

For starters, Roman had pissed me off with his attitude earlier. Then, when I was all ready to go, Dad came through from the kitchen with a full glass of red wine for Mum, tripped on one of Pippa's shoes where she'd dumped them, and splashed wine all down the front of my dress. I had been feeling good about the red mini dress that I'd been wearing, and was not liking the skinny jeans and peacock-green vest top that I now had on.

'Fancy going home after this one?' I asked Pippa.

She gave me a thin-lipped smile and shook her head.

'No, I refuse to be home before Saturday on a Friday night. I'm waiting for a gorgeous guy to walk through that door, I can feel it in my waters.'

'Really? We'll see.'

'Remind me never to come out with you again when Emma can't make it,' Pippa grumbled.

Emma was on a date with Henry, and I'd had to resist the temptation to keep texting her for some light relief. This was their first proper date after meeting.

'It's nothing to do with Emma,' I grumbled. 'I've just had a bad day.'

'Oh and what's Mr. Boss Man done now?' she asked, stirring her straw around in her drink.

'Same as usual, being a miserable bastard. He's had a go at me today for talking to one of the lads.' I looked over my shoulder towards the back of the club where Roman's office was, wondering whether he was behind the door.

'Maybe he's stressed,' Pippa replied with a shrug.

'Well, if he is, he's permanently stressed.' I drained my glass and heaved out a long, drawn-out sigh. 'I know he's worried about the France deal, maybe that's making him worse.'

'Why, what's wrong with it? I thought you said it went well.'

I shrugged. 'I did, apart from the client being a little bit lecherous. It's just that Roman's cut it right down to the wire as far as the costs are concerned. His profit margin is really tight, but he wants to use the best materials possible and French labour and—'

'Yep, okay,' Pippa huffed. 'It's official, you're the most boring sister on the planet.'

I stared at her wide-eyed and slapped at her arm.

'Pippa!'

'Summer!' she said, with her hands on her hips. 'Get a life and get us a drink.'

***

Twenty minutes later, while the crowd had increased, the gorgeous-guy count had not. I was just about to tell Pippa that I was done, when Jack Abbott appeared at our table.

'Hey, Summer,' he cried. 'Not once in nine years and now twice within a week. How're you doing?'

'I'm good, thanks, Jack.'

'This isn't your little sister, Pippa, is it?' Jack pointed at Pippa and grinned.

'Hi,' Pippa replied, a little breathily. 'I remember you, Jack Abbott.'

I groaned inwardly as she licked her lips and shoved her tits out. Jack, ignoring her mating dance, turned back to me.

'How was France? How was Hepburn?' he asked. He sounded

worried, but the way he bit out Roman's name made me think that the question was so much more about his dislike of my boss than concern for me.

I had no idea how France was, apart from confusing.

'It was fine, nothing to worry about.' I smiled, not wanting to tell him about the incident with Alan Cromwell. There was no need—Roman sorted it.

'Really, nothing at all?' he asked, his brow furrowing.

Something told me that Jack may well have been hoping I had something juicy to tell him.

'No, nothing at all.'

'Well, that's good.' He shrugged. 'Anyway, can I get you both a drink?'

Pippa opened her mouth to give her order when I slapped a hand on her forearm.

'It's fine, Jack. Thanks anyway, but we're going soon, and you must be here with friends.'

'Actually, no,' he replied with a sigh. 'My mate, Terry, was with me, but his wife hasn't been well this week, and he felt guilty about leaving her, so he went home after a couple of pints.'

'And you wanted to stay out and continue to have fun?' Pippa asked with another flick of her tongue to her lips.

God, she was so obvious, it was painful.

'Something like that; so go on, don't leave me on my own. Have one drink with me.'

I looked at Pippa, who was silently begging me to say yes. She always did this: gave me those damn puppy-dog eyes of hers and I always gave in. Pippa always got her own way.

'Okay, just one. White wine for both of us, please.'

When Jack went off to the bar, Pippa squealed excitedly.

'Agh, I've always fancied him. He's so fit, oh my God, Summer.'

I looked over at Jack, and she was right, he was good-looking, but he wasn't my type. He was too clean-shaven; he didn't have much muscle; he was a couple of inches too short, and he certainly didn't have a tight, little arse that I wanted to take a bite out of—

Ugh, why couldn't Roman just bugger off out of my head and leave me alone?

'Well, go for it, Pip,' I said, slapping my sister on the back. 'He's all yours.'

Two hours later, the three of us were pretty drunk and Pippa was laughing hysterically at the most ridiculous things. She'd also flirted her backside off and Jack was extremely attentive to her, but didn't appear to be looking for anything other than a couple of drinking buddies for the evening, and someone to talk about himself to. Some of his stories were amusing, but there was only so much Jack Abbott I wanted to be bombarded with. If I was honest, he was pretty boring.

'So as I knocked through the wall,' he laughed, continuing a story about one of his building jobs when he was an apprentice, 'I heard this squeal, and this woman stood up in a bath and held a sponge in front of her, thinking that would cover everything.'

'Oh God, no!' Pippa gasped. 'So you knocked through the wrong wall?'

'Yep,' Jack groaned. 'The gaffer had marked the wrong wall, and I knocked straight through into next door's bathroom.'

Even I laughed at that one. Pippa, ever the one to go over the top, was struggling to breathe and wiping tears from her eyes.

'Something seems to have amused you three.'

With a gasp, I stopped laughing and looked up to see Roman. He was standing next to me with his arms firmly crossed over his chest, his back poker-straight. His eyes were firmly pinned on Jack.

'Fancy seeing you here,' I said with an air of surprise and a hint of sarcasm.

Roman turned his gaze to me. 'I'm sorry, have I never mentioned that I'm part-owner of the place?'

He gave the briefest of lip curls and then looked back to Jack.

'Abbot.' His tone was sharp and pinched, and I got the distinct impression he didn't really like Jack very much.

Jack gave Roman the brightest of smiles and leaned his elbow against the table, looking relaxed and confident.

'Roman, great to see you. I'd heard you bought into this place. Jumping on Henry's coat-tails again?' Jack smiled, but the comment was full of animosity.

'Well, you know me, Abbott, I like to hang around with those that give me a hand up in life.'

My gaze darted between the two men: the dislike was palpable. There was steel in both their eyes, and Roman's body language was defensive, bordering on combative. Jack was leaning leisurely against the table, but there was no disguising the stiffness of his shoulders.

'Hi,' Pippa said a little breathlessly. 'I'm Pippa, Summer's sister.'

'Nice to meet you, Pippa.' Roman gave her a dazzling smile, making me groan inwardly. Mr. Charm himself. 'Do you have a minute, Summer?' he asked, glancing at me.

'What about?' I asked, with a dismissive shrug.

It was Friday night, and I was not in the mood for a lecture about something that I'd done at work; or anything else, for that matter.

'I just need a quick word. You can bring Pippa with you, if you like.'

He nodded at Pippa, whose eyes were sweeping up and down his body without any shame or embarrassment.

'She'll be fine with me,' Jack countered, nudging Pippa with his shoulder.

'W-what?' she asked, quickly turning to Jack. 'Sorry, I wasn't listening.'

God, she was so fickle. For the last two hours, she'd been practically dribbling over Jack, but now her interest was firmly on Roman.

'She'll be fine,' I muttered, pushing up from my stool. 'Come on then, let's get it over with.'

As we walked past Jack, I distinctly heard Roman growl. It was actually quite sexy, giving me just a hint of a warm feeling between my thighs. Obviously I'd had far too much to drink. I followed him towards the back of the club, where I now knew his office was. The thought of going back in there— where we'd had our kiss—set my pulse beating on an erratic rhythm. Was he going to kiss me again? Would I kiss him back? As I watched his bum in his straight-cut black trousers, I was pretty sure that I would definitely kiss him back.

As soon as we were in the office, Roman slammed the door and turned to me. Thank God I didn't stand there with my lips pursed and my eyes closed, because it was clear he was not going to kiss me.

'What the fuck are you doing with Jack Abbot?' he snarled.

'I used to go to school with him. Why?'

Roman rubbed his hand down his face and groaned.

'He's not to be trusted, Summer, and, please, don't leave your sister with him for long.'

His tone was a little softer now, but just as firm in its demand. I was seeing another Roman: a different one than I'd ever seen before. This Roman was worried.

'What's he done?' I asked, 'because he was always okay at school. Is Pippa in danger?'

Roman shook his head. 'No, nothing like that, but he's bad news. He'll just use you, and Pippa, if he needs to. I know someone he hurt badly, and he couldn't give two shits about it.'

'In what way? What way did he hurt her? Did he hit her, or something?'

'No, he betrayed her, and it wasn't the last time he hurt someone.' Roman sighed. 'All you need to know is that he's a fucking shit.'

I didn't know what to say. It didn't sound like the Jack Abbott that I knew, but then I hadn't seen him since he was a good-looking teenage boy, whose main thought in life was feeling a girl's tits.

'Seriously, Summer,' Roman said softly, and he reached for my hand.

I took in a sharp breath, and glanced down at his fingers laced in mine, and then back up to his face. His eyes were soft and pleading, and I think my heart actually stopped he looked so handsome.

'I really don't want you seeing him.'

'What exactly did he do?' I asked quietly. 'I can't just march out there and drag Pippa home by her hair.'

'Does it matter what he did?' he snapped. 'Believe me, he's not to be trusted, and you're not to see him anymore.'

While I'd been willing to listen to reasonable Roman, I was not being *told* what to do by dictatorial Roman.

'I don't think you can actually tell me not to see anyone,' I replied, snatching my hand from his. 'I hear what you're saying, but if I want to see him, I will.'

I had no real interest in seeing Jack Abbott again, but Roman didn't need to know that. But he couldn't think he could just turn around and tell me what to do.

'Why can't you listen to me for once?'

'I am listening to you, but you can't tell me who I can and can't see. You're my boss, Roman, not my dad,' I snapped.

Roman shook his head, and I could see the frustration bubbling in his eyes. Why couldn't he see, that if he'd just told me what Jack had done and then left it at that, I'd have probably come to the conclusion not to see him myself?

'Well, don't ever come to me if he hurts you or your sister,' Roman said quietly, moving to the door and holding it open. 'He's a bastard, and he doesn't care who he hurts. Now, if we've finished, I have work to do.'

He waved me out of his office, not allowing me to respond; then as soon as I was through the door, it slammed shut behind me.

Worry and confusion gnawing at my gut, I made my way back to Pippa. As I approached the table, I could see that she and Jack had their heads together and were laughing. Watching them, after hearing what Roman had said, I found myself looking at Jack through different eyes. His whole demeanour was that of a man confident in himself. He was loud and slick, not a hair in the wrong place, and when I thought about it, we'd talked about him all night. He'd also been quick to pass on gossip about Roman that had been totally unfounded—well, it was unfounded as far as I was concerned. But, being a gossip didn't mean he would hurt me, or Pippa, for that matter. He wouldn't have an opportunity, because even before Roman had spoken to me, I'd already decided I wouldn't be actively seeking Jack out in the future.

As I continued to watch, Jack nodded down at Pippa's glass and then went off to the bar. I took the opportunity to go back to my sister.

'Hey, you ready to go yet?' I asked, knocking back the rest of my drink.

'Now?' She looked at her watch, and screwed up her nose. 'There's only an hour to go, we may as well stay until the end.'

I knew she wouldn't budge, and it looked as though Jack was getting more drinks in, so we'd have to finish those first.

'Okay, but it'll be your fault if we struggle to get a taxi.'

Pippa grinned at me, knowing that, once again, she'd got her own way.

'Anyway, you sneaky little devil,' she gasped. 'You never told me what a little hottie your boss was. No wonder you snogged him. Hey, is that what he wanted you for then?'

Her eyes shone with excitement as she bounced up and down on her stool.

'Did he feel your tits this time?'

I couldn't help but laugh at her stupid antics.

'No, he just wanted to check something about work.'

'Oh really,' she groaned, disappointed. 'I was sure you were necking again. I told Jack I was sure.'

'And what did he say?' I asked, trying to sound disinterested.

'Nothing, he just nodded and said "Oh". Why do you fancy him too?' Her eyes were wide as she stared at me aghast.

'God no, not at all,' I replied a little too vehemently. 'Why, do you?'

I'd seen the flirting and the little glint in her eye. Jack was flash and happy to spend his cash on drinks, and while I loved my sister, I knew that she was a little shallow, and so was worried that she'd find Jack Abbott's money very attractive.

'Maybe,' she grinned around her drinking straw. 'Depends how much money he's got.'

'Pippa, please tell me you're joking.'

Pippa shrugged and winked at me before taking another loud slurp of her drink.

I pushed my empty glass away, hoping I'd be able to do as Roman had asked—well, *demanded*—and not see Jack again. There was something in Roman's eyes that told me I should listen to him, but it all depended on my sister.

CHAPTER 11

When I got to the office on Monday morning, Roman was already there which gave me no time at all to prepare for facing him.

'Morning,' he mumbled as he spooned coffee into a cup. 'Want one?'

I blinked rapidly, ignoring the desire to flee, and nodded. 'Please.'

I sat at my desk and turned on my PC, surreptitiously watching from the corner of my eye as Roman waited for the kettle to boil. After a couple of minutes—which felt like hours—he approached my desk and placed the mug of coffee on it.

'Thanks,' I said, looking up at him.

Roman lifted his chin in acknowledgment and moved away towards his office. I'm not sure what went off in my brain to make me open my mouth, but something did and before I could stop myself the words were out.

'Do we need to talk about Friday night?' I blurted out.

Roman turned and stared at me. As he rubbed at his temple with his forefinger, I knew I shouldn't have said anything. We would only end up arguing, and I was being stupid resurrecting our argument. He'd told me his worries, I'd listened, and that should be it. The problem was, my stubbornness about seeing Jack again—when I never had any intention of doing so—had been playing on my mind. I had to poke that bear.

Roman breathed out a deep sigh of annoyance and moved a couple of steps away from my desk.

'What else is there to say,' he stated quietly. 'You either don't believe me, or you're going to choose to ignore my warning. Subject closed.'

'I'm not ignoring what you said. I just didn't like you telling me what to do, but …' I said lowering my voice, '… I do feel I should apologise for being rude to you.'

Roman tilted his head and gave me a grin.

'Shit, we are definitely making progress here.'

'Yeah, well,' I said, trying to hide my smile. 'Maybe I realised that you were simply trying to be nice.'

'Me, nice?' Roman asked incredulously. 'No fucking way, I'd rather eat shit first.'

We both burst out laughing and thankfully any tension was gone.

'Is it bad what he's done?' I asked, sitting back in my chair and taking a sip of my coffee.

'Yeah, it is. And it's not a one-off incident either. He's a wanker, Summer, and if I was the last person on earth who could help him out of a dangerous situation, I wouldn't.'

I stared at Roman and saw that his eyes were darker than I'd ever seen them.

'You really hate him, don't you?'

'Yes, I do. I know I was a bit heavy-handed about it, but I was shocked to see you with him at the club.'

'I haven't seen him since school, until recently, but he seemed as nice and friendly as he did nine years ago.'

'Yeah well,' Roman growled, 'people change. My advice is to keep clear of him.'

I didn't know whether to tell Roman what Jack had said about him, but I had a feeling that would cause a whole other load of trouble. There was obviously bad blood between them, so I could bet that what Jack had said about Roman had just been him shit-stirring. Roman had rescued me from Alan Cromwell, he certainly hadn't encouraged me to do anything that I wasn't comfortable with.

'Well, I'd better get ready for my meeting,' Roman announced after a few minutes of us both drinking our coffee in silence.

'Okay,' I said cheerfully and watched him retreat to his office.

Finishing my drink, I took the time to contemplate the magnificent specimen that was my boss. He was such a contradiction. Yes, he was handsome and had a great arse, but he was also one of the most surly people that I had ever met, yet could also be quite sweet. Look at the perfume he'd bought for me in France—he'd actually blushed when I thanked him for it. Also, take the situation about Jack. On Friday night he'd pretty much demanded that I never see Jack again; yet today he was much more measured and reasonable. Then other days ...

'Summer!' Roman bawled from his office. 'Damn well get in here now!'

And so it began again.

'What?' I asked, and then stopped in my tracks and inhaled sharply.

Standing in front of me was Roman, with his shirt sopping wet and clinging to his body, giving me a hint of perfectly defined abs. He'd opened the top two or three buttons of his shirt, and the bit of chest that I could see looked like a beautifully-sculpted piece of art: all hard, clean lines that begged you to touch them. So much so that my fingers twitched as I took a step into his office.

'What's happened?' I asked like an idiot.

Roman looked up at me and frowned.

'What the hell do you think has happened?' he spat back at me, pointing at his chest. 'I've spilled coffee down my damn shirt, and I've got a meeting in an hour and it was fucking hot.'

Roman hissed in a breath as he dabbed ineffectually at his chest with a tiny piece of tissue that looked as though it had been used for rubbing dirt off an urchin's face.

'Shit.'

I swallowed and closed my eyes trying to imprint the image in my brain, then realized the man needed help. I pulled a clean tissue from my pocket and started to dab at his shirt, but he hadn't just spilled the coffee, he'd practically drowned himself in it. It wasn't long before the tissue was simply a soggy ball. The problem was I couldn't stop dabbing at him, my fingers itching to spread out over the pecs that were highlighted through the wet cotton.

'Thank Christ, I like a lot of milk in my coffee.'

I suddenly woke from my dreamlike state. 'Sorry, I'll go and get the first aid kit,' I said turning to leave.

'It's fine, I'm fine. Just get me something else to clean off with.'

I ran back to my office to retrieve the packet of wipes that I had in my drawer. Reaching for them, I paused and took a deep breath.

'Do not do, or think, anything stupid, Summer,' I whispered to myself. 'He is your boss.'

'What the hell are you doing in there? Hurry up.'

He is your boss and he is a cantankerous dick.

'Okay,' I bellowed. 'I'm coming.'

I raced back into his office and slapped the packet of wipes against his chest.

'Here.'

'God, be careful. I might have first-degree burns,' he moaned.

'And do you?'

'Well, no.'

'No,' I replied. 'I didn't think so, seeing as you declined the offer of the first aid kit, and actually told me that it wasn't that hot.'

Roman looked down at his chest and started to wipe off more of the coffee residue.

'You'll have to go to my house and get me a clean shirt,' he said, his chin practically touching his sternum.

'I will?' I squawked.

'Yes, you will. I don't have time to get there and back and get everything ready for my meeting. So you'll have to go.'

He threw the handful of wipes that he'd been using to one side, and then reached for the cuff of one of his sleeves. Oh shit, he was going to take it off. Thankfully—because I wasn't sure I would have been able to control myself—he didn't. He simply unfastened the cuffs before moving over to his desk.

'Just a second,' he grunted, leaning over the desk.

As he did, I thought I was going to die: my heart momentarily stopped before suddenly pumping wildly back to life. His *unbelievably* amazing arse was in prime place in the shop window. Christ, you could probably crack a nut open on that arse it was so hard.

'Here, take these and go to my house.'

Roman surprised me by flinging a set of keys at me. I juggled them in the air, finally catching them. In his other hand, he had a T-shirt that looked as though it was covered in paint. I held in a gasp, knowing that he was now going to strip off. In equal measures, I was relieved and disappointed when Roman turned his back to me, pulled off his shirt, and then dragged his T-shirt over his head, before bending down to write something.

'This is the address,' Roman said, turning and passing me a *Post-it* note. 'The alarm code is on there too. And please don't be long, I can't meet the client in this bloody thing.' He ran a hand down the paint-splattered T-shirt and let out a breath.

I looked at all the papers, charts and blueprints that were spread across his already untidy desk. He was right, he wouldn't have time.

'You need to go *now*, Summer.'

'Okay, okay.' I snatched the note from his fingertips and strode from the room to collect my bag.

'My bedroom is top of the stairs, first on the right. All my shirts are hanging in the wardrobe. Bring me a white one.'

'And would there be a "please" with that?' I asked.

Roman sighed. 'Please.'

'Oh, my pleasure,' I grunted, slamming the office door behind me.

***

Once my satnav had got me to Roman's driveway, I breathed out a huge sigh. I don't know whether it was one of relief at having found the house, or trepidation at walking into his private space—I decided that it was a mixture of both. I didn't want to be responsible for him holding a meeting in a dirty T-shirt, but I was a little scared that having an insight into Roman's life might just increase my crush. Why I thought that, I had no idea. He was evidently sending me loopy.

I knew that he lived in one of the new developments on the edge of town, but I hadn't contemplated that it would be quite as big. I looked up at the three-storey, double-fronted house, and, wondering what a single man needed so much space for, I made my way up the drive.

I pushed the key into the lock, opened the door and stepped into the large, square hallway. As I did, the alarm panel next to the door started to beep rapidly. I pulled the *Post-it* from my jacket pocket and quickly keyed in the numbers written down, letting my head fall back with relief when the beeping stopped. As I turned towards the stairs, I almost died of shock as a bark rang out.

'Shit,' I muttered. 'Where the hell did you come from?'

In the doorway to what looked like the kitchen, his head poking through a baby-gate, stood the scruffiest little dog I had ever seen. His grey-and-black fur stuck out in all directions; one ear lay flat, while the other was perked up, and, around his neck, was a blue-and-white spotted bandana.

'Hello boy,' I soothed, holding my hand out to him.

The dog gave it a little sniff and then proceeded to lick it with his hot, sticky tongue. I sank down onto my haunches and put my other hand over the top of the gate to scratch his head and ears. He whimpered joyously, and one of his back legs started to scratch his hind quarters. The more I scratched, the faster his leg moved, and the more high-pitched his whimper got, making me giggle. Suddenly my mobile beeped in my pocket, so I stopped petting the pooch and reached for it. It was a text from Roman:

Grumpy: Stop playing with Doolittle and get my shirt!

With a gasp I quickly looked around for the CCTV that he evidently had set up, but there was nothing. How the hell did he know? Then my mobile beeped again.

Grumpy: It's my mum's dog. I'm looking after him. Everyone loves the little fucker. I'm guessing you do too.

I couldn't help but smile as I stood up.

'Sorry, buddy,' I crooned as I gave Doolittle one last scratch. 'But I need to go and get Roman's shirt.'

At the mention of Roman, the dog started to howl and wag his tail so fast that it was creating a draught.

'Wow, I guess you love Roman,' I said tentatively, testing to see if it was a coincidence. It wasn't, because Doolittle went for it again, his tail wagging even faster this time. Once he'd finished, I gave him another quick scratch before I ran up the stairs, suddenly aware that I only had half an hour to get the shirt and get it back to the office.

As I entered Roman's bedroom the smell of him hit me with force. It wasn't overpowering, but his lemon and musky after-shave definitely hung in the air. I breathed in deeply as I looked around the room. It had wooden floors, grey-and-mustard check bedding, dove-grey walls and chunky cherrywood bedroom furniture; it was typically Roman—manly. I was, however, surprised how neat and clean it was when you considered the state of his desk back at the office. The bed was made, and not just with the duvet thrown haphazardly over it: it had been neatly pulled up and the pillows arranged on top—plain ones underneath and check ones on top. Time was pressing on, however, and I didn't have enough of it to do a critique of Roman's interior design skills. So I went over to the huge, double wardrobe and flung open the doors. Everything was hanging tidily and each type of clothing had its own section: trousers and jeans hung in one, jackets in another, then shirts, and, finally, shelves from top to bottom for other items, all of which were carefully folded.

As I reached for a white shirt, I couldn't help put press my nose to one of his jackets. Shit, this was getting ridiculous—I was starting to act like a stalker! Luckily for Doolittle, I found him adorable and doubted whether Roman had a pan big enough for him.

Shaking my head, I pulled the white shirt from its hanger and, in the process, pulled off the one next to it also, seeing it drop down to the bottom of the wardrobe.

I folded the white shirt neatly and laid it on the bed. Then I went back over to the wardrobe and stooped down to retrieve the shirt on the floor. I couldn't help but notice the three framed photographs lining the bottom of the wardrobe. I put the other shirt back on its hanger and pulled out the first photograph. It was a picture of a younger Roman wearing boxing gloves and standing in a boxing ring. He looked hot and sweaty and his right arm was draped around the shoulders of another man, who was also hot and sweaty. The other man wasn't wearing gloves, but his hands were wrapped in the sort of tape or bandage that boxers wore under their gloves. He was as tall as Roman, with short, buzz-cut hair. They were both grinning widely at the camera and looked happy, and I remembered what Dec at the club had said that Saturday night, about Roman still having it—evidently he had been referring to Roman's boxing skills. Putting the picture back, I slid out the other two in turn. Both were in the boxing ring, but they caught Roman in action: throwing a punch in one, and ducking a punch in the other. I gazed at the pictures, and, as much as I didn't like the idea of him punching someone for fun, I had to admit he looked phenomenal. I'd only had a hint of his toned body earlier, but in these photographs his muscles were honed to perfection: sharp and defined.

Careful to put the pictures back exactly how I found them, I sighed heavily. I was right: coming into this house and seeing these pictures had just made me want him even more.

'Oh fuck, fuck, fuck, fuck, fuck.'

CHAPTER 12

♥

It was Wednesday, two days after the coffee incident and two days after I'd been in Roman's home and seen the pictures of him boxing. It was also two days since I'd started to have erotic dreams about him. Well, to put it plainly, in each one—and there had been three to be exact—he'd shagged me so damn thoroughly I'd woken up breathing heavily with a throbbing between my legs.

The second dream, which had been during my after-dinner, pre-Coronation Street nap, had been so bloody good that I'd had to get Roger, my little battery-operated boyfriend, out from the bottom of my knicker drawer.

Each of them had left me feeling mortified, sure that whenever I saw Roman he was fully aware of what we had been doing in my dreams. They seemed so real and I was having problems separating them from reality. My feelings for him were changing from those of simple lust, and I really had no idea what to do with them. He was still snippy and rude, but I relished our battles, and was finding them more and more entertaining. But I thought that if we kept up with the barbed comments and sarcasm, Roman would never realise that my feelings for him were changing. Being sarcastic was my weapon against turning into a simpering idiot around him. There were some days, though, that I set myself a little challenge to try and get him to smile after one of our spats: because when he smiled, it was beautiful, and gave a little poke to my heart.

Despite the fact that Roman was worming his way into my heart, it still didn't stop those base feeling of lust that I had for him. On a daily basis he would leave me in a hot sweat and breathing heavily, without him even realising the affect that he had upon me. Today had been no exception, particularly because he'd come in dressed to work on-site in well-worn jeans, an open red-plaid shirt with a white T-shirt underneath, and work boots. Shit! Be still my beating heart and throbbing lady parts!

'If Alan Cromwell finally rings, call me. I'm going to be on-site for most of today,' Roman announced as he came in and threw some letters that he'd signed onto my desk.

'You don't say,' I replied.

He might look more appetising than a Las Vegas all-you-could-eat buffet, but today was one of those days that I needed to bite back. The way my heartbeat increased whenever he was near to me was disconcerting and scary. No one had ever had me so tied up in knots like this before: not even Alex when we first met. I felt like a teenager falling in unrequited first love, and I hated and loved it in equal measure. So being a bitch helped.

'Do you wake up every morning with a plan on how you're going to piss me off?' Roman asked without looking up from an invoice that he was studying.

'No, not really.' I shrugged. 'It just comes naturally somehow.'

God, this was just the distraction I needed. Banter and snarkiness were much easier to handle than unrequited lust.

'Well, while we're on the subject of your sunny disposition, I need a favour from you.' He perched on the edge of my desk, his denim-clad backside decidedly too close to my hand.

'What?' I snapped, wheeling my chair to the other end of my desk to look in my drawer for … nothing.

'There's a lunch tomorrow for local businesses and I've been invited to go. I need you to come with me, make notes of any contacts or leads. You know the sort of thing.'

My mouth dropped open as I stared at the inside of my desk drawer. I took a couple of seconds to consider my response, but I had nothing.

'Summer, what the hell is wrong with you? Do you need your ears syringing or are you ignoring me on purpose?'

'I'm thinking,' I snapped, wheeling myself back towards him. 'I was making sure I was available.'

I looked up and gave him the barest of smiles. Roman rolled his eyes and huffed.

'Well, considering it's during working hours, I don't doubt that you'll be available. That is unless you were planning on throwing a sickie or have booked a day's holiday that I don't know about.' He inclined his head and stared at me, brows risen. 'Well?'

'No,' I sighed. 'Neither of the above, so I suppose I'll have to go with you.' My stomach was rolling with nerves at the thought of spending a couple of hours by his side.

'Don't sound so enthusiastic, will you?'

He let out a short laugh and shook his head as he stood up and went back to his own office.

As he settled himself at his desk, I risked a quick glance. I had no idea what was wrong with me, but I was becoming more and more drawn to him.

He picked up some papers and began reading them, his brow furrowing as he tapped a pen against his chin. With a sigh, he sat back in his chair, his eyes still intent on the papers, and when he flicked out his tongue to lick his top lip, I felt myself shiver.

Not sure I could handle much more of watching him without groaning with longing, I got up to close his office door. Just as I rounded my desk, the door to the main office swung open and a tall, statuesque woman, with a curtain of long, auburn hair that hung down to her waist, walked in. Her body was tiny and encased in tight, leather, skinny trousers and a baggy white T-shirt. Diamonds adorned her ears and wrists, but what really caught my eye, were the beautiful pair of *Gianvito Rossi* black suede ankle boots—I could answer questions about shoes on *Mastermind*.

The woman was stunning: she even took my breath away. Holding her hand was an adorable little girl of about five or six, with strawberry blonde curls and Cupid's bow lips.

'Can I help you?' I asked.

'Sorry, is Roman here?' the woman replied, straightening her back and moving the child to stand in front of her.

As I opened my mouth to respond, Roman came through the doorway.

'Caroline?' Roman said, stopping in his tracks. 'What the hell are you doing here?'

Roman's hands went to his hips, as he stared at her, waiting for her response.

'Hi Roman. It's been a while,' the woman said.

'Yeah, you could say that.' He shook his head, looking confused. 'So why now?'.

The woman smiled at him. 'I was passing and thought, why not? Plus I thought you'd like to see Maisie.'

Caroline bent down to speak to the little girl.

'Maisie, you remember Uncle Roman don't you?'

Maisie didn't say anything, but started sucking on her fingers, looking up at Roman with huge eyes.

'Hi Maisie,' Roman said, his frown replaced with a soft smile. 'You've grown a lot since I last saw you.'

'I'm nearly five,' she replied, smiling back. Her eyes were shining as she showed off perfect, little white teeth, before wrapping tiny arms around her mother's legs.

The child was as beautiful as her mother, and Roman obviously adored her.

'Well, you're much prettier than I remember,' Roman said as he scruffed a hand over her head, messing up her curls and making her giggle. God, he really was determined to blow up that one remaining ovary of mine—along with my heart.

Something akin to jealousy pulled at my chest. I would never bond with a child of my own, and I couldn't help but think this woman had been blessed with far too much: beauty, a child and gorgeous boots—yet there was something hard and cold about her narrow-eyed stare.

'So?' Roman looked up at Caroline, crossing his arms over his chest.

She shrugged. 'I really am sorry. It just seemed easier to stay away, the way things were.'

Roman cleared his throat. 'Yes, I guess so. Although I'm sure *he* had something to do with it.'

Caroline chewed on her bottom lip, but remained silent. Finally, Roman spoke.

'So what brings you here, Caroline?' he asked, his voice tight.

Caroline gave him a small smile and sighed. 'I just thought it was silly to stay away.'

'You're both okay, though?' Roman patted Maisie's head.

'Yes, we're fine. Are you free for lunch and a catch-up?' Caroline asked. 'It's a bit early I know, but if the boss can't take a couple of hours off, then who can?'

'Hmm, no can do, sorry.' Roman shook his head. 'I've got to go on-site today, we're running behind on a warehouse conversion the other side of Rickeby.'

As Roman spoke, I noticed how Caroline hung onto his every word, smiling brightly.

'Ah, so the boss is going down there to kick ass, is that it?' she asked with a tinkling giggle.

Roman's mouth twitched up into a very brief smile. 'Something like that. It's really all hands to the pump. Summer's just lucky I haven't given her a hammer and some nails.'

I had to stop myself from gasping. Roman was joking with her: all I ever did was piss him off. Jealousy was no longer pulling at my chest, but was now stabbing at it violently. The conversation between was a little uneasy, but it was clear they'd been close at some stage, but what their relationship had been was difficult to know. Maybe they were exes? They certainly weren't together now. Roman had never mentioned a girlfriend, and he'd kissed me with enough passion to make me think they weren't currently together, but whatever their relationship, it was evidently special.

Roman turned and held a hand out towards me. 'Sorry,

Caroline, this is Summer my PA. Summer, Caroline Peters, an old friend of mine.'

I looked at Roman's face, but it was giving nothing away.

'Nice to meet you, Summer.' Caroline said and looked from me back to Roman. I thought I saw the ghost of a frown on her face, but then it was gone. 'What about a coffee instead then? You got time for that? Then you can tell me all about your work,' she said, draping her arms over Maisie's shoulders.

'Okay, but it'll have to be take-away from the café on the corner. We can have a quick chat while we're walking down there.'

'Excellent, let's go.'

'I'll just get my gear together. Summer, call me if you need anything,' Roman said to me as he went into his office.

'Will do.' I looked up to smile at Caroline, but she was concentrating on tapping something into her mobile.

Leaving his office Roman came over to my desk and leaned over it. My breath hitched as his face was inches from mine.

'I doubt she will, but if my sister calls or pops in, say I'm out with a client. Don't mention that Caroline was here,' he whispered. 'Okay?'

'Yes, no problem,' I replied. Minutes later Roman and Caroline had gone, with Maisie's hand in Roman's, and I was left alone, feeling deflated and wondering what the hell was going on.

CHAPTER 13

'Tell me again why I'm here,' I asked Roman as we stood amongst the crowd of people milling around the Civic Hall.

We were attending the civic lunch that Roman had talked about the day before, and I couldn't honestly say that I was enjoying it.

Once Roman had left the office with Caroline, I hadn't seen him until this morning and he'd been all manner of grumpy. I wondered whether it was his meeting with the lovely redhead, but he'd barely spoken other than to bark orders at me. Not that it was any of my business, but I was hoping he'd tell me how he knew her, and why I wasn't to mention her name to Tiffany. Unfortunately he wasn't spilling any beans or even uttering her name

We'd eaten lunch and now it was 'networking time', although I was desperate to leave because I was hating every minute of it. I was hating it because the whole time I'd had to sit next to Roman, all I'd wanted to do was touch him. I wanted him to tell me that he had feelings for me too, and everything would be perfect. I knew that was never to going to happen, because the only feelings that Roman had for me were those of irritation and disdain.

I didn't want to be that woman: the one who yearned for someone that they couldn't have, but Roman Hepburn didn't make things easy. He looked and smelled so damn good. While I wanted him to touch me, I wanted it to be the way a man touches *his* woman, the woman that he adores and can't keep his hands off. Not because the space between them was so tiny, that every time he lifted his fork to his mouth his elbow brushed the side of her boob, sending her into mini spasms of ecstasy.

Sitting so close to the man that was taking up my every thought meant that the whole lunch had been one long, frustrating strain on me. His accidental touch and that damn aftershave he wore was making me a tad horny. I was so turned on that the poor bakery owner, sitting opposite me, was lucky I hadn't poked her eyes out with my nipples by the time dessert was served.

'I need you to make a note of any contacts or sales leads,' Roman whispered, bringing me back from my thoughts. 'Plus, I heard you talking to the guy from the UPVC window company about the possibility of some sort of affiliation. It's a great idea and I'll be giving him a call.'

My grin was huge and I felt myself grow another couple of inches. I'd been suggesting that to Mr. Barlow for the last couple of years, but he'd told me it would never work.

'Okay,' Roman said, without taking his eyes off a group of three men standing in front of us. 'That over there is Geoff Williams, the guy that is supposedly taking over as Chief Planning Officer for the council, so I wouldn't mind having a chat with him.'

'So go over then.' I took a sip of my rather warm sparkling white wine. 'He looks bored, he might be grateful for some of your witty repartee.'

Roman raised his eyebrow and allowed a small smile to touch his lips before striding over to Mr. Williams.

'Hey, Summer, I thought it was you.'

I turned to see Holly Jenkins, now Robertson, the co-owner of Darrington Hall, a local hotel. Next to her stood her tall, good-looking husband, Liam.

'Hi Holly!' I exclaimed, pulling her into a hug. 'Look at you, you look fantastic. How old is the baby now?' I asked wistfully, the thought of Holly's baby causing my heart to do a little flip.

Liam beamed. 'She's seven months,' he replied. 'She's amazing and gorgeous and looks just like Holly. Do you want to see a photograph?'

'No, she doesn't!' Holly cried as she slapped a hand against his arm. 'God, he's such a doting daddy. Ava is going to be spoiled rotten. She's got him wrapped around her little finger.'

'Well, that's what daddies should be like with their daughters.' I smiled at Liam. 'So we know fatherhood is going well, what about being a husband?'

Liam grinned. 'Equally as brilliant.'

'Oh God,' Holly gasped. 'Even after a month that sounds weird. My husband.'

I couldn't help but notice the look that passed between them: loving and tender. It was beautiful to see, but I also couldn't help feeling a little envious at their obvious love for each other and their little baby back home.

I felt a hand on the small of my back and turned to see that Roman had returned.

'Holly, Liam, this is my boss, Roman Hepburn, he now owns Barlow's.'

Holly smiled while Liam took Roman's hand and shook it.

'Nice to meet you.' Liam said. 'So, how's business so far?'

'It's going well—so far,' Roman smiled. 'Could be better.'

'Ah, well, talking of business ...' Liam said, at which point Holly edged me away from the two men.

'You didn't want to listen, did you?' she asked with a groan. 'He'll talk for hours about refurbs and extensions, and, to be honest, I've heard it a thousand times before, bless him.' Holly looked across at Liam, who was now in deep conversation with Roman, and gazed at him lovingly.

'Nope,' I laughed. 'I'll hear it all word for word when we get back to the office. He'll bellow for me if he needs me.'

'I have to say,' Holly said, looking at me over the rim of her orange juice, 'he's a bit tasty.'

I almost choked on my wine, coughing and spluttering as

Holly grinned at me.

'You fancy him then?' she asked.

'Ssh, he'll hear you, and, no, I don't!' I stressed.

'Well, why not?' she hissed. 'You'd have to be blind not to.'

'He's my boss, I just don't see him like that.' There was no way I was going to tell her that was *exactly* how I did see him, every day and every night. 'We work together and that's it.'

'So did Liam and I.' She nudged me and gave me a cheeky grin. 'And look how that ended up.'

'Well, I can promise you, it won't be the same with me and Roman. He's a misery guts, for starters.'

Holly winced. 'Ooh harsh, but he's still a very good-looking misery guts.'

I shook my head. 'As hot as he might appear, he's too grumpy for my taste,' I lied. Who was I kidding? I was starting to find his sharp tongue quite sexy.

I sighed and took another sip of my wine, just as Liam and Roman re-joined us.

'We need to go, beautiful,' Liam said as he linked his fingers with Holly's. 'I've got that meeting with the landscaper at three and I need to sort a few things out first.'

'Okay. Well, it was great to see you, Sum'. We should meet up for a drink sometime. I know Mags would love to see you.'

'Yeah, that would be brill'. I'll call you.'

Liam shook Roman's hand again. 'Don't forget to call me about the building work, Roman.'

'I will, and thanks for that, I really appreciate it.'

Once Holly and Liam had gone, Roman took out his phone and tapped something into it.

'What was Liam talking about?' I asked.

'Hmm.' Roman continued tapping away.

'Liam, when he said to call him.'

Roman's head shot up and large smile lit up his face. 'They're adding a pool and a gym to the spa and adding some conference rooms to the hotel, plus Holly is desperate to increase the size of the dining room too. He's heard good things about us, so has asked me to quote for it.'

'Wow, that sounds like a big project,' I gasped. 'That would be brilliant if you got it.'

'Yeah, it would,' Roman replied. 'It would take a lot of pressure off, and he doesn't want it started until the back end of the year, so we'd have time to finish The Palisades, the warehouse and the French conversion—if we ever get started with it.'

I smiled at Roman and felt relieved. We'd all been on edge about the amount of work coming in: none of us wanted to lose our jobs. The Palisades was continuing to be a problem: the planning department still hadn't agreed to his idea of flipping the plan. As for the French conversion project, we still hadn't heard from Alan Cromwell and Roman had sent him the final costings five days ago.

'So what did the new planning guy say?'

Roman shrugged. 'Don't know. He wasn't free when I went over.'

'Hey,' I said tapping Roman on the shoulder. 'He's free now. Quick, go and grab him before someone else does.'

Roman rushed off, leaving me to sip my warm wine while staring at his profile as he chatted away.

***

Almost two hours later, we were on our way back to the office in his huge shiny black truck. We were silent, because although I'd tried to ask Roman what the planning officer had said, he wasn't talking. Well, he was, but it was more like one-word grunts.

The tension was intense as Roman punctuated the silence with deep breaths and the occasional sigh.

'Are you going to tell me what Geoff Williams said, or just stay in a bad mood for the rest of the day?' I asked, watching the pulse throb in his rigid neck.

'Nope.'

I hated tension, particularly when there wasn't really any need for it. Why could the stupid man just not tell me what had been said?

'Nope what? You're not going to tell me, or nope you're not going to be in a silent, bad mood all day?' I grumbled, staring out of the window.

'You know something, Summer,' he growled, 'try to remember that you're my PA, and not my wife.'

'Well, that can be easily rectified,' I replied. 'You evidently don't trust me enough to let me know what's going on, so I'm kind of superfluous as your PA. If you want my resignation, consider it done.'

The fact that he evidently didn't trust me, really hurt. I worked hard for him, despite our squabbles and the way that he spoke to me on a regular basis.

Roman let out a long sigh. 'I do trust you. You're the best PA I've ever had.'

'I'm the only PA you've ever had,' I retorted. It was true, but I still felt a little thrill of pride.

Roman barked out a laugh and shook his head. 'That's true, but I mean it, Summer, you're great at your job and I do trust you. I'm just really pissed off and thought it better not to speak rather than bite your head off.'

'Don't stop the habits of a lifetime.' I grinned at him, glad that the tension was now broken. 'So I guess it wasn't good news.'

Roman shook his head. 'Nope. Basically he hasn't had chance to review the case yet.'

We carried on in silence for another few minutes while I watched the shops and houses whizz past in a blur. Then, as we were stopped in traffic, Roman's phone rang out. I glanced at the *Bluetooth* display on his dashboard to see it said: '*Mum*'.

'Hey Mum,' Roman answered, sounding much breezier and happier than he had done in the last half hour in the truck.

'Oh Romy, sweetheart, I'm in such a state. Doolittle has gone missing.'

Coughing to hide a giggle, I couldn't help the smirk as I glued my eyes to the window, concentrating on the street outside to avoid laughing at Roman's mother calling him 'Romy'.

'What do you mean, he's gone missing?' Roman sighed. 'How

has he gone missing?'

'Your dad went to take the rubbish out and he left the door open. Mrs. Robard's Cockapoo, Cilla, is on heat and the randy little bugger just shot out of here faster than Reverend Sheeran when that brothel was raided last Christmas.'

My head whipped around to Roman, who groaned beside me. Reverend Sheeran married my parents and christened the three of us.

'Mum, listen, I have someone in the truck with me, can I call you back later? And, to be honest, that rumour is totally unfounded.'

'You know it isn't!' she protested. 'Your dad's friend, Mike's uncle's cousin, was one of the arresting officers.'

'Mum, I'm going to call you back when I get to the office.'

Roman took in a deep breath and gripped the wheel tighter.

I, on the other hand, thought his mother sounded hilariously batty. She obviously had no filter, and I loved people like that.

'No, you will not call me back. I need you to come over and help.'

'Believe it or not,' he grumbled. 'I do have a business to run. I've just been to a council shindig, and now need to get back to the office. Summer and I need to get some work done.'

'Ooh did you say Summer?'

'Oh fuck,' Roman groaned under his breath.

Roman now had a pained expression on his face. What was that about? His mum seemed to know my name. My heart started thudding. Had he been talking about me to her?

'Hi Summer,' his mum called.

I looked at Roman, who gave me a resigned shake of the head.

'Hi, Mrs. Hepburn.'

'Oh it's ...'

'Mother!' Roman snapped. 'Will you please just let me get to the office, and I will call you back.'

I could see from the tension in his jaw, that Roman's patience was almost at an end, but his mum was evidently the one person he didn't lose it with.

'Okay?' he asked in a coaxing tone.

Mrs. Hepburn sighed, and I was sure she was going to accede to his request, but she didn't.

'Roman, I need you to come and help your father look for the damn dog. *Please.*'

'Just let me take Summer back first.' His voice was almost pleading.

It seemed stupid to me to do that. I wasn't aware of where his parents lived, but with the build-up of traffic, we could still be twenty minutes away from the office.

'Well, where are you now?' his mum asked.

'I can be with you in half an hour,' Roman replied, being rather economical with the truth.

'Half an hour! That's too long, Romy. He could be miles away by then.'

Roman's resolve finally failed as he looked at me.

'Do you mind?'

I shook my head. I didn't mind—far from it. I was now *desperate* to meet his kooky mother.

'Okay, I'm about five minutes away. Get Dad to go looking for Doolittle, and you wait at the house until he comes back,' Roman said as he manoeuvred past a lorry.

'No, I'll go, your dad will have to wait here. His ingrown toenail is weeping again.'

Roman sighed heavily and I saw his jaw clench tightly before replying. 'Well, whatever, but someone wait at the house until I get there.'

'Thanks, Romy. And hurry, because if anyone can find him, you can.'

'So, Romy, we're off to find Doolittle then?' I sucked in my lips, stemming the laughter that was desperate to break free.

Roman briefly took his eyes off the road and glared at me.

'Not a word, Summer,' he growled.

'I wouldn't dream of it ... Romy.'

CHAPTER 14

When we pulled up in his parents' driveway, Roman turned off the truck engine and inhaled deeply before turning to me.

'Summer, I need to warn you about my parents,' he said, eying me warily. 'They're not like normal parents. My mother has weird ideas about things, and my dad is the most uncouth man that you will ever meet.'

I bit down on my lip, trying desperately not to laugh. He really was worried about me going inside the house.

'No family is perfect,' I said. 'My brother is a man-whore, and my sister is an attention-seeking flirt, but I love them both dearly.'

'No, you really don't understand. I have no idea how Tiffany and I turned out so normal. I really don't.' Roman looked up at the house and then back to me. 'My mother's parents were hippies, and my dad was brought up by his two elder brothers without any rules or guidelines whatsoever.'

'I won't repeat anything I see or hear, if that's what you're worried about,' I said, genuinely meaning it. He was my boss, and this must be the last thing he wants—his employee meeting his weird parents.

'It's not that, they're my parents and I love them, but they're just … strange,' he said with a withering frown. 'Dad will fart, belch, and very possibly pick his nose in front of you, and my mum will treat you as though she's known you forever. If she starts going on about things of a romantic nature, just ignore her.'

My smile faded, as I realised that he was more worried about his mum thinking we were an item, than being embarrassed about them.

'I can stay here, if you don't want her to get any ideas.'

'Seriously, Summer, it's not that. I just need you to be prepared and remember that I did try really hard to avoid this. Anyway, if I left you in the car, she'd only come out here and force you into the house.'

Now I was worried. What the hell was I walking into? Maybe I *should* stay in the truck and lock the doors. But curiosity was killing me; aside from which, Mrs. Hepburn was now on the doorstep waving us in.

'Oh Romy,' Roman's mum cried, as we walked up the drive. 'I have no idea where the little bugger has gone. He could be miles away by now.'

'He can't have got that far.' Roman kissed his mum's cheek as he ushered her into the house.

Mrs. Hepburn stopped in the hallway and turned to face me.

'Hello, Summer. Lovely to meet you, dear.'

I smiled, wondering what Roman's melodrama had been all about. His mother was a tiny woman with dark blonde hair pulled into a high ponytail, and she had the brightest blue eyes I had ever seen. The only resemblance to Roman was her mouth: they shared the same full, Cupid's bow lips. She seemed perfectly lovely to me.

'So,' she said, taking hold of my hand. 'Are you Romy's girl?'

'She's my PA, Mother,' he said, with a deep rumble in his voice. 'I told you this on the phone.'

'She might still be your girl,' she huffed.

Roman's flaring nostrils told me that that sounded like a fate worse than death as far as he was concerned—and that pinched just a little.

'No, Summer is merely my PA. Now are we going to look for this dog or not?'

Suddenly Mrs. Hepburn started to giggle. 'Her name is Summer.'

'Yes, you knew that,' he said tightly.

'I know, but think about it,' she sighed.

Roman rolled his eyes and pushed her along the hallway. Okay, giggling about my name was a little bit rude, but still perfectly lovely.

We moved through the lounge/diner into the kitchen, and Mrs. Hepburn pushed me onto a chair at the weathered-pine table.

'Sit here and I'll make you a cup of tea. Romy, do you want one?'

Roman leaned against the door frame, his arms firmly crossed over his chest. His brows knitted together intently as he watched his mother filled the kettle. Looking around the kitchen and listening to Mrs. Hepburn sing while she made the tea, a deep sense of contentment fell over me. Contentment and a little sadness. After just a few minutes, I really liked her, and I felt sad that after this visit today, I'd probably never see her again. In no way did I feel uncomfortable, and I really wasn't sure what Roman had been worried about.

'I thought you were desperate for my help?' Roman said with more than a hint of exasperation.

'You've got time for a little chat first,' his mother said, as she turned back to me. 'So you're Romy's PA and your name is Summer. That is so exciting.'

'Well, it's okay, but I wouldn't exactly say it's an exciting job,' I explained.

'No, I mean ...'

'Mum, no!' Roman barked, and gave her a wide-eyed stare.

I had no idea what was going on, but it was definitely making Roman feel uncomfortable. Whereas I was still feeling amused by it all.

'Oh Romy, you are such a grump.'

I grinned widely. So it wasn't just me who found him grumpy.

'Right, that's it!' Roman barked. 'No more Romy. I am not seven years of age anymore. Now, can we please concentrate on searching for the dog?'

'He hates it so much,' Mrs. Hepburn whispered to me with a small giggle. 'But he'll always be my Romy, just as Tiffany will always be my Tiffy.'

She smiled widely and plonked herself down on the chair next to mine. Grabbing my hand, she clasped it between both of hers, which were warm and soft, and gazed into my eyes. 'You're so pretty. Isn't she, Romy?'

I knew that I should probably be a little freaked out by all her attention, but she was just a little eccentric, that was all. The discomfort in this situation was all on Roman, and I was waiting in anticipation for him to answer the question. He didn't. He linked his hands behind his neck and stared up at the ceiling. I can't say I wasn't disappointed, because I was, but why would he answer? I was merely his PA.

'Oh he can be so rude at times,' Mrs. Hepburn grumbled.

'I'm busy and need to get back to the office,' Roman stated. 'So where's Dad? I thought he was going to stay here.'

'I strapped his toe up and he said even with green pus coming out of it, he'd be quicker than me.'

Roman scrubbed a hand down his face and groaned, his uneasiness growing with each sentence that came out of his mother's mouth. I wanted to tell him to stop being so judgmental of her, but wasn't sure that would be appreciated. At least I was having fun.

'Okay. You stay here and Summer and I will go and look for him,' Roman smiled gently at his mother and gave her shoulder a squeeze.

'Summer can stay with me.' Mrs. Hepburn's eyes twinkled.

'No!' Roman's bark startled us and Mrs. Hepburn actually jumped in her chair. 'She's coming with me.'

'I don't mind staying,' I replied, playing with him. He definitely didn't want me to be around his mother, but I liked her: she was nowhere near as weird as he'd made out.

'I need you to help me. Come on, let's get going. Which direction did Dad go in?'

'Down to the park. Doolittle loves herding the geese, so he thought he might have gone there.' Mrs. Hepburn looked sad again as she led us out of the house .

'We'll go towards the canal, then. Come on, Summer.'

'Oh, and bring Summer back for tea,' Mrs. Hepburn cried as we walked down the path to the front of the house. 'It's sausages and waffles, your favourite.'

'See you later, Mum.' Roman waved a hand over his head and stalked off in the direction of the canal.

After a few minutes of jogging along to keep up with Roman's long strides, I tugged at his elbow and pulled him up.

'Can you slow down, please?'

Roman looked at me quizzically. 'I'm not going fast. It's you; you're unfit.'

'No, I'm not!' I cried. 'I'm actually wearing four-inch heels. You try walking at your pace in them.'

'So why wear such stupid things if you can't even walk in them?' he asked, starting to walk off again.

'I can walk in them perfectly well, thank you. I'm just not very good at running in them,' I huffed.

'Okay, I'll slow to snail pace if that makes you feel better.' He afforded me a small smile, but it was enough to make my heart jump.

He did indeed slow down as we continued on towards the canal, intermittently calling for Doolittle along the way. By the time we reached our destination, the sun had gone behind the clouds and the temperature had dropped a little. For which I was thankful—after jogging most of the way, I was feeling a little bit hot and sweaty.

'Shit, he could be miles away,' Roman groaned as he looked up and down the canal path.

'I'll go and ask that guy mooring his boat over there,' I replied. 'He may have seen him as he was travelling down.'

'Good idea. I'll go this way and ask some of the other people that are moored.'

After twenty minutes of asking people and calling Doolittle's name, we met up again, both shaking our heads.

'Nothing.' Roman kicked at a stone in frustration. 'Mum's going to freak, she loves that bloody dog.'

'How about we go back to the house and start ringing around some vets?' I suggested. 'Someone may have found him and taken him in.'

'He's microchipped, so I'm sure they would have called if they had him, but it's a good idea.' Roman looked over at me and smiled. 'Listen, why don't you wait here and I'll run back for the truck and take you back to the office.'

'No, I want to help,' I protested. 'Plus I'm looking forward to sausages and waffles for tea.'

'Seriously, you want to stay?'

I wasn't really being serious, expecting Roman to simply laugh and make it clear that I wasn't staying, but his response almost sounded more like a request more than a question: it felt as though he'd welcome it. Suddenly, I felt nervous, wondering what that might mean, but decided to push it from my stupid brain and take it for what it was: a thank you for helping to look for Doolittle.

'Yeah, seriously. And I really want to hear your mum call you "Romy" just one more time.'

Roman's eyes shone as he started to laugh softly. 'I did warn you. I'm sorry she's so full on.'

'I really don't know what your problem is, she's lovely.'

Roman groaned. 'Just beware that at dinner she may say some things that are a bit strange.'

I wondered whether some old family secret would be told that Roman didn't want me to hear.

'Is it something that I should be scared about? Are you related to an axe-murderer or something?'

'If only.'

I inclined my head to the side, studying his face. He looked as though he was actually in pain as he bit at this thumbnail.

'It can't be that bad, surely?' I asked.

'Okay,' he breathed out. 'It might not seem bad to you, but it's been the bane of my fucking life since I was a kid. I'm only telling you this because I don't want you to be surprised when she does. And believe me she will make a damn saga out of it.'

I was really curious, but a little concerned at the same time. What could be so bad that it would worry the big, strong, arrogant Roman Hepburn?

'My name isn't Hepburn; well, it is, but it's not my surname, it's my middle name.'

'Oh okay. So what is your surname?'

'My mother is very strange, I've told you that.'

'Yes,' I said slowly. 'Although, I don't wholly agree.'

'Believe me she is. She's especially got a thing about names. As far as she's concerned names are very important and they can tell you a lot about someone.' He paused and rubbed a hand down his face.

'Roman, just tell me,' I pleaded, thinking he was being extremely dramatic, and rather unnecessarily so.

'Well, before she met Dad, she'd already decided that if she ever had a son he'd be called Roman.'

'Okay.'

'So when she met Dad, she knew he was the one because of his name. You see our family surname is actually "Holliday".'

I thought about it and then it suddenly struck me.

'Oh my God, your name is actually *Roman Holliday*? Really?'

Roman nodded and rolled his eyes.

'So where did the Hepburn come from?'

'Mum's obsessed with Audrey Hepburn, so the fact that her future son was going to be called Roman Holliday probably made her pee her pants with excitement.'

I started to giggle at the thought of Roman's embarrassment. I'd always hated my name when I was a child because the kids at school thought it hilarious to call me Winter, Spring or Autumn. But I had to be honest: Roman Holliday was a much bigger burden to bear.

'So,' I said, with a smirk. 'I'm guessing Tiffany is after *Breakfast at Tiffany's*, and Doolittle after Eliza Doolittle?'

Roman nodded. 'Yep.'

'Well, it's a bit strange, but it doesn't make her weird,' I replied.

Roman scratched at his stubble and sighed. 'Listen, she'll tell you this if I don't, but don't take any notice of it. You promise?'

I was concerned, but still nodded.

'Well, Dad wanted to call Tiffany "Summer".'

'Oh, that's why she giggled when I told her my name.' I nodded in understanding.

'Kind of. Dad wanted to call her Summer, but Mum said no. And she said no because she said, when I grew up, I would marry a girl called Summer, so she'd forever be ...'

'Summer Holliday,' I gasped.

'Yeah,' Roman whispered. 'According to her, Summer would always be my destiny.'

My eyes widened and my mouth dropped open. I don't know whether I started to choke because of the great gasp of air that I sucked in, or the fly that flew into my gaping mouth, but either way it wasn't pleasant.

CHAPTER 15

♥

By the time we got back to Roman's parents' house my feet were starting to ache. I could walk around in high heels all day, but ask me to jog a mile or so in them, and then walk another mile along a bumpy canal bank, and I wasn't so good.

'Oh, sit down,' Mrs. Holliday gushed as I hobbled in through the front door. 'I can't believe the big bully made you go with him.'

She shoved me down onto the sofa in front of a large brick fireplace, over which hung a framed pencil sketch of none other than *Audrey Hepburn*. It was evidently some sort of shrine to Audrey, because on both sides of the picture were white taper candles in glass candlesticks, and a fresh red rose lay on the mantelpiece directly underneath it.

'Is that better?' Mrs. Holliday asked as I settled back.

'Great, thank you.'

'Ooh you're so inconsiderate, Romy, I don't know where you get such bad manners from,' she complained.

I grinned at her chastising Roman. I wondered whether I should get her to come into the office and help me deal with him.

'I didn't make her come, and I certainly didn't make her wear such stupid shoes,' Roman grumbled, as he flicked through his phone.

'What are you doing anyway?' his mother asked, as she pushed a cushion behind my back.

'Trying to find some local vets numbers. Summer thought it might be an idea to call them as someone may have found the stupid mutt and taken him in.'

'Oh my word, aren't you clever?' Mrs. Holliday regarded me with pride, as if I was one of her own children and she'd just watched me in my first nativity play.

'It's only what I would do, if my dog went missing,' I replied, a little embarrassed by her adoring gaze.

'Well, it's still very clever. Why didn't you think of that?' she asked Roman, giving him a light slap on his arm.

'Because evidently I'm a stupid moron,' he muttered under his breath, without looking up from his phone.

'Takes after his father in sooo many ways. Now, Summer, my love, let me get you a nice cold drink, and maybe a bowl of water for your feet?'

'Oh no,' I blustered. 'No, just a drink is fine. Honestly.'

'Okily dokily, a nice glass of fresh orange juice coming up. Romy?'

'Hmm?'

'Would you like a cold drink too?' Mrs. Holliday sighed and snatched Roman's phone from his fingers. 'We have a guest, so stop being rude.'

'I'm trying to find your bloody dog.' He snatched the phone back and tutted at his mother. 'Like I said. Stupid mutt.'

'He doesn't mean it,' Mrs. Holliday said turning back to me. 'He loves Doolittle and Doolittle loves him.'

'Oh I know. I only mentioned Roman's name, and he couldn't stop wagging his tail and started howling.' I smiled as I recalled the scruffy little dog.

'Oh how sweet, they've always been the best of friends. They adore each other.'

I looked over at Roman, who had a tinge of a blush at his cheeks, and a warm feeling swept over me. It appeared that Roman Hepburn was nice to his dog, even if he was grumpy with everyone else. It really was quite sweet.

'Mother, my reputation is being seriously annihilated here.'

I couldn't help but giggle, earning me a cocked eyebrow from Roman.

'When did you meet Doolittle, Summer?' Mrs. Holliday asked, ignoring Roman's grumble.

'Oh when I went to Roman's house the other day.'

'Ooh you did?' Her head whipped around to look at Roman. 'So you see each other out of work then too?'

'No, Mum, we don't,' Roman answered with more than a hint of exasperation. 'Summer went to get me a clean shirt because I'd spilled coffee down mine.'

'So you sent Summer?' she asked in an accusatory tone.

'I had work to do!' Roman exclaimed.

'She's your PA, Roman, not your slave, remember that.' Mrs. Holliday pointed a finger at him and raised her eyebrows.

'Yes, mother,' Roman sighed with a shake of his head. 'Whatever you say.'

Their interaction was amusing, and showed the deep love between them. The easy banter reminded me of my own family.

As I crossed my legs and settled into my seat, a voice bawled out from the kitchen.

'*Twinkle, where the hell are you?*'

My eyes shot up and I stared in astonishment at Roman.

'Twinkle?' I mouthed.

Roman suddenly looked panicked,

'I told you, my grandparents were hippies,' he groaned on a deep sigh. 'The owner of that dulcet tone is my dad. Whatever you see and hear from this point forward, please erase it from your brain. *He* is why you shouldn't have agreed to stay for dinner.'

I looked towards the door and wondered if he was right? Maybe I should go home?

'In here, Pete,' Mrs. Holliday called impatiently. 'Sorry, Summer.'

That was all she said: 'Sorry, Summer.' As though no further explanation would be needed. I looked to Roman, whose own face was crumpled with worry.

The door from the kitchen was flung open and in walked what could only be described as Peat Bog Man. Roman's dad was covered in something from head to toe, with only the whites of his eyes showing. It could have been mud, but the smell was horrendous.

'*Pete*! What are you doing, you're getting whatever that is all over my carpet,' Mrs. Holliday screamed.

'Shit, that's what it is,' Mr. Holliday replied as he held his arms out in front of him like an extra from *The Walking Dead*. 'Bloody shit!'

I couldn't help the quiet snort of laughter at the sight of Mr. Holliday stood in front of his wife covered in shit. Despite the dirt, I could see where Roman got his looks from, because he looked exactly like his father—just a taller version.

'Christ, Dad, you smell,' Roman groaned. 'Why don't you wait outside, you're stinking the place out?'

'Shit stinks, son, so what do you expect?'

I had to agree with him—it did. And he did. I clapped a hand over my mouth and nose, trying hard not to inhale the stench.

'Oh my God, it's not like anything I've ever smelled before.' Roman held his arm across his face. 'I'm going to gag.'

'Don't be so dramatic. Shit is shit, whatever it smells like.'

This wasn't so bad: my own dad said 'Shit' quite a lot—usually over the football results, but he still said it. What my own dad didn't do was start to undress in front of strangers!

'Oh God!' I squeaked as Mr. Holliday started to undo the belt on his jeans.

'Dad, no!' Roman cried.

'Pete, we've got guests.'

'Hey?' he said, one finger waggling his ear, while the other one undid his jeans and allowed them to drop to the floor.'

My mortification was complete when I realised that Mr. Holliday evidently liked to go commando!

'Dad, for fuck's sake!' Roman bellowed. 'Summer cover your

eyes.'

'Oh bloody hell,' I muttered, and then started to giggle, as I turned away, and placed one of Mrs. Holliday's cushions in front of my face.

This scene was nothing like anything that would go on in my family home, but I couldn't help but find it amusing. Add to that Roman's obvious discomfort and amusing turned to hilarious.

'Twink, can I move please? I've got something up the crack of my arse that is moving, and I'd like to extract it as soon as possible.'

The snort of laughter that burst out of me must have sounded like a sob, because suddenly Roman was crouching down in front of me, gently lowering the cushion.

'I'm so, so, sorry, Summer,' Roman said, rubbing at his temples. 'I'll take you get your car?'

'No,' Mrs. Holliday practically screamed before I had time to answer. 'She's staying for tea.'

I bit down on my bottom lip, desperately trying not to laugh, but it was becoming increasingly difficult as Roman's parents continued their chat behind us.

'Pete, Roman's right, you do stink. What exactly is it?' I heard Mrs. Holliday ask.

'It's geese shit. The little bastard was herding the geese, just like we thought.'

'This gets worse,' Roman groaned. 'I did warn you about him.'

My shoulders were now shaking as I buried my face into the cushion.

'I managed to get hold of him and put his lead on, and then one of the geese ran towards the park lake, so Doolittle followed him, dragging me in with him. I didn't realise he was so strong.'

'He's not that strong,' a disgruntled Mrs. Holliday responded.

'Well, he is when he's after a geese, or is it goose? What's the singular for goose, Twink?'

'Goose, isn't it? Should I google it?' she asked distractedly.

'*No*,' Roman cried. 'Just get him out of here, please,' he pleaded desperately.

As Mr. Holliday continued to grumble, I heard something plop onto the carpet, followed by a scream from Mrs. Holliday.

'Ugh, what's that?' Mrs. Holliday asked.

'Don't know,' Mr. Holliday replied, 'but my arse feels better now.'

Roman let out a pained whimper, and I let out a loud bark of laughter, doubling over because my sides ached.

'I'll give you a pay rise if you never talk of this again,' Roman muttered. 'In fact, I'll give you the damn company.'

CHAPTER 16

Roman was driving me straight home, rather than back to the office for my car. Over our dinner of waffles and sausages, Mrs. Holliday had insisted on me drinking almost a bottle of wine. Every time I took a sip, she filled my glass back up to the top. I tried to tell her that I was driving home, but she asked why I'd need to drive when Roman had his truck with him.

'But I'll need my car in the morning, Mrs. Holliday.' I just couldn't form the word 'Twinkle' without laughing. 'I need to drive to work.'

'It's Twinkle, and don't give me that rubbish.'

'What's rubbish about that?' Roman had asked. 'Summer doesn't live within walking distance of the office, so she'll need her car.'

'Whatever,' his mum scoffed and nudged Mr. Holliday who was busy scratching his backside.

'Can I apologise again about my parents?' Roman said as he pulled into my neighbourhood. 'I know tonight must have been a nightmare for you.'

I grinned into the darkness. 'I actually found them quite amusing,' I replied. 'Admittedly, your dad's bottom was a little disconcerting, but your mum was lovely.'

'Well, that's a positive. Even I come away from there feeling defiled at the best of times, and I've had thirty-one years to get used to them. I'm just so sorry I had to take you there. I never even asked if you had any plans for the evening.' He let out a sigh, and indicated to turn into my parents' road.

Disappointment hit me. I was almost home and had actually had a pleasant evening. I really didn't feel ready to leave the warmth of Roman's truck—or him for that matter.

'Well, I guess this is you,' he said, as he pulled up at the bottom of my parents' drive and turned off the engine.

'Thanks again for the lift home.' I unbuckled my belt, and turned back to him. 'And please don't worry about your mum and dad, or what I saw, it won't go any further than that your dad doesn't wear undies.'

Roman groaned and dropped his face into his hands.

'Oh God, he's a nightmare, but I did try and warn you.'

He looked at me with an arched brow and a smile twitching at his lips.

'I know, but seriously—it was fine. Plus, it was quite nice to see you aren't just miserable with me, but with everyone else too.'

I laughed and was surprised when Roman joined in.

'Yeah, it's not just you that drives me nuts, my crazy parents do too.'

He was smiling, and it was a really beautiful smile that I wished I saw more often.

'Not sure how I should take that, being called as crazy as your parents.'

'I didn't say you were as crazy as them, just that you drive me crazy,' he corrected, glancing quickly out of the windscreen. 'To be honest, you're right most of the time, and I only do it to yank your chain.'

'Oh my God, really?'

I probably should have been mad, but I liked this teasing Roman. He was much more relaxed.

'Hmm,' he said, wincing. 'I probably shouldn't have told you that, should I?'

'Maybe not. But as a matter of interest, why were you offhand with me on your first day? You were really nice at the meeting you had with Mr. Barlow, and then that day you came to the office, you were like a different person.'

Roman cleared his throat, and rubbed a hand over his stubble, contemplating me closely. His eyes on me sent a thrill throughout my body, and I could feel my bra tightening with my reaction.

'You may want to punch me when I tell you,' he said quietly. 'It really is stupid.'

My breath hitched, worried about what he was going to say. Almost immediately, the thrill his gaze was giving me was replaced with a cold worry.

'It was your name,' he said, tilting his head and eyeing me carefully.

'My name?' I twisted in my seat and pushed back against the door. 'I don't understand.'

'I told you what my mum said about a girl called Summer.'

'And because I was called Summer, you thought you'd be an …'

I trailed off. After all, he was still my boss.

'I know, I know,' he cried. 'But I thought you were called Sarah, and then I found out you were called Summer, and it felt … well, weird.'

I had no idea what to say to him, other than 'you stupid dickhead', but even that seemed inadequate.

'You're a grown man, Roman,' I snapped. 'A businessman, and you've been argumentative and cantankerous with me because your mother thinks your destiny is with a woman called Summer? You are joking?'

Roman bit on his lip and shook his head.

'I know, it's pathetic. But in my defence, I only did it because I was so attracted to you.'

The air rushed from my lungs, and my stomach did its own little disco dance. Never did I expect him to say that. Maybe my reaction was a little over the top, after all, he'd only said that he was attracted to me. Amidst the shock, a little smile pushed through. I was a woman, and what woman didn't want to be told by a sexy, hot guy that he was attracted to her

'Oh.' That was all I could manage: 'Oh!'

Roman's tongue flicked out and wet his lips, as he shifted in his seat.

'Yeah, very,' he replied softly. 'I've tried keeping you at arm's length, but it's getting more difficult each day, Summer, especially after that damn kiss at the club.'

Looking into Roman's bright eyes, I took a deep breath and edged a little closer to him. I could hear my heart hammering in my eardrums, and wouldn't have been surprised if Roman hadn't heard it too.

'Summer,' Roman whispered.

'Yes.' My voice was breathy as I struggled to take in any air.

'I really am sorry for behaving like a prick. I shouldn't have behaved so badly, just because I liked you and my batty mother has some weird ideas. Please will you forgive me?'

His scent was intoxicating and my desire for him was buffering against all my reason. I knew that I should probably make him work harder for my forgiveness, but I was so attracted to this man, I didn't see the point in wasting the time that could be spent getting to know each other.

'Is that your A game that you're bringing to me, Mr. Hepburn?' I said with a shake of my head. 'Because for an apology, that was pretty pathetic, especially after your special levels of misery.'

Roman dropped his head back and laughed loudly. 'Okay,' he said, grinning. 'How about I take you out to dinner, tomorrow evening?'

I tilted my head in the pretence of contemplating his invitation, but really, I had no need to think about it.

'Okay, we'll see whether you can do any better over dinner.'

Roman grinned and leaned forward, dropping a gentle kiss to the side of my mouth. I held my breath, recalling what those lips had felt like before—and they were so much better than I remembered.

'Good,' he replied, his lips still on mine. 'I'll pick you up at eight-thirty to take you into the office.'

'Okay,' I said on a long breath. 'See you in the morning.'

Roman's engine idled as I walked up the drive, and when I turned at the front door, he gave me a wave before he sped away, leaving me feeling like a gooey pool of girliness.

CHAPTER 17

The next morning, I got out from under my duvet faster than I ever had before. The thought of Roman picking me up made me as nervous as a turkey the week before Christmas, plus, I wanted to look my very best. My usual practice of getting up twenty minutes before I was due to leave the house just wouldn't be conducive to me looking fabulous.

Waiting for Roman to turn up, I sat on the arm of Dad's favourite armchair and watched through the window, intermittently wiping my damp palms on my skirt. Today I had gone for a 1950s sexy-siren look: tight black pencil skirt, black-and-white polka-dot blouse with cute, short puffed sleeves, a wide, waist-synching, red leather belt and matching red *Louboutin* peep-toe shoes: my precious babies, who only normally came out for very special occasions—and this was one of those times.

As I finished checking my scarlet lipstick in the mirror over the fireplace, I heard the short burst of a horn outside. I ran over to the window and looked through to see Roman's truck at the end of the drive. It was almost five minutes past eight—any later and I would have thought he'd changed his mind.

'Morning,' I gasped as I plonked myself into the passenger seat.

'Morning,' Roman replied with a cheeky smile. 'I stopped and got you something.' He nodded towards a bag in the footwell.

I frowned at him and reached down for the bag. 'What is it?' I peeked inside and spotted a takeout cup of coffee and a chocolate muffin.

'Oh, thank you,' I said, my heart giving an extra little beat.

'Well,' he said with a shrug, 'I figured I have a fair amount of making up to do.'

I so desperately wanted to reach over and give him a little peck on the cheek, but decided maybe it wasn't appropriate to kiss your boss. Okay, so we'd already had a really hot kiss, and one little sweet kiss last night, but we'd leave it at that for now.

'Thank you, anyway.' His reward was my sweetest smile. 'And thank you for picking me up.'

Roman arched an eyebrow. 'I wasn't sure you'd be speaking to me, to be honest.'

'Why?'

'After that dreadful meeting with my parents?' He gave a little shudder, making me laugh.

'Seriously, it wasn't that bad, and to be fair, you did warn me.'

'Nothing can prepare you, though,' Roman said, starting the truck. 'My mum even called the house this morning and asked to speak to you.'

'What?' I cried, thankful I hadn't taken a sip of my coffee yet.

Roman chuckled and quickly glanced at me. 'I did tell you. She didn't believe we weren't an item, and that you weren't staying with me last night.'

My breath started to speed up at that thought, and I fought the urge to let out a little moan.

'But, like I said to her, all in good time, mother, all in good time.'

That time I did let out a little moan.

***

We had been in the office for a couple of hours, and had barely spoken two words to each other, as Roman was too busy on the phone in his office.

As soon as we'd walked through the door his mobile had

shrilled out and hadn't stopped since. Every time he came into my office, to drop paperwork on my desk, or ask for a cup of coffee, his phone was at his ear, and while he couldn't really speak to me, I sensed that Roman was feeling really stressed. His shoulders were practically hunched to his ears, and his hair looked like he'd just got out of bed after a restless night.

Finally after a few hours of huffs and sighs and much pacing, he came into my office without his mobile.

'Do you want a coffee?' I asked, getting up from my desk.

Roman rubbed a hand over his face and sighed. 'Please, that would be great. Thanks.'

I gave him a small smile and went to make the coffee. As I stood waiting for the kettle to boil, I felt Roman's presence behind me.

'Shit, what a morning.'

I turned to see him raking a hand through his hair—again. He looked anxious and tired, and it wasn't even lunchtime.

'Anything I can help with?' I asked.

'Can you lay bricks?' Roman asked, giving me a small smile.

I screwed up my face, as though thinking. 'Nah, sorry. I can make a mean lasagna, would that help?'

'Unfortunately not, but you can make it for me one day.'

Then he winked at me, and I lost my breath. I liked this Roman: this Roman was sweet and fun. This Roman wanted my lasagna— what more could a girl want?

'If you carry on being nice, I might just make you a cake too,' I joked, turning back to the now boiled kettle.

As I spooned coffee into a mug, I was startled as Roman gently laid his hand at my waist and moved his mouth to my ear.

'Oh, and by the way, I should have said earlier, you look beautiful today.'

As he moved away from me, I inhaled sharply, placing a hand against the thrumming beat in my chest.

It was almost time to finish for the day when Roman returned from a site visit to the warehouse conversion that we were doing. He'd been gone for a couple of hours, and I'd strangely missed him. It wasn't as though I wasn't used to having the office to myself, because I was—he often went on site—but today was different and I craved for his return. Every time the door had opened I'd held my breath and waited in anticipation for it to be Roman. Debbie from Accounts and Maddie from Wages—although lovely—didn't give me the same thrill. So when he finally did reappear, I couldn't help the huge grin that lit up my face.

'Hey, how did it go?' I asked brightly.

'Not good.' Roman took off his suit jacket and threw it at the wall. A cloud of plaster dust fluttered through the air.

'Shit!'

I wasn't sure whether it was the fact that he appeared to be covered in plaster dust, or if it was something else that was 'Not good'.

'What happened?' I got up from my seat and picked up his jacket.

Roman sighed heavily and pinched the bridge of his nose as he perched on the edge of my desk.

'The plasterer that Nige recommended is what happened. His work is shit and so it's all going to have to come off.'

Nigel was one of our more experienced project managers, so I was a little surprised that he'd made such a big mistake.

'Really, it's that bad?' I asked.

Roman nodded and looked up at me with tired eyes.

'It's not evenly spread and bumpier than a farm track in places. It's just not acceptable. That's why I'm in such a mess. I got a little bit angry, shall we say, and kind of attacked it with the decorator's scraper.' He afforded me a small smile as he brushed dust from his trousers.

'How many rooms are we talking about?'

'All five bedrooms; thankfully he hadn't started downstairs.'

'I don't understand why Nige didn't pick up on it,' I replied as I hung Roman's jacket over the back of the chair we kept for visitors.

'He's been off-site for two days trying to source replacement timber for interior doors as the last lot was shit. That's why I went down there, just to check everything was okay.'

'No wonder it's bad work if he's plastered five rooms in two days.' Good plastering was an art, and while an experienced plasterer could work quickly, that amount of rooms in two days was definitely too quick.

'Exactly. The guy reckons it was the bad light and that it only needs re-working in certain areas, but it isn't. It all needs re-plastering and the worst part is, *he's* going to have to do it. I don't have time to get anyone else in.'

Roman looked utterly defeated as he stood up and walked towards his office. He stopped in the doorway and turned to me.

'Any chance of a cuppa?'

I gave him a soft smile and nodded. 'Do you fancy a biscuit too?'

The smile he returned made me falter. It was beautiful and gave some light to his tired features. Unable to speak—because if I did I was sure I'd sound like a budgie on helium—I simply nodded and turned away.

I had no idea what this man was doing to me, but it was causing my heart strings to strum in time with my throbbing nipples.

***

When I got home that evening, I raced upstairs and flung open my wardrobe door. What the hell was I going to wear? Roman had said that he'd pick me up at seven-thirty, but, stupidly, I hadn't even thought to ask what I should wear. Smart, casual, formal, informal—I had no clue. I needed help, so I picked up my mobile and dialled Emma.

'Hey sweetie,' she answered on the second ring.

'Hi Em, I need your help.'

I explained about my date with Roman and then waited for a couple of minutes until she stopped squealing with glee down the phone.

'Oh. My. God,' she gasped. 'All that sexual tension from your kiss has been brewing nicely. Where's he taking you?'

'I have no idea,' I groaned. 'That's why I'm ringing you. I need ideas on what to wear. I'm such an idiot, I should have checked.'

'Okay, calm down,' Emma soothed on the other end. 'If it's dinner and it's Roman, then it's going to be pretty swish I would say.'

'What makes you say that?'

'Just by looking at him. I know I've only met him once, but he doesn't seem the burger-and-chips type of man. He oozes sophistication.'

'Did you damn well sigh, then?' I asked sitting bolt upright.

Emma giggled. 'Maybe. You have to admit—he's bloody splendid.'

'Hmm,' I grunted with a little smile of my lips. She was right— he *was* bloody splendid.

'Hey, you're supposed to have the major hots for Henry.'

'I do.' A very definite sigh echoed down the line this time.

'So how was your date on Friday? All you sent me was one damn text that said: *Sigh* and had a love heart on it, and that you'd call me later, but you didn't.'

'I know, I'm sorry,' Emma groaned. 'But we've been so busy at work, I've not been getting home until gone eight most nights and then just crashed.'

'You haven't even spoken to Henry then?' I asked, my tone dripping with sarcasm. The 'ums' and 'ahs' on the other end of the line gave me my answer. 'It's fine, Em. I get it you really like him and maybe like him more than me now. It's not a problem,' I joked.

'Sorry, am I a really bad friend?'

'God, no. I'm really pleased you've found someone you like.'

And I really was. She was such a lovely person and good friend that I wanted her to be happy. Yes, I would like to be in her position, in the first throes of what appeared to be an easy relationship, but then the man I wanted a relationship with was Roman, who also happened to be my boss.

'We've spoken to each other every night for hours, and then

went out again on Wednesday night,' Emma said dreamily. 'He's so gorgeous and—shit—he can kiss.'

'Still no sexual shenanigans, then?' I giggled.

'No.' Another sigh, but this one sounded a little disappointed. 'I mean we did steam up his car windows when he dropped me home, but no clothes were removed, and while I knew beyond doubt he was excited, I didn't actually touch his hot rod.'

'*Emma, just say it!*' I burst out laughing.

'No, it's his hot rod, his disco stick. What do you want me to call it? Because I'm telling you now, I cannot, and will not, use the "C" or the "D" word. You know I find them offensive.'

'What's wrong with "cock" or "dick?"' I asked, knowing how Emma hated those words.

'Ugh, no, no, no, no, no. Don't say them.'

'Coc—'

'Summer! If you say it, I'll say the "M" word, and, to topple you over the edge, I'll combine it with the "P" word.'

I gasped. 'You wouldn't!'

'I would!'

'You wouldn't dare!' The words actually made me want to vomit and she knew it.

'Moist panties!' she squealed, followed by howls of laughter.

'I hate you. I really feel sick now,' I whimpered.

'I really don't understand you,' Emma laughed. 'You're so common in so many ways, yet you hate the words "moi—"'

'Emma, stop it, don't!'

Emma laughed louder.

'Okay, we're even now. So,' she said, all business-like, 'let's get this outfit sorted.'

CHAPTER 18

Roman placed his palm against the small of my back as he led me into the restaurant. I'd been surprised when we started to drive out of town, expecting to go to one of the local pubs, but as we pulled up outside the beautiful black-and-white house, my excitement levels had risen, and I was glad that I'd worn the little black dress and silver *Manolo Blahnik* sandals that Emma had suggested.

This restaurant, Bennett's, was supposed to be one of the best in the area, having been taken over by the Premiership footballer, Joe Bennett, about a year ago. I couldn't believe that Roman had brought me here on a first date. At least, I hoped that this was a first date; it seemed like it was, but then one never knew with Roman.

'Oh my God, Roman,' I gasped. 'It's beautiful.'

The room was bathed in candlelight, and on each table stood tall, thin vases of flowers. The light bounced off the glasses and silverware and a gorgeous smell of lilac hung in the air. As it was a Friday night the place was busy, but there was still a relaxed atmosphere, with a gentle noise of chatter in the background.

'I've been to Bennett's in town, the first one he opened,' Roman said, 'and really enjoyed it, so thought I'd give this place a try. Luckily they'd had a cancellation.'

'I did wonder how you managed to get a table. I hear it's really popular,' I grinned, 'with women desperate to catch a glimpse of Joe Bennett.'

Joe Bennett was not only a Premiership footballer, but also the England Captain and really good-looking—a bit too pretty for me, but I could see the attraction. He'd played abroad for a while, but came back a few years ago when he rekindled his romance with his childhood sweetheart—amidst quite a lot of furore, seeing as she was engaged and then married to a psychopath, who later kidnapped and beat her up.

'Hmm,' Roman grunted. 'He's a good footballer, but can't say that I'm attracted to him.'

'Me neither,' I sighed. 'Far too pretty for me. I much prefer a man with a bit of scruff and muscle.' Okay, so that pretty much described Roman. I couldn't get any more obvious.

Roman looked at me with wide eyes and then smiled. Shit, there it went again—my breath disappearing from my lungs.

'Sir, do you have a reservation?' the maître d' asked.

Roman gave his name and we were shown to our table. It was situated in the bay of the window and overlooked the tree-lined driveway. Every tree was covered in fairy lights, curling up the trunks and into the branches, and it looked magical.

As we decided what to eat, I gave a contented sigh. 'This is beautiful, Roman. Thank you.'

He looked up over the top of his menu, his eyes twinkling in the candlelight, and I didn't think he'd ever looked more handsome. This new Roman—the happy, relaxed Roman—was a breath of fresh air. Although, bossy, domineering Roman was pretty sexy too!

'You deserve it,' he said after a beat. 'Putting up with my miserable arse, day in and day out.'

'Well, thank you, anyway.'

I swallowed deeply as his eyes narrowed and his gaze became more intense. Heat swept over my body, and I had a powerful desire to reach across the table and drag him over for a kiss.

'Okay,' I gulped, looking back at my menu. 'What shall we

order?'

'So,' I said as the waitress put our coffee on the table. 'How do you know Henry? My friend Emma seems to like him.'

'I think the feelings are mutual,' Roman answered before taking a sip of coffee. 'He hasn't stopped talking about her.'

'Really?'

I was thrilled for Emma, especially after what had happened with Tyler.

'Yep, he's pretty smitten. Emma too?'

'Oh yeah, her too,' I nodded. 'So have you been friends for long?'

'About ten years, we met at the gym that I used to belong to.' Roman's hand gripped his coffee cup as his gaze drifted out beyond the window. When he looked back at me, his eyes were dark and his mouth a thin line. I had no idea what appeared to have upset him, but I chose to ignore it.

'And now you own Ziggy's together?' I said.

'We do.' Roman's grimace was replaced with a grin. 'I never saw myself as a nightclub owner, but Henry needed a partner. He had the vision for it, and I had the expertise to turn the building into a nightclub. I'd been living down South for a couple of years, and decided to come back when Henry had the idea about the club. It's taken us almost three years of red tape, planning, and hard work, but when I look at what we've achieved, it was worth every sleepless night we had over the place.'

'It seems to be doing really well. Why Ziggy's, by the way?'

'Ziggy Stardust,' he replied as if I should have known. 'Henry and I are both David Bowie freaks. Have to admit we both shed a tear when he died.'

While I kind of wanted to laugh at that, Roman's face was so serious that I didn't.

'Well, it's a great club; Emma and I love it,' I replied, making Roman's smile reappear.

'So how long have you been friends with Emma?' he asked.

I continued to tell him all about my friendship with Emma and regale him with stories of my family. He laughed a lot and asked numerous questions, and it was absolutely perfect.

'Can I ask you something now?' I asked, playing with the stem of my glass.

I wasn't sure that I should, but we were getting along, and he wanted to know things about me, so why shouldn't I get to know him too? It was something that I'd been wondering about, I'd had a couple of glasses of wine, and my lips were loose.

'Oh dear, am I going to hate this question?'

Roman sat back in his chair, throwing his napkin onto the table.

'I don't know,' I shrugged. 'I don't see why you would. But, you don't have to answer.'

Deep down, I hoped he would because I needed to know if I was hoping for something that would never happen.

'Go on.'

'How do you know Caroline? Is she an ex-girlfriend?'

Roman was silent for a few seconds, his eyes firmly set on my face. I swallowed, wishing I'd not asked, as he clearly didn't want to answer.

'No, she's not,' he said with a shake of his head. 'She the girlfriend of a friend of mine. Well, he's dead now, but that's how I know her.'

His eyes were downcast, and his voice quiet, so while I wanted to feel some relief—that she was nothing more than the girlfriend of a friend—I had to wonder if he wished that there was more to it.

'Oh, I'm sorry your friend died,' I replied, feeling like a total idiot.

I let out a sigh and resigned myself to the fact that this would probably be a first and last date. I was too damn nosey, and he appeared to be hung up on someone else.

'You don't need to be sorry, Summer.' He said it so softly that I almost didn't hear him. 'It was a long time ago.'

I had no idea what to say, Roman looked so desolate, and I wanted to hug him, but that would just be weird on a first and last date. I took another sip of my wine instead, and tried to think of ways of avoiding him in the office until I could get a new job. Then I felt stupid, because he'd never said it was a date, only an apology for being horrible to me.

'This has been lovely, Roman,' I said, forcing a smile. 'Thank you, and consider yourself forgiven.'

'You're letting me off the hook that easily?' he asked, a smile now lighting up his face.

'Well, you don't want to have to keep buying me expensive meals, do you? Next time I think you're being mean, I'll force you to buy me a cream cake or something.'

'Really.' Roman was now grinning widely, and his brows were arched. 'You'd be happy with just a cream cake?'

'Yes, of course. I'm not a high- maintenance PA, who'd expect an expensive meal every time you lost your temper with me for no reason. Let's face it, you'd be bankrupt by the end of the month.'

Roman nodded slowly and reached across the table for my hand that was still playing with my wine glass.

'So, you think that this was simply an apology for being a mean boss?'

As his fingers wrapped around mine, my mouth suddenly felt dry and I couldn't form any words. His dark, smouldering eyes were drinking me in, as though I was the most desirable woman he'd ever seen. While his thumb rubbed slow circles on my wrist, I could feel the excited throb between my legs.

'That's what you said,' I replied, around a swallow.

Roman's eyes darkened further as he leaned closer to me.

'I think you'll also remember that I said I was very attracted to you,' he said, in a low voice, 'and have been since the first time I saw you in my accountant's office, and have become more attracted to you since that kiss. While I know that this could go royally tits up, Summer, I'd still like to try and see where it goes, because if I've learned anything, it's that life is too short.'

As Roman's thumb continued stroking my wrist, I felt every nerve in my body pulsate, but nothing pulsated more than my *fandango*—okay, so Emma's issues about the nouns for the reproductive organs may have rubbed off on me!

'Are you okay with that?' Roman asked again.

I swallowed and nodded.

'Good. Now drink your coffee because I'm taking you dancing.'

I gave a sharp intake of breath, snatched up my coffee cup, and drank it back in one go, ignoring the burn it caused in my throat because the anticipation of going dancing with Roman was far more overwhelming.

CHAPTER 19

♥

'Good morning.'

I shivered as Roman's breath ghosted against my neck as he whispered against my ear.

'Hey,' I sighed. I turned in my chair and gave him what I hoped was a brilliant smile.

My heart was racing being so close to him, and I was sure that he knew exactly what he did to me. The cocky little grin told me he did.

Friday night had been amazing, and I'd had the best time. After Bennett's, Roman had taken us to a Salsa club in Manchester, where we'd danced for hours. We hadn't got there until late, and I was sure we wouldn't be allowed in, but Roman told me he'd checked it out on the Internet and it stayed open until four in the morning. And we danced until the place closed. We weren't very good at it, and spent most of our time crying with laughter, but were having too much fun to care. When it came time to leave, we almost had the hang of it. We did, however, get the hang of kissing each other—more than mastering it in fact. Just thinking about the way Roman threaded his hands in my hair, or cradled my face while he kissed me, had me feeling hot. It had been the perfect first date.

'Would it be a bit girly of me to say I missed you over the

weekend?' he asked, caging me in with his hands on the arms of my chair.

I sucked in my bottom lip and shook my head. Seriously, if he didn't move I was going to do something stupid: deliciously sexy, but stupid.

'Well, I did. I missed you and your smell.' He moved closer and breathed in deeply. 'Do you know I actually went to a department store and sniffed every fucking bottle of perfume until I found the one that drove me crazy every day, the one that you wear, the one that I bought for you?'

I felt as though I was going to collapse from the vapours: the only word for him was 'swoony'.

He then lowered his head and kissed me. His lips were soft and gentle as I opened my mouth for him, and my tongue searched for his. As his hand came into my hair, I let out a moan and pushed forward in my chair, gripping onto Roman's hand that remained on the arm of the chair. He bit lightly on my bottom lip before gently pulling away, and dropping a sweet kiss to my cheek.

'I shouldn't have done that,' he groaned.

I gasped and looked at him warily, until a huge smile lit up his face.

'If someone comes in, Summer, it's not going to look good is it?' he said, pointing down to his trousers that were showing a definite bulge.

I started to laugh and pushed at his shoulder.

'Get into your office and sort yourself out.'

'Seriously,' he cried. 'You want me to jack off in my office?'

'No!' I gasped. 'That's not what I meant and you know it. Just go and do something with it … I don't know, go and think of something less exciting.'

Roman chuckled, and with another quick kiss to my lips, went through to his office, leaving the door ajar.

'I'm going to bang one out now, Summer,' he called.

'Okay, Roman,' I replied, with a giggle. 'Let me know when you've finished and I'll bring you a coffee.'

His deep laugh was the only response I got, but it made me

smile.

As I carried on reading my emails, and getting my heart pattern back to normal, the phone rang. I snatched it up.

'Hello, Roman Hepburn's office,' I answered breathily.

'Summer, it's Alan Cromwell. Put him on.'

His response was short and curt, but at least he'd eventually decided to call. Roman had been waiting for days for him to ring about the quotation.

'Roman,' I said as he picked up his line. 'Alan Cromwell.'

He breathed a sigh of relief on the other end. 'Finally. Thanks, Summer, put him through.'

***

Unfortunately, a little over ten minutes later I found out that Roman's relief at Mr. Cromwell calling was totally misplaced.

'The fucking bastard,' Roman roared as he slammed out of his office.

'What's happened?' I stood up and went to him, mainly to try and stop him wearing a furrow in the carpet.

'He's given the job to someone else. Whoever it is has undercut me by almost ten grand.'

My mouth dropped open. 'They can't, surely? I know how tight those margins were.'

'Yeah, well, they have. They must be using some shit materials to undercut us by that much, that's all I can say.'

'Can't you look at the figures again?'

As soon as I asked the question, the way Roman's lip curled made me wish I hadn't. It was a stupid thing to say. No way would Roman cut back on quality just to get a job, and, as I'd already pointed out, his profit would be pretty slim as it was. Thankfully, it appeared that Roman was already starting to try and avoid the need to buy cream cakes—he simply shook his head.

After a couple more minutes of pacing, Roman flopped down on to a chair and dropped his head back.

'I don't get it,' he said still staring at the ceiling. 'How the hell can they do it so cheaply? There are some materials that will have to be shipped over, plus the labour costs over there are higher. I'd love to know who got the damn job so I can ask them how they worked their figures out.'

'I don't know what to say, other than I'm sorry.' I took Roman's hand and gave it a reassuring squeeze. 'How bad is it?'

He lifted his head and looked at me, looking utterly defeated. 'Really bad if we don't get The Palisades moving soon.'

'Is there anything I can do?' I asked, pretty sure that there wasn't.

Without any words, Roman pulled me onto his knee and then hugged me tightly to his chest. Evidently my hugs helped.

CHAPTER 20

It had been a week since Alan Cromwell had dropped his bombshell and Roman was gradually getting more and more stressed. He'd asked around all his contacts, but no one knew who Mr. Cromwell had given the work to.

'The building world isn't that big,' Roman groaned. 'I know people all over the damn country, how can no one know who got the job?'

'I don't know.' I bit at my lip wondering what on earth I could do or say to help him. 'Do you think they're keeping it from you, or they just don't know?'

Roman shrugged and walked over to the sink. He turned on the tap and filled a glass with water, before knocking it back in two gulps.

We'd worked late and then gone over to Roman's house, having eaten a Chinese take-away. I say we'd eaten it, but Roman merely pushed his food around the plate. He tried to look interested in whatever drivel I could think of to talk about to try and distract him, but the smiles and nods weren't fooling me. His head was full of the business, and how he was going to turn things around.

The Palisades *still* wasn't moving: the new planning officer appeared to be as obstructive as the previous one. He had refused

Roman's idea of flipping the plan until he was convinced there were no protected birds anywhere in the vicinity, never mind where the nest had been found. On reading the letter telling him this, Roman had stormed down to the council offices and sat outside Geoff Williams's office until he came out for his lunch. Roman then cornered him and demanded a meeting there and then. Unfortunately, Mr. Williams didn't have any good news to impart. Apparently some ornithology specialists were coming from Cambridge University to study the nest. He wasn't willing to allow work to start again until he was positive that it was actually abandoned. Rather than put Roman's mind at rest, it sent him into a major tailspin, wanting to know why it had taken almost five weeks for the experts to be called in. When he arrived back at the office, I was really concerned that he might have committed murder, he was so angry. Thankfully he assured me that he'd left Mr. Williams in one piece—minus the use of a few auditory nerve endings.

'Do you want me to go home?' I asked, placing a hand on Roman's shoulder.

He turned his face to me, gave me a small smile and put his hand on top of mine. 'I'm sorry, I've been shit company tonight.'

'It's understandable.'

I moved closer and wrapped an arm around his waist. My hand moved from his shoulder and I brushed the hair from his forehead. His eyes were surrounded by dark circles, and he looked exhausted from spending all hours worrying about the business. I stood on tiptoe and kissed his lips softly.

'You need to get some sleep,' I whispered.

Roman's arms snaked around my waist and pulled me tighter against him.

'Stay.' It wasn't a question or a command: it was a plea.

I wasn't a nervous virgin, and I certainly wasn't a girl like Emma, who insisted on the five-date rule before sleeping with someone, but the thought of staying the night scared me. It scared me because being with Roman meant something to me. *He* meant something to me. It was nerve-wracking enough him being my boss, which meant part of me wasn't able to relax into the relationship in case it went wrong, ultimately affecting my job.

'Roman, you really need to get some rest,' I protested.

'I don't, Summer,' he whispered. 'I need you.'

He pulled me into his arms and started to kiss me, softly and slowly.

'Oh God, Roman. Is this a good idea?' I gasped as Roman's lips kissed down my neck. 'I mean, you're my boss and — oh shit!'

Roman groaned as his hands gripped my waist and pulled me closer to him. His erection was definitely evident in his trousers, and, as it brushed against me, my fandango did a little dance — quite possibly a *fandango*.

'At this moment, Summer, I couldn't give a damn about whether this is a good idea or not.' He nipped at my earlobe as his hands snaked up my back and into my hair, gripping it tightly.

'What happens if ..?'

'No thinking about 'if,'' Roman said in between hot, delicious kisses. 'Just think about now.'

Thinking about 'now' and how turned on I was feeling, I dragged my hands up Roman's back, taking his shirt with me. My nails dug into his hard muscles making him quiver beneath my touch. My heart beat rapidly at the thought that I could do that to him. I could make Roman shiver with desire, and it made me feel gloriously confident.

'I need you, Summer,' Roman whispered against the swell of my boobs. 'But this won't happen if you're not ready.'

I almost laughed in his face. Not ready? He had to be joking. I was so ready that if touched me in just the right place, I'd go off like a rocket. A very loud rocket at that!

'I'm just worried,' I gasped, as he gently nibbled at my neck.

'What are you worried about?' he said huskily, in between kisses and gentle bites.

'You're just feeling low because of the Cromwell deal. Oh God ...'

Roman's hand brushed over my boob, and my sensitive nipple tingled with joy.

'I promise you, this is not to make me feel better because of some damn deal that's gone south. This is because I can't stop thinking about you and it's getting harder every day to keep my hands off you.'

I had no willpower and caved.

'Okay,' I sighed, dropping my head back and giving him access to more of my neck.

'Good.' Roman pulled his mouth away from me and grabbed my hand, dragging me from our spot against the wall in his hallway, towards the stairs.

He almost took the stairs two at a time as I scrambled behind him. When we got to his bedroom he pulled me to him, my back against his hard, muscled front. One of his arms wrapped around my chest, while his other hand reached for the zip of my dress. As he gently pulled it down, his lips kissed the back of my neck; warmth flooded through me and my stomach fluttered as he pushed the dress from my shoulders.

'You are so damn gorgeous, you know that,' Roman whispered against my skin. 'And you smell amazing.'

I turned my body to face him and saw desperate longing in his eyes. Roman's jaw clenched as I reached up and ran a hand through his hair. As my dress dropped to the floor, Roman's gaze moved to my boobs, barely covered by the pink-and-black lace push-up bra that I was wearing. He drew in a breath and pulled me to him, devouring me with a deep, sinful kiss that was full of promise. I kissed him back just as fervently, and then stepped out of my dress which was pooled on the floor.

'Fuck,' Roman groaned as he looked at me in my sandals and underwear: the knickers I was wearing were as brief as my bra.

'I think you need to get your clothes off too,' I giggled, as I started to undo the buttons on Roman's shirt. 'I feel distinctly underdressed.'

Roman tugged the shirt away from my fingertips, pulled it over his head and threw it onto the floor next to my dress. He unzipped his trousers and toed off his shoes and socks, never once removing his gaze from me. When he kicked his clothes to one side, it was my turn to take a sharp breath. He was stark, buck-naked—not a pair of undies in sight and—oh, lordy, lordy!—he was beautiful. Hard, toned and glorious.

'You've got no undies on.' I stated the obvious, earning a grin from Roman.

'Like my dad, I find them far too restricting,' he replied with a smirk. 'Now get on the bed.'

The stroppy, gobby side of me wanted to protest and tell him to stop ordering me about, but the mushy girly part of me started to melt. God, I liked bossy Roman in the bedroom.

My fingers interlaced with his, I led him to the bed and dragged him onto it with me. Roman pushed gently at my shoulders so that I lay back against his pillows, then pulled me down the bed with his hands at my waist.

'You've been tantalising me for bloody ages,' he said as he crawled backwards.

I smiled at his words. 'Really, is that so?' I whispered.

'Yep, since the first time I saw you, I've been thinking about what I want to do to you and that smart little mouth of yours.'

If his eyes hadn't been twinkling and his lips slightly upturned, I would have thought he was angry.

'Last chance, Summer,' he said softly as he hooked his fingers into the sides of my knickers.

I nodded and then gasped as I was suddenly bare and felt the delicious scratch of Roman's two-day scruff against the inside of my thighs.

'Oh God,' I cried.

'Nah, just Roman,' was the muffled response from between my legs.

Oh my goodness, I hoped my poor fandango would survive the night.

CHAPTER 21

I stretched lazily, warmed by the sun peeking in through the open blinds, and then sighed. Last night had been quite simply wow! It was like one of the scenes from a raunchy novel, except it was all happening for real. Roman had surpassed every one of my fantasies. The sex had been hot, fast and, to quote an elderly American lady: 'darn good'. Now I ached in all the right places and in all the right ways.

'Morning,' came a sexy growl beside me.

I turned to face a sleepy-eyed Roman. 'Hey.'

'You okay?' he asked, running a finger down my nose and along my bottom lip.

'Yeah, you?' I breathed on a sigh.

Roman nodded, snaked his arm around my waist, and pulled me to him. He lowered his mouth and kissed me slowly and thoroughly. My heart thudded, not only because it was a bloody good kiss, but also because it meant he didn't regret what we'd done.

'Do you want some breakfast?' he finally asked. 'I've booked a meeting in our calendars with "a supplier" this morning, so we have plenty of time.'

He winked, and I sighed and snuggled against his chest. 'That's naughty, Mr. Hepburn, but that would be nice.'

'I'll make us some tea and toast, you stay here.' Roman dropped a kiss to my head and rolled out of bed.

As he padded across the bedroom to his chest of drawers, I peeked above the duvet to watch him and sent up a silent prayer of thanks to the God of Bottoms at the sight of his toned arse and muscled thighs. He definitely worked out, and regularly, if his body was anything to judge by. I continued to stare as Roman opened a drawer and took out a pair of striped pyjama bottoms and pulled them on, just high enough that I could still see the two sexy dimples above his bum. He turned towards me and smiled when he saw me watching him.

'You look pretty comfy in there,' he said.

'I am, it's lovely and warm.' I snuggled down further and closed my eyes. 'I think I'll have a little snooze while I wait for my breakfast.'

'You do that.'

I felt Roman's lips on mine and my heart did a little flutter.

***

I don't know how long I had snoozed for, but when I woke, I could hear voices downstairs. I snatched up my mobile from the bedside table and saw it was almost eight-thirty, so I wondered if it was one of the lads from work. Cocking my head to one side, I listened again to the noise below. One of the voices was definitely Roman's rumble and the other was distinctly female: that made my heart thud.

Bringing my knees up, I rested my head on them and waited, contemplating what I should do. Roman and I weren't enough of a 'thing' for me to go down there and ask what the hell was so important that it disrupted a sexy man bringing me breakfast in bed, never mind that it was another woman. However, I couldn't sit up here for hours while they talked. After another five minutes of muffled discussion, I heard the front door close and thought it was probably safe to go down and find Roman.

I looked around the room for my clothes and quickly gathered them together. Then the thought struck me that Roman might have other plans, seeing as he'd covered our morning. Feeling a

little unsure, but going with it anyway, I snatched up Roman's dis-
carded shirt and pulled it on over my head. The sleeves hung
below my hands and the length of it skimmed my thighs, so with
a couple of buttons open to reveal some cleavage, I hoped, but
thought it unlikely, that I looked like a sex kitten as I made my
way downstairs. Following the sound of clattering plates and
cups, I found Roman in the kitchen. His back was to me and the
sight of it made me clench my thighs together.

'Roman,' I whispered to announce myself.

He spun around with a knife in his hand.

'You're up.'

'Yeah, I heard a door close,' I explained, deciding not to let on
that I'd heard the exchange, part of me wanting to test whether he
told me the truth.

'Hmm, Caroline was here,' Roman said, and turned back to
buttering some toast.

'Oh okay.'

I didn't know what else to say, because whatever came out of
my mouth would be bound to sound snippy and bitchy. What the
hell was she doing here at eight-thirty in the morning when
Roman would normally be at work? Did she do this often, just
pop in?

As I watched him, I suddenly felt extremely awkward standing
in my boss's kitchen, in his shirt after we'd spent the night having
epic sex. Maybe this hadn't been a good idea and I shouldn't have
agreed to stay.

'I should probably go home to change and see you at the
office,' I said, and started to leave the kitchen.

'Why?' Roman's voice was hard and loud.

'Sorry?'

I turned back towards him to see him staring at me with the
knife still in his hand.

'Why should you go?' he asked, confused. 'I told you I'd sorted
this morning. Everyone in the office thinks we're at a meeting.'

'But I need to get some fresh clothes, and you probably can't
afford to take the morning off. You must have things to do.' I

looked towards the hallway, as though whatever Roman had to do was waiting patiently in the doorway for him.

'Summer, what's changed in the last forty minutes?' He put the knife down and took a long stride towards me. 'You thought it was a great idea not long ago.'

He was so close now I could practically taste him and my thighs parted instinctively in anticipation. His hands were at his hips and his jaw was tight as he stared me down.

'Nothing,' I finally said, 'I just thought ...'

'Is this because Caroline was here?' he asked taking another step closer. 'Because she only called to drop off some paperwork she needs me to sign, that's all.'

He nodded to a pile of papers on the kitchen table.

'She wants me to be Maisie's legal guardian. Caroline's parents are the only grandparents that Maisie has and are quite old. Caroline asked me so that I could help them, if the need arose.'

'What about her father?' I asked.

'He's dead.' His eyes darkened and he let out a long exhale. 'Maisie has no one if anything happens to Caroline. That's actually why she called in to the office a couple of weeks ago.'

Call me the worst kind of bitch, but I hated that meant she'd have even more of a connection to Roman. There must be someone else who could care for Maisie, did she not have any other family? The way I was feeling about him was giving me a sour taste in my mouth. Caroline was simply trying to make sure her daughter was secure and I was feeling jealous about it.

'Okay,' I replied, not trusting myself to say anything else.

'Come here,' he said, indicating with his head for me to go to him.

Before I'd even taken one step, I was in his arms and he was kissing me with so much passion that my legs literally began to shake. One of his hands grabbed my bum and squeezed it gently, while the other skimmed up my side, finally resting on my cheek.

'Next time you decide to wear my shirt,' he whispered against my mouth, 'forget the damn knickers.'

The next thing I knew, he picked me up, his hands under my

backside, and walked me back towards the stairs. I wrapped my legs around his waist and hung on for dear life as he kissed me all the way back to the bedroom.

'So how are we going to do this?' Roman asked as we sat at his breakfast bar eating fresh toast with huge dollops of strawberry jam on it.

'What do you mean?' I asked, swallowing a mouthful of food.

'Me and you, how do we do it? I mean how do we act at work?'

Roman reached across and wiped something from the corner of my mouth with his thumb, he then stuck it into his mouth and sucked on it as he watched me intently.

I almost moaned out loud as I felt the now familiar pulsing between my thighs. Shit, I'd never been so turned on, never had so much sex in such a short period of time, and had never wanted to lick up a man's body so much in all my life.

'Summer!'

I shook my head to banish the porno pictures that were flashing in my dirty mind.

'Sorry. Well, I guess it's up to you,' I replied trying to gather myself into some semblance of composure. 'I mean if you want to keep it quiet about what's happened, then that's fine. I totally understand.'

Roman looked at me silently; he picked up his mug of tea and started to drink from it, staring out through the window that over-looked the large garden. I fidgeted in my seat, wondering whether I should say something. Finally, Roman put his mug down and turned back to me.

'I think that maybe we should keep it quiet at work.'

'Okay,' I whispered. 'That's fine with me.'

And it was. I totally understood, but a little bit of me felt deflated. I still had a bit of hope that this could have been something more than a one-night fling with Roman. Shit, who wouldn't when they'd had as many orgasms as I'd had in twelve hours?

'Obviously my family are going to absolutely shit a brick,' Roman grumbled, interrupting my thoughts. 'And having met my mother, you know she's going to freak out about this.'

My head shot up from contemplating the leftover crusts on my plate.

'Sorry?'

'My mother. She is going to freak when she realises that we're seeing each other, especially when it's you—"my destiny".' He wiggled his eyebrows and laughed.

I almost choked on the gasp that I swallowed back. Coughing I looked at Roman with wide, watery eyes.

'You okay?' he asked with a grin.

'Aha. Toast. Wrong way,' I spluttered, pointing at my throat.

'So it wasn't my sexy eyebrow wiggle, or maybe calling you "my destiny", or even the thought of telling Twinkle about us?'

Roman chewed at the corner of his mouth, and I could see that he was trying hard not to laugh.

'What's happened to miserable Roman?' I asked, taking a sip of my tea.

'Told you,' he said dragging my bar stool closer to his. 'Life's too short to be miserable.'

'But ever since I've worked for you, you've been ...'

'A miserable bastard,' Roman finished for me. 'Yep, I know.'

He sighed heavily and ran a hand through his hair.

'I wasn't always a misery, Summer. I used to be quite funny, you know.'

'Hah, really?' I laughed, earning me a pouty frown. 'Don't believe it.'

'I swear I was. Then I wasn't,' he sighed. 'Before I came back to town, I'd been in a dark place for a long time.'

'What like Stoke-on-Trent?' I sniggered.

'You are so not funny.'

'But I so am,' I giggled.

'What I mean, Summer,' he said pointedly, 'is that, no matter how much I tried, I couldn't drag myself out of it. But I'm looking at things differently now, and part of that is me going back to being my absolutely bloody hilarious self.'

I traced a finger down his forearm and then linked my fingers with his.

'Do you want to tell me what made life so dark for you?'

He took a deep breath and then slowly blew it out.

'It was when I ... lost Michael.'

'Michael?'

'Caroline's boyfriend,' Roman explained. 'Maisie's dad. We met when we were just ten years old—we started at a local boxing club at the same time. We hit it off straight away, we both loved boxing and were both driven. Michael, though,' he said with a hint of a smile, 'well, he was much more competitive than I was. Always wanted to do more push-ups than me, run further than I did, hit his sparring partner harder than me. He just loved to tell me how much better he was than me. But, I still loved him like a brother and we were pretty inseparable for years, until he and Caroline moved down South.'

I nodded slowly, contemplating yet again his connection with Caroline, but understanding his desire to help with Maisie.

'How long ago was it?' I asked. 'That Michael died?'

'It's been over five years, but I still miss him.'

'How did he die?'

'I can't ... it's—'

'No. It's fine, you don't need to tell me.' I realised it must have been Michael in the photographs I found in the bottom of his wardrobe the day I picked up his shirt. His death hurt so much, Roman couldn't even bare to look at his picture. 'It must have been hard,' I said softly. 'I can't imagine how I'd feel if anything happened to Emma.'

His hand tightened in mine. 'He was my best friend, so, yep, it was hard. I had some counselling and things got better. And,' he said leaning in to kiss me, 'you've helped.'

'I have?' I exclaimed, my heart swelling.

'Yeah, baby, you have. It's been great fun seeing how much I can wind you up every day.'

As my hand went to slap him, Roman ducked and caught hold

of my wrist.

'I'm joking,' he laughed.

'Hmm, I'm not so sure,' I replied, sulkily.

'Really? I am.'

He shook his head and pulled me in for a long kiss.

'Leave the smart mouth for better purposes,' he whispered. So,' he said after a few beats of silence. 'We'll keep it between us for now?'

I nodded and sighed. 'Yeah, okay, if we must.'

Roman smiled and kissed me, with his hands on my bottom, gently squeezing my bum cheeks. 'Okay,' he said. 'Let's do this; we'll just take each day as it come.'

He held his hand out to me and we shook on it, and I thought it was possibly the best meeting that I'd ever been to.

CHAPTER 22

The weekend had been perfect, with Roman and I spending most of it together. I'd gone to the club with Emma on Saturday night, and then gone home with Roman. He'd cherished pretty much every part of my body until we'd eventually fallen asleep, tired but very, very satisfied. Yes, it had been perfect.

The next morning I woke to the fact that Roman's side of the bed was empty. I glanced at the clock: it was only eight-thirty. Not too early, but it was Sunday, and I'd hoped that we would get to snuggle in bed this morning. But, as Roman was really worried about losing the France job and The Palisades not starting, I guessed that he hadn't been able to sleep.

Thinking about the problems the business was having, an idea suddenly came into my head. Believing it was the best idea ever, I reached to the bedside table, and snatched up my mobile.

I punched a number into my phone, and with one ear cocked for Roman returning, I waited for an answer. After a couple of rings, a sweet, happy voice answered.

'Holly Robertson.'

'Oh hey, Holly, it's Summer.'

'Hi, Summer,' she replied cheerfully. 'What a nice surprise.'

'Yeah, I'm sorry to call you on a Sunday morning, but do you have a few minutes? I'm not disturbing your routine with Ava,

138

am I?'

Holly let out a laugh. 'God no, that child is a night owl. Keeps us awake most of the night babbling and gurgling to herself, then sleeps all damn morning. She's fast asleep on Liam's chest at the moment, although how, with him snoring down her damn ear, I have no idea.'

My chest twinged at the vision Holly was conjuring up, and I wondered whether I'd ever get that: a man who loved me, with our child sleeping on his chest.

'Ah, that's so sweet.'

'I know,' Holly sighed. 'Just looking at him makes me want to make another one.'

'Well, before you do, can I ask you something first?' I joked.

'Yes, of course you can. What is it you want to know?'

'The extension and refurb at the hotel that Liam wants Roman to do?'

'Ooh yes, I'm so glad he's finally agreed.'

'I need to ask you a favour, if you can manage it.'

***

Ten minutes later, and I was feeling optimistic. Holly had said she would speak to Liam, and their business partner, Mark, about starting the work on the hotel as soon as possible. As far as Holly was concerned, she was desperate for the work to start: it was just a case of whether they had the money available. Which was where Mark came in, as he was their accountant too.

She also promised not to say anything about my call to her. I trusted Holly, so I had told her everything about Alan Cromwell and The Palisades, and she was extremely sympathetic. The hotel had suffered badly before Liam had started to help her run it, so she knew exactly how stressful business could be.

I had just finished the call, when the bedroom door opened, and Roman walked in.

'Morning baby,' he said, holding out a steaming mug of tea to me.

'Morning.' I took the tea from him and smiled. 'Hmm lovely, thanks.'

Roman chucked me under my chin in acknowledgment, and then walked towards his wardrobe. He flung open the doors and pulled out a pair of jeans, a T-shirt, and what looked like one of his flannel work shirts.

'Are you going on-site?' I asked, eyeing him over the rim of my mug. 'Even though it's a Sunday?'

'Yep, unfortunately. I'm going to check on the re-plastering at the warehouse.' He didn't turn to look at me, but dropped his checked pyjama bottoms and gave me a great view of his rock-hard bum before strolling into the en suite and turning on the shower.

While Roman was in there, I heard a knock at the door.

'Roman, someone is knocking at the door!' I yelled.

The shower was still running, so he evidently couldn't hear me. The knock came again, but much louder and more insistent this time. I quickly got out of bed, found my jeans and T-shirt from the night before, pulled them on quickly and ran downstairs. I just hoped that, whoever it was, wasn't drawn to the fact that I had no bra on. My boobs weren't too big, but they definitely needed some support; plus, it might be May, but the mornings could still be a little nippy.

As I reached for the door handle, the knock resounded again. I flung open the front door to come face-to-face with Brendan Marks, one of our site managers.

'Brendan,' I gasped, the realisation hitting me that Roman and I could no longer keep our relationship quiet.

'Summer.' A smile twitched at Brendan's lips as he scratched the back of his head. 'Surprised to see you here.'

'Erm, yeah.' What else could I say? *It's not what you think*? I was standing in Roman's hallway with bed hair and no bra on. It was *exactly* what he would be thinking.

'So what brings you here?' I asked. 'You taking Roman on-site or something?'

Brendan's face changed and the smile dropped into a thin line.

'No, I need to speak to him about the French job.'

'Come in, he's in the shower.' I stood aside and ushered

Brendan inside. 'I'm not sure how long he'll be, sorry.'

Brendan looked towards the stairs and nodded. I turned and saw Roman descending them. He was dressed, but barefoot, and his hair was still damp—*sheesh*, he looked good.

'Brendan, what's up?' he asked in a low voice, looking from Brendan to me.

'I've found out who got the France job. Thought you'd want to know.'

'Who?' I asked, glancing up at Roman.

Brendan hesitated.

'I'm sure you've guessed—Summer and I are together,' Roman said as he reached the bottom stair. 'So, go on.'

Brendan cleared his throat.

'Jack Abbott.'

I gasped.

'Is that so?' Roman ground out through a tight jaw.

***

Brendan went within five minutes of giving Roman the news, and, within thirty seconds of that, Roman was stalking into the kitchen.

As he slammed and banged mugs around, I watched him from the doorway—guilt and shame stopping me from going to him. I had been the one to tell Jack Abbott about Alan Cromwell.

I couldn't stand it.

'Roman,' I said, moving up behind him. 'I think we need to talk.'

He spun around to face me, and I knew that my deep red complexion had given me away.

'What did you do, Summer?' he asked, his tone quiet and controlled.

'I swear to you, I didn't do it on purpose, or to cause trouble. He was in the pub, and I told him we were going to France and he asked me who the job was for and I said a local man, and he asked for his name ...' I babbled, my eyes wide and pleading with him to believe that I meant no harm.

'And you told him it was Alan Cromwell?' he asked.

I nodded and chewed on my bottom lip.

'And that's it?'

I nodded again, anticipating a temper blowout.

Roman let out a long breath, and leaned back against the kitchen counter.

'It's not your fault, Summer,' he said, rubbing the back of his neck. 'Anyone could have found out. Like I've said, the building trade is a small world. And,' he sighed, 'if I've pegged Alan Cromwell right, I'm sure he'd have been bragging around town about buying the property and what he was going to do with it.'

'You're not mad with me, then?'

I took a tentative step forward, to be snagged at the waist by Roman, and pulled against him.

'No, I'm not mad, but I wish you'd told me he knew.'

'I just didn't think it mattered.'

I snaked my arms around his neck, and reached up to drop an apologetic kiss at the corner of his mouth.

'When did you say you told him? In the club that night I saw you?'

I shook my head. 'He was in the pub a few days before we went to France. I was having a little moan.' I winced, remembering that all my ire had been directed at Roman.

'I can imagine,' he replied, with a cocked brow. 'Did he say anything else, ask you anything else? Because I need to know if I have to tie down any of our other jobs?'

He tilted his head looking at me expectantly. I held my breath for a few seconds, wondering whether to tell him what Jack had said. Telling him could cause a whole lot of trouble, but not telling him was wrong if we were to move forward with our relationship.

'Promise me you won't storm out of here and go and kick his door down.' I framed his face with my hands, forcing him to look me in the eye. 'Roman?'

'It depends,' he growled. 'Did he fucking touch you, or make you feel uncomfortable?'

'God no,' I said on a long breath. 'But he did say you might.'

'What the fuck!'

I told Roman everything that Jack had accused him of, and I thought that he was going to punch the wall. He paced up and down the kitchen, cursing and calling Jack Abbott some words that I'd never heard before: in fact, I'm pretty sure he'd invented them himself.

Finally, he stopped in front of me, his hands tugging anxiously against the back of his neck.

'You know I'd never do that, don't you?'

'God yes,' I cried, 'I admit he had me worried, and when Alan Cromwell tried to come on to me, I did wonder. But you came back and saved me.'

Relief spread over Roman's face, and his shoulders sagged.

'I swear to you, Summer, Jack Abbott's a lying bastard. I've never done any such thing, and there is no fucking gossip that says I did. He made the whole thing up.'

I nodded. 'I know that, I do.'

Roman shook his head.

'What about the night at the club? Did he say or ask anything then, because it can't be just luck that he managed to get it in under my quote?'

I shook my head. 'No, he just spent all night talking about his exploits as a builder. We didn't discuss you at all, even after you took me into the office.'

Roman nodded and watched me carefully. I couldn't blame him: he was probably checking that I wasn't showing any signs of lying.

'There is something else,' I said quietly, deciding to lay everything out there.

Roman dropped his hands to his side and rolled his eyes.

'Summer!' he groaned.

'I know, but this isn't about Jack, and it's good, I promise.'

'I rang Holly to ask for a favour,' I said, looking down at the floor.

'What sort of favour?'

I peeked up to see Roman was now holding onto the sink, and looking through the window. His stance had relaxed slightly, but there was still tension in his shoulders and neck.

'I asked her to talk to Liam and Mark about starting the hotel refurb early.'

He slowly turned to face me. His brow was furrowed, creating two deep lines on his forehead.

'You asked her what?'

I repeated what I'd said.

'And she said?'

'She said, she'd have had you start yesterday, if it'd been up to her, but she needed to ask them. Mark is also the Finance Director, so he'll have the final say, but she said Liam would be okay with it.'

'Really, she's *that* confident,' Roman retorted with a fair hint of sarcasm. 'If he isn't ready, or doesn't have the money she can't force him.'

'Actually, she said it would be a definite "yes" from Liam.' I started to giggle. 'You see, she's got this thing that she does that he likes.'

'Fuck,' Roman groaned and rubbed a hand across his face, before letting out a laugh. 'You fucking women, and your damn magic pussies.'

I burst out laughing, slapping a hand over my mouth. Roman's body visibly relaxed, and the anger that had been suffocating him had thankfully dissipated. As he moved towards me, I watched him intently, trying to gauge his mood. I knew he disliked Jack Abbott, but Alan Cromwell giving his job to Abbott had made Roman off-the-charts enraged. Plus, me calling Holly may have made him a *tiny* bit angrier.

Roman pulled out the bar stool next to me and flopped down onto it.

'I'm sorry for getting angry, you know it wasn't directed at you, right?'

'I know,' I answered honestly. 'I totally understand your reaction. Jack Abbott is a double-crossing snake in the grass.'

He let out a little snort of laughter, and his lips twisted into a half-smile.

'What's so funny!'

'Sorry, but it's just when you said "double-crossing snake in the grass", it made me laugh. It's so old fashioned. Now if you'd called him "a fucking dick-nut", I'd have understood.'

I could see that he was trying desperately not to laugh as he bit down on his bottom lip.

'Stop laughing at me,' I protested.

'I'm not, honestly.'

He *so* was, because as he pulled me against his chest, I could feel it shaking with laughter.

'So what now?' I asked.

'I don't know, I need to think about it,' Roman answered with a shrug, wrapping his arms around me, and linking his fingers at the small of my back.

'I have no fucking clue how I'm going to be able to carry on the business if that shopping centre isn't started in the next few weeks,' he said quietly. 'And when it does kick off, we're going to have to work some damn long hours to ensure the shops get finished on time. If they're not—and I doubt they will be—Arc Trading could enforce some pretty hefty delayed completion penalties on us.'

'I know, I typed up the contract, don't forget. And that's why I thought that if you could get a couple of weeks work on the hotel in the meantime, it would take the financial pressure off.' I gave his shoulder a squeeze, wanting him to know I really was on his side.

'Let's hope Holly works her magic then,' he said, lifting his head and grinning at me. 'And you're right; the money from the hotel will help.'

Roman gave me a small smile and then sighed. 'I just wish you'd told me what your plan was.'

'Why, so you could have told me I couldn't do it?'

'No,' he replied, 'because I should have made the call myself. I don't want everyone thinking it's my PA girlfriend that's got the balls in this relationship.'

For some reason, Roman calling me his girlfriend felt amazing, and I knew that I was blushing.

'I'm sorry. I didn't think.'

Roman's hand curled around my neck and he kissed me gently.

'You were right to ask,' he whispered. 'Just next time, tell me what your plan is.'

'Okay, I will Mr. Hepburn,' I said, giving him a salute. 'Thanks for calling her, though, I really do appreciate it.'

'You're right, I should have told you, or, at least, asked.'

Roman shook his head. 'No, you took the initiative. It was only my own stupid pride stopping me from making the same damn call, so thank you.'

He pulled me closer to him and kissed me. Then, holding me tight, he rested his forehead against my shoulder.

'I just wish I knew how Abbott managed to undercut us so much,' he said. 'He had to know our price.'

'Hey,' I said holding my hands up in mock surrender. 'It wasn't me.'

Roman laughed and leaned up to kiss me again.

'I know, gorgeous, I know.'

CHAPTER 23

♥

After the Jack Abbott bombshell on Sunday morning, I left Roman's house and didn't see him for the rest of the day. We spoke on the phone very late on Sunday evening, but his mood had declined. In fact, he was possibly even angrier than he had been when he first heard about Jack.

The re-plastering of the warehouse conversion hadn't gone well—the quality was slightly improved, but not to Roman's standards. Nige, the site manager, got the full force of Roman's temper for hiring the guy, and then the plasterer himself got an earful and a demonstration on how to plaster from—of all people—Pete, Roman's dad. Apparently, Pete was an extremely skilled plasterer before he retired, and had worked alongside his son when Roman first started in the building trade.

Roman told me on the phone that he should have asked his dad to do the re-plastering in the first place, but hadn't wanted to bother him. In fact, he hadn't actually asked his dad at all. Seemingly, Twinkle had called Roman to find out if he wanted to go around for Sunday lunch, and when Roman had politely declined because he was working, Twinkle had taken it upon herself to turn up at the construction site with Pete and mounds of food for her boy and the lads on the job. It was then that Pete had seen the 'dog-shite plastering' and taken over, working with

147

Roman all day, up until almost ten o'clock that night.

It had been three days since I'd seen him, with Roman being on-site all day and until late into the evening. We'd spoken on the phone every night, and on two occasions even had phone sex, which was the sexiest thing I'd ever done.

The session of phone sex that had me coming the hardest had been the night before, so I was hoping that Roman would be in a good mood when he came into the office, but I was totally wrong.

'I will fucking kill that bastard.'

I winced as Roman slammed the office door, and stood in front of my desk, his fingers grabbing furiously at his hair.

'What now?' I asked, scared to hear his answer.

Roman let out a strangulated growl.

'Fucking Jack Abbott has subbed half the gang from The Palisades' site for the Alan Cromwell job.'

He turned and kicked the wastepaper basket across the room, sending pieces of paper and pencil shavings flying. My throat constricted and my heart rate sped up to warp factor as something occurred to me. This was a major setback, because if, by some stroke of luck, we were given the green light to start back on The Palisades, say, tomorrow, there wouldn't be any damn men to do it. Subbing the men was paying them to work for Abbott instead, and it was cheap shot.

'Can he do that?' I asked with a shaky voice.

Roman swivelled around to face me and his eyes softened.

'It appears that bastard can do what he likes.'

'The little shit,' I gasped.

'Yep,' Roman replied. 'And "little shit" is the nicest thing that I'd call him.'

'Seriously, there's nothing that you can do?'

Roman shook his head. 'No, nothing. They're not cards-in with me, and anyway, who can blame them?'

'I can,' I protested. 'They should have more loyalty.'

'Why? They're not getting full wages while the site is down; I was only paying them a retainer.'

'Exactly, *you* were paying them a retainer and have been for weeks.'

'And this morning I received a cheque from *Mr. Abbott* amounting to the retainer for the ten men he's damn well poached from me. Fucking self-serving, smarmy, condescending bastard! No one damn well does that; I wouldn't, and he's only doing it to prove that he can. Little snide fucker!'

Roman stamped his booted foot and looked around the room — probably for something else to kick. When he couldn't see anything, he swiped the stapler from my desk and threw it at the wall. As staples and pieces of black plastic followed the earlier trajectory of the paper and pencil shavings, Roman thrust his hands to his hips and lowered his head. I knew he was still battling the rage inside him.

'Roman,' I said, taking a hesitant step towards him. 'You need to sit down and consider your options. Maybe call Gareth in to go through the accounts and the budgets.'

Roman exhaled and then looked up at me.

'I know, I've already asked him to come in after lunch. In the meantime, I'm going to make a few calls.'

'Okay,' I replied, as he turned towards his office. 'Are you calling from your mobile, or do want me to put anyone through?'

He hesitated and pinched the bridge of his nose. 'Erm, yeah. Get me the planning office first; I'll see if they can give me any news about the nest.'

As Roman closed his office door, I picked up the phone and dialled the number for the planning office, hoping that, at last, they would have some good news.

***

An hour later Roman appeared, and while his eyes were still hard and steely, his posture was more relaxed, and I hoped he had something positive to tell me.

'Well?' I asked expectantly.

He shrugged and his mouth lifted at the corners. 'Nothing encouraging to tell you, but the ornithologists are arriving on Friday.'

'*Friday*! What the hell is taking them so long?' Now *I* felt like kicking or throwing something.

'Some rare species of parrot somewhere in Asia apparently,' Roman replied with a short laugh.

'There must be other bird lovers who can help?' I protested.

'Possibly, but this group have done a study of Marsh Harriers, so they are specialists.'

His stance—shoulders drooped, hands hanging loosely at his sides— and his quiet tone were that of a man defeated. An image of the Roman in the boxing photographs I had found in the bottom of his wardrobe flashed into my mind. The man in front of me looked as far removed from that confident man as I did from Miss Universe.

'Let's hope that by Friday evening we have news that means work can restart,' I said rubbing my hand gently up and down his arm.

'Yeah, let's hope so.'

My instinct was to put my arms around his waist and hug him, but we were in the office and anyone could walk in, so I kept to rubbing his arm. I made the right decision, because within seconds Gareth, our accountant, walked in.

'Hey, you okay to talk now, Roman?'

Roman nodded and shifted his features into something that looked less stressed.

'Yes, sure, come through. Summer, you may want to join us in case we need any correspondence sending, or files finding. You know how bad I am at finding where you've put things on the shared drive.' Roman gave me a quick, discreet wink and walked into his office.

'Right,' he said, as we all took a seat. 'Let's find out how much shit we're actually in.'

Gareth punched away on his tablet, brought up some spreadsheets and gave them a quick once-over before looking up at Roman.

'We've got some overdue invoices that total twenty four thousand pounds, and two that haven't yet reached the terms of their payment date. They total just over thirty-one thousand pounds.'

'When are they due?' Roman asked as he jotted the amounts down onto his pad.

'Both reach their payment terms in nine days.'

'So, we've potentially got fifty-five-K coming in?'

Gareth nodded. 'I've got Debbie doing debt chasing and reminders as we speak, although, we haven't been able to get hold of Stan Davies for three days. He still owes us three grand of the twenty grand it cost for the extension we put on his factory.'

'Let me know if you get him today,' Roman said gravely. 'If not, I'll go around there myself. We did that job almost six months ago, so how come he still owes us?'

'His terms were ninety days.'

'Yes, but Gareth, that still means he's three months overdue. How the hell did that happen?' Roman threw his pen down onto the desk. 'I should have been told about this before now.'

Gareth pushed his glasses further up his nose and blinked rapidly behind them. 'He paid the majority of it on day eighty-nine.'

'That's the oldest fucking trick in the book, Gareth. We'll be lucky if we see the rest of it. It'll cost me more to take him to the small claims court than he damn well owes me.'

'I'll keep trying him,' Gareth stammered as I watched him highlight a line on his spreadsheet.

'If you don't get hold of him by lunchtime tomorrow, I want to know.'

As Roman sat back in his chair, I flicked my iPad until I got to his calendar to add a reminder to check with Gareth at midday the next day. I saw that Roman had four meetings in for the following day already, so put it into my calendar instead. Three of the meetings were with other building companies, and the other with a pub chain that were renovating one of their pubs in the town. So it looked as though Roman's day was going to be filled with begging for work one way or another.

'Right,' Roman proclaimed, 'who do we owe money to?'

Gareth's face now broke into a smile, only very small, but still a smile.

'Just three grand to Tyrell Bricks, and eight hundred pound to the mobile network.'

'Which means,' Roman said scribbling away. 'That we could have over fifty-one-K in the bank soon?'

We then spent the next half hour discussing the situation and how much needed to be paid out to the contractors who were still on a retainer. At the end of it, Roman didn't look as dejected, but things wouldn't stay in a good place if The Palisades wasn't started soon.

CHAPTER 24

By the time Gareth went back to his office, Roman's hair was a dishevelled mess from dragging his hands through it.

'Why don't you call it quits for today?'

I stood on tiptoe, smoothed down his hair, and then gently brushed my fingertips over his forehead. Roman's eyes closed momentarily and his lips parted as he let out a small sigh.

'I'd love to, but I should make some calls and try and drum up some work, just in case The Palisades goes totally to shit.'

'Who are you going to call?' I asked. 'Let me help you.'

'To be honest, Summer, I have no damn clue who to call. I've tried everyone, even a guy in Chester that Liam Robertson put me on to, but he's at least six months off wanting his work starting.'

'What about Ziggy's' I asked. 'Is that going to be affected by all of this?'

Roman shook his head. 'No, Henry is the major shareholder, and Ziggy's is doing better than either of us ever imagined.'

'Well, that's good,' I replied with a sigh. 'So, are you prepped for tomorrow's meeting with the brewery?'

He nodded and tapped a finger on a plastic wallet on his desk. It was full of papers and spreadsheets.

'Yep, all done.'

'Well then, call it a night. Go and see your mum, she's called four times for you today. She wants you to go for your tea.'

'She does? What did you tell her?'

'That I didn't think I'd see you today to ask.' I smiled and pouted my lips. 'I think that deserves a kiss.'

Roman pulled me to him and placed a sweet kiss on my lips. 'Thank you, you're definitely what I'd call a great girlfriend.'

I giggled softly.

'She gave me the third degree every time, though. I'm sure she knows about us.'

'We could just tell her,' he said with a shrug.

My eyes went wide as I studied him, waiting for a cheeky grin that said he was joking.

'I mean it, Summer. Let's tell her. I know she'll go over the top, and I know we've only been seeing each other a little over a week, but, let's be honest, this thing between us is already much more than casual dating, isn't it? And let's also be honest, it started a lot longer than a week ago.' He reached for my hand, and took hold of my fingertips, waiting for my answer.

I shivered as I thought back to our kiss in his office, knowing that was what he was talking about.

'Are you sure?'

I knew I was, but Twinkle would likely make this out to be so much more than it was at the moment, and Roman would be the one that would have to deal with that.

'Yeah, I'm sure. We can tell her together.'

'Hmm, that I'm not so sure about,' I joked, shaking my head. 'Maybe it'd be better just coming from you.'

I leaned back to look up at him, and there was a huge smile on his face.

'I take that back about you being a great girlfriend. You're a bad one and a shit PA.'

'Oi,' I cried, slapping at his chest. 'That's not fair; I spoke to her four times for you today.'

'Oh well, that's okay then,' he said sarcastically.

Roman started to laugh and wrapped his arms around my back, engulfing me in a strong, gorgeous-smelling hug. He felt warm and safe, and I could have stayed there forever. It hadn't escaped my notice that, even though we were still fairly casual, how I was falling for him, but it wasn't a scary thought. Roman had obviously thought our relationship through, and his confidence in what we were doing was rubbing off on me. Okay, so there may well come times where working together and being in a relationship would be difficult. But Roman was right in that we should just take it one day at a time, and I really wanted it to work.

'So according to your mum, it's *burgers* and waffles for your tea tonight,' I said against Roman's chest.

He pushed me away from his body and looked down on me.

'Knowing that, would you like to come with me?'

I thought about it for a few seconds, and nodded. 'Okay, why not.'

'Shit, you are insane.' His eyebrows almost disappeared into his hairline. 'What?' he asked, as I started to giggle.

'You, you make me laugh. Your mum isn't that bad.'

'Firstly, it's a minor fucking miracle that I can make anyone laugh this week, and, secondly, you've met my parents, they *are* that bad.'

'Whatever. Just go home and take a nap or something, and I'll pick you up at six-thirty. Apparently your "tea will be on the table at seven sharp".'

'Summer,' he rumbled. 'I'm not going home to nap at four-thirty in the afternoon, and I'm certainly not letting *you* pick *me* up.'

'Don't be such a chauvinist,' I responded with a resounding slap on his chest. 'I can drive and you can have a drink. After all, you're the one that seems to need alcohol to get through an evening with your mum and dad.'

He grinned and nodded.

'Hmm, you could be right, although that will change. I'm sure after tonight you'll be knocking back the gin. So maybe I'll concede on the lift, but not the damn nanna nap. I'm a virile young man, not an eighty-year-old pensioner.'

'Not so sure "virile" is the word I would use.'

That earned me a slap on the backside.

'Take that back unless you want me to show you right here, right now, exactly how virile I can be.'

Biting on my bottom lip, I shook my head.

'Nope,' I whispered.

My body was on high alert as Roman's hand trailed up my side and cupped my breast, his thumb rubbing my nipple in small circles.

'Did you just say "no"?'

I nodded my head.

'So you want me to show you, is that it?'

I couldn't speak, my head and body were in such whirlwind. Even if I could have formed words, I would have agreed with Roman showing me.

As his fingers moved to my blouse, and slowly started to unbutton it, I shivered with anticipation. Once the buttons were open, Roman pulled my blouse from the confines of my skirt and pushed it from my shoulders. He then dropped his head and slowly kissed along my collarbone until he reached the bottom of my neck, where he gently nipped at my skin.

'You are so beautiful,' he murmured against my flesh. 'Now get the rest of your clothes off while I lock the door.'

'What did I say about being bossy?' I asked breathily.

'We're at work, I'm allowed to be bossy. Now, get your damn clothes off.'

As Roman went to the outer office door, I unzipped my skirt and let it drop to the floor with my blouse. Next to go was my white bra, and, by the time he returned, I was standing in my white thong and black *Kurt Geiger* stilettos—I told you, I love my shoes.

'Summer.'

Roman breathed out my name reverently as he slowly walked towards me, unbuttoning his flannel work shirt and pulling it off with the cuffs still fastened. His eyes stayed on me as he unbuckled his belt, and then undid his jeans before letting them slip down his muscular thighs. He bent to take off his boots and socks, still eyeing me intently. My fingers twitched with longing to touch Roman's hard, toned body; my lips trembled with longing to kiss his beautifully defined abs, and my fandango screamed with longing for his big, beautiful cock—I would *not* call it a disco stick, no matter what Emma said! Finally, he was naked, and he reached out a hand to me, his finger extended to trace around my nipple.

'I think you should leave the shoes on,' Roman said taking a step closer. 'I want to feel those heels digging into me while I'm inside you.'

He then did something that made my heart beat faster than the wings of a humming bird. He took the sides of my thong in his hand and ripped them apart. Oh. My. Sweet. Lord. My fantasy had been fulfilled, and it was every damn bit as amazing as I'd read and dreamed about. I hadn't even had to ask him to do it, *and* he hadn't needed a pair of scissors.

'Roman,' I gasped. 'Oh shit.'

Before I could say anything, he hoisted me up with my legs around his waist, and carried me over to his desk. He bent forward and, with a sweep of his hand, knocked everything off onto the floor. A tiny part of my brain flinched at the mess of paperwork that I'd probably end up sorting through later on, but the rest of my brain was drowning with desire. I gasped as Roman laid me on the desk, and spread my legs apart.

'Rest your heels of the edge of the desk,' he husked as he bent to kiss my stomach.

I did as I was told, and arched my back as his lips moved downwards, enticing me with kisses and nips on my sensitive skin. Making a slow journey down my body, along my pubic bone and onto the inside of my thighs, Roman drove me to desperation. I tugged at his hair, trying to force his mouth between my legs, but he was stronger than me.

'We're in the office remember,' he chuckled softly. 'I'm in charge.'

'Roman, please.'

Then without warning, his body disappeared from between my thighs, leaving me feeling cold and isolated. I propped myself up on my elbows and saw Roman grabbing his wallet from his jeans on the floor. He flipped it open and pulled out a condom, ripped the foil open with his teeth and then put it on. God that had to be the fastest sheathing ever—if such a time had ever been recorded. Then, like a damn bullet to the chest, the realisation that the condom wasn't necessary as a contraceptive hit me.

My heart was in pain.

I took in a deep breath. Nothing was going to spoil this moment. I was going to put my sadness aside and damn well enjoy being thoroughly sexed by Roman. He was happy—*we* were happy. For now, I was going to forget.

'Lie back, sweetheart,' he commanded.

Before my back hit the desk, he was between my legs again and thrusting inside me.

'Wrap those sexy legs of yours around my back. I need to feel those heels.'

As soon as I'd done as he'd asked, Roman began to show me exactly how virile he was. His hands reached for mine and our fingers interlaced as he pulled them above my head. His mouth dropped to my lips and our tongues and teeth clashed as our kisses became heavy and frantic. This wasn't the slow, languid sex that we'd had before: it was quick, hard and red-hot and every single cell within me buzzed with pleasure. Roman linked his fingers with mine and led me to the best orgasm of my life—*ever*.

With both of us breathing heavily, Roman leaned on his forearms, which were either side of my head, and brushed my hair away from my face. He looked down at me with a huge grin and kissed me gently.

'Okay,' he said. 'Now do you take it back?'

I looked up at him with a lazy, hazy smile and nodded.

'Yeah,' I breathed out. 'But I think you may have broken my fandango.'

'Really, is that so? And what the fuck is your fandango?'

'Well, if I need to explain it to you, then you're not the man of the world that I thought you were,' I giggled.

Roman nuzzled against my neck, and I felt his body shaking.

'Are you laughing at me?' I asked a little petulantly.

'Nope, not at all.' He then looked at me, sincerity replacing humour in his eyes. 'I may have broken your *fandango*, sweetheart, but I think you've just broken the wall around my heart.'

At that moment, if I could have, I would have done a little victory dance. But as Roman was on top of me and nibbling at my neck, I had to make do with a little hip roll and a mental high five.

A few hours after our *'desk sex'*, Roman tightened his grip on my hand as we walked up his parents' driveway, and I could see the tension in his shoulders.

'It'll be fine,' Roman muttered almost to himself as his hand reached for the door handle.

'Roman,' I groaned. 'If you don't want to do this, we don't have to you know.'

'I want them to know, baby, I really do, but you do know she's going to go way over the top.'

'So leave it for now then. Wait for a while.'

Roman shook his head. 'No. I'm sure about you and about us, so whether I tell her now or on our damn wedding day, she's still going to go crazy.'

I started to laugh, but he was right: Twinkle was going to flip about Roman finding his Summer whenever we told her.

Just as he put his hand on the door handle, it was yanked open. 'Roman!'

It was Tiffany, his sister, evidently on her way out, as she looked stunning in tight black leather trousers and a sparkly silver top that fell off her shoulder.

'What are you doing here?'

Roman didn't answer, but held up our conjoined hands in explanation. Tiffany's hand shot to her mouth, and I was sure there were tears pooled against her lashes.

'Really?' she gasped.

'Yes, really,' Roman replied. 'Now can we come in?'

'Oh God, yes. Come in.'

Tiffany backed away from the door and into the hallway. She placed her handbag onto a small console table, and then hugged Roman to her. Roman kissed her cheek and wrestled himself from her arms.

'Okay, Tiff, don't go overboard,' Roman grumbled.

'I'm just so happy for you. You do know Mum is going to go wild about this,' she giggled.

I watched their exchange and wondered what the hell was going on. He was thirty-one years of age and a good-looking man. Surely, she'd seen him with a woman previously? Before I had time to think about it anymore, I was suddenly grabbed into Tiffany's embrace.

'Oh Summer, thank you,' she whispered in my ear. 'We never thought he'd ever be happy again. He was so lost, after Michael; it hit him so hard. We were really worried about him.'

Losing Michael had evidently impacted on Roman much more than I'd realised. It appeared to have affected his family too.

'Romy, is that you?'

A shaft of light lit up the hallway as the door into the lounge was swung open.

'Hi Mum,' Roman sighed, appearing to physically wither in his mother's presence.

'Mum, guess what?' Tiffany gushed excitedly. 'Roman and Summer are together. Look!'

Tiffany stood to one side and pointed down at our hands that were still joined.

'Oh my Lord! Pete, *Pete*, come quickly, Roman is having sex again! And it's with Summer. What did I tell you about her being his destiny?

CHAPTER 25

Telling my parents that I was in a relationship with my boss was proving to be far less eventful than telling Roman's. Where Twinkle had opened a bottle of 'pink sparkling' to celebrate, my mum was making a cup of tea.

'This is a little different to last night,' Roman whispered against my ear.

'I know, I doubt my mum will call my auntie to tell her I'm having sex again.'

Roman grimaced and shook his head.

'So, how long was it since you'd had sex?' I asked with a smile.

'Not as long as she thinks,' he told me. 'But this is different anyway.'

His eyes twinkled as he looked at me before kissing me softly.

'Roman,' my dad said, coming back into the room. 'Perhaps we could have a chat.'

I burst out laughing as I watched my dad eye Roman as though he was a small boy who'd just been caught looking up my skirt.

'Dad!' I exclaimed. 'Stop it.'

'What?' Dad asked, hands on hips.

'Honestly, Summer, it's fine,' Roman said.

'No, it's not. You're not giving Roman the third degree. We're going out, he hasn't asked to marry me.'

'It doesn't matter, Summer,' my dad grumbled. 'I want my daughters to be with men who will cherish them. As your father, I'm entitled to ask.'

'Raymond,' Mum moaned as she came in with a tray of tea and cakes. 'Leave the poor boy alone.'

'Mum!' Now she was at it. 'He's a thirty-one-year-old man, not some spotty teenager.'

'I'm sorry, Summer,' she replied, busying herself pouring the tea. 'But it must be important to you, for you to actually come home with Roman and introduce him to us.'

She had a point. I'd never taken a boyfriend home so early on in a relationship before. I'd been going out with Alex for almost six months before he met the family.

'I think,' Roman interjected, 'Summer was keen because my parents know, and so we wanted you both to know as well. Plus, we're aware it's all very new, but I think we've both realised that this could be something special.'

As my stomach did a little flutter, I marvelled at how sweet Roman was at times. My heart was in free fall. He was right: we were new, but I knew it wouldn't take much to fall in love with this man.

'How will this work in the office?' my dad asked as he slowly prowled backwards and forwards, his hands firmly in his pockets.

'It's worked fine so far, Mr. James,' Roman answered. 'But knowing how moody I can be at work, I'm sure Summer will have to pull me into line on a few occasions.' He grinned and nudged me playfully.

'You see, Summer,' Dad sighed, 'that concerns me. What if you break up and can't stand working together. You'll have to find something else.'

'We'll cross that bridge if we come to it,' I huffed. 'I wish we hadn't come here now.'

'Hey,' Roman said, pulling on my hand. 'Your mum and dad are worried, that's all. But if things don't work out between us, then we'll sort something out. It might be hard, but I think we're both adult enough to be able to work together.'

I gave Roman a watery smile. Even this early on, I wasn't sure I could work with him if we weren't together. The thought of doing so, while he moved on was awful. But I was going to take my own advice and deal with that if, and when, it happened.

Dad sighed, but he nodded and finally sat down to drink his tea. As he did, Roman's phone shrilled in his jeans' pocket.

'Sorry,' he said, reaching for it. 'I'm waiting for a call about a job.'

He stood up and moved into the hall. While Mum and Dad asked me questions about Roman, I had one ear on his conversation, wondering whether it was good news. After a few minutes, he came back into the room. He looked uneasy and he was chewing on his lip. As he reached the sofa, his eyes met mine.

'You got a minute, Summer?' he asked, indicating towards the hall.

'Yeah, sure.'

I followed Roman out, and watched as he paced up and down the hall, a hand running through his hair. After a couple of steps, he turned to me.

'That was Caroline,' he stated.

My heart dropped. Every time I heard her name it plummeted because I felt as though there was a connection between her and Roman that Roman just wasn't telling me about.

'Okay,' I said, hesitantly.

'She didn't tell me the other day, but she split from her boyfriend a few weeks ago. I guess now that's why she asked me to be a guardian for Maisie.'

'And?'

He rubbed at his temple with his forefinger and blew out a breath. 'And, she's been evicted from the apartment that she's been staying in.'

'Okay,' I repeated slowly.

'She has nowhere to go, and has asked if she and Maisie can stay with me for a couple of weeks until she finds somewhere.'

I waited a beat, knowing that whatever I said next could either make me look like an absolute bitch, or I could be handing my new boyfriend to a woman who I was sure had feelings for him.

'Would you mind?' Roman asked.

The fact that he'd asked if I minded, totally surprised me. It really had nothing to do with me, but it felt good that he cared enough to ask.

'It's your house, Roman, and she's your friend.'

'Yes, but you're my girlfriend.'

That made little swarms of butterflies take off. 'Girlfriend', a simple word, but I loved when Roman said it.

He reached for my hand and linked his fingers with mine. 'I can't do nothing,' he said. He looked down at the floor and scuffed his foot along the ornate runner. 'I have to help, for Michael's sake. I couldn't forgive myself if I did nothing.'

Sad eyes looked up at mine, and I could see that losing Michael still affected him, no matter how hard he was trying to move on from his death.

'Of course, I don't mind,' I replied, swallowing around the lie. 'You have the room, so it's logical.'

He let out a breath and gave me a dull smile. 'Thanks, baby. I can't say no to her, so you being fine with it is a weight off my mind.'

'Don't be silly,' I replied, feigning a smile. 'Do you need to go to her now.'

He winced. 'Is that okay? She has to be out of her apartment by morning, so it's best to move her out tonight. She doesn't have much, a few clothes that's all. The apartment came furnished.'

I nodded towards the lounge door. 'I'll tell them you got called away.'

Roman tilted his head back and frowned.

'You're not coming?'

My mouth dropped open and my eyes went like saucers. 'You want me to come?'

'Yeah, of course I do. We had plans tonight, don't forget.' He gave me an eyebrow wiggle.

My initial thought was to tell him he didn't have to say that, just to make me feel secure. The problem was I couldn't: I needed him to make me feel secure.

'Really?'

'Yeah, why not. I'll just have to keep you quiet.'

The next thing I was pulled into his arms, and kissed until my lungs almost gave out.

CHAPTER 26

'Why did Caroline only tell you tonight that she's being evicted tomorrow?' I asked, as we pulled up in front of Caroline's apartment building.

Roman shrugged. 'No idea, maybe she thought she could sort it out by herself. Maybe that's why she came by the office, but then couldn't tell me. We hadn't seen each other for so long, she was probably embarrassed.'

'Why didn't you see each other?'

'We just didn't see eye to eye on who she was living with.'

I was going to ask more, but as Roman was manoeuvring his huge black truck into a parking space, I decided to leave it. Once he turned the engine off, he twisted in his seat to face me.

'She said she hadn't wanted to call me, but had no idea what else to do,' he explained. 'Her parents live in a little one-bedroomed bungalow, so they can't have her. I just …' he trailed off and sighed.

I opened my mouth to suggest she went to a B&B, but when I saw the stress etched on Roman's face as he looked at me, I knew that I shouldn't. He had to do this, and I knew it was for Michael as much as for Caroline and Maisie.

'Michael would hate this,' he ground out, confirming my thoughts. 'He loved her and was so excited about Maisie coming.'

His eyes roamed my face, and I could see he felt conflicted. I'd thought that I'd managed to hide my worry: evidently not. He cared what I thought, but his loyalty to Michael was immense, and I had to respect that.

'Roman, it's fine.' My voice sounded much surer about this than I actually felt. 'She needs somewhere to go and you have the room.'

'It won't be for long,' he said confidently, giving me a gorgeous smile.

'No problem.' My reply was given airily and with a grin, but I still felt worried.

'One thing though,' he said tentatively.

'What?'

'*Please* don't tell Tiff about this.'

My eyes widened. 'Why? Roman, what's going on?'

'Something bad happened between them.'

'Like what?'

I was stunned that he was even considering this if it was going to upset his sister.

'Tiff hates people knowing about it, so it's not for me to tell you. But Tiff was hurt, badly.'

I turned and looked up at Caroline's apartment. 'Then you can't do this,' I protested, turning back to him.

Roman's head dropped to rest against the steering wheel. All he said was: 'But it's for Michael.'

***

When we got up to Caroline's apartment, she was already packed up and waiting.

'Oh hi,' she said full of surprise as I walked in behind Roman.

'Hi Caroline.' I gave her a smile and tried to feel relaxed.

Everything about her had me feeling as taut as a piano wire, and, to be honest, a little insecure. Aside from what I thought *her* designs on Roman may be, she was absolutely beautiful, so why wouldn't Roman be attracted to her? Even now, when she was moving home, she looked gorgeous.

Her auburn hair was piled up on her head; she wore the

skinniest jeans I'd ever seen, and a T-shirt so tight it looked as though it was spray-painted on—and she evidently wasn't wearing a bra because her nipples were sticking out far enough to hang your coat off.

Unable to look at her without feeling even more inadequate, I looked down at the floor. That was when I thought that I might actually hate her. She was wearing my most coveted shoes. The shoes that I had tried everywhere to buy, but could never get them in my size. She had on a pair of *Sophia Webster* Pink Flamingo print, 'Lola' court shoes.

I think I actually whimpered. Who the hell wears shoes like *that* for moving house.

'You okay, baby?' Roman asked.

My head shot up, startled. 'Yes, why?'

'You made a strange noise.'

'Did I? Oh sorry, just thinking about something.'

Roman looked at me with a small frown, and then kissed my forehead. 'Okay.' He then turned to Caroline. 'You ready?'

'Yes, sure,' she said quietly. 'I'll just get Maisie. Most of the stuff is in the lounge.'

'Is there much?' Roman asked, moving and pulling me with him.

'No,' Caroline called over her shoulder.

'Uncle Wo,' a sweet little voice called as we entered the lounge.

'Hey, Maisie, how are you?'

Roman went over to Maisie, who was sitting on the sofa clutching a pink teddy bear. He knelt in front of her and poked at her little pudgy tummy that was sticking out.

'Okay,' she whispered, giving him a shy smile. 'Are we coming to live with you?'

Roman blanched and then smiled at the little girl. 'Yes, sweetheart, you are, just for a little while.'

Maisie's eyes shot to me, so I gave her a little wave.

'That lady was at your work?' she whispered, leaning closer to Roman.

Roman looked over to me, and then back to Maisie. 'That's my girlfriend, Summer.'

Maisie rubbed her cheek against her shoulder, and giggled. 'She's pwetty.'

Roman laughed and tickled Maisie under the chin. 'Yes, she is, just like you.'

Watching him with Maisie, caused a huge ache in my heart. I was falling more and more for him every day, and I could see myself wanting everything with him. Except that wasn't possible. My nose started to tingle, my throat itched and tears threatened as I thought about the children that I'd never have. My head was full of the children that I could never give Roman—if we ever got to that point.

That momentary dull thud of the pain I'd felt in my heart in Roman's office when he had me on his desk was now a searing agony.

As soon as I'd told Alex about my gnarled old ovaries, he'd dumped me, so would Roman do the same? Was it too early to even tell him about it? We were still new, still getting to know more about each other, still enjoying those first exciting and butterfly-filled-stomach weeks of a new relationship. We certainly weren't at a point where we should be talking about having children, but he needed to know.

'We'd better get going,' Caroline said a little impatiently. 'It's way past Maisie's bedtime.'

'Okay,' Roman said, standing up. 'I'll put the boxes and the suitcase in my truck, and you can take Maisie and whatever is left in your car.'

Caroline didn't speak, but simply nodded and moved from the lounge.

'You okay to help me take some of this stuff down?' Roman asked me.

'Yes, of course.' I gave a quick smile to Maisie, who was watching me, and then picked up a box and a bag of toys, and followed Roman back down to the car park.

'Is she asleep?' Roman asked Caroline a little over two hours later.

They didn't have an awful lot of things, so the three boxes and a suitcase were now all in Roman's spare room—which was now Caroline's—while Maisie was in the room across the landing from hers.

'Yes, I don't think I'll be long behind her,' Caroline yawned. 'I'm shattered, it's been a long day.'

'Yeah, I don't think we'll be too late either,' Roman said, stretching and giving me a glimpse of his hard, tanned abs.

'I'm so sorry, Summer,' Caroline sighed. 'This must be the last thing you want, Maisie and I cramping your style.'

I smiled and shook my head. 'Honestly it's fine.'

It didn't feel fine: it felt a little unsettling. But she'd been nothing but lovely all evening, engaging me in an excited conversation about shoes, once she'd seen me gazing in awe at her feet. Maisie seemed to like me too. She had watched me all evening, and then when we eventually all sat down she had insisted on sitting on my knee while she showed me her dolly and told me all about the clothes it had. She was a beautiful child, and just having her on my knee, with my nose in her hair, made me ache for what I couldn't have. Yet at the same time she was a comfort: it was as though she knew that I was anxious and that her cuddling into me might help. God, having them at Roman's house was going to be hard on more than one level.

'Well, I appreciate it, I don't know what we'd do without you, Ro.'

Caroline having a nickname for Roman made my stomach churn with jealousy. I didn't have a nickname for him, and he was my boyfriend.

'I'm off to bed then.' Caroline smiled and walked towards the kitchen. 'Just going to get a drink of water to take up.'

Roman and I sat in silence, Roman flicking through the TV channels, and me listening to Caroline opening cupboard doors looking for a glass before filling it with water.

A few minutes later, Caroline padded back into the lounge, now without her *Sophia Websters*, gave us a wave and went up to bed.

'You ready for bed?' Roman asked, pulling me onto his knee. 'Or do you still have some energy?'

As he kissed up my neck and along my jaw, my nipples tightened and a moan of pleasure escaped.

'I think I have some energy,' I replied, breathlessly.

'Good,' he replied, putting a hand up my T-shirt. 'Because I am nowhere near ready for sleep.'

I threw my head back, revelling in Roman's touch and his kisses, hopeful that having Caroline and Maisie in the house wouldn't stop our alone time, because every day I was getting more and more addicted to him.

CHAPTER 27

♥

It had been over a week since Caroline and Maisie had moved into Roman's house, and Roman and I had seen each other every night.

Obviously, Roman taking me home for tea with his parents felt as though we'd moved on a step, but in the back of his mind I think Roman was also fully aware that I was concerned about him being in the house with Caroline. I really had tried not to show my worry, and honestly thought I'd managed to hide it, but he'd been especially attentive in the past days—not that I was complaining. His extra little kisses and hugs, and sweet little whisperings, made my heart beat a little faster and put a huge grin on my face.

Things were going well between us, and I couldn't remember the last time we had fought, or more to the point, when Roman had been miserable and bossy, probably because things were a little easier in the office too.

Holly had worked her magic and Liam Robertson had decided to push ahead with part of the building work at Darrington Hall. He had asked Roman to go over and talk prices with him about building the extension to the restaurant. Roman came back feeling a little more optimistic. While Liam had agreed the price for the full build, Mark, his partner and Finance Director, would only agree to the extension on the restaurant until later in the year. It was enough to keep us going though, and Roman had agreed to start the work in two weeks.

'This is going to help so much.' Roman let out a long breath of relief. 'Mark has written up a schedule of interim payments too, which will more than keep us ticking over until we get The Palisades finished — if we ever get it finished.'

'We will be positive, today is a positive day,' I replied as I tried to decipher Roman's spidery scrawl so that I could type up the quotation and Statement of Work. 'What does this say?'

Roman leaned over my shoulder to scrutinise the pad that he'd given to me.

'Fuck. No idea.'

He took the pad from me and held it closer. I looked up at him and giggled. His eyes were screwed up, his brow furrowed and his mouth gaping open.

'Ah yeah. "Replacement architrave required on existing doorways."'

He threw the pad back on my desk and then ducked down to kiss my cheek.

'What was that for?' I asked without looking up from the rest of his scribing.

'Just felt like it. You're too delectable not to kiss when the opportunity arises.'

I turned my head to look up at him and gave him a huge smile. He smiled back; his eyes were soft, and he looked more relaxed than I had seen him in days.

'I guess we owe Liam a big thank you,' I said as I took hold of Roman's hand. 'He's given us some breathing space.'

'Yeah, we do, and he has,' Roman sighed. 'I did tell him not to feel obligated, but he said Holly was anxious to get started on the dining room. Their new chef has increased the number of covers from non-residents by ninety-five per cent, and she's struggling to get people booked in. So as soon as Mark gave the go-ahead, he knew he had to get me over there as soon as possible. Then towards the end of the year he wants to start on the new additions to the hotel and spa.'

'Well, it couldn't have come at a better time.'

'Thank you too, baby.' Roman kissed me softly, and ran a finger down my cheek. 'For calling Holly.'

I gave his hand a squeeze and then turned back to the quotation that I was about to type up. As I scanned Roman's figures, he ran a hand down my hair and then stooped to kiss the top of my head.

'Give me a shout if you need anything else translating,' he said.

'Okay.'

Roman was just about to enter his own office, when the outer office door was flung open, and Tiffany burst in, with a face so thunderous they could have named a hurricane after her.

'Please tell me it's not true,' she spat at Roman.

Roman's eyebrows raised as he thrust his hands to his hips. 'And hello to you too.'

Tiffany ignored him and ploughed on.

'You have to be the biggest idiot on this planet,' she cried, pointing a finger at Roman. 'What has possessed you? That fucking bitch, Roman.'

I sat open-mouthed, wondering what the hell she was going on about. Tiffany was normally lovely and pleasant. Whatever Roman had done, it had certainly upset her.

Roman looked at me. 'Fuck.' He turned back to Tiff. 'Caroline.'

'Yes, damn Caroline. Do you agree with it?' she turned to me and asked.

I looked between her and Roman before replying.

'It's nothing to do with me, Tiff,' I replied. 'It's Roman's house, and she's his friend and needs somewhere.'

'Hah!' she huffed. 'Needs somewhere my backside. She just needs in his boxers, that's all.'

I damn well knew it. But being right didn't stop my stomach from clutching.

'No, she doesn't,' Roman scoffed, moving around Tiffany to close the door. 'I'm with Summer and she knows that.'

'Wouldn't stop her—we both know that.' Tiffany looked at

Roman knowingly, and I was anxious to know why. 'Have you been seeing her all this time?'

'God no!' he cried. 'I wouldn't do that to you, you know I wouldn't. She's desperate, that's all.'

'Yeah, like I said *desperate* to get in your pants,' Tiffany snapped back.

'Listen,' I said, rolling my chair back. 'I don't really know the woman, but she's been perfectly pleasant to me. So what don't I know about her?'

Someone needed to tell me, because if she and Roman had a romantic history that I didn't know about, new girlfriend or not, I was not going to be happy about it. My anxiety was growing, and that would topple me over the edge.

'Has he not told you that she's a lying, manipulative, relationship-wrecking bitch?' Tiffany said through gritted teeth. 'Because she is.'

'Tiff,' Roman warned. 'That's enough.'

'No it isn't,' she replied, her voice shaking with emotion. 'She ruined my life, Roman, or have you forgotten that?'

'No, I haven't forgotten and I really am sorry.' He put his hand on Tiffany's shoulder, giving it a gentle squeeze. 'But she has nowhere else to go.'

Tiffany whimpered and shook her head. 'We were talking about getting married, Ro,' she cried, swiping at tears on her face. 'You weren't here, you didn't know what we were like together.'

Things were becoming clearer, and my heart ached for Tiffany—she looked devastated. She must have been deeply hurt by whatever had happened. This, whatever it was, was what she hated to talk about.

'I know, and I hate how much they hurt you, but she was grieving and grief makes people do strange things.' Roman looked down, with his hands on his hips. 'Losing Michael—'

'You can't defend her just because of Michael! She can't get away with shit just because her boyfriend died.' Tiffany pushed a finger in Roman's chest, as tears continued to crawl down her face. 'But, it always comes back to him, doesn't it? When will you just damn well let it go?'

My head snapped to Roman, as he made a stricken noise from the back of his throat. His hands fisted as he looked at Tiffany with pain in his eyes.

'Roman?' I whispered, pushing up from my chair and going to him.

He put out a hand and shook his head. 'No, Summer. I just need a minute.'

He pushed past Tiffany, swung open the door and stormed away, leaving me open-mouthed, staring at his sister.

'What the hell is going on, Tiff?'

As Tiff wiped her face, my stomach churned and a light sweat pricked my forehead. My cheerful, happy mood of earlier had well and truly disappeared.

'I'm sorry,' Tiffany sobbed, dropping down onto a chair. 'But I just fucking hate her, Summer.'

'Caroline, obviously.'

She nodded silently, fished a tissue from her jacket pocket, and wiped her nose with it.

'She took him from me,' she said, her chin trembling. 'Everyone thought, just because we'd only been together a few months that I was fine. And I admit that I am better off without him—I know that now—but he broke my heart. *She* broke my heart.'

I moved over to Tiff and put an arm around her shoulder, hugging her to my side.

'What happened, Tiff?'

She turned her red-rimmed eyes to me and gave me a weak smile.

'After Michael died, Roman went away to work down South, where Caroline and Michael had been living for a couple of years. I don't know, maybe he felt closer to him there. And, of course, there was *her*.'

My heartbeat increased at Tiffany's words and what they might mean.

'Were they in a relationship?' I asked quietly.

'God no, he just wanted to help her and Maisie. He wanted to check up on *her*, make sure *she* was okay.'

She spat the words out as though they were poison. 'He said he owed it to Michael. He pretty much cut himself off from the rest of us—his family. Then about four years ago, he started to phone home and spend Christmas with us, and it felt like we were getting him back. Finally, he came back to live here, said he wanted to come home and have a family of his own, with all of us all around.' She started to laugh through her tears. 'Hah, he always used to say he wanted eleven kids, so I guess his poor wife would need help with a brood that big.'

Bile rose to my throat at Tiffany's words. This was exactly what I'd been dreading. It felt like her words were a death knell to my relationship.

As my head buzzed with the information, Tiffany started to talk again.

'He'd been home about six months, when he told us that she was coming back too. He said that Caroline wanted Maisie to spend more time with her grandparents, get to know them a little better.'

Dread slammed against my already racing heart. I couldn't help wondering whether she'd really come back for Roman. Nausea fought with the nerves in my stomach as I gasped.

'Are you sure they weren't together?' I asked, selfishly forgetting Tiffany's current despair.

'No, honestly. I swear, it was nothing like that,' Tiffany said, shaking her head and grabbing my hand. 'He really only ever kept an eye on her. But when he came home, I think he suggested that she come too. Said it was stupid being there when her parents lived here. So eventually she did.'

'And what happened?' My voice was quiet and timid, still worried about what I was going to hear.

'It was Roman's birthday and she came around to the house with a card and present for him. I was there with my boyfriend. When he saw her, that was it. He told me later that it was love at first sight. He couldn't help it. Within two weeks, he'd dumped me and moved in with her. Maisie even calls him "daddy".'

Tiffany took a deep breath and studied our hands that were still joined.

'It's not losing him, Summer, it's the way I lost him. He was cruel and mean when he told me, and she sat in his car, watching, while he dumped me in the cinema car park. She's never apologised, and still thinks it's okay to prey on my brother's good nature because of Michael. I hate her and I can't believe he's letting her stay at his house. I feel like he's taking her side, all because of damn Michael.'

Roman's loyalty to Michael was admirable, but Tiffany felt betrayed by it, no matter how torn Roman was.

'Now, they're not together either?' I said.

'No, he's dumped her too—in readiness for his next conquest no doubt.' Tiffany shook her head. 'Kicked her out about a month ago.'

'Is he local, because I have to be honest, he can't be much of a human being if he's wiped Maisie from his life, even if she isn't his.'

'Hah!' Tiffany scoffed. 'Jack Abbott has no conscience, Summer, so it's no surprise he doesn't even care about a child who calls him daddy.'

'Jack Abbott,' I said on a gasp. 'You're joking? Roman didn't say he was Caroline's ex.'

'Probably because I asked him never to tell anyone,' Tiffany replied. 'It was humiliating. I'd told people we were going to get engaged and then he dumped me. It was less embarrassing to say we'd drifted apart.'

'Oh, Tiff.'

'I'm not proud of the fact that I've lied, Summer, but it was the only way I could get through it.'

As what Tiff said, ran around my brain, I finally understood why Roman hated Jack Abbott.

While I comforted Tiffany, my phone beeped on my desk, and, when I checked it later, I saw that it was a text from Roman:

Grumpy: Can you meet me at my house? We need to talk.

CHAPTER 28

♥

We were at Roman's house and I was preparing to talk. I was also preparing to leave with my heart broken, because I was sure that Roman was going to end things.

'Here you go,' Roman said passing me a glass of wine.

'Thanks.'

I took it from him with a smile, and settled back into the sofa.

'Where's Caroline?' I asked.

'I paid for her to take Maisie for a burger and then the cinema. They won't be back for a few hours.'

While I was annoyed that Roman had paid, I was also grateful that we could talk without fear of being interrupted, especially by Caroline. It was no comfort that I'd been right about her.

'She's skint,' he said looking at me warily, evidently reading my mind. 'But we need to talk, and she doesn't need to hear what I'm going to tell you. I need to explain things to you, so that you understand why I've done something that has upset Tiff so much.'

I sighed as I recalled poor Tiff, and how she'd still been upset when she'd left the office. This had to be something Roman felt was really necessary to leave his sister in such a state.

'Okay,' I said quietly. 'Tell me.'

Dragging in a breath, Roman looked at me with tearful eyes.

'I told you how Michael and I met, and how close we were.'

I nodded. 'Boxing club.'

'Yeah, we were both really good. Although I had a better technique, Michael had the raw aggression. Then about eight years ago, he and Caroline moved down South. I was doing well on the boxing scene, but Michael felt that our trainer wasn't doing enough for him. I think he thought that Dickie was concentrating on me too much, and getting me all the best bouts on the card.'

'Did you argue about it?' I asked, wondering whether this was what was fanning the flames of guilt.

Roman shook his head. 'God, no. Michael totally understood, but he felt he needed someone who would make him their priority. That's when he found a guy called, Tom Anderson. Tom was based in Camden, so Michael got a transfer with his job and moved himself and Caroline to Essex.'

'Did you lose touch?'

'No, we spoke most days either on the phone or via text. When Caroline got pregnant, he was so excited, he called to tell me before his own parents. Then ...'

Roman took in a deep breath and swallowed audibly.

'I killed him, Summer,' he said, 'with one punch I killed him, and ruined Maisie's and Caroline's lives.'

Air dragged from my lungs as Roman's words registered with my brain.

He killed his friend.

Boxing.

The pictures in his wardrobe.

Tears sprang to my eyes as I saw the pain in Roman's eyes. I wanted to comfort him, yet my own shock wouldn't allow me to move. Putting down my wine, with shaking hands, I shrank back into the chair and placed a hand against my churning stomach.

'What happened?' I whispered.

Roman sat forwards, his forearms resting on his thighs, his hands clutched together. He looked up at me, and there were now tears on his cheeks.

'As much as I don't want to tell you this, you have to know. You mean a lot to me, Summer, and you're meaning more to me every day. I don't ever speak of this, because it cripples me knowing what I did.'

He let out a shuddering breath, linked his hands behind his neck and looked at me. The pain he was feeling was evident on his face. His eyes shone and his chin was trembling as he took a deep breath.

I couldn't stand to see the pain in his eyes. Just thinking about telling me was killing him, and that was making my heart ache for him.

'Roman.' I moved closer to him, placing a hand on his knee.

'I … I … Shit!' he muttered. 'This is so fucking hard, but I want you to know.'

'Hey, it's okay.' I reached out for his hand and pulled him closer to me. 'You don't have to tell me.'

'No,' he said, resting his forehead against mine. 'I want to tell you. I don't want any secrets from you.'

I swallowed back the guilt, thinking about the secret that I was keeping from him. A secret I was keeping for my own selfish reasons: he wanted a big family, and I couldn't give that to him. But if we got through tonight, then I knew I had to tell Roman about the problems that I would have having children. No matter what the cost to my heart.

'Just take your time,' I whispered, bringing his hand to my lips.

'Well,' he started, with another deep breath, 'like I said, I was pretty good. I fought at Middleweight, so I was a couple of stones lighter then.' Roman shook his head and smiled ruefully. I had no idea why because there wasn't an ounce of fat on him, he was all toned muscle.

'Anyway,' he continued, 'I was making a name for myself on the semi-professional scene. More importantly, for some, making a serious amount of money.'

'So you fought in competitions for prize money?' I asked, holding his hand tight. He needed to know that I was there for him, no matter what he was telling me.

'Hmm, kind of,' he replied with a shrug. 'It was all exhibition-type fights—gentlemen's evenings and boxing shows—but the prize money I earned was pretty damn good.'

'But I thought unless you were a professional, and boxing title-fights, boxers rarely made much money?' I'd taken that much in when my dad was droning on about boxing.

'Generally you don't, but Vance, my manager at the time, was bloody good, and I was a good fighter. So as well as the prize money, I'd get a percentage of the ticket sales, which, as I was so good, was always a hefty amount because people wanted to see me fight. The other thing Vance did, unless it was for charity, was to negotiate a percentage of the bets placed.'

'They actually bet on that level too?'

'Yeah, people will bet on pretty much anything, and they were putting big amounts on me, so it was very lucrative. Obviously some bookies wouldn't agree, but it got to a point where Vance had the say on the bookies that could attend, so if they didn't agree to the deal then didn't get in.'

'Wow,' I gasped, 'he was one astute businessman.'

'I owe him a lot,' Roman replied as he raked a hand through his hair. 'I made a shitload of money that helped me to buy this place and, eventually, buy a partnership in Ziggy's and the business.'

'If you were so good why didn't you become professional?'

I shifted on the sofa, and Roman gently pulled his hand from mine. I reached for it again: we needed to have contact. I would not let him slip away from me while he told me the worst thing that had ever happened in his life. As my fingers wrapped around his, Roman gave me a small smile and sighed.

'That's where my nightmare starts, really,' Roman sighed. 'I'd joined a boxing association and had won a few bouts. So now I was fighting in a national championship—the first steps to going professional—and that's when it all went wrong.' He looked at me, his anxiety evident in his eyes, which were wide and staring.

'You don't have to tell me this,' I said, softly, cupping his face.

He shook his head and gently pushed away from me.

'No, you *have* to know all the details.'

I didn't want him to do this. Reliving it was killing him, but he was determined to work through it.

'Okay, but stop if you want to.'

He took a deep, shuddering breath and grabbed my hand back.

'Michael was moving up the ranks too, but I was the one that people were talking about. One day we ended up on the same card. My original opponent had dropped out, and, without me realising it, Michael's manager arranged for Michael to fill the spot.'

He stopped again and took a long swig from his bottle of beer before continuing.

'So, I was fighting for a national title and was winning on points …' he said.

My own breath stalled as grief shrouded Roman's face. I gave him a smile, encouraging him to continue.

He did, with a long inhale. 'There was no way I was going to lose; there were only a couple of rounds left, and Michael was never going to be able to catch up. I knew it and he knew it.'

He paused for a few seconds to look at me and then carried on.

'I should have managed out the fight, stayed away from his punches, and just landed some body shots.'

He stopped again and this time he turned away from me, dropping his head into his hands.

'Baby, what happened?' I asked, placing what I hoped was a reassuring hand on his back.

'I lost concentration and he managed to land a punch on my chin that shook me, so I wanted to be sure.' He paused and blew out a breath. 'I punched him hard, Summer. In the head …'

I gasped inwardly, somehow knowing what was coming.

'… so damn hard that I killed him.'

His words caused me to shoot a hand to my mouth. This was Roman's nightmare. This was where he killed his best friend.

'God, I'm so sorry,' I whispered.

My other hand was on Roman's back. I wanted him to know that I was still there for him. His head turned and he looked at me with tear-filled eyes, warily watching me.

'He was in a coma for almost a week before they decided to

switch off the machine. And do you know what one of the worst parts about it was? His damn family didn't blame me one bit. They said Michael knew the risks the day he decided to take up boxing as a career.'

'And they were right,' I replied. 'He did, and you can't blame yourself for that.'

'Of course I fucking can. I'd won, all but for the final bell. It was obvious. Dickie kept telling me and Vance kept shouting it out to me. But I got cocky and let Michael get a punch in, and because I was such an arrogant dick I went for the head shot. He was my friend, Summer. We'd grown up together, and I did it to prove a point because he always was a fucking competitive bastard who wanted to beat me at everything.'

'But they were right, he knew the risks,' I protested.

'No they fucking weren't,' he whispered, on a shaky breath. 'I killed him, Summer. I killed my friend.'

A wracking sob escaped from Roman's body as he slumped forward with his arms wrapped around his chest.

'Roman, sweetheart,' I pleaded, 'let me hold you.'

Taking a deep breath, Roman grew silent; then he turned and leaned in close against me.

'I'm sorry,' he said quietly after a while. 'I just never talk about it.'

'It's okay,' I soothed. 'It's totally understandable.'

'Do you hate me?' His eyes scanned my face. 'Knowing what I'm capable of?'

'No way, it was just an accident.' I pressed a kiss to his forehead and then pulled him against my chest.

I needed to comfort him, hold him, and tell him that everything would be okay. I could feel his pain, and wanted to be the one to take it away.

'Roman,' I said softly, brushing his hair from his forehead. 'Are you okay?'

He nodded and a soft kiss landed on my cheek. Arms tightened around me—one at my waist and one at my chest.

'I stayed at the hospital the whole time,' he sighed. 'By

Michael's bedside, hoping that the doctors were wrong and that he'd come round and give me shit for something or other. Tell me that my stance had been wrong, or that my jab had been too weak, but he didn't. So after a week his family and Caroline decided that it was time to let him go. They were so damn kind to me, Summer, it made it a thousand times worse. Caroline was a wreck. She was broken and I couldn't bear to look at her and see the pain in her eyes. The blame.'

'But it's like they said, Michael knew the risks,' I replied, wrapping my fingers around his arm at my chest.

'Yeah, I know, but ultimately I was still to blame. It didn't matter, though; they turned the machine off, and we had the funeral and then life carried on. Only it didn't, not for me,' he said on a whisper. 'I hated myself, and the only way I could cope was to shut myself away from everyone. I'd taken Michael from his family, so why should I enjoy mine? The only person I spoke to was Caroline, and that was because of the guilt that ate away at me every day.'

I reached down and kissed his jaw. 'I'm here for you,' I whispered.

'You don't hate me?'

'No, baby, I don't hate you. I'm glad you told me, and I'm sorry that you went through all of that.'

'You're sure?'

'Positive.' I turned to him as he sat up and looked at me. 'You and Michael, you both knew the risks, whatever you might think about what happened. And, while I understand your need to be there for Caroline, you can't keep doing it, especially if it affects your relationship with Tiff.'

Part of me wanted him to give up his Knight in Shining Armour role because of me too. Caroline had gone through a terrible time, but Roman had his own life, and I was determined to be a big part of it.

He gave me a sad smile and sighed deeply.

'I know,' he said resignedly. 'Once she finds somewhere to go, I'll take a step back. The problem is, I feel guilty about the position she's in now too. Michael would want me to help her.'

'How is her splitting up with Jack Abbott your fault?' I asked incredulously.

'I persuaded her to come home, and she only met Jack because he was going out with my sister. Abbott made her homeless, and she would never have met him if I hadn't killed Michael. This *is* all my fault.'

'No, Roman. It's purely on Jack Abbott. Listen, I don't expect you to abandon her, but you can't keep making her your responsibility, because if you do, you'll lose Tiff.'

'But Michael—'

'Michael wouldn't want you to keep this guilt inside you,' I said, laying a palm against his thudding heart. 'His family were right; he knew the risks, and, if he was as competitive as you say he was, then you know he would have been fighting you with the same amount of force and passion.'

'Yeah, I know, but …'

When he didn't say anything else, I continued.

'Promise me that you'll let this guilt go. You have to let go of your need to rescue Caroline all the time. Think about Tiff.'

He nodded. 'Yeah, you're right. This isn't fair on her. Or you. I promise.'

The remorse that I felt almost had me telling him no, he should continue to be there for her, but I was falling in love with Roman and I was a selfish woman. I didn't want to share him with anyone, least of all Caroline.

CHAPTER 29

♥

The next day, Roman called Tiffany and asked to meet up for dinner. He'd asked me to go along, but I thought that it should be just the two of them. Tiffany needed to know that she was her brother's priority, not Caroline—or me, for that matter.

We'd agreed to meet at Ziggy's later, so I was surprised when I got a text just before I left the house:

Grumpy: Things a little better with Tiff. Apologised and explained. Have agreed will speak to Caroline about finding somewhere else. See you later x

The last part of the text gave me a little thrill of joy, I couldn't lie. But I knew Roman wouldn't allow Michael's child to live anywhere awful, so I wasn't holding out any hope of Caroline leaving Roman's house anytime soon. After what she'd done to Tiff, I really didn't care about her, but Maisie was a lovely little girl, and none of this was her fault. Maybe to appease my own selfish guilt, I'd spent some of the afternoon looking at affordable places to rent and printed off the details. Caroline probably would say she couldn't afford them, but Roman wouldn't repair his relationship with Tiffany while Caroline was still staying in his house.

The other riot of thoughts in my head, were about if I should tell Roman about the possible issue with children. He'd laid himself bare to me. He'd told me all about his living hell; he'd trusted me enough to do that, so maybe I should afford him the same level of decency.

The problem was I was scared it would push him away. But if I didn't tell him, it would be a whole lot worse him pushing me away when I was even deeper into our relationship. Alex's rejection, no matter that I was better off without him, had hurt. I hadn't been enough for him and that stung, but I knew it would be a whole lot more than a stinging hurt if Roman felt the same way.

'What do I do, Em?' I asked as we sat in Ziggy's. 'If I tell him now he'll probably think I've gone all stalker on him and already booked the church, and if I don't tell him and we start to get really serious, he'll think I've deceived him.'

'You could drop it casually into the conversation,' she suggested.

I sighed heavily, my gaze wandering around the club, wondering where Roman was. He'd said he'd be here, and I knew he would, but I was desperate to see him. I wanted to check he was okay after his dinner with Tiff, but I also missed him.

'How do you drop something like that into a casual conversation?' I asked, turning back to Emma.

She shrugged and took a sip of her drink.

'I suppose just as he's putting a condom on I could say, "Hey, as long as you're clean, dude, don't bother with that, because, to be honest, I'm as barren as the damn Sahara."'

'Don't say that, and please don't call him *dude*,' Emma chastised, her button nose screwing up in disgust. 'Anyway, you're not barren. It's just going to take a bit more effort, that's all.'

She grabbed my hand and clutched it between both of her own.

'You will have a baby one day, I *know* you will. So tell me, why are you worrying about this now?'

I shrugged. 'No idea,' I lied.

'I call BS on that,' she grumbled. 'It's because you've got deep feelings for him, isn't it?'

Emma gave me a look that I knew meant she already knew the answer.

'Yeah,' I sighed, knowing there was no point in lying. 'And they're getting deeper every day, Em.'

'That's a good thing, unless you don't think he feels the same way?'

'Well, we haven't mentioned love or anything like that, and it's only been a couple of weeks,' I replied. 'But we seem to be on the same page. He wants to spend time with me, and he's told me things that I don't think he would if this was just casual.'

'So you obviously envisage a future together, but you're worried about how he's going to take it if you can't have a baby'

'That's about it. Look how Alex reacted, and we'd been together three years, not a month.'

'Do not compare him to Alex; *he's* a prick! If you think that this is turning into something serious, then tell him. I bet you'll be surprised. But you need to listen to me when I tell you that one day you *will* have a baby.'

I tried to give her a big smile, one that showed my teeth, but I simply couldn't picture myself with a baby, no matter how hard I tried. My biggest fear was that Roman would reject me when I told him, and he'd prove to be no better than Alex. He wouldn't be the man I thought him to be.

'If you say so, but it's not the end of the world, anyway,' I said responding to Emma's optimism.

'Don't pretend to me, Summer. I know that you put on a happy face about it,' Emma said. 'You always make out you don't care, but I know that you do.'

'I don't!' I said vehemently. 'I've come to terms with it.'

Emma's eyebrows rose and her eyes widened.

'No you haven't. Don't lie to me. You've only known for a short time, so there's no way you've come to terms with it. I don't think you ever will. You pretend, but the mere fact that you're worried about what Roman will think shows me that you are constantly thinking about it.'

She was exactly right: it was on my mind a lot, but the more I fell for Roman, the more it was rearing its ugly head. It hurt like a punch to the gut.

'Still doesn't help me to decide whether to tell him now, later or never,' I groaned.

'Well, personally I think you should. If it's going somewhere he deserves to be told,' Emma replied.

'I know.' Sadness engulfed me. He'd finish it, I just knew it. 'Maybe I should just finish things with him,' I blurted out.

Emma's hand came out and grabbed my arm, her fingertips digging into my skin.

'No!' she cried. 'You can't do that.'

'Why?' I asked detaching her hand from me. 'We've only been together a short time, and, yes, the sex is off the charts good, but surely it's best to finish it now before it gets serious.'

Emma slammed a palm to her forehead. 'You've just told me it's already got serious. You've got feelings for him!'

She laughed emptily and shook her head.

'You really like him, you think he might feel the same way, so just tell him.' She pulled me into a hug. 'If he dumps you because of it, then he's not the man for you.'

I bit on my lip and nodded.

'And that's what scares me, Em.'

'Summer, please just tell him.'

I nodded again, not really sure that I could, but knew that I had to.

Giving Emma as big a smile as I could manage, I took a large sip of my wine, almost draining the glass. As I watched the Friday night revellers, I felt Emma's leg jigging up and down next to me.

'What on earth is the matter?' I slammed my hand down onto her bouncing knee and stared at her. 'Do you need the toilet?'

'No,' she gasped. 'Henry and Roman are on their way over.'

My head shot around in the direction in which she was looking. Henry and Roman were making their way through the crowds; both dressed in trousers and open-necked shirts, rolled back at the sleeves, they looked like an advert for men's aftershave. All that was missing was a rock ballad blasting out and both of them walking in slow motion. Handsome as separate entities, together they were stunning.

Henry's smile was gleaming as he looked at Emma, while Roman stared at me with a tight jaw. It was a good stare, though, because although he was a few feet away, I knew that look. It was the one he usually gave me when he was about to set my knickers on fire.

'Hi gorgeous,' Henry said, bending down to kiss Emma's cheek. He then turned to me and held out his hand. 'Hi Summer, great to meet you at last. I've heard a lot about you.'

I turned and smiled at Emma. 'I hope she wasn't too critical.'

'Oh no, it wasn't Emma.' Henry grinned at me and tightened his grip on my hand. 'Anyway, who's for another drink?'

'I'll come with you,' Emma gushed and jumped up, latching herself onto Henry by the lips.

Roman gave a low laugh as he slipped into the booth beside me. He leaned into me, took hold of my chin and then kissed me. I was right about that look: my knickers combusted. It was exactly the right amount of pressure, enough tongue action, some gentle nipping at my lips and a hand tugging in my hair for good measure.

'Hey,' he whispered as he slowly pulled his lips away from mine.

'Hey,' I gasped. 'You okay?'

'Yep, I am now you're here,'

He leaned forward and kissed me again. This time not only were my knickers still blazing away, but I think he actually set my bra alight too.

'Wow,' I whispered.

'Yeah, well, I've missed you.' Roman took my hand and started to play with my fingers, spinning the wide silver band on my right ring finger. 'I thought you were coming with your sister, Pippa, tonight.'

'No, she bailed. I think she's got a new man. So, how did it go with Tiff?' I asked. 'Your text said it went okay.'

Roman nodded and closed his eyes momentarily. 'I should never have said yes to Caroline,' he sighed. 'I really hurt Tiff, Summer. She seems okay with me, and said she understood why, but the conversation was a little bit stilted. Things still aren't right between us.'

I'd been the one left with a sobbing Tiffany in the office, so I knew how hurt she had been. At least now he'd realised it too.

'So how did you leave things?'

'I've promised I'll talk to Caroline. I said I'll help her find somewhere to live and then that's it. I'll always keep a lookout for Maisie, though,' he stated.

I nodded. 'That's understandable, and I wouldn't expect anything else from you.'

And I wouldn't. He cared about Maisie: she was his best friend's child.

'God, this last couple of days has left me knackered.' Roman kissed me softly at the corner of my mouth. 'At least I've got you.'

I forced a smile, one that I really wanted to make huge and wide, but my conversation with Emma was still playing on my mind.

He was being lovely and sweet, but all I could see was a future without him when I told him about my PCOS.

'Roman?'

'Yeah.'

'Why do you like me?'

I had no idea where that question had come from. I wasn't looking for praise, I was simply trying to gauge what he was really feeling. I needed some sort of sign to let me know what I should do.

Should I give him the good news about the fact that my child-bearing hips were somewhat redundant? His answer could mean that I wouldn't have to tell him.

He was silent, and I wondered if it was because he couldn't think of anything. Totally irrational I know, because if nothing else he could have said the great sex. I was beginning to think he had nothing to give, when he finally spoke.

'What's this about, Summer?'

'I just wondered. We spend a lot of time together, and I wondered what stops you from being bored in my company nearly every day and night. Is it because the sex is so good?'

'Okay,' Roman said against my ear. 'I want to spend time with you because you're my girlfriend, not my fuck buddy, not my booty call. You. Are. My. Girlfriend.'

I swallowed and nodded as Roman let go of my hand and cupped my cheek instead. His eyes were dark and the little tic in his jaw had appeared.

'You make me laugh, you're interesting and you don't take my shit. I've started to be nice because you wanted me to be. I've told you this before, but I've been falling for you for months, and I intend to keep falling. For months I've been holding back, considering the consequences, and doing a lot of thinking about you, specifically about those fucking pouty lips, when I'm alone in the shower. So when I finally grew some bollocks and did something about it, I couldn't believe what a fucking amazing woman you were as well as being damn beautiful and sexy.'

This time when he paused I made a little whimper and then, for whatever reason—I have no idea—blurted out.

'We can't see each other anymore.'

CHAPTER 30

Roman blinked. 'Excuse me?'

'We can't see each other anymore.'

Before I could say anything else, Roman was out of his seat and dragging me with him. I stumbled to keep up with him as we travelled through the club, finally stopping in front of the office door that he'd dragged me through twice before.

Once inside the office, Roman pulled out a chair at his desk.

'Sit,' he commanded.

I crossed my arms and stared at him.

'No, you can't tell me what to do.'

'I just did. Now sit down and tell me what the fuck that shit was all about.'

He nodded towards the chair. If his set jaw and furrowed brow were anything to go by, he was definitely not going to take no for an answer.

I flopped down into it with a huff.

'So go on,' he said, his tone a little softer now.

'I just think that it could become too difficult in the office, and I don't want to have to leave my job.'

I couldn't look at him, so I stared down at my hands which were twisted together on my lap. There was no way I wanted to stop what we were starting, but Roman wanted us to become serious—he'd just made that clear. How could I allow that to happen knowing that I'd never be able to give him the children he wanted?

'That's bullshit, the job has been going perfectly well, so now tell me the real reason.'

'It's not bullshit.'

I looked up at him and wished I hadn't. His chestnut-coloured hair was sexily dishevelled, his brown eyes were dark and brooding, and he looked totally confident that I would not be getting my own way on this one. His confidence knocked mine down to the ground, and I couldn't help the little sigh of wonderment that this man wanted me. Roman must have heard it because his lips twitched at the edges.

Despite His Royal Sexiness standing in front of me, I had to be stronger and stick to my guns on this. I'd rather have a few days of misery now than years of a broken heart at a later date. I was already in deep, and if I carried on seeing him, I knew it wouldn't be long before it was full-blown love on my part. When he left me because I couldn't give him a child, my heart would definitely shatter.

'Tell me the real reason, Summer.'

Roman leaned forward and took a strand of my hair that had escaped its quiff and stroked it back into place. His hand rested on my neck and he gave it a gentle squeeze.

'Please, Summer,' he whispered.

The tenderness in his tone and in his eyes broke me, my bottom lip quivered and guilt and sorrow started to suffocate me.

'I have to go,' I breathed as I tried to stand.

My legs wouldn't move, and I flopped back into my seat.

'Roman,' I pleaded, as if he could do something to make my limbs work.

He shook his head, steadfastly keeping his gaze on me. We watched each other for a few beats: I was getting ready to flee and Roman was getting ready to catch me.

'Whatever I said about why I like you seems to have upset you.' he said finally.

I chewed on my bottom lip, not wanting to answer, not able to answer. My head was a mess because I didn't think I could lie to him now, but I also couldn't tell him the truth either.

'If that's what it is, and that's *if*, well, tough, I'm not apologising for what I said. I meant every word, they *are* the reasons why I love spending time with you, why I like you. I do want this to go somewhere and I think you probably do too; in fact, we're well on the way to that already. So tell me the reason that crock just came out of your mouth. I want to know exactly what it is.'

We sat in silence for what felt like hours, but as I watched the second hand on the large clock on the wall, I knew it had only been a mere four minutes. Finally, I opened my mouth to speak because I knew Roman well enough to know that he wasn't going to be the one to crack.

'Things *are* going too quickly for me ...' I started.

Roman leaned down and looked me directly in the eye.

'Please give me enough respect to afford me the damn truth, Summer. Because *that* isn't it.'

I took a deep breath. This was not going to plan. God, who was I kidding? There had been no plan—I'd just opened my mouth and gone for it. There was nothing for it: he wasn't going to let me leave until I told him the truth, or at least a version of the truth.

'Okay,' I replied with a huge gulp. 'Tiffany told me that you'd like a big family, and that's not going to happen if you stay with me.'

Roman inclined his head as though I'd just spoken in Mandarin.

'Sorry?'

'You want kids, lots of them, eleven to be precise, and if this "goes somewhere", as you put it, that isn't going to happen with me.' I straightened myself up and held my shoulders back, aiming to look self-assured, even though I didn't feel it.

'Okay,' Roman replied with a shrug. 'Tiff doesn't know what goes on in my head, and things that I may have told her in the past may not apply now. I think my comment was I'd like eleven kids so that I could start a football team; however, that was when I was twelve years of age and obsessed with the damn game. Yes, I'd like kids, and one of the reasons I came back, was to settle down and hopefully start a family. But if we get to that point, we can compromise on numbers—eleven isn't set in fucking stone.'

'But what if *my* number is zero,' I spat back at him.

Roman looked above my head and blew out a long breath.

'I don't know, it may be something that I'd struggle with, *if* you were adamant.'

That was it: there was my escape hole.

'Okay,' I said standing up, grateful that my legs were working again. 'There's nothing else to say than. I'm adamant that children aren't in my future.'

Roman's hand came down on my shoulder and pushed me back onto the chair.

'The problem with that is I know that's a lie too. Which means that we *can* compromise, which means that we *aren't* ending this just because we have a difference of opinion on how many kids we may or may not have in the future. And, considering we've only been together a short time, while I do want this to go further, a lot further, that also makes your argument unreasonable at the moment.'

'No it's not!' I shrugged Roman's hand away. 'Because if we stay together it's going to be so much harder when we *can't* compromise, and we then have to break up after years of being together.'

My throat began to itch and tears pricked at the back of my eyes. For the last three years I'd wished and yearned for Alex to be the sort of man that I knew Roman was: the sort of boyfriend that made my heart beat faster and my stomach to flutter more. Yet here I was pushing that man, that boyfriend, away, and it was causing my heart to ache.

Roman took a deep breath and crouched down in front of me. He took both of my hands in his and stroked the backs of them with his thumbs.

'Summer, all I want is for you to be honest with me. I know

that zero kids isn't the number in your head.'

'You don't know that,' I argued. 'You can't see inside my head.'

'No, I can't,' he replied softly. 'But, I do see the smile on your face when Maisie is around. You look at that little girl as though she's the most magical thing in the world. I saw how you held her on your knee that night they moved in, and how you smelled her so much I thought you'd become addicted.'

My heart stopped and then did a free fall to the pit of my stomach. How did he see all that? If I remembered correctly, he'd been talking to Caroline about her options.

'You don't know anything,' I whispered, emotion cracking my voice.

'Oh sweetheart, I do. I know lots of things about you. I know that just watching you totter around in those damn shoes of yours makes me smile. I know that your capacity to laugh with my crazy parents, not at them, or even be weirded out by them, makes me think you're fucking awesome. I know that Caroline moving in has been really hard for you, but you smiled and let me help her, and so I know that you are one of the most level-headed and kindest people I've ever met. Everything I know about you has made me realise what my damn therapist couldn't—that life is much bigger than the shit I had swimming around in my head. And so I know now that joy is out there if I want it, I just have to let it in. You've made me smile again, Summer. What I also know about you,' he said with a twitch of his lips, ' is that you have a fucking unbelievable rack.'

I couldn't help the laugh I snorted out.

Roman stroked my hair and sighed.

'Okay, now tell me the truth.'

So I told him, with my eyes shut tightly, because then I wouldn't see the disappointment that would undoubtedly shroud his face.

***

When I opened my eyes after telling Roman everything, I expected him to be disappointed, and I wasn't wrong. He was sitting on the edge of his desk, his eyes looking into the distance as he rubbed the back of his neck.

'I'm sorry,' I whispered and got to my feet and slowly walked to the door.

'Where are you going?' Roman asked.

I looked over my shoulder at him and inhaled raggedly.

'I understand, Roman. I just hope that this won't affect us working together.'

He looked at me quizzically, and pushed himself up to his feet.

'Summer, I don't know what you think is going on in my head, but I promise you it's not how I'm going to replace you as either a PA or as a girlfriend.'

I gasped and shook my head.

'I don't understand.'

I truly didn't. He looked shocked by my news, even a little devastated. So, I couldn't think of any reason whatsoever as to why he would still want to go out with me.

'We're not breaking up because of this,' he explained matter-of-factly.

'But you can't want to—'

'Let me just stop you there and explain something.'

Roman took two steps towards me, and stopped an arm's length away. His eyes were soft and full of emotion. Thankfully, it wasn't pity, because I wouldn't have been able to stand that. When I looked closely I could see that it was desire, and it threw me. There was nothing sexual or erotic about this conversation, this situation, yet his eyes said he wanted me.

'Firstly I can't imagine how you feel about it—something close to heartbreak if the look on your face when looking at Maisie is anything to go by. I hate that you must feel like that and there's nothing that I, or anyone else, can do to help you. Not in the immediate future anyway. Secondly,' he continued, taking another step towards me, 'if you and I ever get to the point where we want kids, then I think it will be because we are in love with each other. And, if we're at *that* point then I've no doubt that I'll be so fucking in love with you, that a life with you and no kids will far outweigh the thought of a life with kids, but no you.'

My breath caught in my throat as his words embedded themselves into my brain. I had not expected this sort of declaration. He wasn't thinking straight.

'But if you get out now, Roman, you can have both with someone else.'

'I'll let you into a little secret,' Roman said taking a deep breath. 'I may have already found my woman, and don't want anyone else.'

I gasped and stumbled backwards and leaned against the door breathing heavily. My heart was beating hard as my hands trembled trying to find the door handle.

The way his eyes were boring into my soul made it clear that I was that woman.

'So the point is, Summer, I can't contemplate, even this early on in our relationship, doing it with anyone else. You make me happier than I've been in long damn time—*you*, not anyone else.'

'Roman.'

I said his name pleadingly, but I had no idea why I was pleading. I think I just wanted him to be sure, but the set of his jaw and the strength in his back told me that he was.

'Of course, you may decide I'm too much of a miserable git to put up with and leave me anyway, and that's something I'll have to deal with. But I won't let you walk away from this without trying it first, because I have a feeling in my gut that we could be pretty epic together.'

Taking the final step to reach me, Roman reached out his arms and looked at me expectantly. 'Well?'

'Are you sure, Roman, because if we do this, and then you change your mind it'll be pretty shit?' I huffed out on an empty laugh.

'Yep, I'm sure. I can't promise that this is going to be forever, but it feels right for now, and we'll work together towards the forever part.'

I chewed on my lip thinking about what Roman had said, specifically that I'd helped him to find joy in life.

'What if you realise it's just sexual attraction, and someone else starts to make you smile more than I do.'

I watched as Roman's lips split into a wide grin that crinkled his eyes at the corners.

'You *were* there on my office desk, weren't you? You know, when I was inside you?'

I nodded and felt myself blush.

'So, you'll be aware that I wasn't actually smiling too much at that time?'

'You're a man, and I don't think I'm a bad-looking woman. I mean, if a woman is willing and is fairly attractive, isn't it pretty easy for a man to get aroused?'

Roman started to laugh.

'I thought the "snake-in-the-grass" was funny, but "aroused" has that beaten.'

'What's wrong with the word "aroused"?' I exclaimed.

'Nothing if you're a sex therapist or wear cardigans,' he quipped. 'But to answer your question—no, contrary to your belief, men don't get "aroused" by every decent-looking woman they meet. Well, I don't anyway. I need something a little more than a great body and a pretty face, and I can promise you, Summer, while you have both of those in abundance, the things that I find most attractive about you are your damn spirit and your generosity.'

'What do you mean?'

I didn't recall being particularly generous: I bought cakes for the office a couple of times, but that was it. The spirit I understood, after all I fought with Roman at every opportunity, when necessary.

'I told you, it's how you dealt with my parents,' Roman answered, interrupting my thoughts. 'They're fucking crazy, but you never batted an eyelid, and that was *before* we were together. And don't even start me on how you handled that clusterfuck of dealing with my shit. *And* you stuck up for my sister,' he said giving me a soft smile. 'You're generous with your time and affection for people you hardly know, and that's why I like you and find you attractive. Plus, the great rack and arse help.'

As we both laughed Roman moved until we were inches apart. I looked up into his eyes, trying to find a hint of uncertainty, but there was none.

'Well?' Roman asked. 'Do you understand that I'm committed to you?'

I nodded my head and was then pulled into another knicker-burning kiss.

CHAPTER 31

A couple of days after our heart to heart at the club, Roman and I arrived at his parents' house because they'd asked us around for supper and a game of cards, but weirdly no one seemed to be home.

'We'd knocked at the front door, but all the lights were off and there was no reply. So Roman led us around to the side of the house and through the gate, where we let ourselves in the back door.

'Hello, anyone home?' Roman called as we came through into the kitchen. 'Are you sure she said tonight?' he asked me.

'Yeah, definitely.'

'Hey boy,' Roman said stooping down to rub at Doolittle's ears. 'Where is everyone?'

Doolittle sniffed at us both and then retreated to his basket under the kitchen table. Keeping tight hold of my hand, Roman guided us towards the door into the dining area of his parents' lounge/diner. He pushed it open, and, as he walked over the threshold, the lights flicked on and we were greeted by a rousing chorus of 'Surprise!' to the backing track of Grease's 'Summer Nights', and a huge banner pinned up across the room that said: 'ROMAN'S HAVING SEX AGAIN!'

'What the f …?'

Roman stopped dead in his tracks, causing me to slam into his back.

'Roman?' I gasped, pointing at the banner. 'Look!'

'What the hell is going on?' he cried, still staring at the sea of smiling faces in front of us.

'We decided that having Summer as your girlfriend was worth a party.'

My mouth fell open in shock, then laughter bubbled up inside me as I watched the horror register on Roman's face as he looked around the room.

Twinkle stepped forward and cradled Roman's cheeks, bringing his head down so that she could give him a big smacker on the lips. Behind her Pete had the video camera rolling, while Tiffany had the grace to shake her head and mouth an apology to me, but barely looked at Roman.

'Mum, what the hell have you done?' Roman hissed between gritted teeth.

'What I said—thrown you a party. Listen to John and Olivia,' Twinkled squealed, 'they're singing your song.'

'Come on, son,' Pete piped in, 'give us a speech.'

Roman turned to me, and gently grabbed my chin between his thumb and forefinger.

'If you want out now, I totally understand. I'll fucking miss you, but I'll respect your decision. Alternatively, we could fake our own deaths and run away to Australia.'

The sincerity in his tone and the sadness in his eyes made me burst out laughing: he actually meant every word. Okay, so a party to congratulate someone on having sex again wasn't on my bucket list of things to do before I was thirty, but it wasn't totally heinous.

'This is not funny, Summer,' Roman groaned.

'Oh it is,' I replied slapping at his chest. 'She's happy for you.'

I really did think it was funny and sweet. This was his parents' crazy way of showing him that they loved him.

'Come on then, Romy, give us a speech.'

Twinkle tugged at Roman's arm and he swung around to face

her.

'You want a *speech*?'

'Yes … speech … go on Roman,' various voices called while John Travolta gave out a breathy 'Oh.'

Roman took a deep breath and looked up to the ceiling. I could see his lips moving, and wondered whether he was cursing or praying. Finally, he looked at Twinkle with a forced smile on his face.

'Thank you for the party. It's really very kind of you, but—'

'Oh no "buts", Romy, your mother went to a lot of trouble,' Pete called from behind his video camera. 'She's spent all damn day cooking and baking, never mind creating a phone bill that I'm probably going to have to sell my body to be able to afford to pay.'

'I only rang immediate family,' Twinkle protested. 'Tiffy did the rest with her Twatter.'

'It's Twitter, Mum, and I did it under protest.' Tiffany glanced at her brother, and then back to Twinkle.

'Well, whatever,' Roman sighed. 'Thank you, *but* I have not just started having sex again.' He waggled a finger towards the banner that was stretched across the archway between the dining and living area.

'You're not having sex with her?' a male voice shouted.

'Well, yes, Uncle Charlie, but …'

Roman looked at me and then back towards the crowd of people in front of us, all of whom appeared to waiting with bated breath. To see big, confident Roman lost for words doubled my affection for him. I wanted to take him in my arms and stroke his head until he felt better.

'We are, it's just …' Roman faltered, evidently worried that he was going to embarrass me. I, however, was the middle James child, who had been born in between two of the most indiscreet people I knew: Dylan and Pippa. Plus, I didn't have much of a filter or get embarrassed easily.

'What Roman is trying to say,' I said, pushing forward to stand by his side, 'is that, yes, we are having sex, but he never stopped.'

'Really?' a short, red-haired woman commented. 'We all thought that you'd become a bit of a monk. Gone all … what's the word I'm looking for, Gloria?'

'Impotent?' Gloria suggested.

'No way,' Pete cried, finally lowering his video camera. 'My lad isn't impotent. You're not are you, son?'

'No, Dad,' Roman sighed his grip on my hand tightening.

'Ooh what is that word?' the red-haired woman asked again. 'You know, when someone stops having sex on purpose.'

There were a few muttered musings while people scratched their heads. Tiffany let out a withering groan, Roman repeated the word 'fuck' quickly and numerous times, while in the depths of the room someone else let out a loud fart. Me, well, I held a hand to my mouth to mask the laughter.

'Ooh I know,' the red-head cried. 'Celibate … that's it! We thought you might be celibate.'

'Fucking shoot me now,' Roman groaned.

***

'I swear to you,' Tiffany pleaded. 'I begged her not to do it, but you know what Mum is like, she wouldn't listen.'

We'd been at the party for a couple of hours now, and the thaw had finally started between Tiff and Roman. Conversation had been stilted at first, but after a few glasses of wine, she'd finally ventured over to talk to us.

Roman shook his head and took a long swig of beer from the bottle that he was gripping onto for dear life.

'I'll let you have that one,' he groaned. 'Let's call it payback for you-know-who.'

Tiffany stiffened slightly before letting her shoulders sag. 'Okay, we'll call it quits. I hate fighting with you, much as you deserve it. So, sorry you've been subjected to this misery.'

'Don't worry about it, Tiffany,' I replied, surreptitiously digging Roman in the ribs with my elbow. 'It's fine. If it makes your mum happy.'

'It's making a bigger deal of it than it actually is,' Roman retorted.

'Oh thanks,' I muttered.

Roman looked at me horrified, and then his hand went behind my neck. He pulled me closer to him and kissed my forehead.

'I didn't mean you. I meant me having a girlfriend isn't a big deal.'

'She's just happy that you're back living here,' Tiff said. 'And that you finally appear to be happy after ... well, you know why.'

I held my breath momentarily at the subject of Michael raising its head again, but Roman didn't react. His eyes softened, as he glanced over at his mum. 'She's just so batty,' he said, turning back to me and Tiffany.

I leaned into him and snaked an arm around his waist, hugging him to my side. He was right: she was crazy, but her happiness made me feel warm and welcome, and I, for one, wouldn't want her any other way.

Roman shook his head and grinned. 'We may as well enjoy it, now we're here. Either of you want another drink?' he asked us.

I glanced at my empty glass and thrust it into his hand.

'Tiff?'

She nodded and passed her glass over too. As soon as he disappeared into the kitchen, I turned to Tiffany.

'How are you doing?'

Colour rose up from Tiffany's neck to her cheeks. She glanced in the direction that Roman had gone, then quickly back at me, before finally settling on watching her feet.

'I'm fine, I just feel like a spoiled princess, storming in like that. But he knows how much I hate her. He did grovel a lot, and I did have the most expensive meal on the menu, seeing as he was paying.'

'You had every right, Tiff.' I gave her back a comforting rub. 'She hurt you, and Roman understands how hard it is for you to think of her in his house. He's asked her to find somewhere else, you know.'

'I know,' she sighed. 'I feel for her little girl, I really do, but if she needs help, then she should go and ask Jack. He's the one that threw her out. She knew that Roman wouldn't say no. I just think she plays on his guilt.'

I nodded, totally agreeing with her. There was something about Caroline that made me distrust her. Even though Maisie wasn't Jack's child, he'd been the only dad she'd known for three years, so I couldn't imagine how he could make her homeless, whether he loved her mother or not. However, I didn't know anything about their break-up, and I barely knew Jack these days, so maybe I was totally wrong. What I did know was that I would only feel comfortable once Caroline had moved out.

'Roman did suggest she ask Jack for help, if only for Maisie's sake,' I sighed, 'but she said she wouldn't ask him for anything. He's already moved on, apparently. I have to be honest, I was talking to him at Ziggy's a few weeks ago, and he gave no indication whatsoever that he had a partner, never mind one who had a child.'

Tiffany grimaced. 'That sounds like Jack; if he doesn't talk about something, then it doesn't exist.'

'Well, it's a good job you didn't get married.'

Sadness swept over Tiffany's face before she quickly plastered on a smile. 'I know, better off without him, most definitely.'

We fell into silence as Roman returned with our drinks, passing one to each of us. As I took mine, he gave me a dazzling smile and leaned in for a quick kiss.

'You sure you're okay with all this madness?' he asked.

I looked around at all the people having fun, laughing, drinking and eating, and I was.

'Have you ever brought a girl home before?' I asked as a matter of interest.

Tiffany snorted and almost spat out her drink. 'No chance,' she coughed. 'And, on that note, I'm going to talk to Auntie Anne about her new boyfriend—he's half her age apparently.'

Roman rolled his eyes and turned back to me. 'No, baby, I haven't. Never wanted to.'

My heart jumped in my chest and the butterflies fluttered awake.

'Really?' I whispered.

Roman shook his head, and pulled me to him. 'No, and not because I was scared of them meeting my parents, although they are pretty scary to meet, right?'

I giggled and waved a hand at him. 'Nah, I can handle them. They're not scary at all.'

'And that,' he said, kissing me, 'is why I brought you home. That, and because you're so fucking amazing.'

That was it. They were the words that did it—I was most definitely in love with Roman Hepburn Holliday.

As we kissed against each other's smiles, my mobile rang in my pocket. I ignored it, simply relishing having Roman's arms around me. Then it went again.

'I better get it,' I said, pulling out of Roman's arms. I looked down and saw that it was my mum.

'Hey, Mum,' I said breezily, grinning at Roman as he linked his fingers with mine.

'Oh Summer, I'm so sorry to bother you, love, but you need to come home.'

As Mum started to cry quietly on the other end of the line, dread hit me. My phone shook against my ear and my breathing started to get shallow.

'Mum, what is it? What's happened?'

Roman looked at me enquiringly, and putting his beer down, he took a step closer.

'It's Pippa, Summer. She's left.'

'What do you mean "she's left"?' I asked, calming down a little.

Pippa was always getting fancy ideas about things like going travelling, or getting a flat with her friends. But she never did any of those things once she realised Mum wouldn't be there to cook and clean for her.

'She's left, and says she's going to live with some man she's met,' Mum replied, sounding desperate.

'Mum, you know she'll be back.'

'No, she won't,' she cried. 'She's packed her stuff and gone, but what's worse is that she's withdrawn three thousand pounds from Dad's and my bank account.'

I gasped and looked around for a chair. Roman put his arm around my waist, instinctively knowing that I needed to his support.

'H-how?'

'It's my fault, I gave her the online banking details because she owed me some money and was going to pay it back in …'

'But she didn't,' I whispered.

'No. We argued about her going, but she was adamant and said we couldn't stop her. When she said they might move to London, your dad asked her what she was going to do for money, because she obviously can't stay at her job if she goes to live down South. She just said she'd got money and stormed out and got in a car with him and drove off.' Mum blurted out everything without taking a breath. 'I just knew somehow. So Dad checked and he saw the money was gone.'

'Oh Mum,' I whimpered, my heart dropping with a thud. 'I'm so sorry. What do you want me to do?'

'I was hoping you'd come over, Dylan is on his way. You two know people around town, you might be able to find out where this man lives and try and talk some sense into her. It's not just that she's taken the money, love. It's the fact that she obviously hasn't got any, and neither has he, or she wouldn't have taken ours. She can't go to London,' Mum cried. 'Not with a man who has nothing.'

Pippa could be flighty and demanding, but taking money from our parents wasn't like her. This felt like a hammer blow to the guts for me, so God knows how Mum and Dad must feel.

'Do you know anything about him?' I asked.

Mum sniffed. 'Just his name, love—Jack Abbott.'

CHAPTER 32

When we got to my parents' house, Dylan was already there with his phone to his ear, pacing the lounge.

'Hey, Mum,' I said, rushing over and pulling her into a hug. 'What's happening?'

'Dylan is ringing someone he knows that might know where this Jack person lives.'

'It's okay, Mrs. James,' Roman's deep voice broke in. 'I can tell you that.'

Mum's eyes startled as she looked over at Roman.

'Sorry,' I said. 'I should have called on the way. Roman knows Jack, he knows where he lives.'

'You do?' my dad cried. 'Come on then, let's go. Dylan!'

Dad made a cutting action across his throat to indicate to Dylan to cut the call.

'No worries, thanks anyway,' Dylan said to whoever was on the other end of the phone. 'What's up?' he asked, pocketing his mobile.

'Roman knows where we can find Jack Abbott,' Mum said.

Dylan looked at Roman, and then walked towards him with his hand out.

'Hi Roman, I'm Dylan, Summer's big brother.'

Roman took his hand and shook it.

'Nice to meet you, although not under these circumstances.'

I chewed at my nail and looked at my poor mum clutching at a screwed-up tissue. At twenty-three, it shouldn't be such a major trauma that my sister had left home: she was an adult after all. I knew that the main issue was that she'd stolen from Mum and Dad, but also she would have no idea how to look after herself, or anyone else for that matter. She was the baby of the family, and had always been treated as such.

'Listen, at risk of being shot down in flames, she is twenty-three. Aren't we being a bit over-dramatic?' Dylan said, echoing my own thoughts.

'She stole from us!' Dad exclaimed. 'All she had to do was ask for it.'

He was right, all any of us ever had to do was ask, and Mum and Dad would help us out.

'I know that, Dad,' Dylan replied, 'and I could kill her because of that alone. But now we know where she is, do we really need to go storming around there?'

'Maybe Dylan has a point,' Mum sniffed. 'Perhaps if we just tell her we know about the money and want to talk to her about it.'

Dad sighed heavily, and I felt Roman stiffen beside me. I kind of agreed with Dylan, but knowing what I knew about Jack Abbott, I did not want my little sister to end up like Tiffany and Caroline.

'Jack Abbott isn't someone we would want Pip to be with,' I told Dylan. 'He went out with Roman's sister for a while, and dumped her in a pretty hurtful way, and he's recently dumped a friend of Roman's. She's currently staying at Roman's because Jack kicked her and her young daughter out without anywhere to go.'

Dad growled and moved towards the door.

'That's it, she's definitely coming home.'

'I didn't realise. Shit.' Dylan caught hold of Dad's arm. 'Just wait, Dad, I really don't think storming around there will help.'

'But she needs to come home, son.' Dad's eyes were dark, and my stomach clenched at the look of distress on his face.

'Can I suggest something?' Roman said, clearing his throat. 'How about Summer, Dylan and myself go? Maybe Summer and Dylan can talk to her, and I might be able to get her to see that he's not the right man for her. I've seen first-hand with my sister what a piece of work he is.'

Dad looked at Mum, who shrugged.

'I suppose it can't hurt.'

Dad thought for a minute and then nodded. 'Okay, but if you see any sign whatsoever that she's in danger, you just drag her out of there.'

'He's not dangerous, Mr. James,' Roman assured him. 'He's just a shit.'

Dad managed a little smile. 'Okay, and it's Ray, not Mr. James.'

Roman nodded and turned to Dylan. 'We can go in my truck.'

Dylan stooped to give Mum a kiss on the cheek, and then followed Roman and I out of the room.

***

Jack Abbott's house was not at all what I'd expected. As a builder, I'd thought that it would be smart and tidy, but it was far from it.

It was on an estate, with an on open-plan lawn at the front and a paved driveway to the side, leading to a garage. The grass was overgrown, as were the flower beds; there were weeds sticking out between the paving stones of the drive, and the black paint of the garage door was chipped and scuffed. The curtains were closed in all the windows, and those in one of the bedrooms were actually hanging off the rail.

The rest of the houses in the estate weren't much better: one even had a cooker and old sofa on the lawn, while the one next door to Jack's had two of the three windows at the front boarded up. Even in the growing darkness, the area looked awful.

'You're kidding,' Dylan muttered. 'She left home to live in this shithole?'

I took Dylan's hand and gave it a squeeze. He looked as desolate as I felt. Pippa may be a princess, but she was still our baby sister, and my stomach was churning wondering what on earth she'd got herself involved in.

'Are you sure this is the right address?' I asked, turning to Roman.

He nodded. 'Yeah, this is where I always sent Maisie's birthday cards. I never visited before, but always got the impression they lived in a really nice area. Caroline said they had some land attached to it.' He looked up at the bedroom windows and shook his head. 'She was obviously embarrassed living in a place like this. Christ, I can't believe Maisie was living here.'

Roman blew out a breath, and I knew the guilt about Michael was threatening to rear its head again. I took a step closer to him, placing my hand on the small of his back. He flashed me a quick smile and said, 'Abbot must have thought all his Christmases came at once when he got the Cromwell job.'

'I guess so.'

'If he's so down on his luck,' Dylan muttered, 'what the hell is he doing with Pippa? She's not exactly got the money to bail him out. The three grand she's nicked from Mum and Dad won't go far.'

'Hmm, that's what I'm wondering,' Roman replied. 'Well, let's knock and see if they're home.'

As Roman and Dylan made their way up the driveway, a thought suddenly struck me. I felt my stomach roil as I remembered the night at the club. I'd pretty much told Pippa everything about the Cromwell deal, and how tight Roman's margins were because he was using local labour and materials. That was what Jack Abbott was doing with Pippa! It had to be: he was getting information from her.

Unsure what to do, I stood hesitantly and watched as Dylan banged on the door with a closed fist. As he did, Roman stooped to look through the letter box, and then stepped back, placing a hand on Dylan's back.

'What is it?' I asked, rushing forward.

'I think they've gone. Take a look.' Roman moved aside for me to look.

As I pushed open the metal flap, I gasped. There was no hall, but the door opened into the lounge, and I could partly see into the kitchen. There was no furniture in the lounge, and the cupboard doors were open in the kitchen: just like Mother Hubbard, the cupboards were bare.

'Fuck!' Dylan hissed. 'Where the hell has she gone?'

CHAPTER 33

The three of us went back to Mum and Dad's to tell them the news, and decide what we should try and do next.

Roman offered to make some calls the next day, hoping that some of his contacts in the building trade might know where Jack Abbott was.

He and Dylan left after a while, and I stayed with Mum and Dad. I was supposed to have been staying with Roman, but they were both so devastated and worried about Pippa that I thought it best to be home with them. So, with a long and lovely goodnight kiss, Roman went home.

As I lay in bed later that night, my mind wouldn't give up whirling the idea around that I was the one that had given the information to Jack about the Cromwell job. Then, when that dissipated, the worry about Roman and I getting serious and not being able to have children reared its ugly head again.

I'd heard his words that night in the club office, but I still couldn't help worrying that I'd never be enough for him.

It was almost dawn by the time I fell asleep, only to be woken about an hour later by a text from Roman:

Grumpy: Think I've got an address for Abbott. It's in Manchester. Am going to go there now. You okay to get a lift to

the office?'

Groggily, I sat up and pressed his number, thankful that he answered.

'Hey baby,' he said breathlessly. 'I called an old mate who used to work for Jack's old boss. He got me the address.'

'That's fantastic, but I want to come.' I jumped out of bed, and flung open my wardrobe door, grabbing a pair of jeans and a T-shirt. 'I can be ready by the time you get here.'

'Summer, I don't know,' he sighed. 'You saw the state of the place he was in. I'm not sure I want you somewhere that might be just as bad, if not worse. He may not even be there.'

'So how did your friend get the address then?' I asked, pulling on a pair of knickers.

Roman was silent for a few seconds and then groaned. 'Abbott met up with his old boss yesterday to talk about subbing some of his gang for the Cromwell job.'

'But he's nicked yours, what does he need any more for?'

'They obviously weren't enough, but do we need to have this conversation now?'

'Yes, we do. Now, are you taking me or not?'

'I suppose so,' he groaned. 'Because if I don't, you'll just damn well keep ringing me.'

I grinned, because he was right, I would.

'Roman?'

'What Summer?' he snapped, his tone irritated.

'How has he been able to afford to do the Cromwell job, and send you that cheque for your retainers on the men, and yet live in that horrible place?'

'No idea, but it crossed my mind too. But for now, just get off the phone and get dressed, because I'll be with you in ten.'

With that the line went dead, and I quickly got dressed.

CHAPTER 34

The address that Roman had been given was an entirely different type of house to the one we'd visited the day before.

This house was a cute black-and-white cottage on the outskirts of Manchester, surrounded by acres and acres of open fields. There was a pebbled driveway in front, with beautiful pink rose tree borders and a huge oak tree shadowing it.

'Oh my God,' I gasped, 'this is lovely.'

'Yeah, I know.' Roman frowned as he banged on the door. 'So, how do you go from that shithole we saw yesterday to this in a matter of days?'

Just as he was about to rap on the door again, it swung open and we found ourselves facing Pippa. She looked okay—other than shocked to see us—but she was clean, tidy, wearing make-up, and a pair of leather skinny jeans that I'd never seen before.

'Buy those with Mum and Dad's money?' I asked, pushing past her into the house.

'Wh-what are you doing here?' she asked, as Roman followed me in.

'Taking you home,' I snapped.

'I'm not coming home. I'm living with Jack now. Didn't Ma and Dad tell you?'

'Yes, they did. They also told me that you stole three grand from their account. How could you, Pip?'

Pippa's colour rose as she lifted her chin defiantly.

'I'll pay them back, and it's not like they can't afford it.'

My heartbeat rapidly increased as I felt the urge to punch her.

'That's not the point!' I stormed towards her and grabbed hold of her arm. 'You are the most selfish little bitch I've ever met. Do you know how worried they've been about you? If you'd just asked, they'd have probably given it to you. Why, Pippa?'

Pippa pulled out of my grasp and moved over to a large, cream velvet sofa that in itself looked as though it cost three grand. She plonked herself down and pulled a throw cushion against her chest.

'I just needed the money to help Jack out, he's going to give it back to me when he gets his first payment from ...' her voice tailed off and she at least had the decency to blush.

'Oh yes, and that,' I said. 'Did you tell Jack about the Alan Cromwell deal? Stuff that I told you?'

Before I realised what I'd said, Roman made a noise behind me. Me and my big mouth. I turned to see him staring at me, his eyes wide and expectant.

'I only told her that your margins were tight, and that you were using local French labour.'

I winced, waiting for him to berate me, but he didn't say anything; he just took a deep breath and turned to Pippa.

'Did you tell Abbott any of that?' he asked.

Pippa shook her head. 'No, I don't even remember you saying that. When did you say that?'

'The night that Jack had a drink with us at Ziggy's.' She didn't look as though she was lying, and I breathed a little sigh of relief and the pounding in my chest lessened. My sister had all the attention span of a Supermodel at a physics lecture.

'I don't remember. All I remember is you boring me to death about Roman, and then him storming off with you to his office.'

She definitely wasn't lying: she flicked her hair when she was lying, and her hands were still in her lap.

I turned to Roman. 'It wasn't her.'

He nodded again. 'Okay, well, whatever. I think you should come home with us, Pippa.'

Pippa looked at him as if he'd just told her Justin Bieber wasn't the greatest pop star on earth—what can I say, my sister loves Bieber big style.

'I'm not coming home, I'm living here now with Jack.'

'He'll hurt you, Pippa,' Roman told her in a low voice. 'He hurt my sister, and he didn't treat the woman he had before you much better. Once he's got what he needs from you, he'll be on to someone else.'

'No, he won't!' she spat back. 'He loves me.'

'Oh for God's sake, Pip, grow up! You've known him all of five minutes.' I shook my head in despair, because I knew she wasn't going to budge.

'Like you've known Roman, and you love him,' she cried, jumping up off the sofa.

My mouth dropped open, and I felt the colour drain from my face. Had I told her that I loved Roman? Should I deny it? If I did, would he be hurt? If I didn't, would he run out of here quicker than my dad at a party when it's announced the buffet is open?

'Summer and I are different,' Roman said, moving up behind me. 'We're in a relationship that's open and honest. Jack fucking Abbott wouldn't know honesty if it kicked him in the balls.'

I glanced at him, wondering what his reaction was to Pippa's words about me loving him, but he was simply staring at her.

'I know about that Caroline woman and her daughter, if that's what you mean?' Pippa said like some stroppy teenager. 'It's not even as though she's his kid.'

My feelings about my sister instantly changed. No longer did I think she was simply a spoiled little brat who played on being the baby of the family.

'You selfish, selfish girl,' I said, my tone laced with cold animosity. 'How could you live here, knowing that the child that calls him daddy doesn't have a roof over her head? How could you be with such a man that would allow that to happen?'

Pippa shrugged, and suddenly I didn't even want her to come

home.

'Where is he?' Roman asked.

'Meeting a supplier for the French job.' She looked down at the floor and folded her arms over her chest.

'Will he be long?'

'Don't know.' She shrugged again.

'Mind if we wait.' Roman said, more as a statement than a question. Taking my hand, he moved over to the sofa, pulling me with him.

'Nice place,' I snipped. 'You pay for this, did you?'

Pippa sighed. 'No, Jack found it, we moved here yesterday.'

'Hmm, I suppose we couldn't have our little Princess living in the other place, could we?'

'You went there?' Pippa gasped.

'Yes, we did,' I replied. 'It was delightful.'

'It was only temporary after she left,' Pippa protested

'Yeah, if you want to believe that, Pip. He's been living there with Caroline. Then some idiot came along and gave him three grand,' I muttered under my breath.

'Summer, enough,' Roman said in a low tone. 'Just leave it, okay.'

He leaned forward and gave me a soft kiss, and I nodded.

'Okay,' I sighed and turned to Pippa. 'I need the bathroom.'

'Upstairs, second on the left, no right, no left. Oh I don't know,' Pippa sighed. 'It's up there somewhere.'

With a squeeze of Roman's hand, I left the room in silence. At the top of the stairs, I opened the first door on the left only to be faced with a couple of clothes rails with some men's clothing hung on them and a pile of shoe boxes. There must have been at least ten boxes.

My blood boiled as I thought of what Pippa had been spending our parents' money on. I lifted up the lid of a *Sophia Webster* shoe box: Chiara' sandals. The damn bitch! She knew I wanted them. I flicked the lid off another: *Manolo Blahnik* loafers, not my choice, but still they were bloody *Blahniks*.

I flipped them over to examine them, and make sure they were real. Yep, real. How could she spend money she'd stolen from our parents on designer shoes? And, what made it worse, was that they were ones that she knew that I coveted? Shoes that she'd never even shown any interest in before.

With anger seeping through me, I checked another box with another pair of *Blahniks* in them, then a box with a pair of *Christian Louboutin* 'Glitter' pumps: all of them were beautiful.

I did a quick count of the boxes. There were actually nine in total, as one box just contained receipts. I don't know why—maybe out of spite—I swapped them all around, mixing different shoes in different boxes: not an act of mindless vandalism, but it was the worst thing that *I* could do with such beautiful shoes.

I then went back downstairs, my rage making me forget that I still needed a wee.

CHAPTER 35

Roman and I waited in silence for almost two hours for Jack to return, but when my stomach started to rumble, and Pippa made no attempt to offer us anything, I forced Roman to leave. I was desperate to rage about the shoes as well as get something to eat.

When we got into the car, I was just about to tell him, when his mobile rang.

'Sorry,' he said, getting out of the car, 'I need to take this.'

I watched in surprise, as he paced up and down, talking into his phone and dragging a hand through his hair. When he finally got back to the car, his face was sullen.

'Okay?' I asked.

'Yep,' was all he said and thrust the car into gear. He then turned the radio up and we drove away.

Every few minutes on the way back to the office, his mobile rang, and he'd have to speak to a site manager or a supplier via his hands-free. We barely spoke to each other. When we got back to the office, he parked the car, got out and stalked inside, leaving me watching his disappearing back.

'What the hell is wrong with you?' I asked as I slammed his office door behind me.

'Nothing,' he replied with a shake of the head. 'I'm busy.'

'Are you mad at me because I told Pippa about the French job?'

'Well, it wasn't your best move, Summer,' he bristled, continuing to look at his laptop.

'So if you're mad, just say it instead of going mute.'

I tried to regulate my breathing, and slow down my heart rate. He was acting like the old Roman, when all he had to do was tell me what the problem was.

'Please, Roman, just tell me what's wrong.' I really didn't want to appear weak, but I couldn't help the break in my voice.

Roman's head shot up.

'Hey,' he said softly. 'Why are you getting upset.'

I shrugged and shook my head. 'I don't know.' Tears pushed past my lashes and slowly crawled down my face. This wasn't me: I was stronger than this. Why was I getting upset about the fact that he was in a bloody bad mood?

I knew why. The silence in the car had spiked my anxiety, and I hated feeling like that, especially as we'd been getting on so well. I knew it was just a blip, a mood, but I hated it. I hated that I might have ruined his business; I hated that he couldn't even tell me that he was mad at me for it, and I hated that I may never give him children if we ever got to that point. And, while I was desperate to get Caroline out of his house, out of our lives, I hated that I was scared to tell him in case he would think that I was just being a jealous bitch.

Roman got up from his desk and came around to pull me into his arms.

'Baby, don't cry.'

'I'm sorry, it's just everything is my fault,' I sobbed against his shirt. 'The business is in trouble because of me.'

'You said yourself that Pippa didn't tell Jack. He found out some other way, and, anyway, we've got the hotel to keep us going.'

I looked up and could see in his face that it still wasn't enough. The darkness around his eyes told me that he was still worried, and that brought on a fresh sob.

'Come on, tell me what else is wrong?' Roman asked, kissing my hair.

How could I tell him without sounding like a batshit-crazy woman, who was thinking about babies with her boyfriend of just a month.

'Summer, please,' he whispered.

Then it all poured out, I couldn't help it. I was at a low ebb, and he was being so sweet, holding me and rubbing small circles on my back.

'Our talk on Friday night has just reminded me of what I'm never going to have, that's all. And I know it sounds stupid, but I'm worried that I won't be enough for you, and one day you'll realise and that'll be it,' I said through my tears.

Roman moved to sit down and took me with him, pulling me onto his knee.

When we were settled, he wiped my sticky face with his hand and kissed me softly.

'You know, when you decide you want a baby, there are medical procedures that could help you,' he said, rubbing his hand rhythmically up and down my arm. 'And if that doesn't work, there is always adoption.'

'I know,' I said, with a break in my voice. 'But it hurts, Roman. The one thing a woman should be able to do, and I can't. I feel worthless.'

'Hey, don't even think that,' he urged. 'You're not worthless, far from it. My nanna used to say that God only gives problems to people who are strong enough to handle them. So you need to look at it from that angle; this is a problem that *you* are strong enough to cope with.' He tapped my arm to reinforce what he was saying.

'Bit of a wise old woman your nanna then?'

I reached up and kissed him. A thank-you kiss for trying to help me. As I pulled away, Roman grabbed the back of my head and pulled me back to him.

'Everything will be alright, you know,' he said, nuzzling his nose against mine. 'Remember what I told you on Friday night.'

'I know,' I breathed out, relaxing against him. 'It's just the thought of never holding a baby of my own … it makes my heart hurt, Roman.'

'Oh, sweetheart.' He dropped another kiss on my lips and held me even tighter.

Enveloped in his arms I couldn't help but let the tears flow. Great, huge, gulping sobs that pulled at my stomach and hurt my throat. As my body shuddered with the pain of it all, Roman cradled me close and soothed me as best he could. Every wasted wish for the future whizzed around my head and then punched me with full force. I'd never hold a baby, I'd never pick my child's name, and I'd never see their first school play. I'd never feel that unconditional love that your child gives to you. I cried for those dreams and cried for myself.

After a while, my tears subsided, and I looked up at Roman with sore eyes.

'Thank you,' I whispered.

'What for? All I did was hold you?'

He rubbed the wetness from my cheeks with his thumb and then smoothed my hair away from my sticky face.

'That was what I needed, just for you to hold me.'

'See,' he said giving me a squeeze. 'I can be a really good boyfriend when I'm not being miserable.'

'How good? Good enough to take me for some lunch now?'

'Yep, that good.'

He kissed me again and pushed us up from the chair.

'You want to go out, or would you prefer me to go and get us something?' he asked, taking his wallet from his desk drawer. 'Because, to be honest, you look a bit snotty.'

Before I could say anything, he started laughing and pulled me against his chest. He then gave me one more kiss to my lips before he moved away.

He got to the doorway and turned and looked over to me.

'Come on then, snotty, what are you waiting for?' he said with a grin.

As he disappeared out into my office I couldn't help but sigh with contentment and allow the thought '*Summer Holliday*' to enter my head.

CHAPTER 36

♥

'So,' Emma said as we sat in The Tea Cup Café, tucking into cake, 'you think you might love him?'

'Yeah,' I sighed dreamily.

I'd called Emma and asked her to meet me because things had been niggling away in my head. The catalyst to me urgently needing my friend—and cake—had been a telephone conversation with my Mum that morning. Apparently Pippa had called and had said she wasn't coming home, but, as my mother said, '*Things are okay now, she's apologised.*' When I protested that an apology shouldn't excuse her, I was told: '*But she's our baby.*'

As we'd sat down with a coffee and a huge slab of chocolate cake in front of us, I'd told Emma everything, from Roman warning me about Jack, me finding the shoes that Pippa had bought, me having a meltdown in the office, and, finally, my annoyance at my parents' inability to see past Pippa being the baby of the family.

'And there were nine pairs?' Emma asked, her eyes huge.

'Yes, including a pair of *Sophia Websters* that she knows I'm desperate for?'

'God that's low,' Emma said with a slight shake of the head. 'But I have a feeling that isn't the real reason you wanted cake today. So what's really upsetting you?'

'Apart from sister running off with someone and stealing money from my parents—I don't know, Emma, what could it be?' I shrugged.

Emma tilted her head and raised her eyebrows. She wanted the truth.

'Okay,' I said with a sigh. 'I want Caroline out of Roman's house, and I feel a bitch about it. I know she has a child, but I'm falling in love with Roman, and I know he cares about me, so this should be our time. Time that we spend alone, getting to know each other, and enjoying that first fluttering of love.'

'And she's cramping your style?' Emma questioned.

I let out a long exhale, thinking about everything. Was she encroaching on our time together? Was Roman holding back because Caroline was in the house? I had to be honest.

'No, that's the thing, she isn't,' I replied, my voice breaking. 'She stays out of our way, and is really respectful of our time together, and Maisie is the cutest little girl, but ...'

I couldn't get the words out as the sob broke through.

'Hey,' Emma said in a soothing voice, rubbing my forearm, 'it's okay, don't get upset, sweetie.'

'But I just want her gone, Em. This is something good that's happening for me and Roman, and I hate having her around. And that makes me such a bitch.'

As I started to cry, Emma got up from her seat and came to my side. She wrapped an arm around my shoulder, squeezing it tightly.

'You need to speak to Roman,' she whispered. 'You shouldn't be getting upset like this.'

'He's spoken to her already, after Tiff got upset, and she said she's going to find somewhere, but she doesn't seem to making much effort.'

'So bide your time, she'll be gone soon.'

I looked at Emma with tear-filled eyes. 'I just don't trust her, Em. I know she's been nice and everything, but I don't think she wants to leave.'

Emma wiped my face with her hand and brushed a stray hair

from my forehead.

'You really need to talk to him,' she said. 'You know you do.'

'But he already feels bad about upsetting Tiff with having her stay. I don't want to make him feel any worse.'

'Well, it's up to you,' Emma said. 'But if you don't say something, then you can't complain about her staying.'

'I just don't want him to hate me for it.'

She studied me for a moment and then said. 'Why would he?'

'Because it's more trouble that I'll be stirring up, as well as me giving Jack the information that he needed.'

'But you said he was okay about you telling Pippa?'

'He was, he is,' I replied. 'But it was still me that gave Alan Cromwell's name to Jack.'

The guilt just wouldn't go away, no matter what Roman said.

'Has he said something to make you think he really is angry about it.'

'Not exactly, and I'm probably being stupid.'

'And didn't you say that Tiffany had already asked him to get rid of Caroline?'

'Yes …'

'But?' she asked.

'After my mini-meltdown in the office yesterday,' I sighed, 'he was lovely and sweet all day. We went out for dinner last night, but he was really quiet.'

'He didn't speak or he was off with you?'

'No, he was lovely and he engaged in conversation with me, but it was as if he was following a script.' I chewed on my bottom lip. 'All really polite, as if we'd only just met.'

'Maybe he's tired?' Emma offered. 'You did say he's been working hard trying to get work moving.'

'Yeah, he has. He's waiting to hear from a brewery about some pubs that need a refurb, and he's constantly on the phone to the council about those damn birds. The nest was supposed to be checked last Friday, but they are coming on Monday now.'

'Well, that's good news.'

'Yes, I suppose,' I sighed. 'As long as they say it's okay to start work.'

'That doesn't sound too bad to me.'

'I know, Emma, but we didn't have sex last night, or this morning.'

Emma laughed and shook her head. 'Oh how dreadful.'

'He did hold me all night, and I fell asleep with him tracing circles on my back, but he didn't even want wake-up sex this morning. And he always wants wake-up sex, especially on a Saturday morning.'

Emma giggled, and with a blush to her cheeks, looked down at her cake. 'Henry loves wake-up sex.'

'There you go, why didn't Roman want wake-up sex with me this morning?'

Emma shrugged. 'Maybe he can't perform with Caroline in the house?'

'Oh he can, and he does.' I sighed and rested my chin in my hand. 'I must admit, Maisie was running around outside his bedroom door this morning.'

'That'll be it,' Emma replied.

I finished the last of my coffee and sat back in my seat, not totally satisfied with that explanation.

'Don't worry too much,' Emma said. 'You'll talk to Roman, he'll ask Caroline to go and you'll get Roman-the-Sex-God back.'

I gave a small laugh, and hoped that she was right.

CHAPTER 37

The day after my chat with Emma, we finally got some good news. Mr. Williams at the planning office called to say work could recommence at The Palisades. Apparently, according to the experts, the Marsh Harriers' nest was abandoned and probably had been for a couple of years. How they knew that was anyone's guess, but it meant work could start again on The Palisades, as soon as Roman managed to get a new gang of workers together, seeing as most of them had abandoned ship to work for Jack Abbott.

I'd expected Roman to be happy, but the problems about finding a new gang was evidently playing on his mind, if his mood was anything to go by.

He'd seemed fine the night before, while watching the film I'd wanted to see. We'd snuggled up on the sofa, Roman lying the full length of it, with me tucked in front of him wrapped in his arms. Thankfully, Caroline had gone upstairs with Maisie to watch TV in her room. Roman had even let out a few belly laughs at the film. A perfect evening had ended with some hot, quick sex on the sofa, followed by one of the best ever goodnight kisses, when I'd finally decided to go home.

Today, however, his mood was dour and he was being a pain in the neck.

'Summer, where the hell is the contract for Darrington Hall?' Roman asked without looking up from his phone.

'In the folder called "Darrington Hall", in the usual place. You know, the one where I put all our contracts. The one that you ask me about almost every week.'

I couldn't help but be snarky with him, he'd done nothing but moan and niggle all morning. At one point he'd even bawled at me to stop singing, because in his words, 'You sound like a damn foghorn.'

Roman's head rose slowly, his dark eyes narrowed as they met mine.

'Is that sarcasm totally necessary?' he asked.

'Yes,' I replied. 'You've been a misery all day.'

'Because, believe it or not, I have more on my mind that what colour nail polish to put on tonight, or what stupidly expensive pair of shoes I'll buy next.'

'Seriously, you think that's all I care about?'

'Well,' he said, shrugging his shoulders. 'Isn't it?'

A thudding started in my temples as my blood began to boil. I cared a great deal about his damn business, and he knew it.

'I can't believe you just said that, you stupid chauvinistic pig.' I pushed up from my chair, putting my hands to my hips. 'How dare you, when you know how much I care about this company?'

The rage I was feeling was beating against my chest now, and I really wanted to slap his face.

'Oh yeah,' Roman scoffed. 'You care so much that you told Jack Abbott about my new client.'

My eyes widened as his words stabbed at my heart. Roman's eyes darkened as he watched me, waiting for my response. Breathing heavily, I shook my head.

'You know what Roman, I think I'm feeling a little sick,' I said. 'And I can't see me feeling better for a while, so you may want to get a temp in.'

Roman's breathing was the only sound in the room as I pulled open my drawer, emptied a couple of things out of it into my handbag, and then banged it shut. I reached the door before he spoke.

'Summer, I'm sorry. I didn't mean ...'

'Yeah, Roman, you did,' I said on a shaky breath.

'Summer,' he pleaded, putting a hand to my elbow.

I snatched my arm away and slammed out of the office, dashing tears from my cheeks as I scuttled through the main building, ignoring the worried glances of everyone else.

***

'Bloody piece of crap,' I cried, kicking at the tyre of my car. 'Argh.'

After storming out of the office I had decided that some retail therapy was in order. So I'd driven the thirty miles or so to the huge shopping centre at the edge of Manchester. It was only once I'd tried on half a dozen dresses and three pairs of jeans in the first store that I'd realised that I didn't actually have my purse. I remembered then it was in my jacket pocket that was hanging in the office. I'd put it in there earlier, when I'd gone to get Roman and myself coffee and toast from the café on the corner, foolishly trying to cheer him up. So, without enough cash on me for even a bottle of water, I'd driven home still feeling pretty irate. The twenty-seven missed calls and ten text messages from Roman hadn't helped either—at least he'd stopped about an hour ago, when I'd finally sent him a text that simply said: *'Get stuffed.'*

I'd made it to within two miles of home when my car slowed down to a dead stop. My luck had run out as I'd been driving on fumes for the last forty minutes, so to get that far had been a bonus. The only problem was the nearest petrol station was probably about three miles away, and I was not in walking shoes, plus, I had no damn money.

With another frustrated kick to the car, I pulled my mobile out of my bag and went through my contact list. It was three o'clock on a Monday afternoon and everyone would be working. I scrolled to Emma's number as she was probably the most likely to be able to come and rescue me. I stabbed my finger at the screen and listened to the dial tone. After getting her voicemail twice, I gave up. It was only then that I remembered that she was actually off work. She had gone to a spa hotel with her mum for the day and was probably, at that very moment, in the middle of being massaged.

Leaning back on the bonnet of my car, I stared down at my phone, wondering who else I could try? Dad was working and today was mum's day for volunteering at a local charity shop-she'd come if I asked, but I wasn't sure I was in the mood for a lecture about keeping a proper eye on my fuel gauge. As for Dylan, well, he'd be saving some poor animal's life, or flirting with their owner, no doubt, and I couldn't possibly drag him away from that. There was no one else that I could think of.

With a heavy sigh, I decided the only thing I could do, was walk the two miles home, and call Dylan later to take me to get fuel and then back to my car. No doubt by the time I got home, my feet would be covered in blisters, but what choice did I have?

Then—call it good luck, divine intervention, whatever—a truck with a ladder and cement mixer on the back pulled up behind my car. I looked at the driver and sighed with relief.

'Oh thank God, Alfie. Am I glad to see you.'

Alfie Chambers walked lazily towards me with a huge cocky grin on his face.

'I knew that you'd want me one day,' he said with a wink. 'Any idea what's wrong with it?'

I grimaced. 'No fuel and no money to get any.'

'Seriously?' Alfie started to laugh. 'You disappoint me, Summer. I kind of expected more from you than running out of petrol.'

I knew he was joking, but my argument with Roman was still playing on my mind, and I wasn't in the mood for any of Alfie's smart comments.

'I know, okay, there's no need to remind me.'

Alfie started to laugh and walked towards the truck. 'Well, maybe next time you'll remember this moment, being stranded. Although,' he said as he looked at my feet over his shoulder, 'maybe a better idea would be to have a pair of flat shoes in the car, so that if it does happen again, you can actually walk to the petrol station.'

I glanced down at my shoes and had to agree, but style always won over comfort as far as I was concerned.

'Whatever, Alfie. So are you going to lend me some money and take me to the petrol station?'

'No need,' he replied. 'I've got some petrol in the back of the truck. Lucky for you. Unless of course your car is diesel?'

'No, it's not.'

Alfie reached inside the bed of the truck and pulled out a plastic petrol can. He came back over to my car and emptied the contents into my tank.

'You can keep this in case you ever need one again,' he replied, opening up my boot and putting the empty, plastic petrol can in it.

'Thanks, Alfie,' I said on a sigh.

'No problem, but I'd say you owe me a date for helping you out.'

Alfie leaned against the bonnet of my car, a glint in his eye and a cheeky grin on his face.

'What?' I asked, as he stared at me.

'I'm waiting for you to agree to go on a date with me.'

He folded his arms across his chest and looked as though he wasn't going to move anytime soon. Tall and blonde, Alfie was definitely good-looking, but there was something about him that had always made me keep him at arm's length. His many women, and the way that he boasted about them, being the main reason.

'Alfie, you do know that I'm seeing Roman, right?'

At the mention of Roman's name, something dropped in my stomach. I hated that we'd argued, but I wasn't putting up with him blaming me for something that he'd insisted on many occasions wasn't my fault. Either he'd been lying before, or he was just being hateful today. I was hoping that it was the latter, but I couldn't help but think otherwise.

'Yeah, I know,' Alfie replied. 'But I figure, you don't ask, you don't get.'

'Well, sorry, but you're not getting.'

Alfie started to laugh and hugged me against his side.

'I'll wear you down.'

His arm around me felt alien, and I twisted to get from under it.

It was at that moment that a car screeched to a halt behind mine. A door slammed, and the next thing I knew an angry-looking Roman was standing in front of us.

'What the fuck is going on?' he demanded, fisting his hands at his sides.

Alfie loosened his hug, but kept his arm behind me. I glanced at him and knew by the cocky grin that he was goading Roman. I shifted away and took a step towards Roman.

'I asked you a question?' Roman demanded.

Alfie looked at Roman and shook his head. 'Sorry?' he asked.

'Roman,' I warned, taking another step closer.

'I said what the fuck is going on?'

Roman was staring at Alfie, not acknowledging me in any shape or form. I knew from the way his eyes were narrowed and the pulse in his jaw was ticking wildly that he was not happy.

'Roman, Alfie stopped to help me,' I said, as I moved in front of him, directly in his vision. 'I ran out of petrol, and he kindly helped me out.'

'I've been looking for you for the last three hours, did it not occur to you that I might be worried sick? Yet here you are with *him*, with *his* hands on you? Thank God I was driving past. And I'll say it again—looking for you.'

I took a deep breath and silently counted to ten. It probably didn't look good, but I would hope that he would realise that I wasn't interested in Alfie Chambers, whatsoever.

'I'm sorry, boss,' Alfie said, 'but what's the problem?'

Roman took a step to the left to get a view of Alfie.

'The problem, *Alfie*,' he growled, 'is that you have *your* hands on *my* girlfriend.'

'Roman!'

I heard a low whistle from Alfie. 'Ah, come on, it's just a bit of fun. We're not doing anything wrong, are we, Summer?'

I turned to Alfie and felt a huge desire to slap him. He was not making this any better by acting this way. He didn't seem to care that Roman was obviously fuming. Admittedly my not answering his calls for the last few hours was probably partly to blame for his anger, but Alfie was making matters worse.

'No, absolutely bloody nothing is going on here.' I turned back to Roman. 'Not that I need to explain, but Alfie was just having a joke with me about running out of petrol.'

I didn't think it necessary to admit he'd been trying to get me to go on a date. There was no point in stoking the fire.

'If it makes you feel better, boss, I did ask her on a date, but she turned me down.'

I groaned and hung my head. The stupid idiot.

'I know that you were aware that we are seeing each other,' Roman said in low growl, pointing at Alfie, 'so what the fuck you thought you were doing asking Summer out is beyond me.'

Alfie gave a short laugh before making things even worse. 'It's a free country, and she can go out with whoever she likes.'

'Yes, she can, but that happens to be me!' Roman snapped, his finger jabbing at Alfie's chest. 'Keep your hands to yourself in future.'

'Like I said, it's a free country,' Alfie muttered.

'Are you for real?' Roman moved to go past me, so I grabbed his arm.

'Don't you dare,' I said, with a bite to my tone.

Roman stopped and looked down at me, his jaw tight and his nostrils flared.

'Just get back to work,' he barked over my shoulder towards Alfie. 'Summer doesn't need your help any longer. I'm here now.'

Keeping my eyes on Roman, I heard Alfie chuckle behind me, and then from the corner of my eye saw him get into the truck and drive away.

'I don't trust that man one little bit,' Roman said as he watched the back of Alfie's truck disappear down the road.

'So you thought you'd mark your territory,' I muttered, shaking my head.

'He'll be sorry if he touches you again.'

'Oh grow up,' I spat out.

'Me grow up? You're the one that stormed off. And why did you by the way?' Roman thundered. 'I've been worried sick about you. You could have least answered your damn phone.'

I reeled back a step, shocked that he even had to ask why I'd left the office. I would have thought it was obvious.

'Really, after what you said earlier, you want to know why I stormed out?' I straightened my shoulders and held my head high. 'Are you that stupid?'

'For fuck's sake, Summer,' Roman sighed, 'I'm sorry for what I said, I didn't mean it.'

'So why say it?' I asked.

I'd done nothing but mull it over since I'd stormed out, and every time I came to the same conclusion: in the back of his mind that was what he thought.

'I'm worried about work, and you just wound me up, so I lashed out.' Roman pinched the bridge of his nose. 'I'm so sorry, baby, I really am.'

'If you really think that, then why keep telling me that you don't blame me?' I asked, determined to get an answer from him.

Roman sighed and raised his hands, palms up. 'I've just told you, I damn well don't blame you. I opened my stupid mouth and my anger took hold of my brain.'

His eyes were pleading with me, and I had to admit that, until today, he'd never once made me think that he blamed me for losing the Cromwell job.

'Well, you hurt me, and you were a chauvinistic pig too.' I crossed my arms over my chest and turned away from him. 'You know how much I care about the business.'

'I know, and I'm sorry for that too.' He moved to stand in front of me, placing a hand on my shoulder.

'You might be sorry, Roman, but you are unbelievably childish too. If you really don't blame me, then you shouldn't have said what you did, just because you're in a bad mood.' Roman shook his head and tutted.

'I am not childish!' he cried. 'And I'm not in a bad mood. I'm fucking worried about my business and have been fucking worried about you all afternoon.'

God, he was infuriating. I'd been asking him all weekend what was worrying him.

'So why don't you just tell me, instead of saying hurtful things that you don't mean? You've been quiet for the last couple of days, but never once when I've asked you have you admitted you were worried.' I breathed out a heavy sigh. 'You kept saying business was looking better.'

'Because I didn't want to worry you too.' Roman said, taking hold of my hand. 'You don't need to worry about it.'

'I work for you, Roman, of course I need to worry. It affects me too. Apart from which, I'm your girlfriend. You should be able to tell me when things are worrying you.'

'I didn't because I'm trying to protect you,' he said, closing his eyes and taking a deep breath.

'I don't need protecting, why don't you get that, you frustrating idiot?'

'Because I fucking love you, that's why!'

My breath caught and my hand shot to my stomach as if to hold back the bats that were flapping around inside it. Roman and I watched each other, our chests heaving. Neither of us spoke, we just stared.

'What did you say?' I finally asked.

'I said, "I fucking love you,"' Roman repeated in a low tone.

'You do?'

I chewed on my bottom lip and took a step forward. Reaching for my hand, Roman entwined his fingers with mine.

'Yes, Summer, I fucking do. I fucking love you.'

'Do you have to swear when you say it?' I asked, my voice breaking.

Roman nodded. 'Yes, I fucking do, because to simply say "I love you" doesn't seem enough. I need you to understand how much I love you, and that just seems to be the best way for me. I'm no poet, Summer, you know that.'

'So you really love me?' My heart was pounding hard, and I wasn't sure whether I wanted to cry or jump him right there on the busy road.

Roman nodded and curled his hand behind my neck, pulling me closer.

'Yes, I really love you. So fucking much,' he said quietly, before kissing me gently. 'I'm so damn sorry for what I said earlier, I really didn't mean it. I'm stupid, but I just don't want you to worry.'

'I get that, Roman, I do, but you can't speak to me like that. I don't deserve it.'

Roman sighed heavily and dropped his forehead to mine.

'I know you don't, I'm a complete dick.'

'Yes, you are, but you're my complete dick,' I replied, winding my arms around his waist. 'And I love you too.'

The words came easily because saying them was like breathing: totally natural. I didn't need to think about whether I meant them, or whether it was the right time. I'd known it for a while, and had only been holding back because I wasn't sure whether Roman was there yet, but evidently he was.

Roman breathed out a sigh. 'Thank God for that.'

'I'm still mad at you, though,' I pouted. 'We really need to talk about your male chauvinism and belligerent attitude.'

Roman smiled. 'Yes, Miss.'

'I'm being serious.'

'I know you are, and so am I,' he replied softly. 'I promise not to lash out at you again.'

'And I need you to talk me,' I said.

Roman nodded and kissed me softly.

'When did you know?' I asked. 'That you loved me.'

'From the minute you saw my dad's bare arse and tackle, and never said a word. Just took me a while to realise it.'

Roman kissed me again, but this time he didn't stop until a van driver leaned out of his window and offered to throw a bucket of cold water over us.

CHAPTER 38

♥

After a fraught few hours and a roadside declaration of love, Roman decided that we were taking the rest of the afternoon off. We were desperate to get down and dirty, but short of going to a hotel, which seemed a little seedy, we had nowhere to go.

Caroline and Maisie would at Roman's taking over the place with her bloody beautiful shoes and Maisie's dolls, so we couldn't go there. If we went to my house, my mum would end up offering Roman all manner of baked goods before we'd even manage to get up the stairs. Besides which, I didn't fancy screaming Roman's name in orgasmic bliss, while my mother polished her china downstairs. So, we decided to go to a country pub for a late lunch instead.

The food was great, but the whole time Roman seemed quiet and within himself, and I couldn't get him to open up. I was pretty sure that it wasn't me that he was mad with. He'd just told me that he loved me—surely he hadn't changed him mind already?

'Do you regret what you told me?' I asked, voicing my fears.

'What?' he asked, looking up from the apple pie he was pushing around the dish.

'Do you regret saying you love me?'

'God no.' He dropped his spoon with a clatter, and reached

across the table for my hand. 'Why would you say that?'

'Because you've been really quiet since then. I can barely get a word out of you.' I bit on my bottom lip, waiting for his answer.

'I love you, make no mistake about that,' he whispered, giving me a brilliant smile.

'So what's wrong, is it the business? You promised not two hours ago that you wouldn't keep things from me.'

'No, well, yes, I'm worried, but that's not what I'm upset about now,' he sighed. 'I just hate that I can't take you home and do what I want to you.'

'Really?' I reached to cup his cheek. 'That's silly, we'll have plenty of time when Maisie's gone to bed and Caroline's watching her TV.' I grinned, but Roman didn't see the funny side.

'That's exactly the point. She shouldn't be there. We should be there now, me inside you making you come until you pass out.'

His words weren't helping. The heat between my legs had just got considerably hotter.

'Thanks, now I'm annoyed too,' I hissed, shifting around on my chair.

'This is my fault, I should have said no. Or at least made her move out. She's not looked at any of those places you found.'

My relief that he wanted her gone as much as I did was immense. A part of me had thought he'd wanted them there, still feeling duty-bound to Michael.

'Thank goodness for that,' I sighed.

'You don't think I enjoy having her there do you? Not when all I want to do is be alone with you.'

A beautiful smile lit up his face, and my heart gave a little flutter of happiness that he was at least smiling.

'I know that this isn't ideal for us, Summer. So, when we get back I'm going to speak to her again. For us.'

My breath faltered and I wanted to cry. He understood and was going to do what I needed, without my even having to ask him.

'Maybe you should offer to go and see some places with her,' I suggested. 'She might look at them if you find them for her.'

'Yeah, that's not a bad idea.'

'I also think we should tell her about Pippa,' I said with a sigh.

He raised his brow as he stared at me. 'You think?'

I nodded. 'I do. Whatever she has to say about Pippa will probably be totally founded, so don't worry about her upsetting me.'

'If you're sure.'

'Yes, it'd be better telling her now. Plus, finding out it's my sister he's shacked up with, might just make her think it's best to move out.' Yes, it was manipulative, but I wanted her gone—we both did.

Roman smiled widely and leaned across the table to kiss my cheek. 'Okay, let's tell her. Then tonight we'll relax and watch that film you wanted to see. Okay?'

'Okay.' My smile was huge, I'd only mentioned the film in passing earlier, and he'd been in such a mood I hadn't thought he'd heard me.

'I'll might even make you some popcorn.'

'A girl can't say no to that, can she?' I said and took my turn to lean across the table and kiss him back.

***

When we entered the house, the chances of me watching the film were slim: Maisie was sitting on the floor watching cartoons, while Caroline flicked through a magazine. Her feet were up on the sofa, and she had a cushion pushed behind her back. She looked totally at home. I could feel my hackles rise as she barely glanced at us when we walked in. It was Roman's house and she was treating it as though it was her own. Call me a bitch, but I wanted her to feel uncomfortable, and to feel the need to get her own space, but she looked nowhere near ready to move out.

Roman stopped besides Maisie, dropped a hand to her strawberry blonde curls, and gave her head a little rub. Maisie grinned up at him, and then turned to give me an even bigger smile.

'Hey, Maisie,' I said, giving her a little wave.

'Summer, it's *Peppa*.' She pointed at the TV and giggled.

'I know,' I replied. 'I love *Peppa* too.'

Maisie chuckled again and turned back to the television.

'You got a minute, Caroline?' Roman asked, nodding towards the door.

Caroline smiled and nodded, closing the magazine. 'Yeah, sure. Maisie, I'm just going into the kitchen with Uncle Ro, shout if you need me. Okay?'

Maisie's eyes never the left the TV. 'Okay, Mummy.'

Caroline dropped her feet to the floor, pushed herself up from the sofa and followed Roman into the kitchen.

I watched them leave and wondered whether I should follow. Roman hadn't said he wanted me involved; after all, it wasn't really my business.

'You coming, baby?'

I turned to see his head poking around the doorframe. I nodded and moved to follow him, almost tripping over a pair of *Ugg* slippers—even her bloody slippers were designer! Between her and Pippa, I was really pissed off.

When I got to the kitchen, Caroline was sitting on a barstool, while Roman paced up and down in front of her.

'I understand, Caroline, but Jack really should be helping you. I know the council don't have anything at the moment, but some of those apartments that Summer found were really nice, and not too expensive.' He was talking calmly, but I could see that he was trying to hold on to his temper. The muscle in his jaw was ticking vigorously.

'But I still can't afford them, Roman,' she whined. 'And I won't take a penny from Jack—not that he has any money.'

Roman looked at me questioningly, and I gave him a slight nod.

'Listen, Caroline,' he said as he stopped pacing. 'You ought to know that he's living in a fancy cottage on the outskirts of Manchester, so I'm pretty sure he has some money.'

Her head shot up. 'Where?' she asked, pushing up from the stool. 'I thought he was local?'

'No, he's just outside Manchester. We went over there,' Roman explained.

'Why? Why did you go there?' She folded her arms across her chest, as she looked between me and Roman. 'You hate Jack.'

'Did you know that he's living with someone?' Roman stated, ignoring her question.

Caroline's eyes widened. 'What do you mean he's living with someone?' she said quietly.

'Exactly that, he's living with a girl.'

'Who? Who's he damn well living with, Roman?' Her jaw was tight and her hand was against her stomach. The thought of Jack living with someone obviously nauseated her, and was a huge shock.

'Okay,' Roman sighed. 'We went to see him because the girl he's with is Summer's sister.'

I expected her to gasp or cry or something, but, strangely, she simply nodded.

'Well, I hope your sister knows what she's doing,' she said to me in a quiet, controlled tone. 'He'll get what he wants and then she'll be history.'

Caroline looked down and sniffed, and I felt some empathy for the fact my sister was the reason for her tears. She swiped at her face and then looked up at us. I was surprised to see that her eyes were already dry. She obviously wasn't that upset, which I found strange considering her ex was living in a nice house, while she was homeless. She must have an incredible ability for forgiveness.

'That's why we went over there,' Roman answered quietly. 'We wanted to warn her, but she wouldn't leave.'

'I'm sorry, Caroline,' I added. 'My sister is a little selfish and she seems to love him.'

Caroline's gaze swept to me. 'Yeah, well, Jack only loves himself, so I'd tell her not to waste that emotion on him,' she said, with a shake of the head. 'Your sister and now Summer's. He certainly has a type.'

Roman shrugged. 'I can't say I haven't considered it a little weird.'

'Surely that's all just coincidence?' I asked.

Roman looked at me and I knew from the way he breathed deeply and his nostrils flared, that he wasn't totally sure. Now, I was wondering too.

'Okay,' Caroline said, walking towards the door. 'I'll take another look at those apartments tomorrow. I'll manage somehow.'

'I am sorry, Caroline,' Roman said, leaning against the counter top. 'But I'll help you if I can.'

She turned and smiled. 'I know, Ro and thank you. And, Summer, don't feel bad about your sister, Jack does whatever he wants.'

I nodded, thinking back to a month or so ago when we'd met Jack in Ziggy's. If only we hadn't gone out that night.

'She's pretty stupid and selfish at times, but hopefully she'll see sense soon enough,' I replied.

Caroline gave me a small smile and left. I knew I should feel sorry for her, but something told me that she wasn't particularly upset, so why bother.

CHAPTER 39

♥

After Roman's declaration of love, and our chat with Caroline, the rest of the week continued in peace. I had spent almost every night at Roman's house, and every day we were growing closer and closer.

Caroline and Maisie were still there, but by the time we got home from work, they'd already eaten and were busy watching kid's TV. That was when we'd eat our dinner, and by the time we finished, Caroline was putting Maisie to bed. She would then go to her own room to continue watching TV. It appeared that she'd realised that three was most definitely a crowd.

Roman and I tried to keep things professional at work, but it wasn't unusual for him to call me into his office, slam the door behind me and then kiss me within an inch of my lung capacity. Also, I don't know how he did it, because we arrived for work at the same time, but every morning there would be something waiting on my desk for me. Sometimes it was simply a *Post-it* note that said: '*I love you*'—or something much dirtier. Other times, I'd had a cupcake with a marzipan heart on top; a packet of *Love Heart* sweets and a bunch of wild daisies—my favourite flower. Whenever I thanked Roman he would grin shyly and shrug, and I loved him a little bit more.

If was Friday evening and Roman was having a night off from Ziggy's. We were walking through town, going for an early dinner as Roman had plans to see an old friend, Marcus, that night. He'd been extremely apologetic when he'd told me of his plans, and I couldn't understand why. I wasn't one of those girlfriends that couldn't bear to be apart from her man. A good night's sleep in my own bed would do me good anyway, if only because I could starfish across the bed for a change.

'Have you eaten here before?' I asked as we walked across the road towards the Italian restaurant where we were having dinner.

'No, you?'

'No, but Pippa said it's lovely.'

My heart sank at the thought of Pippa, who was still living with Jack Abbott. I couldn't believe how stupid and selfish she was being, and just wanted her to come home.

'That's good,' Roman replied, sounding a little distracted.

Although he was holding my hand and rubbing his thumb along the back of it, his concentration didn't appear to be on me, but on the cobbled path under our feet. In fact he'd been pretty distracted all day. Okay, maybe not this morning when we were having shower sex: then he'd been totally concentrated.

'Are you okay?' I tugged on his hand to get his attention.

Roman looked up at me and gave me a smile.

'Yeah, fine.'

His gaze shot back down to the floor.

'Roman, what did we discuss on the side of the road a few days ago?' I pulled us to a halt, a few steps away from the restaurant. 'What do you need to tell me?'

'Sorry,' Roman replied, 'still finding it difficult to not worry you.'

'So,' I said, tugging on his hand. 'Spill.'

He sighed heavily and nodded.

'I'm struggling to get enough sparks for The Palisades. The only electrician I can get is Johnny Mountjoy, and he can only give me a month.'

'I take it Jack Abbott has got most of them working for him?'

'Yeah, the tosser has pretty much bagged the lot.' He rubbed his temple and started us walking again. 'I'm going to contact a few agencies tomorrow and give a few guys I worked with down South a call. It'll cost me more money, but I'll have to do it.'

I leaned into his side, dropping a kiss to his cheek.

'I'll do the agency calls for you, it is my job.'

'I know, and I should have told you.'

Roman halted and pulled me into his arms.

'I am trying, baby,' he said, kissing the end of my nose. 'In fact, I think I'm getting to be quite a good boyfriend, and boss, with your expert tuition.'

I started to giggle. 'Hey, a few surprises on my desk every morning doesn't make you a good boyfriend,' I joked. 'It helps, but more foot massages and pandering to my every need are still required, to be honest.'

'Oh is that right?' Roman said, kissing my neck. 'What about the amazing orgasms that you get, don't they add bonus points?'

I shivered as I thought about them and had to agree they *were* pretty amazing. I bit on my lip and looked up at Roman through my lashes, hoping that I looked sexy and not like a duck with piles.

'How about we forget dinner, and you take me home and remind me how amazing they really are? Then you can go and see your friend feeling satisfied.'

'Fuck,' Roman muttered as his already burgeoning erection pushed against my stomach.

Then, before we had time to turn on our heels and run, a voice behind me shattered my bliss.

'Hey, sis, fancy seeing you here.'

I groaned and rested my forehead against Roman's chest. 'Please tell me that he isn't really here, and I'm just imagining it,' I begged.

'Hi,' my brother cried, shoving a hand into the small space between my and Roman's bodies. 'Great to see you again, Roman.'

Roman took Dylan's hand and shook it. 'You too, Dylan, and in better circumstances.'

'Yeah. I take it that you haven't heard from her since your visit?' Dylan asked, his tone tinged with anger.

I shook my head. 'Nope. She called Mum and Dad again the other day, but she hasn't responded to any texts that I've sent.'

'She's totally selfish,' Dylan replied. 'Anyway, where are you two off to?'

'We're off for an early dinner,' Roman said and placed a hand on Dylan's shoulder. 'You're welcome to join us?'

I took a sharp intake of breath and poked Roman in his side.

'I'm sure Dylan is busy, aren't you, Dyl?'

'Me, nah. I've got a date later, but I was just going to nip to the chippy and get a cod and chips. You know what it's like living on your own, you never want to cook, so dinner would be great.'

'Great,' I said through gritted teeth.

I loved my brother, I really did, but I'd been serious about skipping dinner and heading back for sex before Roman met his friend.

'Come on, then,' Roman said. 'Let's eat.'

As Dylan walked off in front of us, I pulled Roman back to my side.

'I was being serious about skipping dinner,' I hissed.

'I know, but we can always skip dessert. Don't worry, we'll have time.'

'He can be as inappropriate as your dad, you know,' I said grimacing.

Roman shrugged. 'Okay, so then we're quits.'

'Come on, you two, what's the hold-up?' Dylan asked, turning back to us.

'I don't want you to come with us,' I replied.

'Summer,' Roman said with shock. 'You can't say that.'

'Oh she can, Roman. She loves me really, though.'

Dylan grinned, then crossed his eyes and licked out his tongue at me. He knew me well enough to know that I was being truthful, but we also loved each other enough for him not to care.

'Dylan,' I hissed as Roman led the way. 'Please don't talk

about your sex life. I'd really like to eat my dinner without vomiting.'

'Oh really,' he groaned looking disappointed. 'I was going to tell you all about the date that I had with a girl who owns a grey parrot. You should see what she can do with a crochet hook and a bag of grapes. I came harder than I ever have before, but if you don't want any tips, then I won't mention it again.'

I had no idea what such sexual activity entailed, and didn't think I could stomach finding out. As Dylan jogged after Roman, my heart sank, because I knew my brother, and I knew he wouldn't be able to help but tell us—in extremely graphic detail.

***

I'd been right about Dylan, so when Roman took me home, taking advantage of my parents' being out, it took a little while for us to banish the images and stop feeling defiled and have our own sexual shenanigans. I know *I* wanted to drop my brain into a vat of bleach. I'd seen Dylan naked—admittedly, the last time had been when he was ten—but disturbing images of him and Suki, the parrot owner, were far worse than those of him nude by a mile.

Despite Dylan's conversation, we'd had a lovely meal, and Roman was much more relaxed. However, I was still worried that he was concerned about finding some more electricians. So, I sat in my bedroom debating whether to text him again or not.

I say 'again' because I'd already texted him once. Just a chatty, *'Hope you're having a good night with Marcus'* type of text, but hadn't received anything in return. That didn't worry me too much, but Roman always had his phone with him, and never failed to reply to my messages. Apart from this evening.

'Sod it,' I muttered and tapped out a text:

Me: Hey, going to bed now. Hope you enjoyed yourself. Missed you and see you in the morning. ILY xx

After ten minutes of staring at my dormant mobile, I decided to do exactly as I'd said and go to bed. I doubted whether I'd sleep well because now I was feeling a little anxious that he hadn't replied. A thought that he might be 'occupied' with Caroline flitted through my brain, because, after all, they were alone in the house together, but then I realised I was being stupid. Roman loved me, he was an honourable man, and it was more probable that he'd let his battery go dead. With a sigh I turned out my light.

I tossed and turned for a while, until eventually I must have dozed off because, just after one in the morning, my phone rang and woke me: like a real sap I still had it clutched in my hand. When I saw who was calling though I didn't care how sappy I was.

'Roman.'

'Hey,' he whispered on the other end. 'Sorry it's so late, and sorry I've woken you. I just needed to hear your voice.'

'It's okay.' My words came out fast and breathy; pure happiness that he'd called sent me into a girly tizzy. 'I missed you too. Did you have a good time with Marcus?'

'Yeah, it was okay, good to catch up.' His voice sounded strained and I could swear I could hear him inhale sharply. 'Did you just chill out?'

'Yeah, I did,' I lied. Roman not texting wasn't conducive with me chilling out. 'Was a bit boring, to be honest.'

'Oh sorry I didn't answer your text, by the way,' Roman replied. 'The bloody thing lost power.'

I'd been right, I could understand that happening: he was always talking on the damn thing or emailing from it.

'That's okay.'

'No, it's not, Summer. I preached to you about not keeping in contact with me when your car broke down, and then miss your text. I'm so sorry, sweetheart, I really am.' Roman's voice was pleading.

'Hey, it's fine, honestly.'

I heard Roman take a quick breath again.

'Roman, are you okay?'

'I'm fine, but, like I said, I'm missing you,' he replied and then stifled a yawn. 'Oh God, sorry.'

'You get off to bed,' I whispered. He didn't sound right, and maybe he was simply tired, but worry was gnawing at me. 'I'll see you later, we've got the whole day together.'

'What do you want to do?' Roman asked sounding a little lighter.

It was Saturday and we'd agreed that we'd do something together—well, I'd actually told Roman that he wasn't working because he needed a break. He'd been stressed out about the business, and working so hard that he was looking exhausted and frazzled, hence I'd put my foot down.

'How about I come over at about eleven and we decide then.' I smiled to myself, already having decided what we would be doing before we went anywhere.

'Okay, sounds like a plan.' Roman yawned again. 'See you later, and I love you.'

My heart jumped and my smile got wider.

'Love you too.'

And with a smile on my face, I finally fell into a deep sleep.

CHAPTER 40

I let myself into Roman's house, fully expecting to find him in his office tapping away at his laptop, but the house was in silence, apart from a light snoring drifting down the stairs.

Caroline must have taken Maisie out because the usual annoying, jolly singing of some guy dressed as a clown wasn't blasting from the TV.

I gave a contented sigh, thankful that we had the house to ourselves, and that Roman was getting some much needed rest. I decided to make myself useful and cook him his favourite: bacon and egg sandwiches—if he had anything in his fridge, that was.

I went into the kitchen and pulled open the fridge door, surprised to see it was full. At the back, nestled amongst bottles of beer, cooked chicken and the eggs that I needed, was a large dish of lasagne with a note on it: *'Summer's favourite'* —Twinkle had obviously been cooking and shopping for her son. With a huge smile, I found some bacon and took it and the eggs over to the cooker and placed everything down on the countertop. I then went to the sink to wash my hands and stopped dead in my tracks. There were dried droplets of blood along the draining board to the edge of the sink, and in the sink was a bloodied bandage. With my thumb and forefinger, I picked up the edge of the bandage and held it up, studying it. It wasn't soaked in blood, but there was a band of crimson about four or five inches in length dotted through the centre. I looked around to see whether there was any more blood anywhere else. I wondered if that was where Caroline was—maybe Maisie had cut herself and she'd taken her to A&E? Surely she'd have woken Roman if that was the case? It may even have been Roman. Whoever it was, there didn't appear to be enough blood for it to be a serious injury, but I still wanted to check on him. I quickly washed and dried my hands and made my way up the stairs to his room.

His bedroom door was slightly ajar and, apart from a thin sliver of light coming through a gap under the blind, the room was in darkness. I crept inside and the first thing to hit me was the smell: the yeasty aroma of alcohol mixed with the faint smell of sweat. Crinkling my nose, I looked over at Roman's body in the bed. He was lying on his back, one hand resting on his bare stomach, while the other lay on the pillow above his head. The duvet was twisted between his legs and one of his pillows was lying on the floor.

As his chest rose and fell, matching the rhythm of his snores, I noticed that there was a plaster across the knuckles of the hand on his chest. So, that was where the blood had come from? It was Roman's blood, but what the hell had he been doing? My eyes then wandered to his bedside cabinet where I noticed a bottle: there was the reason for the smell of alcohol.

I moved over to the window and pulled up the blind before reaching to open the window to let in some fresh air. I was about to close the blind again, so that Roman could continue sleeping, when I heard movement behind me.

'Summer?' a croaky voice asked.

Stopping what I was doing, I turned towards the bed to see Roman lifting onto his elbow and rubbing his eyes with the heel of his hand.

'Hey, sleepyhead, seems like you had quite a night,' I replied sitting on the edge of the bed next to him.

'Shit, what time is it?'

Roman flopped back against the pillows with a groan. I

brushed my hand through his hair, pushing it away from his sticky forehead. He was hot and clammy and didn't smell too good.

'It's almost eleven-thirty and you stink.'

Roman cursed under his breath and rolled on his side towards me.

'I'm so sorry, I intended to be up and dressed by the time you got here.' He reached a finger out to stroke my cheek and sighed. 'God, I missed you.'

'Well, it appears that you tried to drown the loneliness with alcohol,' I said nodding towards the almost empty bottle of what I could now see was whisky. 'And what did you do to your hand?'

Roman looked first at the bottle and then down at his knuckles and cursed again.

'I had a little argument with a wall,' he muttered.

'Why, what on earth happened?'

'Me,' Roman hissed. 'I stupidly revisited the past and didn't like the memories.' His eyes darted towards the open wardrobe door. I saw that the framed photographs of Roman boxing, the ones that I'd found previously, were lying haphazardly on the floor.

'Roman,' I said softly. 'It wasn't your fault.'

'So I'm told by lots of people, but it doesn't make the pain any less.'

'I thought things were getting better in there.' I tapped gently against his head.

'They are, but sometimes the blackness still likes to visit.'

He rolled onto his back and put an arm over his eyes before inhaling deeply.

'I'm sorry, I didn't want you to see me like this.'

He was so deep in his turmoil that I knew words weren't going to be enough to drag him out it, so I gently took his hand in mine and looked down at the plaster stretched across his knuckles. There were little spots of blood on it, and his hand looked a little swollen.

'Can you move your fingers?' I asked.

He flexed his fingers. 'Yep, nothing broken.'

'And what about the wall, is that broken?' I said with a smile, trying to lighten the mood.

Roman shook his head. 'No, stupidly I took on an outside wall.'

'Why didn't you tell me how you were feeling, when you called me? I would have come over.'

'I don't know, I thought I was coping, and then, after speaking to you, I just started drinking whisky and got buried even deeper.'

'Did Caroline bandage it for you? You didn't scare Maisie, did you?' I asked, concerned.

'They weren't here,' he groaned. 'Left me a note to say she was having some sort of get-together with old friends and staying over, so her parents were having Maisie for the night.'

I felt a breath of relief that Maisie hadn't had to witness Roman losing it, but realised he probably would have kept a lid on his emotions had she been around.

'Did something happen while you were out with Marcus to start you thinking about it?'

Roman chewed on his lip and stared up at the ceiling. 'No, I've no idea what triggered it,' he said finally. 'But it ended with too much alcohol.'

We sat quietly for a few minutes, Roman with his eyes closed, and me looking down at him, wondering whether I should say anything else and if so what? Eventually, Roman opened his eyes and gave me a beautiful smile before pulling himself into a sitting position.

'I should get showered; you're right, I do stink. Plus, I promised you that we'd have a day together, and lying here in my pit is not fulfilling my promise to my beautiful girlfriend.'

He reached up and kissed me, pulling me closer with a hand to the back of my head.

'I love you,' he whispered against my mouth.

'I know,' I replied. 'I love you too; now get in that shower.'

Roman laughed and pulled the duvet back, throwing his legs out of bed. I watched as he walked, naked, across the room to the en suite bathroom. One of these days I was going to test that theory of being able to crack a nut on his beautiful arse.

***

Once he was showered and dressed, Roman looked a lot better. His eyes were still tired, but he didn't stink. Well, he did smell, but it was a gorgeous lemon and musk scent. As he pulled me into his arms, I noticed a small cut on his lip.

'What happened to your lip? I didn't notice that upstairs.'

'Think I remember falling into the wardrobe door last night, I caught my side too,' Roman muttered, fingering his lip.

I pulled up his T-shirt and my eyes travelled down his body. I spotted a sizable blue bruise on his right side, just below his ribs. 'God, you really did clatter yourself, didn't you?'

Roman winced. 'Yeah, I was absolutely wasted, so we could find other wreckage around the house throughout the day.'

I sighed and kissed the small cut on his lip.

'Do your ribs need strapping up? I asked.

'No, they're fine. My head hurts more.'

'Well, next time you feel like that just ask me to come over, and I'll distract you away from the demon drink.'

'Oh you will, will you?' he laughed pulling my hips closer to his. 'And how will you do that?'

'I have lots of little tricks.'

'Yes, you do,' he groaned before capturing my mouth in a searing, hot kiss.

Roman's hand slid down to cup the cheek of my bum and gripped it firmly, his other hand was at the side of my head, his thumb gently rubbing against my jaw. I stood on tiptoe, pushed myself against his firmness and moaned against his mouth.

'Roman.'

'God, you feel and taste good,' he said as his lips moved to my neck. 'I'm not sure I want to do anything today, but keep you naked.'

'That sounds good to me.'

My fingers wove through his freshly washed and combed hair, and as I felt the zip on my skirt slide down, I knew that Roman was going to get his wish about keeping me naked *all* day.

CHAPTER 41

At eight on Monday morning, when we walked into the office, Brendan was waiting outside the door.

'Hey, Brendan,' Roman said, unlocking the outer office door. 'What brings you here? There isn't a problem at the site, is there?'

Brendan's gang was making a start on the restaurant extension at Darrington Hall, and he usually liked to have them start at seven in the morning.

'No,' Brendan said with a sigh, 'but I thought you ought to know.'

My heart started to thud erractically, wondering what shit news would be coming Roman's way now. If it was anything to do with Jack Abbott, I wasn't sure I'd be able to stop Roman seeking him out and doing him damage.

'Okay, lay it on me.' Roman's shoulders sagged as he opened his own office door and ushered Brendan in.

He flopped down into his chair, indicating for Brendan to sit also. I hovered in the doorway, in case strong black coffee was required.

'Well, as I'm his immediate boss, it was me the police called.'

'The police?' Roman asked. 'Don't tell me one of the lads has been nicking stuff, please.'

Brendan shook his head. 'No, boss, I wish it was that.'

'What is it, then?' Roman's eyes narrowed as he laid his hands on the arm of his chair, ready to push himself up.

'It's Alfie,' Brendan said quietly. 'He's been beaten up and is in hospital, and whoever did it has apparently made a real mess of his face.'

My heart was in my throat, as Brendan explained that Alfie had been found in an alleyway, beaten up and unconcious. He hadn't come around yet, but they thought he may have got a few punches in because his knuckles were bruised.

Roman listened to everything Brendan had to say without comment, then he sat back in his seat and pinched the bridge of his nose.

'Fuck,' he muttered.

'Yeah, I know,' Brendan replied. 'He's a pain in my damn arse, but I wouldn't wish that on him.'

'Does he have any family?' Roman asked.

He then turned to me.

'Summer, if he has family, can you arrange for some flowers to be delivered.'

I nodded, but couldn't move, and my eyes went instinctively to Roman's own hand that that had scabbing knuckles. I couldn't help the 'what if's' that were running around my head.

'He doesn't have anyone, Summer,' Brendan said, breaking my thoughts. 'He lives in a flat just outside of Rickeby, but he lives there alone. The police said his parents are both dead.'

'I'll send them to the hospital instead,' I replied, snatching a glance at Roman.

He was looking into the distance, his fingers steepled and his chin resting on them. He looked troubled, which scared me to death.

Surely he hadn't done this? He'd had the run-in with Alfie, but it was nothing serious, and we'd both been really happy since that day. I hadn't even spoken to or seen Alfie since then, so what reason would he have to do something like this?

'Do the police have any ideas who did it?' Roman asked, his eyes suddenly on Brendan.

Brendan shook his head. 'Nah, but I'll bet it's some angry boyfriend or husband. You know what Alfie's like, he doesn't give a shit whose woman he comes on to.'

Bile rose in my throat as Brendan's words registered. I could hardly breathe as thoughts of Roman beating Alfie to a pulp filled my head.

'Yeah,' Roman said on a long sigh. 'He really doesn't do himself any favours, does he? Okay, Brendan, keep me informed. I'll call the hospital and see if there's anything he needs.'

Brendan nodded and got up. 'Okay, boss, and sorry to bring you such shit news, first thing on a Monday morning.'

'No problem.' Roman turned to me. 'Summer, can you give the hospital a call, and see if they'll give you any information?'

'Yes, okay,' I replied quietly and returned to my desk.

I sat staring at the phone for a few minutes, wondering what I should do: whether I should ask Roman straight out if he'd done it.

I also wondered whether I was being an awful girlfriend, to even think it could be possible, but I'd seen Roman almost break a man's nose for putting a hand on me, and we weren't even together then.

Roman wasn't stupid, surely he wouldn't risk everything just because Alfie had put his arm around me, would he? I turned to look at his office door, which was now firmly closed.

I should just ask him.

Getting up from my seat, I took a deep breath, and put a hand to my stomach to try and quell the uneasiness. I knew that I had to do this, otherwise it would create a huge wall between us.

I knocked on the door and waited; after a few seconds Roman shouted for me to go in.

He was leaning against his desk, looking at a blueprint. 'Is it news from the hospital?' he asked, turning to me.

I swallowed and shook my head.

'I haven't called yet, I wanted to talk to you first.'

Roman's brow furrowed as he pushed up to his full height and faced me.

'Okay.'

Moving inside his office, I felt for the door behind me and closed it.

'I need to ask you something.' I took a huge breath and then licked my lips. 'Did you beat Alfie up?'

There, I'd said it: the horrifying thought that had been going through my mind had been spoken.

Roman's eyes widened, as his hands went to his hips.

'Say that again.'

His voice was incredulous. As he spoke, he shook his head in disbelief.

'I asked if you beat Alfie up.'

Chewing on my bottom lip, I took a step closer to him.

'I'm sorry, Roman, but I need to know.'

'And what the hell made you come to that conclusion?' His eyes were dark, but there was slight curve to his lips, as though he found the idea hilarious.

'Your busted knuckles, your bruises and cut lip.'

'And I told you how I got those,' he replied, dropping his gaze to the floor.

I gasped, because I knew that he was lying.

'Oh my God, Roman. What the hell have you done?'

Nausea swirled in my stomach as I pictured Roman punching Alfie. I whimpered and slapped a hand to my mouth.

Roman was in front of me within a stride.

'I did not damn well beat Alfie Chambers up,' he stated. 'And I can't believe that you would even think that. What the fuck sort of a person do you think I am?'

'I don't know,' I cried, 'I thought I knew you, but I know you're lying about how you got those injuries.'

For the second time, Roman's eyes stared down at the floor.

'Roman, please just tell me the truth, because I know you didn't get those cut knuckles by punching a wall.'

His head shot up and his eyes were full of remorse, making my heart drop.

'You really think so little of me?' he asked, and I could see his devastation. Tears pricked at my lashes as I reached for his hand.

'No, Roman, I love you, but I need you to trust me.'

He reeled away from me, pulling his hand free and stormed over to his desk. He snatched up his mobile and walked back to me, all the while flicking at the screen.

'Here,' he said, thrusting it at me.

I took it tentatively and looked at the screen. At first I didn't understand it, but reading it a third time, the words sank in:

Marcus: You're fighting at 11pm. Can get you another bout for next week if you do well.

'You were boxing,' I whispered, looking up at him.

Roman shook his head. 'No, Summer, I was bare-knuckle fighting.' His tone was laced with ice, and, at that moment, I wished I'd waited and thought carefully about questioning him.

'So, no, I didn't beat up Alfie Chambers.' Roman took his phone from my hand and pushed it into his pocket.

'You could have been badly hurt,' I said.

'No, I couldn't. Apart from being a damn good fighter, I didn't do it.'

He turned and walked away from me. Stopping in front of the filing cabinet and stared up at the ceiling.

'Roman,' I said softly. 'Please talk to me.'

He swivelled around towards me and took a deep breath.

'It was an unlicensed bare-knuckle fight,' he replied.

'An illegal fight?' I muttered. 'W-why would you do that?'

'Money, Summer. Because I need it for this business. "I was approached by Marcus to do this one-off fight,' he continued. 'It was more money than I'd ever made in a licensed fight, so I took him up on it.'

'But if you didn't fight, what happened to your knuckles and your side?' I whispered, recalling the state that I'd found him in.

'I really did hit the wall. The bruising of my ribs was courtesy of my opponent. I hit the wall at the warehouse where the fight was held, because once I got into the ring, I couldn't go through with it—it brought back too many memories of … my last fight.'

Roman's voice broke as he spoke of his fight with Michael. I moved to him, holding out my arms, but he put a hand up to stop me, and it felt like a knife had been stabbed and twisted in my heart.

'I let my opponent get one punch in to the ribs and then walked out. And then I hit the fucking wall. As for my lip, that was courtesy of Marcus for losing him a shitload of money.'

He stared at me with a coldness, which made me shiver with fear at what he was going to say.

'I'm so sorry, but I had to know.'

'I'm sorry I lied to you, Summer, but you should know that after what happened with Michael I would never hit anyone to hurt them like Alfie has been hurt.'

'The guy at the club, the one who touched me,' I replied. 'You almost broke his nose.'

Roman shook his head. 'You may not remember, but I didn't punch him; I slammed the heel of my hand against his nose. I knew it wouldn't break it, just make it bleed a little.'

He was right, he had done that.

'God, I'm sorry. I should have realised. What happened to Michael—'

'Forget it,' he said, interrupting me and taking his suit jacket from the back of his chair. He put it on and started to walk out.

'Where are you going?' I asked, trying to grab his arm, but Roman shrugged it off.

'Out, and I think it best we don't see each other tonight. I'll be on-site for the next few days, so it'll be a good time to get some space.'

'Roman, please.' My plea was a whimper as tears licked at my lashes.

He didn't stop. The door slammed behind him, leaving me alone in his office and wishing I could rewind the last half hour.

CHAPTER 42

I carried on through the rest of the day on automatic pilot, holding my breath every time the door opened or the telephone rang, but it was never Roman.

I called him and texted him, but none of my calls or texts were returned. I knew he'd read the text messages because I watched the three little dots bouncing around, but no matter how long I continued to look at the screen, no message came back.

As the day went on I felt sicker by the minute, allowing the tears to flow freely. Thankfully, no one came into the office to see what an emotional wreck I was.

I couldn't lose him: I loved him so much, and couldn't contemplate what things would be like without him loving me. In just a few weeks, Roman had shown me the sort of man that I wanted to be with, and it was him. He was sweet and gentle with me, and had boosted my confidence when it was at its lowest over my possible infertility. He'd made me think more positively. The way he looked at me, and the words he spoke to me made me feel desirable—his love made me glow. Now I might have lost him.

Half an hour before I was due to leave, I turned off my PC, snatched my coat from the coat stand and left the building, even pretending I hadn't heard Amanda from Wages calling my name as I weaved my way through the desks of the main office.

Once I was locked inside my car, the pain in my chest took over. I laid my head against the steering wheel and sobbed.

'He should have damn well told me,' I said to myself, through my tears. 'He should have trusted me about the fight.'

And he should have, but I knew that I should have trusted him too.

After a few minutes, I pulled myself into some sort of semblance of calm, and started my car.

I'd felt the pain, now I was feeling the anger. How dare he ignore me? I was going to tackle this head on. I was going to speak to him.

***

As I pulled up outside Roman's house, I saw that his truck wasn't there, just Caroline's Range Rover. I considered going in and waiting for him, but I didn't want her knowing that there was a problem between us. I still didn't trust her feelings towards Roman.

I decided that I would return later, but before driving away I sent one more text:

Me: Roman please talk to me. I'm sorry, so sorry. I love you xx

I no longer felt angry, I was sad and heartbroken. As I watched the screen, this time there were no dancing dots.

I drove around for a while, not wanting to go home. I didn't want Mum and Dad to know I was upset—I couldn't stand the thought of answering all their questions.

Finally, after an hour and a half of aimless driving, I made my way back to Roman's, hoping he'd be home. My optimism dipped as I approached the house: there was still only the Range Rover in the driveway. With a sigh, I drove past and decided to turn back at the next turning.

I pulled into a nearby street, wondering where Roman might be, and whether I should go looking for him? As I contemplated this, I almost slammed on my brakes in an emergency stop. Standing next to a white van was Jack Abbott.

'What the hell is he doing around here?' I whispered.

He was distracted by his phone, so I was able to check him out, and make sure it was definitely him as I drove past. It was.

I watched in my rear-view mirror as he locked his van, and then walked up towards the road that Roman's house was on. Quickly checking for traffic, I swung the car around in a quick U-turn. Slowing down, I waited for Jack to reach the junction, wondering which way he would go. He turned towards Roman's house.

As I got to the junction, I saw him stride up Roman's driveway. I turned onto the road, flipped down my sun visor, and pulled on my sunglasses which were sitting in the centre console: if Caroline spotted me, it would be doubtful that she'd recognise my car. Just as I came level with the house, the front door opened, and Caroline ushered Jack in. He paused in the doorway, dropping a kiss to her lips, while she cradled his face.

'You bloody bitch,' I muttered, laying a hand against my thumping heart.

My first instinct was to call Roman, but as my finger hovered over his number, I knew it was pointless. I tapped my phone against my chin, as I tried to think who I should call. Finally, I dialled a number. After a couple of rings, a bright, breezy voice answered.

'Hey, Summer.'

'Hi, Em,' I sighed, 'how do you feel about doing some spy work?'

CHAPTER 43

♥

I met Emma in a pub a few streets away. She was already there waiting for me with a large glass of orange, by the time I got there.

'Okay, spill,' she said, pushing the glass towards me.

I told her everything about Alfie, about Roman's aborted fight and about him storming out of the office, leaving what I'd seen at his house until last.

'And she definitely kissed him back?' Emma asked, shocked.

I nodded. 'Would you hold the face of the man you hated while you kissed him?'

She shook her head. 'What the hell are they up to?'

'No idea.' I shrugged. 'But before I speak to Roman about it, I'm going to find out.'

'Just tell him,' she said.

'He's not speaking to me, don't forget.'

'He'll listen to this.'

'But what does it prove? Caroline kissed her ex, so what?'

Emma's eyes widened. 'It proves that she is up to something. What I have no idea, but it's obviously dodgy. Think about it, she asks for a roof over her head, and he nicks Roman's new client. That can't be a coincidence. And imagine what Roman would say if he knew Jack had been in his house?'

I exhaled, knowing that she was right, but I still wanted more to take to Roman. Something that would ensure that he'd listen to me, and not just tell me to go away and stop being dramatic. The way he felt about me at the moment, I wasn't sure he'd ever speak to me again, anyway.

'We need to follow them,' I said, the idea growing in my head. 'I need *you* to follow *her*.'

Emma grinned and bounced in her seat. 'I've always wanted to be a spy,' she said, clapping her hands excitedly. 'Dad owes me a few days off, I can do that.' She fished around in her bag, finally pulling out a pad and pen. 'Right, tell me what you know about her routine.'

'Well, she takes Maisie to nursery on a Tuesday and Thursday, so that she can do "her jobs", whatever they are.'

'Okay, so that's tomorrow sorted. What time does she take her?'

I told Emma everything I knew and watched as she wrote it all down.

'What about you?' she asked, drawing a line under her notes. 'Are you going into work as normal?'

'No,' I replied, with a thin-lipped smile. 'I'm going to see what Jack Abbott is up to.'

***

The next day, I pulled up in front of the cottage that Pippa shared with Jack, I had to wonder whether I was doing the right thing, and what actual difference it would make. So what if they were really together? So what if Jack had pinched Roman's job, and the two things were connected? What difference would it make, other than Roman losing Caroline as a friend—it wouldn't get him the Cromwell job back? Yes, I'd be happy about Caroline being out of his life, but would it matter if Roman and I weren't together? If he never spoke to me again?

Despite all those thoughts, I knew that I had to try and find out what was going on. I had considered that maybe they were simply in the process of reconciling, but something about the way she kissed him made me think that they'd never been apart, or at least had been back together for a while.

While I was convinced it was all to do with getting at Roman, they were also making a fool out of my sister. Yes, part of me felt she deserved it, after taking money from Mum and Dad, but she was a foolish princess who believed herself to be in love. I wanted to sort this out for her and Roman. The biggest part of me, though, was doing it for selfish reasons: because I felt I needed something to redeem myself with the love of my life; because I couldn't stand the thought that he might never speak to me again.

What I hadn't thought about was whether Jack would be home. I just hoped that he'd be at work, seeing as he had so much to do after stealing the French job. Plus, it was a Tuesday morning, Caroline's day of 'doing her jobs' and I had a sneaky suspicion that Jack Abbott may be one of those jobs! I heaved a sigh of relief when there was no sign of his van.

'Summer,' Pippa gasped, as she opened the door.

Her face lit up, and I couldn't help but pull her into a hug. She had done the worst thing possible, but she was still my little sister and I loved her. I didn't like her very much at the moment, but I did love her.

'Hey, Pip,' I replied. 'Can I come in?'

'God, yes. Come in.'

She ushered me into the lounge, indicating for me to sit on the expensive-looking sofa that I'd sat on during my previous visit.

'Can I get you a drink? Tea or coffee?' She was angled towards a door, that I assumed led to the kitchen. 'I'd offer you something to eat, but we don't have much in until we go shopping later.'

'Just water thanks.' Caffeine wouldn't do as I had a pounding headache. I suspected it was from all the crying that I done the day before, but the stress of the whole situation didn't help either.

A couple of minutes later, Pippa came back with a large glass of water for me, and a glass of orange juice for herself.

'How are Ma and Dad?' she asked, a blush touching her cheeks.

'They're fine,' I replied. 'They're going to the caravan this afternoon. Spending a week or so there.'

Pippa nodded and picked at the designer rips in the knees of her jeans.

'I rang them, you know. To apologise.'

'I know,' I sighed. 'You shouldn't have needed to apologise, though, Pip. You shouldn't have taken the money in the first place.'

She opened her mouth to say something, and then closed it again, before giving a quick nod of her head.

'So,' I said, breaching the silence that I didn't have time for. 'Where's Jack?'

Pippa looked at me and frowned. 'Work, where do you think?'

'Hah, the work that should have been Roman's'

'Please don't start, Summer.'

I held my hands up. 'Okay, I'm sorry, I'll shut up. He's your choice, and we have to accept that, whether we like it or not. I came to see you, to check that you're okay, that's all.'

Pippa's shoulders relaxed as she moved back on the sofa, bringing her legs up.

'I'm fine, just a bit bored with Jack being at work getting ready for France.'

I bit back the sniping remark I wanted to make and nodded.

'I bet. So, when does he go?'

'Day after tomorrow.' Pippa sighed heavily and pouted. 'He's going to be gone for at least two weeks, initially, which is shit.'

Two days didn't give me much time to figure out what was going on. Once Jack was in France, I'd have little chance of proving he was still with Caroline.

'What are you going to do while he's gone?' I asked, my eyes skimming around the room — for what I had no idea.

Pippa shrugged. 'Don't know really. I won't even have a car, Jack's driving his van over there.'

'Pip, you can't stay here for two weeks without transport. You're at least five miles from the nearest shop.'

'Jack's going to take me shopping tomorrow, to get everything I need.' Pippa's eyes were focussed on her glass. She couldn't look at me because she knew I'd see in her face how unhappy she was about the situation.

'Why don't you just come home?' I said on a long breath. 'Just while he's away.'

She paused for a few seconds, as though she was thinking about it, and then shook her head.

'No, I'll be fine. It's only two weeks. I'll spend the time looking for a job.'

'Yes, about that. What did Mr. Devine say when you just upped and left?'

Pippa worked as a secretary for a local solicitor, and while her boss, Mr. Devine, was lovely, I'd no doubt he'd be annoyed at her leaving without notice.

'He wasn't happy,' she replied, a guilty blush touching her cheeks. 'He told me that he had been going to sponsor me towards becoming a paralegal. He was going to tell me at the end of the week.'

My mouth dropped open in a gasp.

'Pippa, you have to go back. That's a fantastic opportunity.'

'No,' she said, shaking her head. 'My life is here now. With Jack.'

'Jack and your designer shoes,' I muttered, slamming my glass down onto the coffee table with some force.

'Hey, what does that mean?' Pippa asked, her brow furrowing.

'All those bloody shoes you've bought. You obviously used Mum and Dad's money wisely.' I knew my tone was bitchy, but she damn well deserved it and more. I thought she was being let off lightly after what she'd done.

'I haven't bought any shoes,' she replied, her own tone hard and forceful. 'I gave all that money to Jack for some materials. I certainly haven't bought any *shoes*. You're the one that spends stupid money on that sort of thing, not me.'

'You gave *all* the money to Jack?' I asked, my eyes wide with disbelief. 'You really haven't bought anything?'

'No,' Pippa said with a pout. 'I just told you that.'

My heart thudded hard as I thought about the boxes of designer shoes upstairs. If they weren't Pippa's, then they had to be Caroline's.

'I need the loo,' I said, quickly getting to my feet.

'Okay, you know where it is.'

I nodded and rushed up the stairs.

Quietly I pushed open the door to the bedroom where I'd seen the shoes. They were still there, neatly piled up, all nine boxes of them.

I stared at them. I loved my shoes, and there would be no way that I would leave nine pairs of designer shoes with my ex-partner. Especially if I hated him as much as Caroline was supposed to hate Jack. I'd be scared he'd do something to them. Plus, if I was as hard up as she claimed to be, I'd put them on *eBay* and try and make myself some money. That way, I'd be able to put a roof over my daughter's head.

They were all neatly stacked too. What man would take the time to stack boxes of women's shoes? Especially if they belonged to an ex. And why had he brought them from his other house to this one? Why didn't he just dump them, or sell them? He evidently hadn't given them to Pippa, otherwise she'd have said so when I mentioned them to her downstairs, surely?

I moved over to the boxes and flipped one open. It was empty—so was the next one, and the next one. My heart sank: maybe he was selling them after all, and not keeping them for Caroline?

'Why isn't he selling them in the boxes then?' I whispered.

I looked around the room, but there was nothing that gave me any hint as to what was going on. I had no idea what I was looking for, anyway; I just knew something wasn't right. It also struck me that the clothes rails were now also empty.

Tiptoeing out of the room, I sneaked past what I assumed was the bathroom, and down a short corridor to another room: Pippa and Jack's bedroom. It was clean and tidy, unlike Pippa's room at home, where clothes were strewn everywhere; maybe Jack did have some positive influence on my sister.

I opened the wardrobe and looked inside, and apart from some of Pip's clothes that I recognised, it was half empty. Moving over to a chest of drawers, I searched them and found only women's underwear. So, unless Jack had some sort of fetish, all his stuff was gone. There were also two cabinets either side of the bed, one side was full of make-up, a hairdryer and straightening irons, while the other was empty.

Either Jack Abbott had never lived here, or he'd packed up an awful lot of stuff for two weeks in France.

Knowing that something strange was going on, I ran back down the stairs, and into the living room, where Pippa was still on the sofa, looking out of the window.

'I think we need to talk,' I said.

Pippa turned to me, and I saw then that she was crying.

CHAPTER 44

'Pippa,' I said, softly. 'Tell me what's wrong.'

'Oh Summer,' she cried, 'it's been awful. I've been here all alone, without any money, barely any food.'

'What the hell has Jack been doing?' I rushed to her side, dragging her into my arms. 'He's not been here,' she snivelled against my shoulder. 'He brought me here, made some excuse about going back to Rickeby to finalise some paperwork and never came back. He only came back yesterday to get his things.'

Her sniffs suddenly became full-on sobs, as she snuffled against my chest getting my top wet.

'Oh Pippa,' I said, soothingly. 'Why didn't you ring one of us, or tell me and Roman, or me now, when I first arrived?'

'I didn't know he wasn't coming back when you and Roman came around, and I'm just so embarrassed.'

She pulled away from me and wiped at her face with her hands.

'He said last night that he was sorry, and he'd make it up to me when he got back in two weeks.'

'But he left you here with no car or any money.'

'He said,' she replied with another sniff, 'that he'd left me some cash by the bed, said to use it on food and taxis, but it was only after he'd gone that I went up to check and there wasn't any.

277

That's when I saw he'd taken everything, all his clothes, everything. He's not coming back, is he?'

'The bastard!' I hissed. 'I take it you were telling the truth when you said you'd given him all of the three grand?'

Pippa nodded, and started to cry again.

'I feel such an idiot, Summer. It's not as though the sex was that good.'

I wrapped Pippa in my arms again and slowly rocked her until the tears subsided.

'Okay,' I said finally. 'Let's get your stuff together and get you out of here.'

'Ma and Dad are going to go beserk, aren't they?' she asked with trepidation.

'Probably not,' I sighed. 'They'll just be glad you've come home, but please don't do anything so stupid in future.'

'I won't, don't worry. I'm off men for a while.'

I gave a little laugh and shook my head; unlikely if I knew my sister.

'What do I do about this place?' Pippa asked, as she started to gather up a few of her things that were dotted around the room. 'I think he rented it in my name.'

'Yeah, probably,' I said, snarkily. 'Don't worry, I'll ask Roman to sort it.'

Then tears pricked at my lashes. I couldn't ask Roman as he wasn't speaking to me. Before I could think anymore about it, Pippa dragged me into a tight hug.

'You're the best sister ever, you know that don't you?'

'Whatever, but just remember that next time I want to borrow your *MAC* lipstick. Anyway, let me call the 'rents and tell them that you're coming home.'

'You won't be able to here, there's no damn signal,' Pippa complained, pulling away from me. 'To be honest, I'd rather you didn't just yet. Let them enjoy the rest of their holiday.'

'I won't call them today, but tomorrow I will.'

Pippa opened her mouth to speak.

'No, Pip, they've been worried enough.'

She nodded and left the room to pack her things.

I fished my phone out of my pocket, and considered sending them a text, but Pippa was right, there was no signal. With a sigh, I put it back in my pocket and went to help Pip.

***

'God,' Pippa groaned, as we pulled into the drive of our family home. 'How many alerts did you have? You should have let me just answer the damn thing for you.'

She was right: my phone had been going off with voicemail alerts, texts and unanswered calls since we'd hit a signal spot a few miles away from the cottage, and I'd not had it connected to my hands-free.

'You go in and I'll check who it is.' I guessed it was possibly the office. Stupidly, I hadn't called in that morning, and with Roman on-site, they were all probably wondering where we were.

I looked down at my phone and saw messages from Emma and—unbelievably—Roman. With my heart beating faster than was probably healthy, I bypassed Emma's five messages and went straight to the first of Roman's *seven*:

Grumpy: Can we talk?

Grumpy: Take it your lack of response means no. I'm sorry for storming out but felt hurt.

Grumpy: You can't ignore me forever xx

Grumpy: Now I'm getting pissed off. Answer your phone. I've said I'm sorry xx

Grumpy: I missed you last night, it was shit – I stayed with Mum & Dad shows how lonely I was without you. I love you so much and am sorry for being a dick, now stop being damn precious and answer your phone xx

I smiled at that one. How could one man be so sweet and yet so grouchy in one text?

Grumpy: Seriously, baby, I'm getting worried now. I rang Emma and she said you're following Jack Abbott!! WTF!

Grumpy: Summer, please let me know that you're okay. I'm scared shitless here that something has happened. If he's hurt you in any way, I'll fucking end him xx

I saw that there were also eleven missed calls from him, so, without hesitation, I pressed the call button.

'Summer,' he answered breathlessly. 'Oh God, baby, are you okay?'

'I'm sorry,' I replied, unable to stop stupid tears from falling. 'I do trust you and I love you, and I know you wouldn't hurt Alfie.'

'Forget about that, I should have told you about the fight.' His voice had a tremor in it: a mixture of relief and love. 'Just tell me that you're okay, and that he hasn't hurt you.'

'Roman,' I said on a quiet sob, 'I'm fine, honestly. I didn't even see him.'

'Oh shit, thank God.' He breathed heavily, and I heard a muttered curse. 'Where've you been, then?'

'With Pippa,' I replied. 'He conned her Roman, took the money from her, and then left her at that cottage alone. She's had barely enough food to eat, and no car, or money, but was too embarrassed to call us.'

'Fucker!'

'I know, but she's home now. She's just worried that he's rented the house in her name.'

'Tell her not to worry,' he said, quickly. 'I'll sort that out for her.'

My heart doubled in size, because I knew he would help, and I hadn't had to ask.

'There's something else,' I chewed on my bottom lip, hoping that I hadn't got this wrong. 'I think Jack and Caroline are still together. I don't think they've ever been apart.'

There was silence for a couple of seconds, and I expected Roman to scoff and tell me that I was being paranoid, or even just plain bitchy.

'What makes you think that?' he asked.

I told him about the kiss and the shoes.

'You could be right, because, as far as I know, you don't go around kissing your ex if you hate them. As for the shoe thing, well.' He paused and laughed. 'I have no fucking clue how her shoes being neatly stacked in boxes proves that they're together, but, hey, you're Miss Marple, not me.'

I smiled widely and let out a huge breath of relief. He didn't hate me and he was laughing.

'I'll explain it to you one day,' I replied with a giggle.

'Yeah, I think you'll need to. One thing that Caroline is going to need to explain is why the fuck she let that little shit into my house. Whether they're together or not, she knows how I feel about that little wank-stain.'

'Roman!' I chastised.

'Well, he is. Anyway, less about them, where are you now?'

'Just dropped Pip off at home, why?'

He took in a breath and I could hear the emotion shuddering through his lungs.

'I need to see you; I've been so worried about you. Would you meet me at my house, just so I can see that you're okay?'

God, I loved this man. 'Yes, baby, I will,' I whispered.

'Okay, I'll see you there in ten minutes, I'll leave the site now.'

As we ended the call, a huge weight lifted from me, and the lightness of being loved by Roman made my smile huge.

CHAPTER 45

My car had only just come to a standstill, when I flung the door open and shot out of it, running towards Roman, who was pacing up and down his drive, obviously waiting for me.

'Shit, I'm so sorry,' he said, kissing me hard on the lips. 'I shouldn't have stormed out.'

'It's okay, I'm sorry too. I shouldn't have accused you.'

Roman shook his head. 'No, it was a natural thing to think. You know I don't like Alfie, I looked like I'd been fighting, so I totally get it.'

He laced his fingers through my hair and changed the kiss to a slow, deep one, making me whimper with desire.

'Fuck, I missed you,' he whispered against my ear, wrapping his arms around me and hugging me tightly to his chest.

'What the hell were you thinking, going after Jack Abbott like that?' he asked.

'I just wanted to see whether I could find out anything. Emma is watching Caroline today, so— Oh shit,' I cried, pulling away from Roman, 'Emma has been calling me too.'

'What do you mean she's watching Caroline?'

I waved him away as my phone rang out against my ear. Finally, Emma answered.

'Em, I'm so sorry, there was no reception at the cottage where

Pippa was. I saw your messages, but it totally went out of my head to call you back.'

'It's okay,' she replied, sounding a little breathless. 'Did Roman get hold of you?'

'Yes,' I said, grinning. 'I'm with him now.'

'Oh that's why you forgot to call me back,' Emma giggled.

'Yeah, but I am sorry. So, what's happening?'

'I watched her all morning and she just pottered around town. She bought a few things, picked up some dry cleaning and then went for a coffee.'

'And that's it?' I asked, dejected that I'd been wrong.

'No!' Emma exclaimed.

'No!'

'No!'

'What's going on?' Roman asked.

'Emma saw something.'

'Yes, I did,' Emma said proudly. 'So, she went for coffee, and then, ten minutes later, was joined by Jack Abbott.'

'No way?'

'Yep. I managed to get a table a little bit away from them, but I could see everything.'

'Did they see you?' I asked.

'No, they were too wrapped up in each other. Holding hands and kissing, it was a bit gross to be honest,' she replied with a tone of disgust. 'He left before her, so I carried on following her. She picked up the little girl from nursery and then dropped her off at a bungalow.'

'She's taken Maisie to a bungalow,' I relayed to Roman. 'Could that be her parents' place? Didn't you say they lived in a bunga-low.'

'Yeah, could be,' Roman said with a shrug.

'What then, Em?'

'Well, then she went back to Roman's house. I waited just down the street, because I had a feeling that she was going to leave again.'

'And?' I asked, almost jumping up and down on the spot.

'She did. She put three suitcases into her car and about four or five boxes and drove away. I'm following her now—she's parking in the retail park just outside town.'

'Oh my God, we'll come to you.' I glanced at Roman who shrugged and shook his head, clearly wanting an explanation.

'Shit, she's got out of the car and is going towards the travel agents. And Jack is waiting is here too, he's by the door.'

'Emma, stay in your car.' Then something struck me. 'You are on hands-free, aren't you?'

'No,' she snapped, 'Henry is driving. Say hi, Henry.'

'Hi,' Henry shouted.

'Will someone tell me what the fuck is going on?' Roman asked, exasperated.

'It's fine,' I sighed. 'Emma and Henry have them in their sights.'

'Who? And why hell isn't Henry taking the mixer delivery at the club?'

'Henry, why aren't you taking the mixer delivery at the club,' Emma asked, hearing Roman's loud bawl over the line.

'Because I'm playing *Dukes of Hazzard* with you.'

'Because—'

'Yeah, I heard,' I giggled. Then something struck me. 'Oh shit!'

'What?' Emma asked.

'When we moved her in here, she had a couple of boxes and one suitcase.'

I turned to Roman who was trying to listen in to our conversation.

'Get inside quickly,' I said, pointing at the door.

'What's wrong?' he asked, striding towards the door, with his key in his hand.

'I think Caroline might have taken some of your stuff.'

'Oh no,' Emma cried, 'you think?'

'Maybe,' I replied, 'but, Em, you need to keep them there somehow. Just until we get there, okay?'

'Roger and out.'

The line went dead as I heard a roar and crashing from inside the house. I rushed in to see what was wrong.

'Roman?'

He stormed into the hallway from his study.

'The fucking bitch! She's taken my laptop and she found the safe.'

'Safe?' I enquired, 'I didn't know you had a safe?'

'Yeah,' he said with flaring nostrils, 'a safe that *did* have ten grand in it.'

'Oh my God, how the hell did she find it and get into it?'

Roman held up wire with what looked like a pen on the end of it.

'This maybe?' He held it towards me.

'What is it?' I took it from Roman and, at the same time, we both said: 'A camera'.

'How did you find it?' I asked.

Roman shook his head and his cheeks pinked. 'I might have had an epic temper tantrum in there. Let's just say my books are no longer in alphabetical order.'

'Oh God.' I laid a hand on his shoulder and frowned. 'You put your books in alphabetical order? You weirdo.'

CHAPTER 46

'I'll fucking kill them,' Roman snarled as he manvouevered through the traffic. 'Just give me one damn pop at him, and he won't know what's hit him. Forget not wanting to hurt another man with a punch—he's getting one of my best.'

I laid my hand on his knee, hoping that it would calm him down, but he was too far gone to even realise it was there. I could have got my boobs out and wiggled them in his face, and I don't think he would have seen them through the red mist.

As we screeched into the retail park, my eyes searched for Emma's car. I had to giggle wondering how she'd remained incognito in a pink *Fiat 500*. Then I had to wonder how the hell the six-feet tall Henry had managed to get behind the wheel: he was probably driving from the back seat!

'There they are,' I screamed, making Roman jump.

'For fuck's sake, Summer. You just burst my eardrum.'

'Sorry,' I whispered. 'There they are.'

He turned to me and grinned. 'God, I fucking love you.' I grinned back and gave him a coy smile.

When we parked up a few cars and a row down from Emma, Roman stopped me from getting out of the car.

'I want you and Emma to stay in the car, okay?'

'No, not okay,' I replied, crossing my arms, 'he's made a fool of my sister.'

'I mean it, Summer. I don't want you getting hurt if things get nasty.' His voice was a deep, sexy, growl, and if this was a different time and place, I'd have jumped him.

'Well, things won't get nasty,' I replied. 'They can't, I don't want you to get into trouble for hurting him.'

Roman looked at me for a second, then he put a hand behind my head, pulled me to him, and gave me a searing hot kiss.

'Like I said,' he whispered against my lips, 'I fucking love you.'

'Okay,' I whispered back, and opened the door, surreptitiously fanning myself.

'Hey,' Roman said by way of a greeting to Emma and Henry. 'What's happening?'

Henry shook his head and raised his eyebrows.

'*Daisy Duke* here has let all their tyres down.'

'Good thinking,' I said, high-fiving Emma.

'Yeah, but she wasn't sure which white van was Jack's,' Henry replied, glancing sideways at Emma. 'So she's let them down on all three white vans that are parked here.'

Roman groaned and pinched the bridge of his nose.

'And you couldn't stop her?' he asked Henry.

'Have you tried stopping Summer when she's adamant about something?' he cried. 'Emma just bats those damn eyelashes at me, and I can't deny her anything.'

I high-fived Emma again. 'I offer blow jobs,' I whispered conspiratorily.

Roman looked at me and shook his head. 'Okay, I think we need to call the police, and let them deal with it.'

'Yeah, me too,' Henry agreed.

Emma and I both moaned, but I knew that Roman was right. I didn't want him to throw any punches, and hopefully the police being here would stop that.

He tapped out a number on his phone and, smiling at me, waited for a reply. He told the dispatcher that he thought someone had stolen from him and that they were in a restaurant, but the dispatcher didn't seemed to think it warranted a squad car.

'But I know she's taken ten grand of my money,' Roman barked down the phone, 'I found a camera.'

He sighed heavily and walked towards his truck. The phone still at his ear, he pulled out a hammer from his tool box in the covered flatbed and walked over to Caroline's car.

'So, you won't send anyone?' he asked, pausing for the reply. 'Okay, well, I think you should know that I've just smashed the window on her car and am about to punch her partner.'

He ended the call, put his phone in his pocket, and smashed the windscreen of Caroline's car.

Emma and I gasped, and Henry bent over, resting his hands on his knees and shaking his head.

'Bloody hell, Ro,' he moaned.

'Well, maybe they'll send someone now. When they get here, I'll make them search her car, and I bet the damn money and my laptop, and whatever else she's nicked, are in there.'

A couple of minutes later, Jack came storming out of the travel agents, his face dark and angry as he spotted all of us around Caroline's car.

'What the fuck do you think you're doing?' He stopped in front of Roman and stared at him. His jaw was tight and I was scared that he'd be the one to throw the first punch—then Roman would be bound to fight back.

I wasn't scared that he'd hurt Roman, rather, the other way around. Roman was a boxer, he knew how to punch. I just hoped that boxers knew how to punch *not* to hurt someone too.

'I want my property back,' Roman said, moving toe to toe with Jack.

'Have no idea what you're talking about,' Abbott replied, with a scoffing tone. 'Now, I think you owe me for a new windscreen, don't you, Hepburn?'

'Why do I owe you?' Roman asked, narrowing his eyes. 'I thought that this was Caroline's car, and that you two were no longer together. Aren't you with Pippa now?'

Jack's sneer disappeared as he glanced at me and then back to

Roman.

'Yeah, we know all about you stringing her along. What was that for anyway?' Roman poked him in the chest. 'Just for kicks?'

Jack took a half pace back, and I grabbed the back pocket of Roman's jeans, trying to stop him from advancing on Jack.

'Well? Why do it, Jack?'

'I don't have to answer to you,' Jack replied and looked towards Supabreaks Travel, where Caroline was now hovering in the doorway.

Roman followed his gaze and glared. 'You!' he shouted to her. 'Get over here and give me my property back. Now.'

Caroline hesitated and then walked over to us. She was wearing the *Manolo Blahnik* loafers that I'd seen in the box at the cottage.

'I don't have anything of yours,' she said, standing behind Jack. 'I don't know what's wrong with you? You're crazy.'

'No,' Roman said. 'The only crazy thing about me is ever helping you. Now where's my money and my laptop?'

Caroline looked at him and lifted her chin defiantly.

'Don't have it, so you've just caused criminal damage for no reason.'

'Don't lie, you bitch,' I spat out.

I couldn't help it, even though I knew I should have kept quiet.

'I'm sorry,' Caroline said, shaking her head dismissively, 'and it has what to do with you?'

'She's my girlfriend,' Roman answered. 'So it has plenty to do with Summer.'

'Plus, you've both been taking my sister for a ride. Why was that, by the way?'

Jack and Caroline glanced at each other, and then turned back to us. Caroline swallowed, and I could see the jealousy flash across her face.

'You weren't too happy about that part of the plan I take it?' I said. 'Your partner sleeping with my sister. For what I'm not really sure; its not as if she knew anything of importance.'

Caroline looked at Jack, her eyes wide and her mouth slightly open. Jack shifted under her gaze and turned to Roman.

'Caro' is right, you're crazy and you owe us to repair her car.'

Emma sidled up beside me and whispered into my ear. 'She was a bit shocked about Pippa, wasn't she?'

I gave Emma a quick nod and turned back to Caroline.

'Didn't he tell you that Pippa hadn't given him any information,' I said, moving forwards a step. 'She didn't know anything. I'm not sure where he got the details about the Cromwell job, but it wasn't Pippa.'

Caroline swung to face Jack, and pulled on his shoulder. 'You said she was the one who told you all the figures, and the combination to the safe. What the—'

'Shut up, Caro',' Jack said in a low tone, his eyes flashing with anger.

'No!' she cried, pushing against his chest. 'You said it was all just to get the details we needed. And you swore to me you hadn't slept with her, you bastard!'

'Sorry to burst your bubble on that one,' I interjected, 'but according to my sister, he wasn't even that good.'

Jack turned to face me, his nostrils flaring and his hands fisted. 'You fucking bitch—'

He took a step forward, and I felt Roman move at the side of me.

'Ro, no!' Henry caught hold of his arm. 'He's not worth an assault charge.'

'You fucking talk to her again, or even attempt to touch her, and I'll kill you.' Roman's tone was low and menacing, and Jack Abbott flinched visibly.

At that moment, a police car pulled up alongside of us, and two officers got out.

'Okay, everyone, what's going on?' A tall, grey-haired officer asked.

'She has property of mine, which may be in her car,' Roman explained, never taking his eyes off Jack.

'He smashed my partner's car windscreen.'

'Jack, tell me how you got the damn details, if it wasn't from her sister?' Caroline demanded angrily.

'Can we all just calm down,' the second police officer, a younger, blonde-haired man, said. He turned to Roman. 'Sir, did you smash this windscreen.'

Roman nodded. 'Yes, to get you here, because otherwise they'd have got away with my money and my laptop.'

'Do you have any proof they have your property, sir?'

Roman shoved a hand into his pocket and pulled out the pen camera. 'This was hidden in my study where my safe is; I'm assuming that's how they found out the code number.'

'You told me that girl gave it to you!' Caroline practically screamed. 'You said a few glasses of wine and she was telling you anything you wanted to know. You damn liar!'

'Miss, please calm down,' the younger officer said softly. 'Are these acusations true, sir?'

'Of course not,' Jack snapped. 'Caroline, just shut the fuck up.'

'Hey.' The grey-haired officer put up a hand. 'I suggest you don't speak to the lady like that.'

'How did you get the information?' Roman asked. 'If it wasn't Pip who told you about the Cromwell deal, and how much I was paying my gang, so you could poach them from me, then who was it?'

'Yes, Jack,' Caroline said, tears now rolling down her cheeks. 'Who the hell did give you the information? Was it that idiot, Alfie Chambers?'

CHAPTER 47

Roman cursed, and I gasped at Caroline's mention of Alfie, as we both looked at each other and came to the same conclusion.

'Roman,' I whispered.

Roman grabbed my hand and gave it a squeeze.

'Let him hang himself, baby,' he said quietly.

Jack turned to Caroline and took a deep breath. 'I don't know what Alfie has to do with all of this. I did what I did for us. For you, because you damn well wanted him to pay for what he did to your precious Michael. You were supposed to move in and find out about the rest of his deals, but you couldn't manage it, so I thought of the fucking camera.'

At the mention of Michael's name, I heard a noise come from Roman, and his body tensed up next to mine. Caroline looked at him and her eyes went cold.

'All this because of an accident,' I said quietly.

'He was my life,' she replied on a sob. 'And *he* took him away from me.'

I looked up at Roman, and there were tears in his eyes. He'd punished himself enough, and now Caroline was doing it all over again. I knew she must be in pain with her grief, but Roman didn't deserve any retribution for what had happened in the ring.

'You selfish bitch," I snapped. 'How dare you blame all this on

Roman and what happened to Michael!"

Caroline's eyes widened. 'What the hell has it got to do with you? You didn't even know Michael.'

'No I didn't, but I'm sure if he was half the man I think he was, he'd be disgusted with you. It was an accident. He knew the risks.' I took a step closer to Caroline, pointing my finger at her. 'How could you do this to Roman, knowing how he's hated himself for what happened?. In fact how could you do it to Maisie?'

'What the hell does my daughter have to do with it?' .

'She has everything to do with it.' I cried, swallowing around the lump of emotion brought on by the thought of Maisie having such awful parents.

'You are so lucky to have her, yet you've been so blinded by bitterness and the need to get at Roman that you've not even considered what effect all this will have on her. '

'You know nothing,' Caroline scoffed.

'I know your twisted plan took her away from the only father she's known, simply to feed your own twisted sense of justice. To be honest, as parents, you're both shit.'

Caroline's gaze followed mine to Jack.

'Poor Maisie, having you two as role models. What the hell would Michael think?'

Caroline's bottom lip trembled as she stared at me and guilt shadowed her face. The mention of Michael had tipped her over the edge.

'This is all your fault,' she screamed, at Jack. 'You promised me that we'd be away and free. That he'd never know we took the money. You made me take the laptop and the other stuff to make it look like a burglary. He made me do it, Roman. I swear.'

Roman stiffened at my side. 'What else did you take?' he demanded.

'Shut up!' Jack snarled. 'You're lying to save your own skin. She's lying.'

His cheeks were pinking, and you didn't need a body-language expert to tell you that he was the one who was lying.

'I think we perhaps need to take this down to the station,' the older officer said, 'and get things cleared up.'

'I'm not going,' Jack said, shaking his head vehemently. 'You've got nothing on me.'

He was clearly rattled, and started to back away from us. The young officer moved to stand behind him, gently placing a hand on the small of his back.

'I think you should come with us, sir,' he said.

'No, no way.'

Caroline was sobbing now, as she and Jack started berating and pointing at each other.

'Ask him about Alfie,' Roman said just loud enough for everyone to hear. 'Go on.'

'We'll talk about everything down at the station, sir.'

'Please just ask him about the near beating to death of Alfie Chambers. Go on.' Roman's voice was hard and adamant.

The older policeman studied Roman, and then started to talk on his radio, while the younger one kept a hand on Jack's shoulder.

Jack struggled against his touch, but the policeman's grip tightened; with his other hand he gripped Jack's arm and pulled it behind his back.

'Get off me,' Jack shouted, attracting a few passers-by.

'Okay, roger that,' the older officer said into the radio. 'Sir, we'd like you to come down to the station with us. Voluntarily, if possible.' He indicated towards Jack. 'Get him cuffed, and we'll take him down to the station.' The younger man nodded in response.

'You can't take me,' Jack cried. 'You have no damn proof. We're booked on a ferry tonight for France.'

'What did you do to Alfie?' Roman asked, his jaw twitching. 'Tell us, Jack.'

'Yes, tell them all about how you paid Alfie Chambers, Jack,' Caroline added bitterly.

Jack looked at her and then the police officers and his shoulders dropped in defeat.

'He's a fucking idiot.'

I thought he was talking about Roman, but then he spat everything out.

'He got me the information I wanted. Stroke of luck that *she*,' he pointed a finger at me, 'was typing up the quote when he went in to see her. He said she made it so easy, leaving him alone in the office.'

My heart sank as I remembered that day. It had been my fault after all. Sensing my guilt, Roman kissed the top of my head, and wrapped his arm around me.

Jack, in the meantime, continued to rant.

'But Alfie got damn greedy; he wanted more money from me, otherwise he'd tell *him* what he'd done. I gave him three grand, but he wanted more—'

'My mum and dad's money!' I gasped.

'Ooh you horrible man,' Emma hissed.

'Yeah, your sister was good for one thing at least,' Jack snarled. 'I needed that damn job, I couldn't let Hepburn get it back. Have you tried keeping a woman like Caroline in fucking shoes.'

'Okay, let's go.'

The next thing Jack was being read his rights, had handcuffs on his wrists and was being led to the squad car by the older officer. The younger one stayed and read Caroline her rights before guiding her towards the squad car.

'This is not my fault.' Caroline shouted, trying to drag herself away from the officer's grip. 'I told you it was all Jack. He made me do it. I'm not going anywhere. I need to see Maisie."

'Pity you didn't think of that before,' I said.

Caroline looked at me and her resolve disappeared as she started to cry.

'But my daughter is with my parents,' she pleaded. 'Please let me go home to tell them, and to ask my dad to get me a solicitor. I'm begging you.'

'You'll get your phone call, don't worry,' the officer replied, leading Caroline away.

Roman turned away from her and shook his head. 'Well, at

least it means that poor Maisie has someone she can rely on; they're really good people.'

'Sir.'

The young policeman returned after putting Caroline in the back of the car with Jack. 'I think you'd better come down to the station too, sir. We need a statement from you about the damage you've caused.'

'He hasn't done anything wrong,' I protested.

'Summer, it's fine. I'm happy to go.' Roman turned to the officer. 'When can I get my money and stuff back?'

'We've got a tow truck coming for the car. It'll be searched as soon as the detectives get here,' he replied. 'We'll look after it until then, but as I said we'd like to see you down at the station.'

Roman agreed before leading me to his truck, with Emma and Henry close behind us.

'Thanks, you two,' Roman said, slapping a hand on Henry's back, and then hugging Emma.

'Oh I thoroughly enjoyed myself. We should do this more often, Henry.'

Henry led Emma back to her car, laughing all the way.

As Roman went to move, I took his hand, pulling him to me. 'Are you okay?'

'Yeah, I'm fine. I wanted to kill him when he made a move towards you, but I'm okay.'

Roman stooped down and kissed me gently.

CHAPTER 48

It was almost a month after the nightmare with Caroline and Jack, and Roman and I were sitting in his lounge with both sets of our parents and siblings. We were finally getting back to some normality: if having both families around for drinks and food at Roman's house could be called normality. Nevertheless, things were good

Once Jack Abbott had been questioned, he told the police everything, or to use the criminal vernacular, he'd 'sung like a canary'.

As his own business had been failing, he'd paid Alfie to get him information on the Cromwell job: our conversation in the pub alerting him to it and giving him the idea. Apparently, he and Alfie drank in the same pub, and realised that they both knew Roman. Alfie, always out for some easy money, had been more than happy to take Jack up on the offer. It was then that Caroline came up with the idea of being evicted and moving in with Roman. Apparently, their break-up wasn't real, but they'd come up with the plan to pretend they had, so that they could swindle Roman.

Unfortunately for Pippa, Jack conveniently forgot that that fact.

What made me even madder was the little thought Caroline had given to Maisie, separating her from the only father she'd

297

ever known, even if he was a shit.

Moving in with Roman was supposed to give Caroline the chance to find out anything they could use to steal jobs from him. Her main aim: to ruin the man who'd killed the love of her life. When she hadn't managed that, Jack planted the video camera in Roman's study and got the bonus of seeing Roman use the safe.

On the same day that Alfie managed to get the information Jack needed, we bumped into Jack at Ziggy's. That was when he decided to make the play for Pippa. He told Caroline it was to get information, not letting on that he already had what he needed. According to Caroline's statement, Jack said he was simply taking her out and getting her drunk, getting little pieces of information each time.

As if my sister would be privy to Roman's business details, or moreover his safe combination. Personally, I felt that for someone who had the brains to know a damn good shoe when she saw one, Caroline was a little stupid to believe that Jack Abbott was merely taking my sister on dates.

Also, in her statement to the police, Caroline said that she had no idea that Pippa had left home to live with Jack. To be fair to Jack, he hadn't asked her to, Pippa just decided. That was why he moved them out to the cottage, so that Caroline wouldn't find out. Lies within lies.

As for Alfie, well, he was still in a bad way from being beaten up by a thug that Jack had hired. He was now conscious and still in hospital, but was going to be all right, albeit missing a couple of teeth and having a crack in his skull.

This family get-together should have been a happy occasion: Roman hadn't been charged with any criminal damage and all the money and items stolen by the 'Gruesome Twosome' had been recovered. However, if I could wrench my own teeth out with pliers, I would have felt more relaxed.

On the surface everyone was getting along fairly well, but I could see lots of different scenarios playing out. Every time Pete called Twinkle 'Twinkle', my mum gave a girlish giggle. Dad kept throwing sly glances at Roman—Roman was having sex with his daughter and that's what dads did. Pete kept making dirty jokes that had Pippa snorting with laughter and Roman groaning with despair.

Finally, my brother, Dylan, was also getting right on my knockers with the cheeky innuendos that he kept throwing Tiffany's way. Tiffany was not in the slightest way interested in my brother, which, in turn, was stressing him out, but slightly improving my mood.

'Is she a lesbian?' Dylan had whispered to me in all seriousness.

I didn't even deign to give the egotistical idiot an answer. It was a surprise, though, that she wasn't affected by him, as most women were. Even Twinkle giggled coquettishly every time he looked at her. Then again, Twinkle wasn't most women.

'You're a dick, you know that,' I hissed out of the corner of my mouth to Dylan. He'd just winked at Tiffany and huffed when she simply smiled back and then carried on her conversation with Pippa about the best bits of *Magic Mike*: namely Channing Tatum, which I wholeheartedly agreed with.

Giving Roman a smile, I pushed up from the sofa to go and check on dinner. I was cooking, which was a little scary seeing as I rarely cooked. I lived at home with my mother, why would I ever cook? So I'd opted for something easy which Roman had loved when I'd made it once before: chicken curry.

'You okay?' Roman asked, catching hold of my hand.

'Yeah, just going to check on the curry.' I leaned down and dropped a kiss on his lips.

'Need any help?'

'No, you stay here. I'll only be a minute.'

I went into the kitchen and moved to the cooker hob to check on the food. Lifting the lid of the huge stainless steel pot, I gave it a stir, and inhaled the gorgeous aroma of garlic and spices.

'Can I do anything?' Tiffany's voice came from behind me.

I looked over my shoulder at her. 'No, everything is under control.'

I flashed her a smile. We'd started to get closer, and I'd really grown to care a lot about her, especially because I knew how much she loved her brother; something that we had in common.

'So,' Tiff said, sidling up to me. 'Your brother?'

'Ugh,' I groaned. 'I'm so sorry about him and his ego. He actually asked me if you were gay because you weren't interested in him. He's not used to it.'

'I'm not surprised,' Tiff gasped. 'He's bloody gorgeous. He looks just like a lighter-haired Micah Truitt, *and* he saves animals.'

The disappointment that Tiffany had been hypnotised by my brother hit me like a train.

'Not you too?' I moaned, banging my forehead against the extractor-fan hood. 'Tiiiiffff, no.'

'What?' she laughed. 'He's really hot.'

'But not *you*, I thought that *you* were immune to him. Please don't tell him, it's so much more fun that he thinks you don't fancy him.'

Tiffany looked horrified. 'Oh my God, no way would I let on. No matter how fit he is, I would not go there. I know he's your brother, Summer, but I get the impression he's only into one-night stands, and that's not what I want.'

I breathed a sigh of relief. 'Thank the Lord above for that.' The thought of getting caught in the after-burn of a hook-up between Dylan and Tiffany was not something I would relish. 'Do me a favour though, Tiff.'

'Yeah, what's that?' she asked opening the fridge for another bottle of wine.

'Please, please, please, ignore him as much as possible. He needs bringing down a notch or two, and you not falling for his charms would do that perfectly.'

'Consider it done.' Tiffany grinned at me. 'This is going to be so much fun.'

Dinner had gone surprisingly well, with Pete and Dad having thirds—thank God I'd made enough to feed half the town. My mum had even suggested that I make it at home one evening, to give her a night off from cooking. Roman sat with an arm around me, his thumb gently rubbing circles on my shoulder as he gazed at me proudly. Everyone thought that my blushes were because of the praise that they were all heaping on me, but it was actually because Roman's touch was starting a fire in the pit of my stomach.

'Well, now you know she can cook, son,' Pete said taking a bite of a poppadum, 'maybe you should think about marrying her.'

I gasped and quickly looked at Roman. This was not the conversation that I wanted to have. Not now, not here. Yes, I wanted to believe that someday we'd get married, have a future together, but I didn't want Roman to feel pressurised into saying something that he didn't want to.

'Oh Pete,' Twinkle said, 'shut up and leave them alone.'

'Says you, who keeps telling me she's his destiny.'

'Dad,' Roman said, getting his father's attention, 'shut up, hey?'

Roman's face was hard as he stared at his dad, daring him to speak. It was blatantly obvious that marriage to me was definitely not in his life plan.

I forced out a laugh, and stood to collect the empty plates.

'I take it everyone wants dessert?' I asked and left the dining room.

Once I was in the kitchen, I let out a long breath and cursed Pete for ruining my fantasy.

'Summer.'

I heard the door click shut and then felt Roman's arms wrap around my upper body before he dragged me back against his hard chest.

'I'm so sorry,' he whispered against my ear. 'My dad is an absolute space cadet. He's totally unaware of other people's feelings at times.'

'It's fine,' I said, trying to sound light. 'He was only joking.'

I laid my head back against Roman's shoulder and grabbed hold of his arms as they enveloped me. The comfort that being in his embrace brought to me was like nothing I'd ever experienced before. I hadn't even felt this safe and loved as a child when my parents had held me. At the time, I had never thought that anyone would mean as much to me as my mum and dad did, no one would ever be that important. But Roman was: he was my world.

'He still shouldn't be saying those sort of things. Joke or not,' Roman replied. 'Something like that is between us. As if I'd discuss it with him, in front of everyone, anyway.'

'Don't be mad at him.' I turned in Roman's arms and snaked my arms around his waist. 'He was just being your dad.'

'Yeah, a total dick.'

Roman brushed hair away from my forehead and studied my face for a few seconds.

'I love you so fucking much,' he finally said on a shaky breath. 'You've totally changed my life, and I can't imagine one moment without you in it. The thought of you not being here petrifies me. Life would be dark and drab without you.'

'Oh Roman,' I whimpered and sucked back the tears of emotion that were threatening. 'You don't ever have to think about it, because it's never going to happen. You're stuck with me.'

'You swear?' he asked earnestly. 'You promise that you're not going to get some ridiculous notion into your head that I should be with someone else?'

I knew what he was getting at, and I thought back to the night in the club, when I'd tried to end things. I knew that night that I really cared about Roman, but it was only a fraction of what I felt now. The thought that he could have agreed made nausea roll deep in the pit of my stomach.

'I know the children thing is going to be hard and heartbreaking, but I wouldn't want anyone else holding my hand while I go through all of that,' I replied. 'I know you're my future and, as long as you want me, I'm yours.'

'That'll be forever then,' he said.

My heart stuttered and a rush of excitement filled me as Roman stared down at me, his eyes full of love.

'Just because I told my dad to shut up, it doesn't mean that I don't agree with him about marrying you one day.'

'Really?' I asked around the ball of emotion in my throat.

Roman nodded. 'You're my life. You're the one I want to fulfil my dreams with; the one I want to wake up to every day for the rest of my life. The one I want to laugh with and the one I want to cry with. So whatever life brings us, we're doing it together, okay?'

Roman's eyes were bright as he looked down at me with a heart-stopping smile. His love was evident, and we would get through whatever life threw at us, just as he'd said — together.

'Deal,' I said and stuck out my hand. 'But, beware, once we shake on it there's no going back.'

'Of course, that's a given,' he laughed and shook my hand.

As we hugged, a small knock sounded on the door.

'Ro.' It was Tiffany. 'Sorry to interrupt you, but Doolittle has been sick in the hall. I think Dad gave him lime pickle chutney.'

Roman sighed, looked up at the ceiling and then cursed under his breath.

'Okay, Tiff. We'll be one minute.'

***

'Well, the bloody trouble you get yourself into,' Twinkle said as she handed Roman a cup of the coffee I'd just made. 'I never have any trouble with Tiffy, it's always you.'

Roman grinned at me over the rim of his mug and collapsed back into the sofa.

We'd finished our meal and were now all back in the lounge, everyone listening to Roman telling them about the bare-knuckle fight that he almost took part in.

'Well, at least you got that contract back, Roman,' my dad said.

'Yeah, and at twice the price now.' Roman grinned. Alan Cromwell had been so desperate for Roman to take the job back, once Jack was arrested, that Roman had had no qualms about upping the price. He'd got The Palisades *almost* back on schedule too, so things were a lot easier business-wise.

'Poor Summer,' Twinkle sighed, 'she must be wondering why on earth she got herself caught up with you.'

'That'll be because of my huge penis and bedroom skills,' Roman whispered so only I could hear.

I slapped at his arm and leaned into him, kissing his bicep. The same arm came up and hooked around my neck and started to tickle my neck. I wriggled and giggled, causing Doolittle to start barking and jumping up, wanting to join in the fun.

'Doolittle,' Roman commanded, 'be quiet.'

Doolittle stopped, stared at Roman, and I'll swear he smiled, and then started again.

'Doolittle,' Pete bellowed. 'Shut the fuck up, you little fucker!'

'Oh,' Mum gasped.

'Dad,' Roman groaned.

'Well, he is a little fucker,' Pete complained.

'Peter Holliday, you foul-mouthed little man. How many times do I have to tell you to watch your language?'

'Probably every day for the rest of our lives, Twink. If I'm being honest.'

'Women, hey, Pete,' my dad said, earning a nudge from my mum. 'What? Oh damn it, I've spilled my coffee now.'

He jumped up, pulled a hanky from his pocket and started to dab at the front of his trousers. Suddenly, Doolittle jumped up at my dad and started to lick the crotch.

'Oh fuck me,' Roman muttered under his breath. 'Someone help me, please.'

I looked around and simply laughed from the pit of my belly. Who cared that a scruffy dog was attracted to my dad's groin, or that Pete had a foul mouth, or that my mum looked like she'd eaten a lemon plus the pips and the peel, or that Twinkle was simply batty? The main thing was I was happy, I had Roman, and we were going to live a beautiful life together.

CHAPTER 49

'Summer where the hell are you?'

I rolled my eyes as Roman's dulcet tones thundered down the hall, up the stairs and through the bedroom door. I stormed out of the bedroom to the top of the stairs and looked down on him.

'Why are you home so early?' I asked, thrusting my hands to my hips.

'Charming greeting after being away,' he said mirroring my stance. 'And why haven't you been answering your damn phone? I've been calling you for the last hour.'

He had been away for a few days on-site at a new job that had just started. We were building a small estate of fifteen houses, and while it had a brilliant site manager, Roman always liked to keep an eye on things.

'Stop!' I cried holding my hand up. 'Don't come any closer.'

Roman stopped and heaved a sigh.

'What've you done, bought or broken that you don't want me to see?'

'Nothing.' I couldn't help the little smirk that twitched at my lips. God, when he decided to be a grump, he was damn good at it, but I loved him for it.

'Summer,' he growled as a warning and took another step up.

'Please, just give me two minutes.' I held up two fingers and gave him my poutiest, pleading look, adding an eyelash flutter for good measure.

'Two minutes.' His eyes twinkled and I knew he was desperately trying not to smile. That look nearly always got me what I wanted, and he knew that when I did get my way, he was rewarded handsomely later.

I quickly scooted back into the bedroom and sighed contentedly. My life was so good, there were days I wondered whether it was all a dream.

Roman and I were married only six months after everything happened with Caroline and Jack. Once he asked me, we didn't want to waste any time. There was a slight hitch when Roman asked my dad for permission. Apparently Dad thought that it was a little too soon and tried to persuade Roman to leave it for at least a year. According to my mum, Roman listened to Dad's reasons, then thanked him, but said, while he didn't want to disrespect Dad, he was going to ask me anyway and the only decision that mattered was mine. Mum, unbelievably, was on Roman's side and told Dad all she'd ever wanted was for her kids to be happy and Roman made me happy. It was at that point that Dad seemingly gave a long sigh, shook Roman's hand, and welcomed him to the family.

The proposal itself was beautiful, to me it was, anyway. There was no fancy dinner, or treasure hunt to find the ring, and he hadn't written a poem or a song as a way of asking me: it was simply Roman. We were at home—as I'd moved in with him by then—and we were watching a wildlife programme about swans. The voice-over artist was talking about the fact that swans mate for life when Roman turned down the sound and turned to me.

'That's us,' he said quietly.

'What is?' I asked.

'We're like swans. I only ever want you for the rest of my life,' he said giving me a beautiful smile.

'Ah Roman,' I sighed, 'that's such a gorgeous thing to say.'

He brushed my hair from my eyes and then kissed me gently.

'Will you marry me?'

After taking a couple of seconds for Roman's question to sink in, I threw myself at him and showered his face with kisses, alternating each one with the word 'Yes'.

Afterwards, Roman did tell me that he'd planned to ask me at Bennett's, where we'd had our first date, but doing it at home in front of the TV just felt right. Bonus: we went to Bennett's anyway to celebrate.

Our wedding was beautiful. We got married in the evening, by candlelight, at the local church, and I wore a stunning 1930s-inspired silk sheath dress with halter straps and a deep V at the front that was beaded at the edges. The skirt skimmed my hips and then fell into a beautiful swirl around my legs: I felt like a Hollywood siren at a red carpet event.

Roman … well, he took my breath away. He had his usual two-day groomed stubble, his hair was cropped short at the sides and sexily ruffled on top, he wore a pair of black wing-tipped brogues, a sharp, grey suit with a deep heather-coloured waistcoat and a crisp white shirt, open at the neck. When I saw him I practically ran down the aisle on my dad's arm, and was glad that I'd been practising walking in my *Freya Rose* 'Valena', silver leather shoes that Roman had bought for me.

After the ceremony, during which Twinkle had read one of her own poems—it was actually quite sweet, even though she rhymed 'wedding' with 'bedding'—we went to Darrington Hall where Holly and Liam Robertson gave us the best wedding reception *ever*. It was by far the most amazing party I had ever been to, and the bar bill, which Roman paid for, vouched for what a good night it had been.

Our married life then started with two weeks in Bermuda, and it was absolute bliss.

We were happy. Yes, we bickered a lot, but we laughed and loved an awful lot too.

There were some difficult times in the beginning, when Roman would go quiet and moody if he thought about Caroline and Jack, or someone mentioned them.

Jack had gone to prison for his part in beating Alfie up, and for aiding and abetting Caroline in stealing from Roman. She not only took the money from Roman's safe, and his laptop, but also a Rolex watch that had been his grandfather's. And the bitch had taken a pair of leather *Tom Ford* boots that I'd left at the house. I'd loved those boots, but I could never wear them again once we got them back from the police.

Caroline pleaded guilty and was only given a short prison sentence. She was now living with her parents who took care of Maisie while their daughter was locked up. They were all living in Jersey now, so, I suppose, you could say Caroline nearly got to France in the end.

While Roman missed a lot of sleep over the fact that he nearly lost everything because of Caroline and Jack, and he hated them with a passion because of it, most of his anger was because they'd dragged Maisie into it.

While Caroline was in prison, we'd regularly visited Maisie at her grandparents' house and taken her out for tea or ice cream. We loved the time we spent with her, but once Caroline was freed, she didn't want us to have any further contact with Maisie. Roman was going to fight her decision, but legally he had no rights. The guardianship papers had simply been part of Caroline's plan to get closer to Roman. They'd never been filed, so Maisie disappeared from our lives. It hit us both hard, but Caroline's mother still sent us the occasional photograph of Maisie. She looked healthy and happy, so we had to be content with that.

But thoughts of Caroline and Jack, and how they nearly ruined Roman were surfacing less and less. When he did think about them, it took a lot for him not to go and punch a wall. Luckily for our walls, he usually went down to the gym in the basement of our beautiful new Victorian house—which, I have to boast—is in the same village as a couple of the members of the megastar band, Dirty Riches. When he was in the gym, Roman took a whole lot out on the punch bag, then came back upstairs looking damn sexy, all sweaty and breathless—I know it's bizarre to fancy a sweaty man, but he *is* awesome!

Pippa was okay and had now settled down with a really nice guy called Jacob. He loved her but didn't pander to her 'princess' status, and so was really good for her. She was also back working for Niall Devine, after much grovelling, and was working towards becoming a paralegal.

As for Dylan, he still liked to say he was playing the field, but we all knew that he'd been seeing a girl called Katie for a couple of months—a lifelong commitment in Dylan years. She was lovely and sweet, and he seemed absolutely smitten. Tiffany was still single, but seemed happy just dating and enjoying life; thankfully, she never did take my brother up on his offer of some 'amazing sex'.

'Okay,' I shouted. 'You can come up now.'

I heard his work boots pounding up the stairs and then across the landing as he looked in our bedroom, then back across the landing towards the room that I was in.

'Fuck,' he whispered as he stopped in the doorway. 'Summer?'

I chewed on my bottom lip and gazed at him through tear-filled eyes. I'd been sure that I'd keep it together, but now he was here and seeing what I'd done, the enormity of everything hit me.

'Oh my God, does this mean what I think it means?' Roman asked.

I nodded as a tear dropped off the end of my chin. 'Yep.'

The room was painted in white and cream, and halfway up each wall was a frieze of teddy bears. There was a white chest of drawers and, at the large bay window, were cream-and-white gingham curtains. In the corner, sitting on a deep cream-coloured nursing chair, was a huge cuddly bear that matched those on the frieze.

Roman took two long strides and pulled me into his arms.

'Are you sure?'

I nodded, unable to speak because I knew if I did I'd cry. I reached into the pocket of my trousers, pulled out the pregnancy test stick and passed it to Roman.

He stared down at it, looking at the word *'Pregnant'* in awe.

'We did it, Sum',' he whispered. 'Shit, a baby.'

I gently stroked away the tears on his cheeks and kissed him gently. After eighteen months and two previous rounds of unsucc-essful IVF we were finally pregnant. Third time was definitely a charm because we'd agreed to give up if this session didn't work. Roman hated what I had to put my body through, and we both hated the effect the stress of it all had had on us mentally.

'Did Mr. Henderson call you?' he asked. Mr. Henderson was our consultant, and he'd been with us every step of the way: from our first consultation right through to both of those awful, sad meetings when he'd had to tell us we weren't pregnant.

'He rang the morning you left to go on-site, he couldn't wait for our appointment next week. So I rushed out and bought a pregnancy kit and everything else.'

'Shit, Summer, why didn't you ring me? I'd have come straight home.' Roman hugged me tightly against his chest, and I heard him take a long, ragged breath.

'Because I wanted to surprise you. So I rang Emma and Henry, and they both spent the last couple of days helping me to do all of this. I know it's early days, but I have a really good feeling that everything is going to be fine. I just know it.'

Roman started to laugh and loosened his grip on me so that he could look at my face.

'You couldn't just tell me like any other normal person, could you?' His smile was dazzling as he looked around the room.

'Nope, you know me, it has to be a grand gesture.'

I smiled as I thought about Emma and Henry helping me to pull everything together. Sadly, they weren't a couple any more. Henry had called things off two months ago because the club was so busy, he hardly had time to breathe, never mind spend time with Emma. They were still great friends, though, and if the very long, sexy, lingering kiss I'd seen him give her yesterday was anything to go by, I'd say they'd be back together soon.

Emma loved him still, and he'd told Roman that he was still madly in love with her. Apparently he'd said he just couldn't do a relationship *and* the club justice. I believe Roman told him to 'grow a pair, man up, and get his woman back'.

Roman sighed and kissed the top of my head. 'Who else knows?'

'Apart from Emma and Henry, no one, but I have invited our families around for a take-away so that we can tell them together. I told them it was an early birthday treat for you, seeing as we'll be in Paris on your actual birthday. In fact,' I said, lifting my arm to look at my watch, 'they're all going to be here in about half an hour.'

'Really?' Roman asked incredulously, '*all of them? Tonight? On my first night home?*'

'Sorry, I was just so excited, and you've only been away two nights.' I giggled at his pouty mouth.

'I know, but I want to show you how much I love you.'

His mouth was on my neck, dropping soft kisses along it and down to my collarbone. All the time he had one hand on my hip, while the other laced through my hair. My pulse started racing and the blood in my veins began to heat up.

'Oh you can show me,' I moaned as he nipped at my earlobe. 'You'll just have to be quick.'

'Okay, Mrs. Holliday, quick it is, but later when we're alone it's going to be long and slow. You okay with that?'

'Oh God, yes. The longer and slower the better.'

As Roman led me to our bedroom, I knew that whichever way he showed me, it was going to be epic. Roman Holliday never did anything half-heartedly and was completely awesome all the time, even if he did have a stupid name.

EPILOGUE

♥

Seven months later

'No, mother, we are not calling her Sabrina, Regina, Holly or Eliza,' Roman grumbled at Twinkle, his eyes never leaving the beautiful round face of our daughter, lying asleep in his arms.

'Well, if not after an Audrey character, what about Audrey herself? That's a lovely name.'

I nearly burst out laughing as I heard my own mum almost choke.

'Nope, not that, or any type of holiday either. She's going to have a normal name.'

'I agree with Roman, Twinkle,' my mum said somewhat apologetically, 'a nice normal name that she won't get embarrassed about.'

'Like what?' Twinkle demanded. 'And are you trying to say my children are embarrassed by their names?'

'Oh goodness, no, I just think that … well …'

Mum looked to me for help, but I was having far too much fun watching and listening.

I'd just spent the last nine hours pushing another human being through my fandango, so this was a nice relief.

'Roman is right, Twink,' Pete said, resting a hand on his wife's shoulder. 'She should have a lovely normal name—I'm not saying our kids don't have normal names—well, okay, they don't really ... but Roman and Summer, well, they have enough to put up with ..., you know, ...with their own names.'

We went by the name Hepburn for business, but to everyone else we were Roman and Summer Holliday.

Roman grinned at his dad and passed the baby to me. He gently laid her in my arms and then kissed me softly.

'I love you,' he whispered. 'She's perfect and so are you.'

With a contented sigh I reached up and kissed him back. 'I love you too.'

'So,' my dad said, breaking our moment. 'What *is* her name?'

'Everybody, we'd like you to meet Emily Constance Holliday,' I whispered against my daughter's head.

'Nanna's name,' Twinkle sighed.

'Yes, Mum. Nanna's name.'

Roman hugged his mum to his side and kissed her temple. 'You see, a perfectly normal name can be just as good as anything Audrey-related.'

'It's beautiful, sweetheart,' my mum said as she gently ran a finger down Emily's cheek.

'You don't mind?' I asked her. 'That it's after Twinkle's mum.'

'God, no, I wouldn't want you to call her after mine,' she gasped. 'Who wants to call a child "Nerys"?'

'Ooh, was that your mother's name, Sue? I like that. I'll have to remember that whenever Tiffy has a baby.'

'Oh shit,' Roman groaned against my ear. 'I'd better warn Tiff that it has been decreed that her first-born daughter is to be called *Nerys*.'

We both started to giggle as our parents gazed down at their granddaughter.

'Oh Romy,' Twinkle suddenly squeaked.

'Hmm,' Roman said distractedly, without looking up from staring at Emily.

'When Emily is six weeks old, I'll be able to get that banner out of the loft.'

'Which banner?' he asked cautiously, his attention now on his mother.

'The one that said *"Roman's Having Sex Again"*.'

As everyone burst into fits of laughter, including Mum, I sat back and watched them.

My weird and wonderful family — I was so lucky to have them.

But best of all I had my gorgeous husband by my side and my beautiful daughter in my arms, and I couldn't be happier.

THE END

ACKNOWLEDGMENTS

♥

With each book, this part gets harder and harder: not because I have no one to thank, but because the list gets longer and longer. The more time I spend in the writing community, the more wonderful people I get to meet.

So this is to everyone I've ever met who has given me encouragement, kind words, answered my never-ending questions and personal messages, and generally been decent. Thank you, thank you, and thank you.

As usual, the biggest thanks goes to you, the reader, and hopefully reviewer, of this and any other of my books. You're amazing people and my gratitude knows no bounds.

Finally to Mr. A. — love ya loads and you know that Roman's bum is yours! Xxx

1

MORE BOOKS BY
NIKKI ASHTON

Guess Who I Pulled Last Night?
No Bra Required
Get Your Kit Off
Rock Stars Don't Like Big Knickers
Rock Stars Don't Like Ugly Bras
Cheese Tarts & Fluffy Socks

All books are stand-alone stories, with 'guest' appearances from characters from Nikki's previous book

Please visit Nikki's Facebook Page: Nikki Ashton Books for news, snippets and pictures

www.nikkiashtonbooks.co.uk

NIKKI ASHTON

Nikki is a romantic Piscean who lives with her husband, two dogs—Millie and Hector—and her mother-in-law, in Cheshire. She divides her time between writing and working part-time as a trainer for a software company. Writing and training may seem completely at odds with each other, but Nikki feels her training work allows her to meet lots and lots of interesting people, and makes character creation easy. If Nikki's not working or writing, she loves watching football—and not just for the men in shorts! She also adores spending time with any of her 16 nephews and nieces—but maybe not all at once as they're a lively bunch.

Nikki's proud to be a romance writer and proud of the characters and stories that she creates. Her books might not contain life-changing messages, or be thought-provoking, or even win a literary prize, but they might just make you smile and put a little flutter in your heart. And that makes Nikki happy.